The Versailles Formula

Also By Nancy Bilyeau

THE GENEVIEVE PLANCHÉ SERIES
Book 1: The Blue
Book 2: The Fugitive Colours
Book 3: The Versailles Formula

STANDALONES
Dreamland
The Orchid Hour

The
VERSAILLES FORMULA

Nancy Bilyeau

LUME BOOKS
A JOFFE BOOKS COMPANY

Lume Books, London

A Joffe Books Company

www.lumebooks.co.uk

First published in Great Britain in 2025 by Lume Books

Cover art by Cherie Chapman

ISBN: 978-1-83901-602-8

For my daughter, Nora

PART ONE

Prologue

Twickenham
June 1766

It's approaching midnight, and I am keeping watch for a ghost. This ceased being amusing some time ago.

I stand pressed into the corner of a castle armoury. This is a place of yawning shadows, hardly surprising when the owner of the house told me he *intended* it to be this way. He even coined a word for the desired effect: *gloomth*.

If it weren't for the faint gleam reflecting off a suit of sixteenth-century armour and the moonlight filtering through a stained-glass window, I'd be smothered by impenetrable black. That would prevent me from making the necessary observations. I admit that it would also make this silent space more unnerving.

I have no one to blame but myself for this predicament. I'm a guest in this house, and over the last several hours, I have said too much, argued too much, and drank too much. Standing guard here, at this spot, was *my* idea. My head tightens with the first approach of a headache. Is it wine or the onset of remorse? The other guests are keeping watch in their appointed places for the supposed ghost. I thought that by doing so, we'd prove to our frightened host what I firmly believe: spirits don't exist. The dead are quiet. They are still.

They certainly don't run through long galleries and libraries at midnight with the objective of reaching a painting that hangs in an armoury next to a set of stairs. Our host is famous for possessing one of England's most elaborate imaginations. The disturbing fact is, he's not the only one who's seen something difficult to explain in this house. We heard the witness statements at dinner.

Just a few inches from my head hangs the painting that plays some bizarre yet pivotal role in this drama. It depicts an angel by Jean-Honoré Fragonard, France's most sensational living painter. Since the French are supremely confident of their superiority in art, literature and science — everything, in short — this could make him the most sensational painter in all of Europe, as far as the French are concerned.

But I don't care for it. Even if I put aside the fact that the frame is too large and gaudy, this angel makes me uneasy — and I can't articulate why. That concerns me. I am an artist, and I've had a reasonable amount of training, as much as is allowed for any female. I've taken every opportunity to learn while working in oil and watercolour. Fragonard's superb details and mastery of shade and light should impress me. They don't. Even in this dim space, something about how the light reflects off the blue sky and white clouds feels artificial. I'm relieved that it's too dark to make out the painting's central figure, an angel with a smile that strikes me as anything but innocent. I detest that smirk, for it keeps making me wonder if I've committed a serious error tonight — one that I will pay for.

Enough.

I take a deep breath. It's time to call a halt to this ghoul watch. The other people in the house may be waiting silently for me to put an end to this ridiculous exercise. I ponder the right words to use.

Knock. Knock. Knock.

My breath quickens as I remember what our host said at dinner: "First, you hear the rapping, the knocks. And after … you see the spirit."

I cling to logic and the scientific principles my husband Thomas and I hold dear. Trust what you can hear, see, smell and touch. Gather evidence.

Our host said the painting is always the destination. The spectre is drawn to the angel, and at this moment, I'm beneath the angel in the painting. That must mean it is coming to me.

But this cannot be real. There are no ghosts.

I need to ease away from the wall. If I walk six feet or so, I'll be able to see the wide staircase and entry hall. I pluck up my skirts, readying myself to take a few silent steps, when I hear it again. Another knocking sound and, seconds later, a series of soft, light steps like someone scampering up the staircase.

My heart beats so fast it is like a pianoforte thundering in my ears. My knees begin to tremble. My throat is tight and dry — I can't speak even if I want to.

A memory flashes of words spoken not long ago in a parlour many miles from here. A spoiled, somewhat disagreeable young woman had said, hugging herself, "Fear makes me feel alive."

I realize that she was talking about *this* house, *this* moment, all without knowing it. She had no idea what it would be like to experience this fear.

And nor did I. Until now.

Chapter One

Two weeks earlier

When I arrive at the Lichfield house of Dr Erasmus Darwin and his wife, Polly, in my ramshackle carriage that morning, all I feel is relief that my son and I managed to make it to town before the rain began. I peered at the sky the entire trip, watching the clouds thicken. I can feel my dress sleeves sticking to my arms. Pierre's cheeks glisten.

The Darwins' is a large, red-brick house with an expansive terrace and a medicinal herb garden. The doctor himself pushes open the front door as Pierre and I approach. "Genevieve, Pierre, always such a pleasure to see you," he booms, filling the doorway as few men can. Dr Darwin is tall, barrel-chested, and broad-bellied. His energy is prodigious. He's a physician, yes, and also a natural philosopher, geologist and published poet.

"Oh my, have you been injured?" he asks, scrutinizing my right cheek.

How unfortunate that he noticed. Minutes after setting out for Lichfield, I'd pulled hard on the reins, hoping my horse would bear left and the carriage would avoid an encounter with a menacing tree branch hanging over the narrow lane. In response, the horse quickened — and veered hard to the right. My five-year-old son ducked in time, but I was not as fortunate. The branch's thick leaves slapped my cheek with a surprising sting.

"Don't worry," I tell Dr Darwin, dismayed that my poor carriage driving left a mark. "A scratch. It's nothing, I assure you."

"Very well, but I promised your husband that I'd look after you." Ordinarily, I would bristle at such a statement. However, Dr Darwin is our patron, arranging for my husband, Thomas Sturbridge, to teach science at a local academy and for us to lease a stone cottage north of town. During the summer holiday from those teaching duties, Thomas is staying in Warrington near Liverpool, collaborating with a fellow teacher on chemical experiments. Six weeks is a long time to be away from his family, but I'd told Thomas I'd be busy with my garden and my painting. His work always has my support.

Turning towards his waiting carriage, Dr Darwin says, "We don't want to inflict any distractions on the geniuses while they are at work, do we, Genevieve? If this goes well, he stands a chance of being nominated for the Royal Society. I've received three letters from Sturbridge already. Progress is most promising!"

And so, I step into the house and greet Polly Darwin in not the best of moods. Her husband has received three letters from Thomas compared to my one. I'd already begun to feel that my husband wasn't writing to me as he used to on our being parted. I'd made excuses, telling myself that it was because he was too busy. But it seems he had the time to write to Dr Darwin. When we were first married — and in the years we lived in London — we shared a closeness of not just affection but belief and ideals. True partners. I never wanted to be a wife who concerned herself solely with the hearth and home, and I don't want it now.

"Is it possible you've grown slimmer since I last saw you, Genevieve?" exclaims Polly.

I shrug and force a smile. I suppose some women feast on compliments on their figures when they are past thirty. I'm not one of them. Whenever Polly remarks on my waistline, I suspect she's thinking that in seven years of marriage, I've produced only one child. Over nine years, Polly has given birth to five, all while impressing everyone as a gracious hostess and tireless charitable force. She is much closer to being the perfect wife and mother than I am. Even if I put all effort into such a goal, I could never compare. Still, I do not envy her. Unlike her husband, Polly has an air of fragility.

"Pierre, you're wanted upstairs," she says, clapping her hands. "Charles has the most splendid invention to show you."

Pierre scrambles up the stairs obediently. Only a mother's eye could detect his slumped shoulders. He has more fun playing with the other children who live along our lane than the Darwin sons. I hope the day isn't too tedious for him. I had insisted we keep our appointment because in my one letter from Thomas, he reminded me of his wish that our son spend time here to encourage his interests in science.

Polly leads me, arm in arm, as we go to the parlour, where the gaggle of young ladies awaits their lesson in watercolour. This is the other reason for my being here: once a month, I teach painting to a small group of genteel young ladies acquainted with Polly Darwin.

I need to try harder to establish a friendship with Polly. The trouble is, I've never possessed a gift for intimacy with other females except for Evelyn Devlin, now Lady Willoughby. We've always understood each other, ever since we met at Derby Porcelain Works. Not even her marriage to Sir Humphrey Willoughby, the master spy catcher of England and a man with whom I have a tense history, could damage my friendship with Evelyn.

Polly says, "I know you and Thomas worry, but I don't believe boarding school will be necessary for Pierre."

Her words are so baffling that I assume she has my family confused with another. Pierre is enrolled at the academy where Thomas teaches. Why should our son be sent away?

"There'll be no boarding school for Pierre," I correct her.

"I quite agree. A summer of being in my son's company will put him on the right path."

Something in my expression makes Polly pause. We've reached the parlour, but before going in, she pulls me closer to whisper, "Do not be angry with Thomas for confiding in us your fears. That spark you look for in Pierre is there. I know it. He couldn't be Thomas's son and not have a passion for knowledge."

What on earth has Thomas said to her? As I struggle to respond, she releases me and says brightly, "Mrs Sturbridge has arrived! Our lesson can begin."

To me, the four slender figures sitting in chairs, little tables set up in front of them, are only blurs. I take a breath and say, "I must see to the colour cakes." With that, I turn my back on everyone and sort through the paints for the day.

Doing so buys me some time, for I can hardly draw breath. As I move the paint palettes around on the table, not even seeing them, furious questions roar in my skull. How *could* Thomas tell the Darwins he was worried about Pierre missing a "spark" for learning? Thomas has never said that to me. And it is ridiculous. Our son is bright and quick and perfectly normal. At age five and a half, is Pierre supposed to solve problems of physics rather than climb trees and collect pebbles? Pierre does not need to be pushed into rooms occupied by the Darwin children to learn from his "betters". And while I know some boys begin their education at boarding school at the age of seven, the thought of *my* boy being sent away fills me with equal parts rage and panic. With a painful thump, I think again about Thomas's letter and how insistent my husband was about our son coming with me to the Darwins' for the day. When did he stop sharing his true opinions with me and turn to subterfuge?

"Excuse me, Mrs Sturbridge?" asks the young woman closest to me. It's Charlotte, newly married to a barrister and keen to enhance her talent for painting, which is truthfully modest. Her lovely brow is creased with concern as she looks at me.

"Have you been hurt?" she asks.

"A trivial scratch," I say, touching my cheek and trying not to flinch. It is tender, more so than immediately after that branch struck. But there is nothing to be done about it now.

"Give me one more minute, everyone," I say, rallying.

I've no choice but to begin the watercolour lesson. For the first time, I peer at the flowers Polly Darwin placed in the middle of the parlour for the young ladies to paint today. She and I agreed she would select something in full bloom. As the daffodil's time is past, I expect today to see elegant red roses gathered in one of the Darwins' vases or boisterous pink hydrangeas. But that's not what Polly chose.

The flowers are blue.

"Aren't you pleased?" asks Polly, smiling proudly. "Blue larkspur are uncommon."

"Indeed they are," I say, my voice flat and strained. I wish Polly had picked any other flower than these, with their delicate cone-shaped blue petals fluttering on long spikes.

Lydia, the young woman sitting closest to the vase of flowers, speaks for the first time this afternoon.

"I know a strange story about the colour blue," she announces. I fight down a scrambling of alarm. This is precisely what I do *not* want to discuss.

"It's a story that will intrigue you all, I promise," Lydia says with a little smile.

Does this girl know about Thomas's formula for a new, revolutionary shade of blue? He developed it in secret eight years ago. Looking at Lydia, I tell myself that's impossible.

At seventeen, Lydia is the youngest of the ladies who gather at the Darwins' house to paint. The daughter of a wealthy merchant, she often seems caught in a private sulk, despite being at the peak of prettiness with her heart-shaped face and fashionable wardrobe. Today, she wears a violet gown with a delicate white-lace fichu at her bodice. To my faint surprise, I spot a book with a dark brown cover lying on the table in front of her.

Polly says, "Do tell us your story, Lydia."

"Yes, tell, tell, tell," the others plead as Lydia smiles and shakes her head, enjoying the attention.

While they clamour, all I can think is that Thomas created that new blue pigment in a laboratory in Derby, only a day's ride from Lichfield. Despite all the agreements of secrecy, word might have leaked out. What will Under-Secretary of State Sir Humphrey Willoughby do if he finds out the people here have discovered that a chemist created a colour blue that led to murder, kidnapping and treason? And what if Thomas, as its creator, is revealed? That would put an end to our quiet life in the country.

Lydia, fingering her lace fichu, says, "What I read is that many, many years ago, perhaps the medieval age, three knights were travelling through the countryside in Italy when a dragon attacked them.

11

After a long, terrible battle, they destroyed it. They almost lost their lives fighting. When they wiped their swords in the grass, they saw the dragon's blood was blue. The blood in the grass mingled with the creature's venom, and the mixture soaked into the ground. A few days later, a flower sprang up there. And *that* was the first blue larkspur."

The others ooh and aah, but I can only laugh with pure relief. I've been stricken with fear before. And it is not only worry over Thomas's colour experiments being revealed but that my unfortunate history as a spy might come to light. While I've felt a growing restlessness in the country over the last eighteen months, I've no wish to become a pariah. Fortunately, just as every other time, I'm safe from censure.

Lydia asks, "Mrs Sturbridge, may I ask why you find what I've said amusing?"

Her mouth set in an angry pout, Lydia glares at me, sizing me up. I can guess what this imperious girl, nearly half my age, sees: my straw hat slightly dented, my cheek grazed, my two-year-old dress patched in two places, looking less than crisply fresh after the ride to Lichfield in the heat.

"I apologize — I'm not laughing at you, Lydia," I say. "I'm just marvelling at the minds of those who thought up the story so long ago. That's what people did when they couldn't explain something rationally — before anyone understood things like chemistry and botany. Blue is rarely found in the natural world, so to explain the existence of a blue flower, they must create a story of dragon blood."

I thought I'd done a decent job explaining, but every face turned towards me is bewildered. Even Polly Darwin, an educated woman and wife to an erudite thinker, stares at me in confusion.

"But blue isn't rare, Mrs Sturbridge — the colour is all around us," says Charlotte, the barrister's wife.

Crack.

The window shutters swing wildly as a gust of wind wallops the house, bringing with it a torrent of rain. Polly and her maid rush to close the windows, and I do my best to help.

The cool wind clears my head, and I proceed with the lesson, distributing the colour cakes and little water dishes. I explain the importance of capturing the larkspur's purplish-blue petals, thick stems and winsome green leaves. No one brings up the subject of blue's rarity again, though Polly Darwin makes a point about colour.

"Mrs Sturbridge has created such a wide selection for all of you," she says. "You have more than ten shades here. What an artist's eye she has!"

I try not to wince as I'm flooded with memories of my silk-painting workshop in Spitalfields. Using a book of one hundred and nineteen colours for guidance, my small team of artists created the most original designs to adorn gowns from Bristol to Boston. I had the skill to take on the fashionable tastes for shades of pink, purple, and lime green and employ them with subtlety in a design for a silk dress.

I push down those proud memories of my London business. Nostalgia just makes my life in Lichfield more trying.

I clear my throat and say, "Remember, ladies, watercolour calls for control. Plan your paint strokes."

They don their smocks and plunge into painting, and I move among them, offering praise and correction. Lydia is the only one who falters.

I don't want to call attention to her lagging behind. Still, when the Darwins' maid appears, telling Polly the family has an unexpected visitor, and Polly leaves, I draw closer to Lydia's table.

"I thought your story about the legend of blue larkspur would serve as an inspiration," I say gently.

She shrugs. "Watercolours, playing the spinet, doing embroidery … Not to be rude, Mrs Sturbridge, but I'm only here because my mother insists I add to my female accomplishments to capture a husband."

I had grabbed a brush from my grandfather's cup and began painting at age eight. It filled my life from then on. I hate to hear art described as a "female accomplishment", even if it no longer brings me as much joy as it once did. My painting has languished since we left London.

"Tell me, Lydia, what would you rather be doing?" I ask, hiding my annoyance.

She picks up the book and caresses it, red flaring in her cheeks. "This. I've never read anything like it."

There is no writing on the book cover. She turns it so that I can examine the writing on the spine: *The Castle of Otranto*. She carefully opens the book to show me the title page: *The Castle of Otranto, A Story. Translated by William Marshal, Gent. From the Original Italian of Onuphrio Muralto, Canon of the Church of St. Nicholas at Otranto*. I've heard of this novel, of course. It's been a sensation for the last year at least.

Lydia says in a rush, "They *found* the manuscript, do you realize? The story of what happened in the castle was written long, long ago in Italy and two years ago translated into English and published as a book."

"As long ago as the story of the knights and the dragon?" I ask teasingly.

With an impatient frown, Lydia says, "Oh, I know the dragon is a legend. But *The Castle of Otranto* is based on events that took place. It was all written down in Naples in 1529. Oh, it's a work of the *sublime*, Mrs Sturbridge. There are curses and ghosts that seem to step out of paintings and what Prince Manfred desires from …" She shivers in delight. "You said we must be in control. I don't *wish* for that."

14

"You prefer to be frightened?"

I keep my tone light, but Lydia takes the question seriously. "Fear makes me feel alive," she says, hugging herself.

I hear the rustle of skirts, and Polly Darwin taps my arm. I immediately tense at her sombre expression. I can't imagine who or what would wipe the customary cheerfulness from Polly's face.

"You'll have to come with me," she says. And then, louder for the group's benefit, "Someone needs to speak to Mrs Sturbridge."

"Is it my husband?" I stammer idiotically. Thomas Sturbridge wouldn't break away from a laboratory experiment in Warrington to see me at the Darwins', but if he did, Polly would be happy to see him.

She shakes her head and leads me from the parlour, walking quickly. I try to catch up so I can ask her the visitor's name, without success.

While she's in front of me for several seconds, Polly blocks my view of whoever stands in her foyer. It is only when she steps aside and gestures to me, her expression remaining guarded, that I get a proper look at them.

I feel a flutter of recognition replaced by a sickening stab of disbelief.

Under-Secretary of State Sir Humphrey Willoughby, the spy catcher of England, a man who speaks directly to the prime minister, stands defiantly, rain-spattered, in the house of Erasmus and Polly Darwin. I've not laid eyes on him for eighteen months, yet he's gone to considerable trouble to find me.

"Genevieve, I need to speak to you," he says. "In private."

Chapter Two

I am consumed by dread as Polly Darwin leads us into Erasmus Darwin's study and then backs away, firmly closing the door behind her.

The room is shadowy, for there's but one small window and the storm has turned the summer sky greyish-purple. But I don't offer to light the desk lamp beside the doctor's pile of papers and well-thumbed books. It's not up to me to make this unforeseen interrogation go smoothly.

And it can only be an interrogation.

There's no point in clinging to foolish hopes that Sir Humphrey seeks me out in Lichfield for friendly purposes. I've seen Evelyn, my close friend, and his wife, *sans* Sir Humphrey, six times in the last eighteen months. Evelyn makes a point to stop and see me on the way to Derby for visits with her mother, usually bringing their six-year-old daughter, Diana. Her husband is always too busy in London to accompany them now that he's been made an under-secretary in His Majesty's government.

Now, just short of forty years of age, Sir Humphrey is a trifle heavier than the last time I saw him, but otherwise, he is unaltered. What marks him unmistakably as a Londoner and one of importance? He is wigged and wears a waistcoat and long jacket, but so do the gentlemen of Lichfield. I refuse to accept it being his noble family. No, I fancy the details of dress set him apart: at least a dozen ivory buttons fastening his waistcoat and silver shoe buckles that gleam, magically undimmed by the mucky weather.

My nervousness over Sir Humphrey's silence since we've entered the room hardens into resentment. Years ago, the British government hashed out a formal agreement with the French that, among other things, permitted Thomas and me to return to England. We lived in London for the first three years, which Thomas disliked. His health suffered from the layers of smoke swallowing the city and he has never liked crowds. After my silk business collapsed and Thomas was offered the position in Lichfield, we moved here and made a place for ourselves. Why should I still feel this degree of guilt?

"I've done nothing wrong," I blurt. "And neither has Thomas. He does no experiments with the colour blue."

Sir Humphrey blinks in surprise. "Genevieve, no," he says. "I'm not here to accuse you of wrongdoing." He takes a deep breath. "I'm here to ask for your help."

Something in his voice, a pain I've never heard from the superbly confident Willoughby, sends me flying across the room.

"Is it Evelyn?" I ask. "She's ill — in some danger?"

"She is no longer in danger," he says carefully.

I yank hard on Sir Humphrey's sleeve, and for the first time, he looks me full on. Paunchy creases etch his eyes, the sort that comes with worry that devours sleep.

"She ... lost ... a child," he says hoarsely. "She suffered greatly, Genevieve. The doctors say she's healed, but her spirits are so low. You are the friend who has always ... meant the most to Evelyn."

"I did not know she was with child. I've had weekly letters!"

"There have been two other losses in the last four years. She didn't want anyone to be informed until the baby quickened. But just when that should have occurred ..." He couldn't continue.

"Tell me what I can do." A plan leaps into my head. "No, no, I shall tell you. I'll write to Thomas today and tell him I'm needed, and I'll come for a visit. It won't take me that long to make the necessary travel arrangements. I merely—"

"No need for that," Sir Humphrey cut in. "I can take you today — now. We will proceed to your house so you can pack a trunk."

"Surely you didn't come all this way to fetch me?"

"No, of course not," he says impatiently. "I've been on official business, called north. But as I'm returning by way of Lichfield, I thought I'd stop off to try to collect you."

It sounds plausible, but I feel odd. It might be the suddenness of his appearance and his offer to sweep us away. It's been no secret that Sir Humphrey distrusts me. I don't feel comfortable with him either. What unites us is our devotion to Evelyn.

He says, "Evelyn told me your husband would be away, working near Liverpool, for six weeks. It seemed a window of opportunity for you — and Pierre, of course — to come to us for a week, perhaps a fortnight."

As I stand there, absorbing every word he's said and its meaning, the drumbeat of rain stops. A loud patter of feet hurtles down the steps on the other side of the door.

"I understand, Genevieve, that this is unexpected. But you need to decide at once, because whether I go with you or without you, I need to leave Lichfield as soon as possible."

Now it's my turn to stay silent. Why can't I make my own arrangements? I am of an independent nature. Both my late grandfather and my husband — the two men who've known me best — understand that. Many others disapprove.

Taking this as a "no", Sir Humphrey opens the door and jerks his head towards the foyer, his lips tight with disappointment. Following me out, he nearly collides with my son, jumping up and down at the sight of Sir Humphrey, his wavy red hair bounding off his shoulders.

"You're Diana's father," cries Pierre, his eyes shining. I can't remember seeing him this excited. "You've come from London, haven't you? Do you have a house near the Thames? Do you see many big ships? Have you ever seen one with three masts?"

I'm not the only one who misses London. Setting aside my suspicion of Sir Humphrey, I want to give Pierre this opportunity. When will he have another chance to travel south?

With that, I make my decision. "Pierre," I say, "how would you like to take a trip in Sir Humphrey's carriage? We're invited to London for a bit. I'm sure you'll see some ships."

After calming down an ecstatic five-year-old, I make my apologies to Polly Darwin. Now that she knows the intimidating Sir Humphrey is here to convey me to the side of his wife, her natural poise returns, and she insists that a watercolour lesson cut short is nothing to fret over.

How delightful to step outside the Darwins' house into the bright sun. The same ferocity that drove the storm to Lichfield seems to have chased it off, too.

Standing right behind me, Sir Humphrey calls out, "Ah, there you are, Howard. It's all settled."

A man in his early thirties strides towards us, eyes fixed on Sir Humphrey and hands shoved deep into his pockets. He's not dressed with the same London aplomb as Willoughby, but he's no servant either. He has a long face and unpowdered black hair; his attire is plain, nearly severe, but I suspect by choice rather than in deference to holding lower rank. It's as if he were wearing a uniform created by a religious order that no one knows but him.

"You've identified Mrs Sturbridge's horse and carriage?" asks Sir Humphrey.

"I've had that pleasure, yes, sir," says the man called Howard, his tone indicating the opposite.

"I beg your pardon?" I demand.

Sir Humphrey makes a placating gesture in my direction and says to the younger man, "Very good. Meet us at Mrs Sturbridge's house. We aim to be on the road headed south by three o'clock."

Without the flicker of a glance in my direction, Howard says, "I'll do my best, sir. I can't vouch for the horse and carriage in question making it to the end of this street."

Sir Humphrey laughs and says, "If anyone can manage it, you can!"

Not only are they talking as if I am not here but also finding amusement. Irritation boiling over, I say, "I don't recall granting permission for anyone to take control of my horse and my property. I shall be the one to—"

A small hand grips mine tightly. "Oh, Mama, Mama, just *look* at the coach," cries Pierre in awe.

Four fine bay horses pull a coach — gleaming black and trimmed with gold — to the Darwins' house. The liveried driver salutes Sir Humphrey. A smiling boy of about sixteen leaps down from the back of the coach, and two black-and-white spotted dogs suddenly appear at the boy's side, tails wagging.

It's almost more than a joyful Pierre can take in. However, I don't share his ecstasy. I've lost sight of Howard and can only assume he's returned to the stable to commandeer my horse and carriage.

Sir Humphrey plunges into conversation with his driver and coach boy. Telling Pierre to wait, I march towards the stables, only to be seized by Sir Humphrey and bundled into the coach beside Pierre. With Sir Humphrey, there's a constant push and pull of who is in charge.

We set off for my cottage. Whether it's the coach's plush seat material or the gentle springs of the wheels, I have to admit this is by far the most comfortable coach ride I've ever had. Even the *smell* is pleasing: faint pine with a trace of aged cognac. White's gentlemen's club in London would pale in comparison.

None of which prevents me from lodging a complaint about Howard taking charge of my horse and carriage. I've never been very good with either, but that doesn't mean I want a stranger taking over.

"Genevieve, if I haven't made it clear to you already, speed is of the essence. We'll reach your house much faster in the coach, and you can start packing a trunk before Howard catches up in your carriage. Spending the night in Lichfield will set us back." Glancing at Pierre, he says carefully, "I want to reach Lady Willoughby as soon as possible."

It's the one argument that could make me swallow my annoyance with all this high-handedness. Still, I can't resist pointing out, "Our cottage is off a narrow country lane. After such a storm, it might not be able to handle your grand conveyance."

"We stopped there first. Your serving woman told us you were at Dr Darwin's. We are aware of the conditions."

I don't care for how he says, "the conditions". My spiteful side almost hopes Willoughby's coach gets mired two feet deep in mud. But no, the surge of summer heat following the storm has already dried the roads sufficiently for us to rumble up the lane to my cottage.

Sir Humphrey is the first one out, turning to offer me his hand as I step down. I wince as I survey the cottage and, rising behind a thin line of shrubbery, the barn. The fierce rainstorm bruised my home, leaving it looking dilapidated. One of the window shutters, torn loose, hangs from its casement. In my garden, the larger plants sag into the lumpy earth. Rivulets of silty water drain off the vegetable beds. My lavender plants look squashed.

Worst of all, a dishevelled Alfred, our servant, stands between the cottage and the barn, staring at the coach, his mouth hanging open. Next to Alfred is our largest pig, its mouth also agape. A chicken squawks in outrage, unseen but heard.

Sir Humphrey's eyes dart everywhere, taking it in. For just a second, I witness surprise and dismay before he clears his face of expression. I am mortified, and if he had said a word at that moment, my pride would have compelled me to cancel our trip entirely. He prudently maintains silence.

I throw some clothes and toiletries into the trunk alongside Pierre's things and then gather practical items for my son, who has grabbed nothing but his favourite toys and a pair of old breeches.

Thankfully, Sir Humphrey stays outside while I organize the packing. I could not bear for him to see how small the rooms are. After a bit, I hear him talking to another man and realize it must be Howard.

I head outside to check on the buggy and have a word with Alfred, neither task I look forward to with pleasure. It will certainly be a relief to get time away from Alfred and his wife, Edith. I have always felt their disapproval, nowhere more than in how they regard my garden. I try to nurture the vegetables, flowers and herbs native to the Languedoc. Where are the carrots, turnips, beets and onions, they want to know. Needless to say, Alfred and Edith had never met a Huguenot before and have no understanding of the heritage of French Protestant refugees.

At the sight of me, Howard breaks off what he's saying to Sir Humphrey, nods at me curtly, and points to the barn. Then he turns on his heel and stalks to that woeful wooden structure.

More irritated than ever by his manner, I make my way to the barn. The man's planted himself in the middle, not in the deepest shadows but away from the patch of sun stretching inside from the door.

As I approach, Howard finally looks me straight in the eye. From the side, his nose is too long, but from this perspective the sharp planes of his face come into a sort of harmony. Some light-minded females might consider him good-looking due to his arrogant bearing and slim waist, but I could never be counted among them. Right now, his lips are pressed together as if I've done him a personal injury.

"Mrs Sturbridge, are you aware of the state of your horse's bridle?" he demands. "It's in tatters. I wonder if you've been able to manage him at all."

"Bridle?" I repeat.

"Look at the bit." Howard pivots to the tackle shelf, where he's placed the offending bridle. He holds it up for my inspection, and I pretend to see what he's seen.

Howard presses on. "The left wheel of the carriage is loose — that's not helping matters. And this stall hasn't been pitched out in an eternity. That can make a horse sick. Don't be surprised if the unfortunate creature gets lockjaw!"

Seething, I say, "I'm not accustomed to being handed a list of household offences from a stranger, a person who has not even been introduced to me."

He executes a bow, his sweeping flourish mocking me. "Captain Howard, at your service." I had thought "Howard" was his first name.

Now I realize it isn't so — and he has an army rank. Not that that impresses me.

"But I doubt my name matters a whit to this poor horse, suffering due to neglect."

"We never practice neglect here," I protest. Before settling in Lichfield, I'd limited experience with horses, that's true. But I would never want an animal to suffer.

Captain Howard turns his back on me to go to our horse. I brace myself for more fault-finding. Instead, he strokes the horse's neck with disconcerting gentleness, she twitches her tail in response, and he disappears from the barn.

I stare after him, both offended and a little alarmed. When Captain Howard bowed, I spotted a pistol in his belt. I wonder where the men were before coming south to Lichfield. Quite a coincidence that they had important government business to attend to so close to my home. Sir Humphrey made a persuasive case that his business had nothing to do with Thomas and me. Although I've agreed to go with him to London, I can't help but nurture suspicion.

Hovering outside the barn are both Alfred and Edith. I inform them that Pierre and I will be away for about a fortnight and that, during our absence, the garden must be tended and the animals cared for. The two of them nod, looking dazed by the coach and the party of people and dogs who've descended on the cottage.

"Listen to me, Alfred," I say, my voice rising. "See to repairing the bridle for the horse and check the carriage wheels. Clean the stalls too. We don't — we don't want distemper!"

The coachman ties my trunk to the top of the coach, and an impatient Sir Humphrey pulls Pierre and me inside. Within minutes, we are on the road heading south. It is rather hard for me to believe that this is happening. I woke up expecting nothing more eventful today than a watercolour lesson at Dr Darwin's house. Now I'm barrelling towards London, a city I left eighteen months ago, without time to write a letter to my husband. But I can't deny that the blood pumps faster through my veins as I gaze out the window and watch familiar surroundings drop away.

We are an hour on the road before Sir Humphrey mentions that we are not, in fact, going to London. He and Evelyn have let a house in Twickenham for the summer, a town some twelve miles west of the city, nestled on the Thames. Although few aristocrats stay in the heart of London through the heat of the summer, and this should provide a better place for Evelyn to convalesce, I don't appreciate learning our true destination in the coach. It adds to my growing sense of unease that I have put myself entirely in Sir Humphrey's power.

And I have fresh cause not to trust him. I want to help Evelyn, my closest friend, in her hour of need. It's inconceivable that Sir Humphrey would concoct a story of his wife's intimate suffering. But, stroking the swollen bump on my cheek, I reflect on something disturbing. When Sir Humphrey asked me to come with him south, he said he knew from Evelyn that Thomas was staying with a fellow teacher near Liverpool for six weeks.

But I am certain that while I wrote to Evelyn that Thomas was going to be away for part of the summer, I never specified exactly where my husband was going or how many weeks he'd be away.

How did Sir Humphrey learn it and why does he care?

Chapter Three

Fortunately, Captain Howard rides atop the carriage next to the driver, sparing me his presence for much of the journey to Twickenham. Pierre and I accompany Sir Humphrey Willoughby, sitting on those plush seats. I listen to everything Sir Humphrey says quite carefully for further revelations of knowledge he should not possess. I catch no slips until supper at the White Stag Inn.

Sir Humphrey speaks of the importance of reaching this particular inn shortly after we set out. Its tavern is known to serve a hearty venison stew that he holds in the highest esteem. Now, tavern kitchens on the main travellers' roads are not known for their attention to fine cuisine. So, while I could not blame him for his fixation — some men think of their dinners for half the day ahead — I soon grew weary of hearing about it.

Pierre, though, catches Sir Humphrey's enthusiasm. After the coach rolls up to the White Stag Inn, we hurry inside and take a table in the tavern. Sure enough, the cook has venison stew bubbling in a pot hanging above the fire. Over plates heaped with meat, onions and carrots mixed in a hearty broth, Sir Humphrey and Captain Howard, shedding his grimness, regale Pierre with stories of grisly dinners and snarling stablemen they'd encountered while I half listen.

"But what about the highwaymen?" Pierre demands. "Have you ever shot one?"

"None to date." Captain Howard grins, patting the handle of his long pistol. "But be assured, I'm ready for them."

My son laughs in delight, much to my chagrin. I find the man's boasts as unlikeable as every other facet of his character. I fume to witness how other people respond to the captain. Men working for the inns instantly respond to his barked orders, and even worse, the tavern women blush and giggle in his presence and seem to crave his attention.

"Pierre, that's why we take careful precautions," says Sir Humphrey. "We don't keep the coach on the road after sunset."

"But my father rides at night after his meetings in Birmingham," says Pierre. "So do all the Lunar Men."

And that is when it occurs. Sir Humphrey and Captain Howard exchange a sharp look.

Captain Howard speaks next. "What are 'Lunar Men'?" He articulates those two words as if they were never pushed together before, but I would wager a princely sum that he's pretending ignorance of the concept.

"When Father and his friends want to talk about science, they pick the night of the month when the moon is full so they can best see the road to ride home," explains Pierre.

Sir Humphrey, his hand resting on a spoon, says, "Those must be important meetings to make night travel necessary."

I jump in, telling them, "There's nothing a chemist likes better than droning on about his newest experiment. In the Lunar Society — that's what they call themselves — everyone gets a turn. Naturally, the meetings run late. Now finish your stew, Pierre."

I see it again, that meaningful look passing between the two men. But I can't work out why they would care about Thomas and his friends. The Lunar Society members aren't concocting secret formulas that could concern Great Britain's Under-Secretary of State for the Southern Department, which covers activities in countries stretching from France to the Ottoman Empire. As Sir Humphrey already knows, Thomas is preoccupied with the study of electricity. That is the basis of the project with Joseph Priestley and their planned book. It's not a new field. Chemists have been experimenting with electricity for over ten years.

I shake my head, stirring the stew left in my bowl. I've no appetite to finish. That night, sleep eludes me. I can't remember the last time I felt so torn. I want to hurry to Evelyn and help my friend through her crisis. But is it safe to ignore Sir Humphrey's secret motives? If only I could discover what they are.

Doubts continue to bedevil me up to the time I arrive at the Willoughbys' home in Twickenham, where Evelyn and Sir Humphrey and their child Diana are spending the summer. Even in the dim light of dusk, I perceive it's a beautiful house: three storeys of pale stone and precisely spaced windows bracketed by four-panel black shutters. Captain Howard sees to the carriage — the people, horses and dogs, and luggage — as Sir Humphrey hurries inside.

I collect Pierre, and we linger on the steps outside the door. We're both tired and hungry, but I can't see us wandering the house alone. The Evelyn I know welcomes guests at the threshold. Yet the minutes crawl by, and she doesn't appear. I fear she's too weak to greet us … or she isn't even here. That possibility chills.

The first human being to materialize is a stout man of middle years, introducing himself as Joseph, the family's major-domo. He apologizes for not ushering us inside sooner. "Let me take you upstairs — Sir Humphrey sent word ahead, and we've prepared the guest room."

"Is Lady Willoughby here?" I ask, unable to restrain myself.

"Yes," Joseph answers, not meeting my gaze. The room he takes us to is spacious and sweet smelling, but I barely notice, for I am deeply worried about Evelyn. Is she not able to get out of her bed?

After what feels like an eternity, Sir Humphrey silently leads me to his wife's sitting room. There, standing in a simple dressing gown, is Evelyn. A wave of relief washes over me at the sight of her, but it is quickly replaced by concern as I notice the pallor of her face and the deep shadows under her eyes. Her arms feel weak as she hugs me.

"I was happy to hear that you and Pierre were coming, but I am sorry for imposing on you and disrupting your summer, Genevieve," she says softly.

"*Imposing?* You can't be serious. I want to be here! Remember when Daphne died three months after we moved to Lichfield, and you went out of your way to come to my side? You knew she was much more than a housekeeper to me. Without you, I couldn't have struggled through."

Soon both our faces are wet with tears.

Over the next six days, Evelyn steadily gains strength. I am relieved to witness her recovery, and my time away from Lichfield fills with quiet pleasures. On the second day of my visit, she and I take a turn in her garden. On the fourth, we manage a walk through the village of Twickenham, visiting the shops nestled along the Thames. But she carefully avoids talk of deeper emotions connected to her lost child, her seven-year marriage, or any other intimate subjects. She and I are alone for much of that time, giving her many opportunities to open up. Not a peep. I keep reminding myself that Evelyn is a very proud person. I must be patient.

It is not until the seventh day of my visit that we learn more about each other's lives. It begins with a delightful surprise in the breakfast parlour.

"Here's our morning treat," Evelyn says as the kitchen maid brings in two large cups of foaming chocolate. Oh, but the pleasure of the concoction! I never prepare it in Lichfield, for Thomas disapproves of chocolate. A deep sigh escapes as I take my first sip, and Evelyn winks across the table. Women who adore chocolate to the same degree enjoy a friendship that can't be shaken.

We first shared morning chocolate in Derby when I stayed at her stepfather's house, the banker who financed the porcelain workshop. She handled the business's accounts. I was placed in both home and workshop as a favour to my Uncle Andrew, the artisan who created Derby's first beautiful figurines.

I didn't have any interest in painting porcelain. I agreed to take the position in order to spy on the factory and uncover its blue formula for Sir Gabriel Courtenay. The last thing I expected to find was a kindred spirit. I remember the many long conversations with Evelyn that continued into the late hours. Most young women thought of nothing but marriage. But we felt little desire for one. We knew that husbands had all the rights; they controlled the money and property and could demand obedience from a wife, with the courts supporting the man. No, Evelyn and I were happy to escape the fate of an arranged marriage. My *bourgeoisie* grandfather was too indulgent of me to force one. Evelyn's stepfather was too indifferent. We chose our husbands ourselves.

"What shall we plan for today?" says Evelyn. "You haven't been to Hampton Court yet — they open the palace for visitors if you get special permission. Or would you prefer Alexander Pope's house? It's much closer."

These outings serve as diversions from deeper discussion, but if Evelyn enjoys them, I am glad to participate. I choose Pope in a heartbeat, and a few hours later, we are exploring outside the house built by Twickenham's most famous resident. The poet's been dead for over twenty years, but the house's present owner, mindful of Pope's following, kindly allows the devoted and curious to roam about the grounds. I've only read a few of the man's poems, but various sayings roll around in my head. I always relished, "Blessed is he who expects nothing, for he shall never be disappointed."

Pierre and Catherine Willoughby play in Pope's gardens, watched by the Willoughbys' governess. Evelyn and I descend to explore the grotto, the intricate chambers Pope had carved out under his villa. It feels like stepping into a demented fairy tale. Four flickering oil lamps hang from the top of the cave's ceiling, illuminating the pools of water and the strange and whimsical walls: brick, covered by jagged stones, and then dotted with seashells encrusted with bits of broken mirror or bright stones.

It's while standing next to a damp, glittering cavern wall that Evelyn says, "Marriage can be complicated, wouldn't you agree?"

I peer at her sideways. Over the past week, Evelyn has transformed from wan and melancholy to her old self: practical, highly intelligent, a touch acerbic and deeply loyal. Perhaps we couldn't plunge into this conversation until she was ready.

"What is it like to be married to someone who is now in the ministry?" I ask.

"Oh, I have no difficulty with Humphrey. I never have. But on occasion, I must join him in society. And that is where I do have difficulty. Humphrey says it's because I'm too honest."

"Too honest?"

"Women of society — the nobility — lie about everything. They take lovers and run up gambling debts and spread vicious gossip about their closest friends. I do none of those things, and that marks me as an outsider." She pauses. "I know I am confirming your contempt of the nobility."

"Oh, I'm sure it is *entirely* mutual. A refugee from Spitalfields? *Quelle horreur.*"

Evelyn laughs, but then grows serious. "Genevieve ... I must tell you that when I said marriage was complicated, I wasn't talking about *mine.*"

I turn to her, astonished. "Mine? Really? But why do you think something has gone amiss with Thomas and me?"

"A difference in your letters to me. A restlessness of spirit during your visit here. And I know you, Genevieve. Leaving London wasn't *your* idea. You're not someone who ever craved the simplicity of the country."

At first, I feel a rush of gratitude that someone has grasped my struggle with leaving London. I have no one to talk to but Thomas and he is incredibly busy. While living in Lichfield, I know I should seize the opportunity to work on my painting. But since I was very young, the vibrant, dangerous, scandalous city of London has served as inspiration for my art. The streets fed my muse. After moving, I can find nothing in my new surroundings that I want to paint.

This feels impossible to explain. Instead, I say, "After I was forced to close the silk-painting business, Thomas secured this teaching position in Lichfield, and, really, what else could we do? Living there's been good for Thomas and Pierre. We can put into practice the theories of Rousseau — Pierre can be formed by nature rather than trapped inside a house in East London. Thomas's health is much improved in the country air. You should see him throw himself into his work in Lichfield. It was the right thing to do, without question."

Evelyn says nothing for a bit. The only sound is the steady trickle of the underground spring, which feeds the grotto's shallow pools. Her following words are gentle. "That all makes perfect sense. I don't dispute it. I must say, Genevieve, I wish your first concern wasn't putting Thomas in the best possible light."

I burst out laughing. It takes me a minute to catch my breath sufficiently to say, "That is precisely what I think you always do with *your* husband." Now it is her turn to laugh. But underneath my joking, I feel a sharp pang. I want to tell her about my upsetting discovery that Thomas fears our son lacks intelligence. But before I can confide in her, the door at the grotto's end eases open, and a trio of people push in. Evelyn and I return to the children. We leave the grotto for the emerald-green lawn that stretches between Pope's handsome pale-yellow villa and the Thames. A barge glides by on the placid river. Our children are playing near a tree with branches arching so far, they touch the ground.

"It's beautiful here," I say. "You'd never know we were near London at all."

Evelyn says, "Pope's house is so famous, it's attracted many people with means to live in Twickenham."

"Like you and Sir Humphrey?" I tease.

Evelyn bites her lip and says, "We took the house at the suggestion of a very good friend of Humphrey's. He's a neighbour. Which brings me to a special request to make of you."

Special request? My pulse jumps. The way she puts it rings a warning bell. At the back of my mind I've wondered if there is some other reason for my presence in Twickenham, if Sir Humphrey had his eye on my husband despite his denials.

My friend continues, "Because Pope settled here, Twickenham is particularly popular for other writers, including Humphrey's friend. Have you heard of Sir Horace Walpole?"

I say carefully, "The MP? Of course. He's quite the letter writer. Supposed to have one of the finest wits in England."

"You'll be able to judge for yourself, Genevieve. He's having a dinner party tomorrow at his house, Strawberry Hill, and *you* are invited."

Evelyn smiles brightly, but her eyes are worried. That bell rings again. I'd been worried that Sir Humphrey harbours an ominous interest in my husband. Now, interest is swinging in my direction. I don't like the sound of this dinner. Evelyn is a straightforward person, but I feel as if she's hiding something from me.

I say, "Why? I'm a painter from Spitalfields, married to a chemist. I have never travelled in grand circles. I've brought no clothes appropriate for a dinner hosted by Sir Horace Walpole."

"I thought of that. I have a dress that would suit you with a few stitches."

The children wave. Evelyn and I must settle this before Pierre and Diana cease their play and join us.

I say quickly, "I must first learn why I'm invited. Did Sir Humphrey tell him I'm staying with you? Why would he do that?"

She frowns. "Genevieve, the two men are *friends*. It would be only natural to mention you are staying with us."

"So Horace Walpole's only being polite — 'Bring her along'?"

"Honestly, it's more than that. I believe your invitation has to do with your being an artist. Horace is, well, troubled about some private matter. He wouldn't say what, but he wants to discuss it over dinner with Humphrey, myself, you and … three other people who he's invited."

"Who are the three others?" I ask, now becoming alarmed.

"He wouldn't say," says Evelyn, biting her lip again. "He is rather … eccentric. But Sir Horace Walpole is not a bad man by any means. I wouldn't want you to come to Strawberry Hill if he were. And it's important to me that you do come. Frankly, I need you by my side."

I think about what she said in the grotto about finding the aristocrats difficult. "Ah, you'd like me to serve as reinforcements?" She nods, smiling ruefully.

"Of course. I shall be there. And who knows? I may find a bit of titled debauchery entertaining."

She laughs. "Sir Horace Walpole's greatest vice is gossip. But he does like to play games, and this airing of a problem over dinner in front of a carefully chosen group without explaining ahead of time is very much in character."

The children run towards us, laughing, and my friend says, "Come to my room later. We must go to Strawberry Hill well prepared, and I have something that will help."

Chapter Four

After the children are set up with an early dinner, I seek out Evelyn in her upstairs sitting room. She has a book for me. The cover is dark, reminding me of …

I start with surprise. Yes, it is *The Castle of Otranto*, the same novel that my watercolour student, Lydia, was reading in Lichfield. I'm surprised that Evelyn would be drawn to a book of ghostly melodrama, but after all, it's very popular. Lord knows she's needed something diverting.

"If you can turn your mind to it, I think it would be helpful to read some of Horace Walpole's book before the dinner," Evelyn says. "It's not long."

"I should read Mr Walpole's copy of the book? Why that one in particular?"

Evelyn smiles patiently. "No, it's *his* book, Genevieve. He's the author."

I take a deep breath. "I'm confused. Someone wrote this book in Italy centuries ago. It was recently found and translated into English." I open the title page. "Do you see? Here's the name of the author and this other person, an English translator."

"Genevieve, I'm sorry. I thought you knew. I shall explain."

It seems that this tale of terrifying escapades in a medieval-era Italian castle was, in fact, a literary hoax. The book was entirely written a few years ago by Sir Horace Walpole, son of the first prime minister and a Whig member of Parliament. At first, the public was led to believe that the manuscript, printed in Naples in 1529, was found in a northern castle owned by an "ancient Catholic family". But the story wasn't true. Responding to whispers, Sir Horace Walpole admitted he wrote the novel. Somehow, the news of true authorship of *The Castle of Otranto* had not yet reached me — or Lydia — in Lichfield.

"The Italian name is a partial anagram of Horace Walpole," says Evelyn. "I told you. He likes to play games."

I can't help but laugh. This is the last thing I thought an MP would spend time doing. Still, his audacity amuses me, and for the first time, I look forward to meeting this celebrated — and strange — man. If only I knew why he was so keen to include me.

That night, after my son's asleep, I light a fresh beeswax candle on the other side of the room and open *The Castle of Otranto*. Twilight's last grey lightening of the sky is extinguished. Through the open window, I hear the night creatures stirring. It's not as loud as the shrill choir of summer crickets I've grown used to outside our Lichfield cottage. But Twickenham is sylvan enough to produce a ripple of nocturnal noises.

Walpole's story begins violently. A young bridegroom, the son of the tyrannical Prince Manfred, who rules the ancient castle, is crushed to death shortly before his wedding — by a giant knight's helmet.

A giant knight's helmet?

I'm unsure what to make of the invention, nor this: terrified servants later report seeing a man the size of the giant lying in a castle gallery. Less fantastical but more disturbing to me is what follows: the prince attempts to seduce the lovely young bride-to-be, Isabella, hours after his son's grisly death, saying he'll divorce his wife to have new sons with Princess Isabella.

In one passage, Prince Manfred grabs Isabella's hand, *cold with horror*, and she pulls away. As the older man tries to seduce her, a sound is heard: a human sigh. It comes from the painting hanging over the bench where the two had been sitting. She takes this opportunity to flee into underground tunnels.

I reach the part of the book when Prince Manfred offers his young daughter in marriage to Isabella's father to try to persuade him to force Isabella into Manfred's bed. Disgust with predatory princes mingles with exhaustion, and I put the novel aside to find sleep. But my dreams are full of endless panicky running to escape some faceless enemy.

When I appear in the breakfast parlour the following morning, Evelyn says, "Genevieve, you look a trifle peaked."

"I suppose you can blame Sir Horace Walpole for that."

My friend says, "I wasn't sure *The Castle of Otranto* would be to your taste."

It wasn't. The finest novel I've ever read is *Tom Jones*. I relish its frankness about human greed and desire, its touching love story and rollicking wit. There isn't the faintest suggestion of humour in *The Castle of Otranto*. I wasn't moved by the book's star-crossed lovers or impressed by a story about a nobleman trying to seduce the fiancée of his dead son. It seemed like a third-rate version of *Romeo and Juliet* with ghosts suffused with menace. But hours away from stepping over his threshold, it doesn't seem wise to denigrate Sir Horace's effort.

"I shall be ready to discuss his book," I assure Evelyn. "You'll be astounded by the way I sing its praises."

She laughs. "Oh, I shall miss you, Genevieve, when you're back home in Lichfield."

Home. I put down my cup of chocolate. The ease I feel with my friend, her acceptance of my nature and our support of one another, shall soon be gone.

"Yes, I suppose it's time to make the travel arrangements," I say. The moment the words are out of my mouth, I feel a dull ache of dread. It was such a balm to my spirits to spend this time with Evelyn. In some ways, I've returned to my old self, before marriage. I know this cannot continue, but it's still difficult to embrace my return to what has been a fairly lonely existence.

"I've kept you long enough," she says wistfully. "You must wish to get back to your painting."

The image flashes before my eyes: a bare easel against the wall, faltering half-finished sketches piled on the chipped table, the brushes and prints out of sight in the table's drawer.

"Genevieve?" Evelyn leans across the table. "You have lost all your colour."

"It's nothing." I can't work out my inability to paint — how could I explain it to anyone else? "It could be the thought of Sir Horace Walpole inviting me to his home because he thinks I have special knowledge about art that fills me with apprehension."

"But you *are* knowledgeable, Genevieve."

"A woman painter can only go so far in England, and I have not gone far enough to pose as any sort of expert. That's the truth. Every time I've tried to advance in the sphere of men, it's been a mistake. Or worse. Throwing myself at the feet of William Hogarth to plead to be his apprentice was a mistake. Trying to enter the circle of Joshua Reynolds was a *disaster*."

How bitter I sound! Forcing a smile, I tell my worried-looking friend it's nothing but a bout of morning melancholy. We decide to take the air with the children before preparations begin for dinner. Pierre is always pleading for a chance to watch the boats pass by. A stroll to the Thames becomes the plan.

To reach the riverbank from the Willoughbys' house, we follow a path through two small orchards, raspberry beds on the left and apple trees on the right. I'm told the orchards are nothing compared to those of the Willoughbys' neighbour, Secretary Johnston, who built extensive gardens and, according to Evelyn, a grotto. Along the river, large trees afford shade, but Pierre will have none of sitting — he races back and forth, eager for a sighting of a sail or even a tiny rowing boat. Anything nautical will do.

Sir Humphrey, trailed by one of his colourless aides, joins us. After chatting with his wife, he says, "Genevieve, a letter arrived this afternoon for you." He hands it to me.

My name is written in my husband's script. Turning the letter over, I feel the edge of a broken seal as it flaps open.

"Sir Humphrey, what is this?" I ask, shaking the letter at him.

He displays no embarrassment. "Rules must be followed. Because of my position, all mail is opened straight away by my staff. We've had some … unpleasant correspondence. Can't take chances."

"But this is *my* letter," I say, temper rising.

"Addressed to *this* house," he shoots back.

I think of the day before yesterday when I saw Evelyn break letter seals by herself, at least one of them from a stranger. My suspicion sparks again. Did Sir Humphrey read Thomas's letter because of his mysterious interest in my husband's activities? But I can't take this further now, not in front of Evelyn and the children.

I unfold the parchment. Thomas tells me his work goes well before getting to the point:

> *Your loyalty to your friend does you great credit. I under-*
> *stand why you would respond to a call to go to her side. I*

comprehend that Pierre is too young to be left behind with servants. Yet I do not want his head turned by London amusements or to indulge his obsession with ships. When you return, I hope there are opportunities for him to spend time with the Darwin children. Pierre would benefit from their company. I cannot wait to see you both and resume our precious life together in the country, Gen.

Your loving husband, Thomas

I refold the letter, reflecting that, beneath these affectionate words, Thomas lacks a deep understanding of his wife and son. Or perhaps he grasps that we have feelings and "obsessions" that he cannot share and wants to draw us closer.

"Sir Humphrey, Sir Humphrey!" Pierre shouts. "A barge just went by."

"You'll miss the boats on the Thames when you leave, won't you?" says Sir Humphrey, ruffling my son's wavy red hair.

"I am not going to leave," announces Pierre, stamping his foot.

I jump in to say, "Pierre, I've just had a letter from Papa. He misses us. We will go back home soon so that we can be with him." I try to emphasize his returning to his father, whom Pierre adores. But that doesn't work.

"I hate it there — and you hate it too, Mama," Pierre shouts. "I know it. Why are you pretending?"

On the word *pretending*, his voice breaks, and he turns and runs back to the river's edge, a confused Diana Willoughby in his wake.

The wobble in Pierre's voice calls forth a prickling of tears. I can't trust myself to speak. At just five years of age, my son knows my heart. I, too, recoil from the prospect of returning to Lichfield, but we simply have no choice.

Sir Humphrey says quietly, "It's hot today, and the boy's overtired, I'm sure."

Evelyn chimes in, saying, "We had too many sweets. When you mix that with exercise in the sun, the result can be a choleric temper. Let me coax him into the shade."

She moves towards the children, leaving me with Sir Humphrey. "You know," he says, "with such an interest in ships, a career in the Royal Navy might be just the thing."

"His father would perish at the thought."

"Naturally," says Sir Humphrey dryly. "The Navy is the pearl of our empire." If he read Thomas's letter, as I suspect he did, he knows how much Pierre's father wants to extinguish this interest.

After a moment, he asks, "What do *you* think, Genevieve?"

Gazing at the Thames, I say, "I'd miss him dreadfully and worry every day he was at sea. But if it is what Pierre wants, I'd try to understand and to help him."

"Well, I'd be happy to look into it. Very young boys can accept commissions as midshipmen."

"I know that. It's imperative to enter the Royal Navy at the right age, or else one falls behind."

I can feel Sir Humphrey's eyes on me. I turn from the river and freeze at his expression: incredulous and even ... unnerved.

"What's the matter?" I ask.

"Sir Gabriel Courtenay told you that, didn't he? 'Imperative to enter the Royal Navy at the right age'? It's as if I can hear his words but said with your voice."

"I've no idea who told me that. But it certainly wasn't Sir Gabriel. I haven't spoken to him in seven years!"

Evelyn returns with the children at that moment, and he drops the matter, thank God. Pierre seems sorry about his outburst, and we return to the Willoughbys' house holding hands tightly.

It's not until I am going through the measuring, fitting and stitching of Evelyn's gown for my wearing it to Strawberry Hill that my thoughts return to Sir Humphrey's accusation. I lied. I knew at once it *was* Courtenay who told me about boys taking commissions in the Royal Navy. Ah, Sir Gabriel Courtenay. He was Sir Humphrey's nemesis: the well-born Englishman spying for King Louis XV of France. England fought a long and bitter war with France that only ended three years ago. During part of that time, Louis depended on Sir Gabriel for intelligence on England.

I didn't know that Sir Gabriel was a spy for the French when he persuaded me to go to Derby Porcelain and obtain its chemist's formula for blue. I thought I was doing it for a rival porcelain factory. I knew that Sir Gabriel turned to spying at the highest level to earn enough money for a grand house on Grosvenor Square filled with the family heirlooms, beautiful furniture and carefully chosen paintings that meant so much to him. How could I truly judge him? I wanted to earn enough money to make a life for myself in Venice as an artist, free of disapproval and sneering.

Yes, I know Sir Gabriel said that about the Navy. What's more, I knew exactly *when* Sir Gabriel said it: on the boat's deck crossing the Channel, with Thomas down below. Sir Gabriel had kidnapped us both, forcing us to travel in secret and in great danger smack in the middle of a war. The genius chemist, Thomas Sturbridge, would have to work for Sèvres Manufactory Works in Versailles, developing his revolutionary formula for the colour blue, the colour of France. I was taken along to ensure his cooperation since Thomas was in love with me. While that pressure point proved useful to Sir Gabriel, he was angry with me for breaking off my spying for him. With Sir Gabriel, what started as teacher and pupil — or even master and minion — darkened to us treating each other like enemies.

Except when we didn't, like that night on the boat, the stars ablaze in a velvet sky. I'd already learned of his turning point, that he chose a life built on spying after his future vanished at the age of eighteen. He'd expected to be the heir to a wealthy uncle who was childless until, in old age, the relation managed to marry and beget a boy. That night, Sir Gabriel told me that the other respectable paths he could have chosen at the time were blocked. He didn't pursue a commission for the Royal Navy because he feared he was already too old.

But I don't want to hear Sir Gabriel's words in my head. Most of all, I don't want to picture him on the deck of that boat, tall and lean, his long black hair hanging past his shoulders. I don't want to remember hearing those admissions about his troubled life just two days after we'd fought with such fury: Sir Gabriel threatening to tie me up if I didn't cooperate and my screaming that I hated him. Or his late-night confession the month before that he needed me to "save" him.

I put Sir Gabriel firmly out of my thoughts.

As I am preparing for the dinner, Joseph pops into the room to discuss arrangements for passage on a travel coach leaving Twickenham. The Willoughbys insist on paying for our coach fare home. It looks as if the best time to go is in three days' time. As soon as I am able, I dash off a letter to my husband saying that I will be home within the week. I am determined to be pragmatic about returning to Lichfield, no matter my feelings — or poor Pierre's — and to enjoy my last days in Twickenham.

After Evelyn's toilette is finished, her lady's maid, Rachel, shifts to performing mine. The truth is, I wouldn't have minded showing up at Strawberry Hill with an unpainted face and hair pinned up. I recoil from the artifice of London society, where women are transformed into grotesque dolls. But evidently, we must prepare with great care for an evening with the prime minister's son. Rachel pads my hair with several matching pieces and threads my curls with light lace ribbons. As for my face, she applies a whitening formula, followed by triangles of rouge. A painful tweezing precedes a darkening of eyebrows. Finally, she stains my lips with a burgundy concoction.

"Mrs Sturbridge, you look *beautiful*," says a startled Rachel.

Realizing that this could be interpreted as an insult, she says, "I don't mean to say you're not lovely every day, Madame."

I pat her arm with a laugh. "You are highly skilled."

The looking glass testifies to Rachel's skills. My hazel eyes are brighter, and my features are softer. My chestnut brown hair looks lustrous. And the swiftly altered lavender gown flatters me in both colour and fit. While I'll never win attention for voluptuousness, my figure appears trim rather than bony.

My glum mood of the day finally lifts. It might be amusing to join the beau monde turned out like this. I'm an actress in a play that is to be performed for one night only.

"Genevieve, just *look* at you," exclaims Evelyn, elegantly gowned and coiffed, when I join her in the downstairs parlour. I spread my skirts carefully as I find a place on the settee. I can hear Sir Humphrey coming down the hall in conversation with another man. A few seconds later, I discover who that man is.

Evelyn says, "Oh, here you are, Captain Howard, and a splendid sight for our dinner."

While, again, his hair is unpowdered, and he has chosen garments dark and unadorned to the point of severity, Captain Howard's waistcoat gleams with silver buttons. He greets Evelyn with warmth before bestowing a curt nod in my direction. Whether it be his brusqueness or his swagger, Captain Howard's presence threatens to dim my hope of a diverting evening.

"I did not know you were among my fellow guests, Captain," I say. My effort at a light tone does not succeed. Anyone with the power of hearing could perceive my dismay.

His eyebrows rising, Captain Howard says, "Does Sir Horace Walpole make it a habit of running his guest lists by you, Mrs Sturbridge?"

Evelyn coughs delicately and suggests we have a sherry together before leaving. When the two men launch into a conversation about the latest act of defiance from the colonists in America, Evelyn pulls on my sleeve and whispers, "I had no idea you disliked Captain Howard."

"He has few qualities to commend him."

"Really? Humphrey trusts Captain Howard as he does few others."

"So I have noted."

She says in an even softer voice, "You are of course entitled to your views. But I can tell you that life has been difficult for him. There are so many obstacles to overcome in England when one is a Roman Catholic. He and his older brother, Lord Robert Howard, required an Act of Parliament before they were granted commissions to serve as officers in the army. His brother was killed alongside him in Québec in the midst of a battle. They were devoted brothers. It was terrible."

I peer over at Captain Howard, his hand on his hip. At that instant, he glances in my direction with that imperious lift of the chin. I am sorry he's had a difficult life, but I doubt Captain Howard and I could ever be friends. I shall still do my best to enjoy this dinner party even though he is among the guests.

Chapter Five

Leaning as far out the coach window as I dare without looking gauche, I get my first glimpse of the Walpole property: wrought-iron bars are dotted with carved strawberries, leaves and fruit, which curl around scrolls.

Once inside those gates, after the coach rumbles past a clutch of trees, my impression is of dazzling white slabs jumping out from sullen grey. It creates such a stark contrast that I blink.

What I see seems impossible, but it is undeniable. When Sir Humphrey said, "Horace's castle," I assumed it to be a joke. But now, our carriage is drawing up to a medieval castle just off the Thames River.

In this quiet town, a retreat for the prosperous writers, merchants and statesmen of George III's kingdom, rises a collection of sharply rectangular pale brick buildings, supporting arched windows filled with stained glass, towers, turrets and *battlements* — yes, the castle boasts parapets with regular gaps for shooting arrows. All that is missing is a moat and drawbridge.

Evelyn leans over to say, "I didn't tell you what Strawberry Hill is like. It's quite something to see it for the first time."

I ask if Sir Horace Walpole inherited this property from his family.

"Just the opposite," snorts Sir Humphrey. "Horace built it out of practically nothing. Twenty years ago, what you saw here was a couple of cottages owned by some toy seller."

Captain Howard laughs appreciatively at Sir Humphrey's remark, and my cheeks flush. How am I supposed to know the history of the property?

We come to a halt next to a carriage stone. The men hop out and Sir Humphrey extends his hand to his wife. She grips it as she carefully descends the carriage-stone steps in her filmy gown.

"Mrs Sturbridge?" As he says my name, Captain Howard thrusts forward his arm to support my descent.

I reluctantly rest my hand on his forearm. I don't want to rely on Captain Howard, but neither do I want to slip and stumble onto the ground in these slippers and ruin the dress.

Captain Howard's suit coat is made of some sort of velvet. It makes for a soft layer atop his hard, muscular arm.

"Thank you," I mutter.

A smirk quivers as if he can tell how much I regret the need to accept his help.

Sir Humphrey gestures towards a chapel-shaped doorway carved into the pale wall. It's time to meet Sir Horace Walpole at last. I'd assumed the doorway opened into the house itself, but that isn't the case. I move into a long roofless passageway between sharp-edged stone walls, and at the end stands our host, Sir Horace Walpole.

Like the fantastical castle he built, the man is not what I expect. He is rather tall and thin, with dark brown hair peeking out from his white wig and brown eyes flicking from one of us to the next with lively intelligence. The fine lines etched on his face suggest that Walpole has passed forty years of age. Yet, he wears a light turquoise coat, heavily embroidered, and matching tight breeches in the latest fashion for foppish young men. There's nothing wrong with that. But he places himself, quite deliberately, before a thick wooden arched door that looks like it belongs to a Plantagenet-age cathedral, complete with a stained-glass window above. The contrast feels odd.

After greeting Sir Humphrey, Evelyn, and Captain Howard, Walpole turns to me, and we are formally introduced.

"At last, Mrs Sturbridge, at last. I've wanted to make your acquaintance for so long," he says, kissing my hand with a courtly flourish.

"I thank you for the invitation, sir. I'm delighted to see your incredible home," I say with a curtsey.

"My little Gothic playhouse," Walpole says, waving a hand dismissively, though he dimples a smile that betrays his pleasure at my compliment.

It is time to ask my question.

"Sir Horace, I confess to some curiosity about why I have been honoured with this invitation and how you could wish to meet me for a long time."

Sir Humphrey frowns at me, clears his throat, and says, "Mrs Sturbridge possesses a certain boldness of manner. It's a trait we've all had to get used to, and—"

Walpole interrupts him with the cry, "Oh, but it's her boldness that I am in great need of." He turns to me. "Mrs Sturbridge, I shall call on your forthrightness as well as your special background tonight."

My throat tightens. "Special background?"

He laughs. "Don't look alarmed! It was Joshua Reynolds who told me about you. He painted my portrait years ago and I've maintained a friendship ever since. He reported on your artistic talent and perceptiveness. I pray that your powers of perception will help me with my little problem."

Just hearing the name *Joshua Reynolds* is unpleasant. The great portrait painter befriended me two years ago. He kept it a secret at first, but wanted to meet Thomas because he'd heard that my husband was a master chemist who could work wonders with errant colours. After Thomas refused to work for him, the artist had no use for me.

I peer over at Sir Humphrey, who knows a couple of unsavoury things about Joshua Reynolds. At this moment, however, Sir Humphrey's interest does not seem to lie with me or Reynolds but with his friend. He says sombrely, "I know you relish a mystery, Horace. Now that we are here, it's time to tell me — to tell all of us — about this problem. Why are we here?"

Sir Horace Walpole's welcoming smile vanishes under the force of his friend's question. He shakes his head and says, "No, not yet, not here. I can't speak of it outside. At dinner — with my other guests — I shall explain. I can tell you what's happening to me *once*. Please, I must do this the proper way."

Walpole rubs his hands and says shrilly, "First allow me to give you a tour of Strawberry Hill!" He turns and rushes inside the entrance, calling to a servant. Captain Howard pulls back Sir Humphrey and says in a low voice, "I think the man is ... ?"

"Afraid," finishes Sir Humphrey. "Yes, he most definitely is afraid. I don't think I've ever seen him in such a state, and I've known him for over twenty years."

When I follow the others into Strawberry Hill, I'm engulfed by a small, dim hall, its floor paved with hexagonal tiles. The only windows are narrow, filled with stained glass and sealed tight. Two austere saints stare down at me, and I feel the warm, clammy air of the hall closing in.

"My good man, would you consider fixing a candle here near the entrance?" asks Sir Humphrey. "It's hard to see a thing."

"That's quite intentional, Humphrey," says Horace Walpole. "It's here in the hall that my Gothic castle achieves the perfect state of 'gloomth'."

"Perfect state of what?" I ask.

"The word is my own invention, Mrs Sturbridge. I am endeav-ouring to strike a balance between 'gloom' and 'warmth'. Now, on with our tour."

Captain Howard says, "Can we hear anything of your problem first?"

"No, you may not." Walpole shakes his head with vehemence. "Mrs Sturbridge has never set foot in Strawberry Hill before today. It would be the height of rudeness to deny her my tour."

Captain Howard sighs as if I am to blame for our host's procras-tination. No doubt he also feels I am responsible for rain from the sky and a sour song in the tavern.

Sir Horace Walpole charges forward. I wish I could say that the tour is so fascinating that it is well worth everyone's time. But I find it unsettling to the degree that at a certain point I long for it to be over.

We walk through various square or round rooms directly leading to one another or connected by short corridors. There are settees, chairs and desks in each room, but furniture is not the point. The walls are lined with portraits and shelves bearing historical curiosi-ties — centuries-old busts, coins, medals, articles of clothing and other personal treasures. This is not a house for comfort. It's built to showcase what Walpole calls "the spoils of my collecting". Each room is kept immaculately clean, or as far as I can make out in the dim light of Strawberry Hill's *gloomth*. Yet a pungent, musty smell emerges from the depths of the shelves, and from some of the rooms' corners too. The house is new, but these objects are not.

I seem to be the only one who is not enjoying Strawberry Hill. The others in my party appear to be at ease here. Sir Humphrey and Sir Horace banter like two people who have known each other most of their lives. Despite her confessing some nervousness three days ago, Evelyn fits in perfectly. Captain Howard, too, has a connection to Walpole going back in time, as they discuss a distant relation of the captain named Henrietta Howard, who is in poor health. After that, I notice Captain Howard often falls into silence, though it could be just his brooding nature.

Sir Horace Walpole talks more and more as we weave our way through these rooms packed with curiosities. At times, he verges on agitated. Our host constantly credits his "Strawberry Hill committee", the friends who he says helped plan the castle and track down his acquisitions. I have no doubt, though, he is the leader of the committee. To live like this would require devouring obsession.

How could these long-ago centuries exert such a powerful grip? It seems to extend beyond serving as a setting for *The Castle of Otranto*. I never imagined someone of means and sophistication would prefer to occupy himself with acquiring the objects of those who lived two or three hundred years before and more. I appreciate the workmanship of these clocks, busts and helmets, but they were fashioned during a time when people were trapped, blighted. Most couldn't read or write. They lived by the cruel whim of kings or the army of priests, monks and friars who tried to control every deed and every thought. This is the best century in which to be alive. Great thinkers like Voltaire and Rousseau have blown away the thick cobwebs and challenged us all to think for ourselves and shape our own destinies. In the world of art, William Hogarth has used prints and paintings to attack the injustices of today's society. *That* is what art should do.

Yet here we are, dressed in our finest, acting as if excited by a crusader's mesh glove or a cardinal's scarlet hat.

I am in Sir Horace Walpole's Holbein room when the reason for my presence once again becomes unclear.

Like all the other rooms we tour, it is eccentric in the extreme. Small and circular, the room boasts walls painted purple, the colour of royalty, Walpole reminds us. In the centre of the room is an ebony table and six matching chairs, and in the centre of the table sits a tray holding four combs made of ancient ivory or tortoiseshell with long teeth. It's as if the table awaits the arrival of a bevy of maids of honour who must perform the toilette of an imperious queen.

And then there are the miniature portraits by Hans Holbein, the famous court painter to Henry VIII — except not even half of them are originals. Most are obviously sketched reproductions of the German painter's work. There must be forty in all hanging in precise rows on the deep purple walls.

"Genevieve, what do you think?" asks Evelyn, beckoning me to come closer to one of the copies. "You said you liked Holbein."

I say carefully, "Hans Holbein was an important artist of the sixteenth century because he made the people he painted look more natural than the other artists who had gone before."

Sir Humphrey squints at a sketch, which is of an unsmiling man of middle years wearing a feathered cap. The feather is the only object showing detail. "This fellow doesn't look all that natural to me," he says, shrugging.

How do I respond to this? I'm a guest of Walpole's, not here to criticize. Still, hadn't he said he valued my boldness and artistic knowledge? That's supposed to be the reason I was invited.

"It's likely that the original painting or sketch is more lifelike," I say, stealing a glance at Sir Horace.

"Oh, no doubt, no doubt," says our host immediately. "I couldn't purchase most of the available Holbeins for my house and not because of the price. They are in the Queen's collection, on display in Kensington Palace. I was granted permission for a friend to make miniature copies."

Sir Humphrey lays a hand on Sir Horace Walpole's shoulder. "My friend, isn't it time you took us into your confidence?"

Walpole stands motionless for a moment, his head bowed. "I will," he says finally. "Of course I will. That's why I asked you here. But it won't make any sense until we reach the armoury. It's like drinking port before the aperitif. Simply never done."

He darts out of the room, and the rest of us have little choice but to follow.

I don't get very far.

As I step out of the Holbein room, a quiver of dizziness trembles at the base of my skull. It's so warm and airless in this dim corridor. But instead of hurrying to join the rest of my party and hopefully reach a cooler part of the castle, I hesitate. It feels like too much — the intricate rooms, the rush of objects to see, Walpole's nervous chatter — all with the tension running underneath of our host's unarticulated fear *and* the mystery of my invitation. Walpole was no more interested in my artist's perspective on the Holbeins than when looking at the large portraits along his gallery. And apart from the deep oddness of this house, I'm filled with suspicion about Sir Humphrey Willoughby.

As clammy and claustrophobic as it feels at this spot, I need a moment to be alone. I close my eyes and breathe. Thankfully, no one taps my arm, asks questions or fusses over me. They've all gone ahead.

When I feel steadier, I move to follow them towards the next room.

"Walpole may have designed it to keep visitors a little off balance," says a quiet voice inches to my left.

Captain Howard is standing in an alcove so dark I can barely make out his features. I find this startling, though I realize that he must have paused to wait for me. I'm grateful, but wariness remains.

"What do you mean?" I ask as he emerges.

"It's the way the corridors twist, or that the rooms' ceilings are set high, then, in a second, they become low, or how the stairwells turn into halls," he says. "A person can lose their bearings."

I realize how right Captain Howard is. But then, this was a man who identified all the weaknesses of my Lichfield stable within seconds of stepping inside. That still rankles.

Still, I am emboldened enough by our conversation to ask Captain Howard if he knows the reason for his invitation as we are all here for a special reason. He considers before answering.

"I have no facts, but I do have a theory." Captain Howard grimaces as he continues. "If I am correct, I'm *not* going to be pleased, and a visit to Cardinal Wolsey's hat won't be enough to calm me down."

I laugh at that. He's as suspicious of his invitation as I am of mine, and no more enamoured of the peculiarities of Strawberry Hill. The last thing I expected to find here was common ground with Captain Howard.

It's time to join Sir Horace Walpole and the Willoughbys. We are back to the beginning: the small hall at the entrance to Strawberry Hill. Two things have changed, however. The sun is even fainter outside — whether it's a rainstorm gathering or the coming twilight, I can't tell — so the dull light filtering through the stained-glass portraits of saints barely throws squares of red, blue or gold on the tiled floor.

There *is* a light source, however, thanks to a woman wearing a housekeeper's cap standing on the landing of the second-storey staircase and holding aloft a glowing oil lamp.

Sir Horace Walpole calls out, "Ah, there you are, Margaret." He beckons for us to follow him up the stairs, through an archway and into a long, narrow vestibule. Yet another stained-glass window provides the only light source. It lands on the shoulders of a full-length suit of silver armour hanging in the centre, surrounded by family crests.

This must be the armoury.

Walpole reaches for my hand and gently leads me to the end of the vestibule, directly opposite the stained glass.

"Mrs Sturbridge, what do you think of this painting?"

It's a small square oil painting within a gilded gold frame. The subject is a cherub, a golden-haired angel wearing a white tunic, perched on a billowing cloud, peering over his shoulder as he smiles. The angel's tunic is incredibly detailed, as are the clouds, not just the one he rests upon but the misty clouds stretching across the painting below the blue sky. A ray of sun pierces that upper cloud with a vigour that makes my stomach flutter.

"Could I possibly have more light here?" I ask.

Seconds later, Walpole's housekeeper, Margaret, is by our side, holding aloft her lamp. When she does, the depth and subtlety of the sunray turn my suspicion into certainty.

"Is this painting a Fragonard?" I ask.

"Bravo, Mrs Sturbridge!" cries Sir Horace Walpole. "He is a coveted artist in France, but not so well known here. I purchased it in Paris six months ago. Ah, Joshua Reynolds was right about you!"

My knowledge of Jean-Honoré Fragonard is based on pictures in books. I've yet to see one of his works with my own eyes. I'm relieved that I have passed the test put to me. But I have a question for my host. "Why would you hang a painting of such beauty here?" I ask.

Walpole explains that the wallpaper design of the vestibule is a re-creation of the tomb of Arthur Tudor at Worcester Cathedral. The room honours the prince's memory. I can barely make out any design in this faint light. Just as it's hard to make out all the details of the Fragonard.

Evelyn asks, "You felt the prince's tomb had need of an angel?"

Clutching his heart dramatically, Walpole says, "Arthur was a pure and noble soul. If only he had lived. I had a dream. In it, I stood here in this exact spot, and a gigantic hand thrust itself from the wall. That was the sprouting of inspiration for me — that dream became my novel, *The Castle of Otranto*."

Sir Humphrey Willoughby says, impatience roughening his voice, "You've told me about that dream. But you went through this a few years ago! And *Otranto* is just, forgive me, it's just a novel. What are you frightened about *today*?"

Walpole nods as if he's agreeing to do something. I tense with excitement. Finally, we will learn what Walpole fears.

He lifts his right hand and points without even looking in that direction. It's as if he can't bear to see. At first, to my shock, I think he points at *me*. But I realize his finger is aimed at the Fragonard over my shoulder.

"For the last month," he says, "this house has been visited by the angel in the painting. Either I'm bearing witness to a spiritual being taking physical form, or someone is going to great lengths to drive me insane!"

Chapter Six

The tension that had been making my head throb pours out of me, much like a waterskin empties after being gutted with a blade.

I'd both longed for and dreaded learning what Sir Horace Walpole fears, only to discover it's nothing but the fancies of an excitable man who, as proven by the house in which we stand, is obsessed with the medieval age. In those times, people were convinced that supernatural beings paid visits to human beings day and night. Naturally, he would be vulnerable to such beliefs. Sir Horace Walpole's confession is sad and a bit embarrassing but nothing more serious.

I am sure of one thing: angels do not visit the living. John Calvin, whom the Huguenots have followed from the beginning, famously said, "Angels do not appear to us and do not conspicuously descend from heaven." Protestant teachings about ghosts, demons or similar supernatural beings are even more condemning. My husband, sceptical of facts that cannot be measured using scientific methods, does not need church sermons to disbelieve. He calls ghost stories "ghoulish grub".

"Zounds," mutters Captain Howard, shaking his head.

Sir Humphrey looks at Howard with reproof, and the younger man stiffens. Moving to Walpole's side, Sir Humphrey asks, "What did you mean when you said someone could be meddling with your sanity?"

"Yes, Mister Under-Secretary, I thought that would be the part you'd seize on," Walpole says, smiling strangely. "Well, that is one of the possible explanations."

Evelyn says, "And you think the other possibility is … an angel appears here in this house?" As hard as she tries to be polite, her scepticism can be heard. Evelyn is thoroughly logical. It's one of the things I like best about her.

Walpole is not offended. Nothing anyone has said seems to disturb him. "I can't explain any more to you now," he says. "I wanted you to see the armoury and the painting, so you'd understand their significance. You haven't had a bite to eat, making me a horrendous host. Let's retire to the refectory. Then I can tell you — and the others can too."

"Others?" Sir Humphrey asks.

Walpole says, with elaborate innocence, "Oh, didn't I mention that there are a number of witnesses?"

A chill moves up my spine. How could an imaginary sighting of an angel be shared?

"On to the refectory!" Walpole says gaily and leads the way to the room where we will dine. At least twenty-five feet long, it is dominated by a medieval-era chimney piece, an ebony black dining table and high-back ebony chairs. The walls are of pale stucco, and a long candelabra infuses the entire refectory with yellow light, turning it into the room with the warmest feel in the house. Its lack of *gloomth* makes it my favourite room so far.

Joining us at the table are two new people. One is Mrs Anna Campion, wearing the simple black dress of a widow. She is a long-time friend of Walpole's from an antiquarian society and fellow admirer of the Tudor royal family. They dive into discussion of the long-dead Prince Arthur.

The other new guest could not be more different: a man who looks several years younger than I am, blond-haired and broad-shouldered. Sir Horace introduces him as Lars Longfren, "one of the leading followers of the Swedish philosopher Emanuel Swedenborg".

"You know Swedenborg?" I ask, excited. "I've read his book *Heaven and Hell*. He has so many interesting beliefs on the human soul. But I don't understand some of the book. I have questions!"

"I can think of nothing better than answering your questions, Mrs Sturbridge," he says in his strong accent, his eyes sparkling.

More good news awaits. The dinner I consume at Strawberry Hill is one of the most delicious of my entire life. Yes, I come to this table ravenously hungry. The first course, *Potage à la Reine*, balances the meats, onions and herbs perfectly, with the lightest of creams blended in. The main course, the capons, are roasted to golden crispness, the tender flesh infused with garlic and tarragon. The wine accompanying our meal is both dry and sweet, and I drain my goblet with enthusiasm.

Much as I'd like to, I cannot question Longfren about Swedenborg's philosophy, for this is the sort of dinner party where one conversation takes place. Sir Horace Walpole leads it, but not into the arena of the supernatural.

At least not yet. As he's covered the refectory walls with paintings of his family and closest friends, Walpole uses them as promptings to entertain us with amusing stories. One tale that sends us all into gales of laughter is that of Walpole, when but a child, informing his father, the first prime minister, that he very much wanted to meet King George I. And while any other child in the kingdom would have got a pat on the head and told it wasn't possible, ten-year-old Horace Walpole was presented to the old, German-speaking King of England in his royal bedchamber one night, with George's terrifying mistress looking on.

"By the time I had turned ten years of age, I'd heard that story of Horace from *my* father," Sir Humphrey says. "He held you up to me and my brother as an example of a properly ambitious child."

Walpole laughs. "You've far surpassed me in service to the realm, Humphrey. You are such a success I even forgive you for being a protégé of William Pitt, who had the audacity to say, 'Not a shot should be fired anywhere in the world without the British government knowing why.' That prime minister set you on this path."

Sir Humphrey Willoughby gives a tight smile. Even with his life-long friend, Willoughby will say nothing about his spymaster role.

But Walpole, a bit agitated from the evening's high drama, pushes on. "I submit that I perform two important functions that no one else could. The first is to build Strawberry Hill and try to share my little Gothic enthusiasms. The second is to make introductions for Sir Humphrey Willoughby. Haven't I put you in the same room as anyone you wanted to meet in London? My only failure is getting you an audience with that experimenter Henry Cavendish! But really, the man is a recluse's recluse."

This news is like a thunderbolt cracking open the plaster and papier mâché castle of Strawberry Hill.

Henry Cavendish is a man of *science*. He published a paper that I know was the subject of passionate discussion at meetings of the Lunar Society. Dr Erasmus Darwin joked with me that if they couldn't recruit the standoffish Henry Cavendish, then the shy Joseph Priestley would be the next best thing for a new member, and that was what Thomas was trying to do with his summer experiments.

Sir Humphrey Willoughby has denied having any interest in what Thomas and his friends are working on. And he's denied that his government business in the Midlands before approaching me had anything to do with the Lunar Society.

If I had any doubts that I've been fed falsehoods, the fleeting, uneasy glance between Willoughby and Captain Howard following Walpole's comment settles them. They must wonder if I understand the significance in Sir Humphrey Willoughby wanting to meet Henry Cavendish.

I have been both anxious and angry about their lying to me since the day I left Lichfield, and now I shall flush the men out.

I say, "Sir Horace, tell us more about Mister Cavendish. Why is he such a challenge for you?" My voice rings out stridently across half the length of his dinner table, but I don't care. Out of the corner of my eye I spot Willoughby putting down his wine goblet.

Horace Walpole shrugs and says, "Not just for me, Mrs Sturbridge. Cavendish is from one of the three richest families in the kingdom. Still, he insists on living in isolation — or the closest thing he can find to it — while he devotes himself to experiments. He communicates to his servants purely through notes. He will talk to only one person at a time in a room, and that person can never be a woman. Humphrey asked me a number of times to persuade him to meet, but all my efforts failed, I fear."

"What?" exclaims Longfren. "This fellow sounds like a madman!"

I won't let Cavendish's peculiarities take over the conversation.

"We all know Sir Humphrey Willoughby is committed to the safety of the realm," I say, glaring at him down the table. The spymaster fixes me with narrowed eyes in return. With Walpole and all these people listening, he won't be able to intimidate me easily. I intend to take advantage of that.

"Why this deep interest in Cavendish's scientific experiments?" I ask. "It seems not very relevant to protecting us from the French and other enemies, or am I missing some vital intelligence?"

It's not Sir Humphrey who answers me but Horace Walpole. "Well, Mrs Sturbridge, all I know is—"

Captain Howard, who's said little throughout dinner, says, "I think the time has come to hear more about your angel, Sir Horace."

A scornful laugh escapes me. "Is that so, Captain Howard? You're eager for the details of a spiritual visitor all of a sudden?"

He replies icily, "I am here to help our host, to come to his aid in any way I can. Isn't that why *you* are here as well?"

Furious words bubble up, but it's at that moment I catch sight of Evelyn shaking her head. Her expression is bewilderment, sprinkled with mortification over my conduct. She has no idea what's behind my scolding comments. I bite my lip to stop from blurting something I could regret.

"Children, children, don't quarrel," says Walpole lightly. "I fear I'm to blame for creating a fraught atmosphere. I've withheld the facts from you too long. That shall be remedied now."

Walpole tells his housekeeper, Margaret, to bring in "Little Emma". While she's gone, our host launches into the story of the first "sightings". Sir Horace was the first one to become aware of an intruder. Unable to sleep one night, he heard a series of loud knocks. Leaving his bedchamber to investigate, he then heard someone running up the main staircase.

His usually clear and drawling voice dropping to a strained whisper, Sir Horace Walpole says, "I saw with my own eyes a slight figure — larger than a child, smaller than a man — running across the armoury. I didn't see him reach the painting. I admit that I — I fell back. I did not confront the intruder. I was overly distraught."

Up to now, Walpole's antiquarian friend, Mrs Campion, has seemed a warm and comforting presence, even a maternal one, though she's at most ten years older than Walpole. But the flickering candlelight that had seemed to flatter every face at the table now seems to emphasize the deep lines of anxiety etched into her forehead and pulls at her mouth.

She says, haltingly, "My dear friend, this doesn't sound to me like the actions of a guardian angel. Aren't they supposed to ... protect human beings?"

Walpole says, "As much as I would like to have a benign angel watching over me — though not *every* single thing I do — I have become convinced that this apparition, while it looks like an angel, is *not* one, neither guardian nor otherwise."

"Because the angel runs through your house at night?" asks Evelyn. "No one has been harmed, correct? Or felt directly threatened?"

"No physical harm," says Walpole. "But I've barely been able to sleep for weeks. How can this be happening? I keep asking myself. Why does the apparition seek out the armoury and always try to reach the Fragonard painting? Is there a message? A reproach? Was it *The Castle of Otranto*? Have I gone too far? Is someone trying to destroy me?" Walpole tugs at a lock of hair, knocking his wig to the side a good inch. I can't be sure, but I think I see tears shining in his eyes.

At that moment, Margaret finally returns to the refectory, her arm around the shoulders of a thin girl who looks to be around sixteen. The girl stares at the floor.

"Emma, in your own words, tell my guests what you saw," says Walpole.

"Is she the first to witness it after you?" asks Sir Humphrey.

Walpole replies, "Lord no, the first was my elderly valet, David, who suffered such a shock from it, he took to his bed and is too poorly to return to service. The next witness was another of my servants, a young footman named Jonathan, who left Strawberry Hill two days afterwards. He foregoes a letter of reference, so desperate was he to leave. Emma, to my gratitude, is staying with me."

The young girl raises her chin and smiles shakily at Sir Horace. He nods encouragingly.

Evelyn asks, "You have ruled out a child of the estate being put up to this? Someone having a laugh?"

"Long ago," says Sir Horace. "I know it's difficult, Emma, but tell us what you saw."

"I sleep next to the kitchen," Emma says so softly I can barely hear her. "Something woke me. I didn't know what. Then there were three knocks upstairs. I was scared because Jonathan had just left, but I … I wanted to see. I'm sorry."

"Don't apologize for being curious — it's a wonderful trait," Walpole insists. "Go on."

Her breathing quickening, she says, "I saw some … person … wearing a white robe. He had golden hair. Running up the stairs in the hall so fast, faster than anybody. Small, like a little child. A boy … He stopped. He then turned into the place on the second storey, the place where Sir Horace hangs the man wearing big shiny armour. I fell back then. Too scared."

Across from me, Mrs Campion reacts with horror, her hands pulling at the base of her throat. Everyone else's attention is on Emma and Margaret, standing behind Sir Horace Walpole at the head of the table. But I am caught up in Mrs Campion's reaction, so extreme that I must wonder if Emma's story reminds her of some episode in her past. I lean forward to speak to her, but the woman shakes her head as if to warn me off.

Sir Humphrey Willoughby says, "Emma, you said you were awakened by a noise? Could it have been a dream? Don't be afraid to say so."

She sticks out her lower lip. "No, sir. I was awake."

Walpole says indignantly, "Are we *all* dreaming? I've seen the apparition three times. Wearing a white tunic, blond, the size of a child, running towards the armoury and Fragonard's painting before slipping away. Even my housekeeper has borne witness!"

"You *have*, Margaret?" asks Evelyn.

We all scrutinize Walpole's housekeeper, obviously a highly capable woman who manages a house with many unusual features and keeps a highly strung owner happy.

"It is what I've heard, not seen, Lady Willoughby," Margaret says. "These accursed knocking sounds, if you'll pardon my strong language. I try to find where they're coming from, and I never can. I did see a figure one night at the other end of Sir Horace's gallery. It was dark, I'm not sure what I saw to be honest. I thought I saw someone wearing white. I called out for the person to stop, and I picked up my skirts and ran to try to catch him, but I'm not a young woman. I couldn't run fast enough. No one was there at the other end of the gallery."

Sinking his head in his arms, Walpole says, "Oh, no, no. Every time I hear that story …"

Sir Humphrey Willoughby says, "Margaret, I'm not sure giving chase was wise."

"Sir, this is *my* house!" she cries, a hand on her hip. "I don't mean that Sir Horace didn't build it and fill it with his treasures. I'm not daft. But I'm the housekeeper of Strawberry Hill. I do not take kindly to mischief, whether it's from this world or the next. My staff is in an uproar, and Sir Horace is beside himself. It needs to stop!"

For the first time since I arrived at Strawberry Hill, I feel a chill race up my arms. This ghost sighting did not spring from Walpole's imagination. The varying accounts, and the emotions under-running what they say, are persuasive. I reach for my wine to fortify myself.

Sir Humphrey Willoughby says, "Unquestionably, something is

happening here. We need to form a plan of attack on the problem, Horace."

"Well, I have an idea of something to try," says Walpole. "It will require your participation, Herr Longfren."

The Swedish philosopher blinks in surprise but smiles. Of all those sitting at the table, he has been the least disturbed by anything said or heard, I realize. When I think about what I know about his mentor, Swedenborg, I remember that along with his writing and his background in science there have been tales of mystical visions. Does our host expect Swedenborg's pupil to produce a vision tonight?

Sir Horace says, "I was thinking we could try an approach I heard about in France. They call it a sitting — a *séance*."

"No."

I am thinking it, but someone else says it.

Mrs Campion utters the word. Not only that, but she also presses her palms hard against the edge of the table to push herself up. She says, "I must go to my room. I have known you for years, Horace. I know I cannot dissuade you once you have an idea in your head. But I can't be a part of this. Margaret, will you take me?"

The housekeeper hurries to Strawberry Hill's guest while Walpole says, "There's no need to withdraw. No harm will come to you, I can make sure of that."

"No, Horace. You can't protect anyone from danger if you proceed." She takes a tottering step away from the table, then another, steadier one. Margaret silently leads her to the door of the refectory.

Mrs Campion makes a lurching stop and turns, her eyes scanning our faces at the table.

"I fear you may all regret what happens here tonight," she says and leaves.

Chapter Seven

Sir Horace Walpole may regret frightening his friend. But not two minutes after Mrs Campion leaves the refectory for her guest bedchamber, Walpole returns to pleading with Lars Longfren to lead a séance. He seems desperate to communicate with the spirit to learn its intentions.

Herr Longfren puts down his wine with a sigh and says to Sir Walpole, "I have a question. Why do you think I have special ability with the dead?" I feel a twinge of sympathy. Longfren thought he was here to do what guests at other aristocrats' houses do — stroll a well-groomed garden, devour an excellent meal and flirt with married women. How wrong he was!

"Of all the philosophers I've read, Emanuel Swedenborg holds beliefs that are the most receptive to spirits of the afterlife being among us," replies Walpole. "Voltaire barely believes in God. Both he and Rousseau are certain that science can explain the natural world. While Swedenborg …"

Captain Howard completes the sentence with sarcasm: "… thinks someone can whistle up a dead soul?"

I open my mouth, intending to slam the captain into place for his ignorant contempt of Emanuel Swedenborg's brilliance, but Herr Longfren calmly explains that his teacher believes a spirit is the soul of a human being that continues to live on in our world after their physical body stops functioning.

Walpole lights up. "Ah! And could that not be the case with this visitation?"

While I understand why Sir Horace would be intrigued, I spot a flaw. "But why would the spirit be drawn *here*?" I ask. "Has anyone died within the walls of Strawberry Hill?"

Sir Horace Walpole sighs. "No. Not in the house. I'm the only one who lives here apart from the staff."

Uncomfortably, it is at this moment that a young servant walks into the room carrying a huge silver tray of desserts. A French puff pastry on a delicate black-and-gold porcelain dish is placed in front of me. Discussion of death notwithstanding, I can't resist. Its sweet creaminess melts on my tongue.

Sir Horace Walpole says, "Since I built Strawberry Hill, only a gardener has died near the property. Of dropsy. Last year. I can't believe Old Jack would make mischief. He was always such a sweet old fellow, dragging his seedlings around in a wagon. Hardly a spry young boy."

I turn my head to observe the young man serving us dessert. He is expressionless. I wonder if Walpole even realizes he's among us — and that he might have known Old Jack too.

Evelyn says, "Forgive me, I haven't read any Swedenborg. His are interesting theories but only theories, surely. When it comes to setting up some form of communication with the dead, that seems impossible."

I say, "I've heard that Emanuel Swedenborg has perceived things through visions that might seem impossible — but are true."

"Yes, Mrs Sturbridge is correct," says Longfren with a grateful glance in my direction.

"You see?" crows Walpole. "I knew I had invited the right man tonight."

Longfren holds up his right hand and says, "Swedenborg is strict on the subject of breaking through from living to dead. The spirits live on after the death of the physical body, but on a different plane. It is close to ours, but it is still separate. Very, very separate. For the living to try to reach out to the spirit is dangerous."

I put down the pastry. That's the second warning someone has issued tonight.

The Swede pushes back his chair and stands, the smile wiped from his handsome face, and says, "I am grateful to be a guest here, but I cannot lead efforts to speak to the spirit world. It would break my teacher's trust in me."

"We can't have that, can we?" murmurs Sir Horace, deeply disappointed. "Please sit down. You are still a welcome guest."

Sir Humphrey Willoughby, who has been patiently silent throughout this bizarre turn in the discussion, now takes charge.

"We should look into the possibility that someone is trying to frighten you, Horace," he says firmly. "This seems to me to be a human disturbance, not a ghostly one."

"How can you be so sure that the spirit world does not exist?" counters Walpole.

I expect Sir Humphrey Willoughby to spout blunt wisdom. Instead, he says with a rueful smile, "I find I agree with Samuel Johnson. He wrote: *It is wonderful that five thousand years have now elapsed since the creation of the world, and still it is undecided whether or not there has ever been an instance of the spirit of any person appearing after death. All argument is against it, but all belief is for it.*"

"Clever, clever," scolds Walpole. "Perfectly quoting Johnson! Well, I still have you to turn to, Peregrine Howard."

Peregrine? Rarely has a man looked less like his given name.

"Sir Horace, why do you place me in the category of believers in ghostly visions?"

Howard asks the question slowly, his body held so still that I brace myself for what's to come.

Walpole seems too distressed to pick up on Howard's seething. He says shrilly, "Please do not pretend you are unacquainted with ghosts. Your family home, Stanham Castle, is said to be the most haunted in the north of England. Why do you think I had it in mind as the place where the manuscript of *The Castle of Otranto* was uncovered when I was pretending I found it instead of telling the world that I wrote it?"

Howard peers into the dark end of the refectory as if someone were there to tell him what to do. His long nose seems to lengthen further, and a nerve dances in his throat. The struggle for control is apparent. Was this the reason he feared was behind his invitation to dinner?

Finally perceiving Howard's state of mind, Walpole says, "I didn't name Stanham Castle in the foreword of the novel and never have identified it to anyone. I know how important privacy is to your family."

Captain Howard takes a deep breath and turns back to face us, sitting ramrod straight. "Thank you, Sir Horace. We've no choice but to lead discreet lives. As to ghosts, the servants told stories. But neither my brother nor my sister nor I — or our parents, for that matter — witnessed any spirit in Stanham Castle, day or night. We had more pressing matters at hand."

With Howard's dark clothing blending into the black chair, his long white face and blazing eyes stand out like a tragic masque. There's an intensity about him, a brittle dignity, like no one else present. Being a Roman Catholic means that he was most likely raised on superstitions that embraced angels and ghosts. Yet he's shown no indication of such beliefs or an openness to discussion. I find him more unfathomable than ever, despite his solicitude to me outside the Holbein room. For my family, Protestant England has always been a shining sanctuary to the Huguenot refugees, and I've never understood why a born Englishman would choose to be Roman Catholic.

At the same time, I acknowledge my own contradictions. Earlier this evening, I felt smug and secure in the Protestant doctrine I was raised on, which insists that there is no such thing as a ghost. Yet weren't the stories of Emanuel Swedenborg's impossible-to-explain visions what drew me with a thrill to learn more about his beliefs? My own inconsistencies make me hesitate to judge Captain Howard.

Sir Humphrey Willoughby says, "I've listened patiently to all of your theories of ghostly invasion, Horace. Let's analyse the problem from the plane of *human* activity. You said the house is open to the public three mornings a week, when Margaret gives tours. So someone could get a grasp of the layout. And I've noted that this is not the most secure residence. There are several ways someone could slip into Strawberry Hill."

"Oh, I'm no stranger to crime. My house in London was once robbed — and, you remember, Humphrey, that my carriage was held up by a highwayman in Hyde Park," says Walpole. "But why would someone want to break into Strawberry Hill just to frighten me?"

For the next half hour or so, Willoughby and Captain Howard question Sir Horace closely about enemies he may have made, whether literary, political or personal. None of the names bandied about mean anything to me. Evelyn and Herr Longfren, both perceptive listeners, hurl their own questions into the conversation. Evelyn also points out the similarity between Sir Horace's experience and the infamous Cock Lane ghost, which haunted a London house with a series of strange knocks. It all turned out to be a family's elaborate scheme to frighten and slander a man to whom they owed money.

"My good woman, no one owes me a penny," cries Sir Horace in mock horror, leading to a much-needed round of laughter at the table.

I, too, have turned away from ghosts as a cause of Walpole's torment. I'm following my own reasoning, for I think I have as good a chance as anyone — equal to Sir Humphrey Willoughby — at untangling this mystery. I possess the advantage of having read part of *The Castle of Otranto* last night. Horace Walpole has confessed after he was unveiled as its author that the novel's inspiration came to him in a dream. In it, he found himself standing in the armoury he'd created and saw a giant hand thrust out of the wall.

He carried that bizarre image into the novel. As I recall, in the story, the villain, Prince Manfred, was trying to seduce the horrified Isabella when a figure sighed and stirred in the portrait hanging on the wall above the bench where the couple sat.

With this "angel" trying to make its way to the armoury, to seemingly leap back into the painting, I ponder a link to the novel.

No, it can't be the plot of his novel. The point must be personal. My gaze settles on the man sitting at the head of the table, someone who used his share of Walpole wealth to raise a replica of a medieval castle. Our host is more interested in honouring an obscure Tudor prince than celebrating the achievements of his Whig forebears, even buying a Fragonard painting of an angel to pay tribute to Arthur Tudor.

Something clicks. It's a thought that first occurred when Sir Horace stood before the painting in the armoury, but I was distracted from pursuing it with all the talk of spirits.

At the next pause in conversation, I say, "Pardon me, Sir Horace, but how did you come to purchase the painting by Fragonard? Did you meet the artist himself?"

Walpole squints as he summons up the memory. "No. An intermediary heard of my interest and approached me."

"Your interest in a Fragonard painting?"

"Yes, yes," Walpole says. "I was attending the Paris salon of my dear friend, Madame du Deffand. The poor lady is blind, as you may know. But that doesn't diminish her interest in many things, including my progress at Strawberry Hill. I told Madame du Deffand, the pièce de résistance for my armoury would be a Fragonard angel. A month later, I had a gracious letter from a vicomte — that's the French version of viscount — saying that he had heard of my desire and knew of such a painting. He introduced me to the man who sold me a small portrait of an angel by Fragonard."

I grip the ebony table with my fingers and lean forward, my heart beating fast.

"But Sir Horace, Jean-Honoré Fragonard is *not* famous for his paintings of angels. He is celebrated for his use of light and command of detail, but his fame is recent. It is Francois Boucher who paints angels. It is something he's been known to favour painting for years, along with his penchant for Cupid and Psyche."

Walpole shakes his head peevishly. "I know my French artists! Fragonard paints angels — just look at the one I own. Isn't that proof?"

I bite my lip. I shouldn't have suggested that Sir Horace doesn't know the artists of today's Paris very well. England may have defeated France in war three years ago, but the French are still the acknowledged leaders in literature, fashion, design, fine art — and cuisine. Our dinner tonight was filled with the same dishes one would consume at a Paris chateau.

Sir Humphrey Willoughby demands, "What could it matter who painted the angel?"

"I don't know yet," I admit. "But there's something odd about a painting that I think is out of character for an artist suddenly being offered up to Sir Horace."

Sir Humphrey waves me away as if I were a persistent insect buzzing in his ear. He says, "The most important thing is to capture the person who enters Sir Horace Walpole's house at night. He must be seized and held for interrogation. We have a good plan. I can arrange for a couple of alert and reliable men to station themselves inside Strawberry Hill at night and wait for him to try again. Just give me a couple of days."

"What's wrong with tonight?" I ask.

It pops out of my mouth without deliberation. But my pulse leaps at the thought of trying to capture the "spirit" ourselves. With all that we have said and gone through in the last few hours to try to solve Walpole's mystery, I'd hate to leave the house and, worse, go back to Lichfield not knowing the truth. This challenge has rallied my energies like nothing else in months. And not only that. My instincts tell me this has to do with the Fragonard. Sir Humphrey's "alert and reliable men" won't know how to question anyone about French painters. I need to be a part of this.

Sir Humphrey barks a mirthless laugh. "I have connections at Whitehall but not the power to produce men in an hour."

"You mistake me, Sir Humphrey," I say. "There are six of us around this table. We could lie in wait *tonight* for the intruder to Strawberry Hill."

Willoughby stares at me in disbelief.

"Well, it's a thought," murmurs Captain Howard, to my surprise. He's never taken my part in anything up to now.

"It's a bad thought," retorts Sir Humphrey. "We must assume that Strawberry Hill is under observation. You think this person will make their way inside while my carriage sits outside?"

Evelyn says, "We could send the carriage home. It would look as if we've left, but we'll all be quiet inside. Then, when we're ready, we could ask Sir Horace to send someone on horseback and give the word for our driver to return."

Now Sir Humphrey Willoughby turns his incredulous stare on his wife. "After a long night of much wine, you propose to capture a possible criminal with your own hands?" he asks.

I detect the barest quiver of a smile before Evelyn says, "Everyone agrees the intruder is quite small, my dear."

My heart leaps in gratitude; I dare not look at her for fear we would burst out laughing.

Lars Longfren clamours for a part to play in the initiative. "Your role will be to stay close to *me*," announces Sir Horace. "I've no intention of putting myself in the path of this scoundrel alone."

With that, Willoughby, shaking his head, consents to what he dubs "Genevieve's scheme". I try to conceal my flush of triumph.

It turns out that six people do not present an overwhelming advantage in a place like Strawberry Hill. Sir Humphrey and Captain Howard identify several places where someone could sneak into the sprawling castle.

I insist that I be the one to wait in the armoury, the destination. At first, Howard and Willoughby refuse to consider it. "Won't one of you gentlemen have grabbed him long before he reaches me?" I demand, which finally persuades them.

But I'm not in the armoury alone for fifteen minutes before I begin to regret it. This is a small, dark vestibule without even a bench to sit on — unlike the passage from *The Castle of Otranto*. The moonlight from the stained-glass window throws a faint diamond of purple, gold and green light onto the massive shoulder of the man's armour stuck to the wall. But that's it. The painting I was so keen to examine once more is barely visible.

Without question, I drank too much wine this evening. That lightheaded feeling of confidence that I had discovered something significant is sinking. It's unlikely that we will see an appearance in the house tonight. And even if we capture the intruder and Sir Humphrey Willoughby discovers what malicious person put him up to it, what does it matter to me? I'm still taking my son home in two days' time. The picture is painfully clear: Pierre unhappily wishing he were back in the south, glorying in the boats; Alfred and Edith staring at my garden without comprehension; the young ladies of Lichfield asking their patronizing questions as they dabble in watercolour.

The dark house is silent. If any of the others whisper together, I can't hear it. Perhaps that's for the best. They may be exhausted and wish I had not suggested this.

As the minutes crawl by, I'm finding it difficult to stay alert myself. Why did I insist on doing this tonight? But I can't bring myself to call a halt to the ghoul watch quite yet.

Knock, knock, knock.

A cold, hard slap of fear knocks the weary cynicism from me. I back up to the end of the room, inches from the Fragonard painting.

This is how it begins. That's what Sir Horace, Emma and Margaret said. But it was also how the fraudulent Cock Lane ghost made its presence known, I remind myself.

You are not a ghost. You are not a soul on another plane. You are a human, and I will not be afraid of you.

The knock is louder now. Whoever — or whatever — makes this noise is drawing closer. It seems to emanate from the entrance hall below. Why are Captain Howard and Sir Humphrey letting this happen?

There's not another sound for half a minute. Trying to rally, I decide to make observations and gather evidence as scientific inquiry demands. I push myself forward, my throat dry. After I move past the suit of armour, the unmistakable sound of feet patter up the staircase. As I stand rooted to the armoury floor, my hands trembling, a small figure clad in white darts into the vestibule, not ten feet away.

My mouth opens, but no sound comes out.

A second later, a much larger dark figure leaps into the armoury. My ears ring with the sounds of shouts, grunts, thumps and scuffling blows. Straining to see, I make out a third large figure, and a familiar voice shouts, "Evelyn, the lamp — the lamp!" Suddenly, the armoury swarms with people and voices I know. Evelyn, carrying an oil lamp, transforms the space from swirling black chaos to one flooded with painfully bright golden light. Now I can see Captain Howard sprawled across the floor, his arms pinning down someone much smaller.

Wearing a tangled and smudged white tunic, that figure jerks free and sits up. Lank, stringy blond hair flies around a narrow face pitted with pockmarks.

"Get your hands off me, you bloody knob," the figure hisses.

Chapter Eight

Strawberry Hill is not a place resplendent with practical chairs, but one materializes for the captured intruder. Captain Howard marches him down to the main hall and pushes him into a seat.

"We have questions, and you'd do best to answer them," says Captain Howard, a bit out of breath.

"I won't answer, not one," declares the intruder, his arms folded.

We've formed a semi-circle around him, lamps illuminating the hall. There's never been less *gloomth* than now. Margaret appears, her housekeeper cap askew, and Sir Horace Walpole clings to her arm, his face a picture of horror. It's hard to know which is more shocking to not just Walpole but the rest of us: the intruder's soiled tunic and sallow plainness or his absolute defiance. I cannot take my eyes off him.

"We'll begin with your name," says Captain Howard.

He grins, displaying two brown upper teeth. "Call me Zophiel," he says.

"Your full name," says Howard.

"Awww, don't you know? Angels just have one name, knob."

The name *Zophiel* makes my head spin. I've heard it before but in the context of art or books. I can't seem to place it.

But one thing I'm clear about is Zophiel is from the streets. It could be East London, which embraces Spitalfields. It could be Southwark, or even a Central London neighbourhood like St Giles, whose infamous Rookery is teeming with so many thieves and murderers that constables will not set foot there. He's been through hardship. Zophiel is young but not *that* young. I'd put his age at twenty. He is shorter than I am by six inches, with bony, dirty arms hanging loose from his tunic. I'd wager his small size resulted from growing up poor, half-starving and often ill.

Which means he is as tough as they come.

I know that the worse things become for someone like Zophiel, the cheekier he will get. He's already burrowed beneath the skin of Captain Howard, who says, his voice rising, "You're in no position to refuse to answer questions."

Zophiel puffs out his cheeks and blows, making a rude sound.

Standing next to me, Evelyn makes a "tsk-tsk" disapproving sound. As for me, though he absolutely terrified me mere minutes ago, and he has disturbed Sir Horace Walpole and his staff, Zophiel doesn't frighten or disgust me under well-lit scrutiny. In fact, to my own surprise, I feel sorry for him. This may be nothing but a nasty prank gone too far. But he's about to be crushed to dust by England's most powerful.

Sir Humphrey takes a step towards Zophiel. He quietly says, "You have committed a number of serious offences, young man. I am Sir Humphrey Willoughby."

"Ah, here's our Captain Grand making his play, trying to shake me," Zophiel crows. His eyes, light blue, spark with a new malice. "Yeah, I haven't stolen a single thing or hurt anybody. What's the crime of having fun?"

"You've broken into a private house, Zophiel. Sir Horace Walpole is an important man — a member of Parliament. The court will send you to prison. There's no question."

Incredibly, he lets out a loud yawn. "Say you're right. A lot of my friends are in the Clink. I'll be in good company."

Zophiel's bravado does not fool me, nor Sir Humphrey Willoughby. He informs the young man that to make things better for himself, he needs to disclose the name of whoever hired Zophiel to sneak into Strawberry Hill.

"Nobody hired me," insists Zophiel. I spot his right leg tapping rapidly against the leg of the chair. Obviously, he was picked by someone for his unique gifts: his size, colouring, speed, and comfort with breaking laws. This feels less and less like a prank. While Zophiel is mocking his captors on top of defying them, I sense a serious plan and particular intent behind these "hauntings".

Sir Humphrey says, still calm and reasonable, "Why don't you tell me this: How did you decide when to slip into this house and run through the halls?"

"I kept an eye on things. There's a place where no one can see you. Somebody was nice enough to dig a hole."

Captain Howard breaks in. "That's where you've been living, Zophiel? All these weeks? In a hole in the ground?"

"Course not." Another brown-toothed grin. "I got my own private cave."

"A *cave*?" Sir Horace Walpole repeats. "This is absurd. There are no caves in Twickenham. I demand that you tell us who put you up to this at once! Is it a conspiracy? Will you be selling a story to the newspapers?"

"Cock and pie — there's a notion!" Zophiel howls. "I'll be the boy of the hour. I'll go to the *London Advertiser*, then the *Daily Gazetteer*. See who will pay more. 'How I Played Ghost at the House of a Trembling Tatler'."

His joke so closely tallies with Sir Horace Walpole's worst nightmare that the owner of Strawberry Hill falls back, his face in his hands.

"All right," says Sir Humphrey Willoughby. "Enough for tonight."

Willoughby gestures to Captain Howard to stand guard over Zophiel and directs the rest of us to a place in the hall out of earshot. With his usual decisiveness, he sends Sir Horace Walpole off in the company of Lars Longfren for a "heartening brandy". It's Margaret he most needs to speak to now. Sir Humphrey wants to lock up Zophiel for the night in Strawberry Hill as the hour is too late to seek a constable for a crime like this, one that appears to be a bizarre prank and involved no violence. "I don't think Twickenham even has a night watchman, sir," says Margaret, agreeing to help. He thanks her and promises to return to Strawberry Hill first thing in the morning to handle things.

"A night locked up alone will straighten out the little bugger," says Sir Humphrey.

"My dear, I know you're tired, but please," murmurs Evelyn, and her husband apologizes for his language.

Margaret hurries off to prepare a pantry storeroom that she confirms has no window and a door that can be padlocked. Although Sir Humphrey suggests we women wait in the carriage that's just arrived, I insist there's no need and Evelyn agrees. Wasn't the capture of Zophiel the product of *my* plan?

"Think about what awaits you if you refuse to tell the truth," Sir Humphrey informs Zophiel at the door of the small, pitch-black room smelling of flour and cloves. "You can run as fast as any human I've seen, but you won't be able to walk as a free man unless I get answers."

Howard starts to push Zophiel into the room when I cry, "That's it! The name's from *Paradise Lost*."

"What are you saying?" asks Sir Humphrey.

"John Milton," I say. "*Paradise Lost* is about Heaven and Hell — the poem is packed with angels — and Zophiel is the fastest. Milton calls him 'cherubim of swiftest wing'."

For the first time, Zophiel looks right at me. His face is only half-lit by the lamp. For a fleeting second, I see pain, anger and fear leaping in his eyes, but Margaret lowers the lamp. I wonder if he was unable to keep up the façade of indifference any longer.

But when he speaks, it's with the mockery he's doled out since Howard grabbed him. "She's a smart one, Captain Grand," he drawls. "Maybe she should be in charge!"

With that, Zophiel whirls around, squares his shoulders beneath his dirty white tunic, and marches into the room. Margaret closes the door with a bang and locks it. After scrutinizing the lock, Sir Humphrey nods, satisfied, and we leave Strawberry Hill at last.

For more than half the carriage ride, the four of us sit in silence, partly stunned by the events of the night and partly overcome with sheer exhaustion.

Evelyn rallies herself to say, "Humphrey, I believe you should thank Genevieve. You wouldn't have captured Sir Humphrey's tormentor if it wasn't for her."

"Hmm, yes," says Sir Humphrey, nodding at me. It's not the most profuse example of gratitude I've heard, but I'll take it.

"I think he'll tell you everything in the morning," says Captain Howard. "He's had his joke. Once it sinks in that he could go to jail, he will cough it up."

I say, "It's sunk in already."

"You think so?" asks Howard doubtfully. "He seemed a dim sort to me, only good at guttersnipe insults."

I remember those naked feelings that leaped in his eyes for only a second.

"He's scared now and probably quite desperate," I say. "It's a good thing there's a lock on the door. He's hell-bent on escape. I wouldn't want to be the one in his way."

Sir Humphrey and Captain Howard look at each other and break out laughing. Evelyn joins in. "We're not laughing *at* you, Genevieve," she says, gasping. "It's just that he was such a little creature. More like a gnome than a man. Spiteful, yes, but I don't think anyone needs to fear him now that he's been uncovered as the mischief-maker of Strawberry Hill."

My cheeks flush with anger. Even after acknowledging that my "scheme" captured Zophiel, why does no one take me seriously? I wonder if it's because, at the end of the day, I am always going to be a Huguenot artisan from a refugee family living in East London. They're not realizing that it's my very background that may give me insight into Zophiel that they lack.

The carriage is coming to a halt. I should stay quiet, but I can't resist a parting shot. "I trust it hasn't escaped you that Zophiel is in the pay of a man who names a minion after a minor character in an epic poem written a century ago."

"Well, I instructed Margaret not to unlock the door until I arrive, and I'm quite sure I can handle him," says Sir Humphrey. "As for the Milton devotee, I am confident I will have that name by noon tomorrow."

I don't have the will to dispute Zophiel's abilities any longer. It's well after midnight, and my limbs ache. All I want to do is reach my room upstairs. I'm nodding off while Evelyn's maid undresses me and removes my hair weaves. My fingers are numb as I cream the face paint off my skin.

My little son is in such a deep sleep that he doesn't hear me or see my candle light up the corner of our room. His mouth is half open, and an arm is thrown over his head. So much happened tonight, and Pierre is utterly oblivious — and should remain so. We will be leaving Twickenham in a few days — two days, as it's after midnight. How can I return to my Lichfield life after going through this drama? That's my last coherent thought before I find sleep.

I'm in the middle of the latest in a series of complicated dreams when I feel someone shake me. It's a wide-eyed Pierre. I look past him at the window. A lovely pinkish-gold light pours in below the curtain.

"Something's wrong, Mama," he says.

I hear what he hears then — people talking loudly in the house, shouting even, in a spirit that is nothing like the first stirrings of the house.

I throw a wrap around my nightgown and slip out of the room to investigate.

I spot Evelyn, half-dressed herself, out in the corridor, talking to two servants.

"Oh, Genevieve, it's terrible," she says, her face chalk white. "Zophiel attacked Lars Longfren. The man is bleeding and unconscious."

A shudder ripples through me, but in a few seconds, it's gone, and I feel grimly focused.

"Evelyn, are you saying Zophiel's escaped?"

"Yes. He's disappeared. Sir Horace sent a messenger here. Humphrey's dressing to ride over at once. We sent word to Captain Howard at his cousin's house." She claps her hand over her mouth. "Heaven above, you said this would happen."

"It gives me no pleasure to be right." I snatch Evelyn's hand. "Listen. Tell your husband I'm going with him." I turn to rush back to my room to change.

"Genevieve, why?" my friend calls down the hall. "Can you help Longfren? Have you experience as a healer?"

"Yes, yes, I do," I say over my shoulder. "I can help." Once in my room, I frantically throw on my simplest dress, fastening the laces and buttons myself. I don't have any healer knowledge besides the ability to nurse my husband and son through their various illnesses.

"I'm going to help some people who need me," I tell Pierre. "You should have fun with Diana in the garden, or maybe the nurse will take you down to the river to see ships."

"It will be the last time, won't it?" he asks, his face a picture of dejection.

I will keep us here, my son, believe in me! Plunging into the search may help serve as a reason to postpone our leaving.

I don't know where that thought came from or how I can fulfil any such promise. But my heart is hammering wildly. Somehow, new possibilities are emerging. I know that I have a better chance of finding Zophiel than any of the rest of them. He is someone I understand. I throw my arms around Pierre, kiss him and run downstairs.

When I catch up, Sir Humphrey Willoughby is about to shut the door to his carriage. Four of his servants or retainers are riding on top or clinging to the sides. "Genevieve, I believe Sir Horace has sent for a physician," he says. "Besides, I didn't know you even had healing skills."

Holding onto the door, I scramble into the carriage with no grace whatsoever. "You'd be surprised what abilities one picks up in the country," I reply, landing in the seat next to him.

"You wouldn't have come up with an excuse in order to interject yourself into the search, now would you?" he says, scowling. "You've been known to make yourself a nuisance in my investigations before."

"You *need* me."

"Oh. And why is that?"

"Because you don't have a grasp of Zophiel, and I do, Sir Humphrey," I declare, brazening my way through his disapproval. "You underestimated him. And it seems Herr Longfren did, too."

Sir Humphrey's face darkens in anger, and my throat goes dry. "What a perfect fool Longfren proved to be," he says. "I was clear that no one should open the door until I got there."

"Why did he do so?" I ask, relieved I am not the object of Willoughby's wrath.

"The little scoundrel was moaning and pleading for water. He woke up the servants, cursing and calling for his saviour. Then he shouted for a cup of water, but Margaret and her staff knew enough to keep the door locked. Longfren showed up and said no one should go without water. He was sure he could cope. The minute the door was unlocked, Zophiel bashed him on the head with a rolling pin."

"A rolling pin was left in the room overnight?" I ask in disbelief.

"Margaret didn't see it when she readied the room. But Zophiel found it under a shelf or something and without any light." Sir Humphrey's voice carries a hint of grudging respect. "We should have tied him up."

To my relief, Herr Longfren is conscious when we arrive, his head cleaned and bandaged, and full of remorse for opening the door.

"A Londoner such as Zophiel is full of cunning and can be quite vicious when cornered," I point out.

"I've not encountered any such person as him in Sweden," he moans, holding his head.

Sir Humphrey focuses on the search for the escapee. He directs two of his men to fan out across the Walpole property and that of the neighbours, asking if anyone had seen a small young blond man wearing a white tunic. The others are to hurry to the village of Twickenham and search there. Someone as unusual looking as Zophiel would surely stand out in daylight. There must be a trail to pick up. Few hackney coaches can be hired in Twickenham, especially on a Sunday morning. He's trapped here.

For several hours, I alternate between tending to the abashed Lars Longfren and the distraught Sir Horace Walpole in the breakfast room overlooking the river. "Such violence under my roof, it is *unthinkable*," he tells me. I extend sympathy to both. That is the female's role, to comfort and tend. I admit that I wish I could be among the party of male searchers outside instead. I am convinced more than ever that I understand Zophiel like no one else at Strawberry Hill.

It's a relief when Mrs Campion appears, and Walpole can focus on telling her every detail of the night before. Then they move on to discussion of his new purchase of the clock that Henry VIII gave Anne Boleyn as a wedding gift.

Freed of conversation, I peer out the bay window and listen for a cry outside, an excited shout that says they've located Zophiel.

But that doesn't happen.

At about noon, Sir Horace Walpole appears. I can tell from the slump of his shoulders and pressed lips that the news is bad.

"A boatman says that one of his friends on the river took a fare towards London early this morning. He saw him too: a very short man, wearing a cap on his head and smoking a pipe."

"A pipe?" says Walpole. "I can't picture it. And hiring a boat all the way to London would be very costly and difficult. It's a hard row."

"He had a diamond ring to pay," says Sir Humphrey Willoughby. "Our witness thought it was unusual for a young well-dressed man to offer to pay with a costly ring — and to have pocked skin and brown teeth."

I should be as dejected as the others. To my amazement, I feel a perverse pride in Zophiel's cleverness in getting out of Twickenham.

"Oh, that is him," says Walpole miserably. "Now, what do we do?"

"Wait for the boatman to return to Twickenham and question him," says Sir Humphrey, wiping the sweat from his face. "Nothing more to learn here."

"With all due respect, I'm not so sure," says Captain Howard from the doorway. It's the first time I've seen him today, and he looks amazingly fresh and rested, considering what we've all gone through. "I've found the spot where Zophiel hid while he watched the house. It's of interest."

When the men leave the house this time, I go with them. I want to see what Captain Howard has discovered. In all the chaos, he's focused his efforts and come up with a success. I must hand it to him.

The sun beats down on us from a cloudless sky. Howard leads us to a place behind a line of elms with a wood of young trees to the side. He points at a shallow, square pit dug into the ground and criss-crossed with wooden beams. A pile of bricks stands nearby.

"This is where I'm preparing to build my chapel in the woods," says Walpole indignantly. "My workmen took a few weeks off. They have another commitment this summer."

"When Zophiel said 'hole in the ground', he meant this," says Captain Howard. "Look what's tucked beneath the beam." He jumps down and, seconds later, holds up the dirty white tunic Zophiel wore last night. "I can't see him sleeping on the bare ground for weeks, and I don't spot much here, just a sack with a slice of cold meat and a chewed-up apple core. I'd be surprised if he kept a good set of clothes here."

"His real store of clothing and supplies is elsewhere, the same place he's been sleeping," says Sir Humphrey Willoughby. "Anything else down there?"

"Yes, but I don't know what it tells us. Objects he's been keeping here."

"Objects?" I ask.

Sir Humphrey turns towards me, frowning. He must not have realized I came along until that moment. Howard picks up something small, then another, and carries them out of the shallow pit. The pieces glitter in his hands.

"Those are seashells," says Sir Humphrey.

Sir Horace Walpole, fascinated, turns the pink and white shells over and then holds one up to the sun. "Where did he get these?"

It does not take me long to form a possibility. A wild excitement bubbles up, just as it did when I silently promised Pierre we wouldn't need to leave. I know where I have seen those shells — it was a few days ago, during our day spent at Alexander Pope's villa.

"When Zophiel said 'cave', he meant something else," I say.

"What?" asks Captain Howard, swinging towards me with the shells in his hands.

"He meant grotto."

Chapter Nine

Before we take the carriage to Alexander Pope's villa, I tell the others my doubts.

"I think the shells came from there, but I don't know how someone could manage to live in Pope's grotto unobserved for weeks," I say. "The public is allowed in several days of the week."

Sir Humphrey Willoughby nonetheless wants to begin our search there. "It's a short distance from Strawberry Hill, and if we are learning one thing about Zophiel, it's that he is resourceful," he says with quiet bitterness.

I feel a surge of pride, although I realize it is seriously misplaced. Zophiel is a criminal. He hurt Herr Longfren and would have hurt anyone else to escape, including me.

Sure enough, the grotto is open for visitors, and this Sunday afternoon, some two dozen awestruck admirers of the great poet are wandering among the dark pools. Sir Humphrey immediately reacts to the walls covered with glittering seashells, precisely like the shells found in the pit behind Strawberry Hill. "This *must* be the place where he stayed."

However, our search of the entire grotto reveals no article of clothing or other sign that someone has ever slept there. A quick conversation with the person in charge of showing the nymph pools to the public confirms that no one matching Zophiel's description has been spotted in the grotto, even as a visitor.

Above ground, Sir Humphrey pulls the two of us into a quiet place within the shade of Pope's meticulous garden to discuss the next step. I can't help feeling defensive about declaring that Zophiel must have hidden in a grotto all this time. I say, "There could be man-made grottoes at other houses in Twickenham — it's a fashionable thing for the wealthy to have. And shells in the walls are commonly used to create the desired effect." A memory sparks. "I believe Evelyn said that the property near your house, Mr Secretary Johnston's estate, has its own grotto."

Sir Humphrey winces. "That house is presently owned by an admiral who dislikes company. Asking permission for a search is not a conversation I relish having."

At this point, Captain Howard suggests we abandon the search for Zophiel's hiding place altogether, saying he doubts we will find the name of the man who hired him among his sorry belongings.

"Good point," admits Sir Humphrey. To me, Howard is making sense as well, though I can't bring myself to say so.

Encouraged, Captain Howard pushes on, saying, "And to be honest, sir, I wonder if this matter should be pursued any further at all. He's been scared off, that's for certain. Zophiel's not going to run to Grub Street to try to sell his story because he knows that will bring about his arrest. His recapture doesn't seem that essential in my view."

I tense, waiting for Sir Humphrey's answer. I suppose I couldn't blame him if he put a stop to this.

"No, we will push forward for at least the next two days," says Sir Humphrey at last. "Even if Sir Horace Walpole weren't a close family friend, I'd want to do it. We need to make every effort to find out who was behind this. Yes, Zophiel made jokes after we caught him, but the underlying intent of these 'hauntings' doesn't seem mischievous. There's a serious intent to the way this was planned and directed, which is very strange. It troubles me."

I share that fundamental unease about Zophiel's late-night runs through the house, always ending in the armoury within sight of the Fragonard angel. He was such an unlikely angel when captured and scrutinized. I need to get a closer look at the painting. There's something unlikely about it, too. Artificial.

Captain Howard remains unconvinced that the challenge is worth such effort, leading Sir Humphrey to further explain his thinking.

"Consider the diamond ring," says Sir Humphrey. "We all saw Zophiel, his obvious poverty. Anyone of his background would find a ring like that hard to resist. Horace confirms he had never seen it. Yet Zophiel had it in his keeping. He kept it until it could be used to finance a rapid escape. I suspect he was given it for just this purpose. I don't think his master is in Twickenham — my instinct tells me he's in London, where Zophiel fled to. But how did he last so long? Why didn't he take the ring early on, abandon this ridiculous haunting of Strawberry Hill?"

Captain Howard says, "Because he's been promised a substantial payment at the end of the … whatever you want to call it. The assignment. He's greedy and has his eye on the prize."

Sir Humphrey nods. "But there's another reason. Tell me what it is."

Captain Howard shifts from one foot to the other, struggling to come up with something.

"Zophiel is scared," I blurt.

"Exactly," says Sir Humphrey. I brighten, but I can feel Howard pulsing with resentment beside me. I wish I could convey to him that I am not trying to make him look bad. That might have been true on the trip from Lichfield and even while we sipped sherry before the dinner party. It's true no longer.

"Zophiel doesn't dare steal that ring for himself," says Sir Humphrey. "The key to this is the character of the man who supplied Zophiel with the ring, who hired him to break into Strawberry Hill. I want to track down that man — or men. If we can find where Zophiel's been hiding himself for weeks, we may discover some clue. We can't afford to pass up that opportunity."

With that, the three of us take the carriage the short distance to Mr Secretary Johnston's estate. Since the Willoughbys' house runs next to it, I've heard of this place but not seen anything past its high walls. Some fashionable Twickenham houses are open to the public on certain days and at certain times. Others who live here enjoy entertaining their friends and neighbours. The owner of Mr Secretary Johnston's estate welcomes no outsiders of any kind.

Using a mixture of cajoling and browbeating, Sir Humphrey gets a servant to open the gate. Once we've reached the main house, Sir Humphrey tells Captain Howard and me to wait in the carriage. "If a group appears to pester the admiral, it's hopeless," he says before leaping out.

Captain Howard says not a single word to me as the minutes crawl by in the uncomfortably warm carriage. He appears to be deep in thought and not a very pleasant one, going by the way he presses his lips. I am about to ask him the reason for his scowl when the driver opens the door for Sir Humphrey, gesturing for Howard and me to get out quickly. Sir Humphrey was apparently successful.

A faint breeze caresses my face as I extricate myself from the carriage. A majestic oak tree throws a cloak of deep shade over all of us. At first, I exult in the cooler air. But with a pang, I realize this length of shadow means it is now late afternoon, and we've nothing to show for our efforts since we left Strawberry Hill.

Standing behind Sir Humphrey is an elderly man dressed in servant's livery. He's stooped in posture, a wispy white beard floating from his chin, but his milky blue eyes examine us with lively curiosity.

Sir Humphrey says, "Josiah will take the two of you to the grotto to execute a search. I need to get back to Strawberry Hill. I'll send the carriage to wait for you on Richmond Road just outside the gate."

Unhappy with this plan, Captain Howard also tries to make a case for his return to Strawberry Hill.

"You can't expect Genevieve to crawl around an abandoned grotto alone, surely?" asks Sir Humphrey.

I am quite capable of searching by myself and try to tell Sir Humphrey Willoughby as much, but I am drowned out by Howard, who says, "Sir, I am increasingly unconvinced that anyone will find anything useful here!"

"But I do think it possible, and it's due to *her*." Sir Humphrey points at me. "She has a sense of Zophiel that neither of us possesses."

I feel a rush of pleasure that Sir Humphrey is acknowledging my insight. It's something I've rarely heard from him. In fact, I believe it would have pained him to admit my worth at times. But he follows it with the directive: "Have the carriage drop her afterwards at my house, Howard, and you can carry on to Strawberry Hill to report. She is set to begin the journey back to Lichfield day after tomorrow, and I'm sure she needs to pack and prepare."

My soaring spirits descend to earth with a thud. How will returning to my home, a cottage buried in the countryside, compare to charging around Twickenham on the trail of a sharp-witted quarry?

It isn't easy to rally myself to search for Mr Secretary Johnston's grotto after that, but I need to enter the spirit of things. Moving with surprising agility, the elderly Josiah leads us past the large square house of ideal symmetry, just the shape that Sir Horace Walpole rejected in creating the eccentric Strawberry Hill. Separate from the residence and overlooking the garden stands the only unusual building: a massive octagon made of red brick and white stone. A ring of urns is fixed to the top.

"Were you in service here when Mr Secretary Johnston was alive?" I ask our guide as we start on a path leading into the vast garden, criss-crossed with canals and dotted with fishponds and statues. It's more extensive than Pope's garden. I hope the grotto isn't located too deep in this expanse.

"Oh, yes, Madame," Josiah says, delighted with the question. "I've been employed at the Twickenham house by three families, first by the Johnstons. James Johnston was Secretary of State for Scotland and served the crown well. He was quite a popular gentleman. We had a coach and six pull up to the house every day when the family was in residence — every single day."

A terrier catches up with us, tail wagging furiously. It pushes a wet nose into my fingers, and I bend to pet its warm, throbbing back. The dog then dashes off towards a greenhouse that appears to be closed.

Josiah halts his rapid hobbling for a minute and looks not at the greenhouse but back at the stylish octagon, a dreamy look in his eyes. "Back then, we had to line up by rank and station outside to receive the guests. Mr Secretary Johnston built this octagon, the entire house and the gardens to impress the finest people in England — especially King George I and his son, then the Prince of Wales. He would visit with his wife, the princess."

"Not an easy man to please," mutters Captain Howard.

I don't understand the message behind Howard's sarcasm — perhaps it's just a matter of his being bad-tempered because he's stuck with me — but I do know how one person would respond to viewing such aristocratic grandeur: my husband. As the three of us, plus a terrier, push deeper into the garden, I think about how Thomas always hates to see fortunes lavished on amusing and entertaining while so many live in wretched poverty. I was drawn to Thomas's enlightened mind and fiery spirit from the first. We talked for hours about our shared vision of a better, fairer England. When did he stop telling me about his passions? Now, I feel he prefers to pour out his soul to friends who share his scientific background. My domain is the home and caring for Pierre. And he has his own opinions on raising our son, ones he doesn't confide in me.

"Mrs Sturbridge?"

Captain Howard is saying my name as if he's had to repeat it to get my attention. Josiah is about ten feet ahead of us, but only his head is visible. A high, thick hedge hides the rest.

"I'm sorry, Captain Howard?"

"I asked if you'd noticed the state of the walkways."

Feeling embarrassed by my preoccupation with my marriage, I scan the ground. It is crawling with aggressive weeds. "Hmm, things are not so well tended here," I say.

"Just so. Away from the icehouse and the greenhouse, the shrubbery and everything else got a little … wilder," he says.

Now that my focus is on the garden, I spot that weed, the flowering nettle, choking the banks of roses and hydrangea. Still, I don't quite understand. What does it matter if the property is a bit neglected? But watching Josiah disappear entirely behind the shrub, I realize the significance. Curious visitors are not permitted here, as they are in Alexander Pope's garden and grotto. It doesn't look like even the main house's servants venture into the garden's heart.

That could have made it an excellent hiding place for Zophiel.

"Captain!" shouts Josiah. "Something you need to see here."

My pulse leaps. Even though the man shouted for Howard, I scramble towards Josiah just as quickly as the captain.

Our guide stands in front of a grey archway connected to a small stone structure covered in vegetation. It looks like a single room in the middle of a vast garden. As I get closer, I see Josiah's hand on an old wooden door behind the tangled ivy.

It's then that the underlying smell of the garden hits me: the dank ponds mixing with the scent of noxious nettle and more benign flowers. It's enough to make my head swim.

"The door's supposed to be locked, but it's not," says Josiah, his loud voice dropping to a whisper, though we are far from the house. The dog that seemed so happy to follow us has disappeared. It must be my imagination, but the birdsong has faltered. An eerie stillness drops over us.

Shaking myself free of fancies, I push the door open. It slowly creaks wide to reveal stone steps leading down into darkness.

Captain Howard pushes me behind him. "I'll go down first."

"If this is where Zophiel hid, he's there no longer," I say. "We know he hired a boat to London. I'm in no danger."

"You're in danger of breaking your neck and then I'll have to answer for it." Captain Howard extricates a wick, wax and a long stick from his coat. Josiah assists him in lighting it, and, stick held aloft, Howard walks down to the bottom of the steps. He then turns right and disappears.

I understand that Captain Howard wants to prevent me from coming to any harm. Why can't he be less rude about it though?

I remain at the top of the stone steps, straining to listen to Captain Howard's measured steps as they fade into silence. Josiah, breathing heavily, wrings his hands as he waits with me. What's strange is the sickly smell. After a few minutes, we hear Captain Howard walking back.

"Mrs Sturbridge will need to come down," he announces before coming into view. I swallow.

"What did you find?" I call out.

"Easier to show you."

I hadn't had any difficulty with exploring Alexander Pope's grotto, either with Evelyn or with the two men today. But making my way down these crumbling steps fills me with dread *and* a growing excitement over the chance of a discovery. It's an unnerving mixture of feelings.

Captain Howard waits for me at the bottom, holding aloft his flickering stick to illuminate the steps.

Once I reach him, I see at once it's a great deal smaller than the Pope grotto. It hasn't been an attraction of interest for years. Someone has drained the ponds, thank heaven. I can think of nothing more disgusting than dank, putrid underground ponds thickening over time. But seashells and bits of broken glass glitter on the walls. Most likely, digging them out wasn't considered worth the trouble.

The far end of the grotto, where stone ends and dirt begins, is our destination. I spot the evidence when Captain Howard raises the candle.

"Zophiel was here," I say.

"For a number of weeks, yes."

I see thick blankets stacked on the ground, sets of clothing piled neatly and two crates. One contains the fruit Twickenham is famous for: strawberries, raspberries and cherries. The other holds tins and sacks of what appears to be dried meat and flatbread. Candlesticks lie beside them. At least a dozen shells are assembled in two rows next to the blankets.

I find the neatness and practicality of Zophiel's secret home surprising. When captured, his insults and defiant jokes, not to mention his violent escape, suggested a wild personality. But everything I see here supports an organized and prolonged effort to make this absurd hiding place liveable.

"What do we have here?" says Captain Howard, holding up a newspaper. One of the articles is circled. Holding up the lamp, I see a name underlined, that of Sir Horace Walpole. Howard says, "Reading this article, anyone would know that Walpole is at Strawberry Hill. It's a serious assignment of keeping watch. Hard to believe, but the little crook could read."

A closer look at the shells makes my throat tighten. "I think he was playing a game here. Noughts and crosses, something like that."

He was a criminal, but he was not much more than a boy.

"Sir Humphrey will want to examine everything," Howard says and begins putting the clothes and shells into the crate containing supplies of food. He opens a burlap sack positioned alongside and removes a pale square dotted with burn marks and holes.

"Do you think those supplies will tell anyone anything?" I ask doubtfully.

"This hard tack tells *me* something. These are the supplies that soldiers are given when on the march. I haven't seen such since Canada. Someone took this enterprise very seriously, outfitted him and instructed him not as if he were a practical jokester but more like a valued ..."

Captain Howard's voice trails off. But I believe I know what he is thinking.

"A valued spy?" I ask.

Chapter Ten

It isn't too hard to persuade Captain Howard to bring me to Strawberry Hill. I would like to think it's because of his respect for my contributions, but it could be that he's simply tired of arguing. In any case, the person I am most worried about is Sir Humphrey. Fortunately, when we come through the entranceway, the sight of the crate filled with Zophiel's belongings captures Sir Humphrey Willoughby's interest so much that he barely notices I have returned.

The two men set up a table there in the entrance hall to prevent their activity from disturbing Sir Horace Walpole's household. As they pick through the clothes and food containers, searching for some clue as to his real name or, more importantly, that of his master, I make my way upstairs to the armoury.

Nothing about the fictitious haunting of Strawberry Hill makes sense. The more we search for clues, the less I understand why anyone — and who knows how many people are involved — planned this and put it into action.

While the men obsess over the devilishly clever Zophiel, I will focus on Fragonard. This painting plays a role in the mystery, and while everyone else seems to have forgotten about it, I can think of nothing else.

With the light of late afternoon pouring through the stained-glass windows on the main floor and in the armoury, I can appreciate what Walpole was trying to accomplish with the trompe l'oeil wallpaper. The artist Walpole hired had worked diligently with shading to create deep dimensions. As you walk up the staircase of Strawberry Hill, you are meant to feel that you are entering Worcester Cathedral and Prince Arthur Tudor's burial place. But I'm here for the painting, not the wallpaper, and my heart sinks as I approach Fragonard's angel. I can see the painting now better than I could yesterday evening, no question. But it's still too much in the *gloomth* to assess correctly. Only Horace Walpole would hang a painting by Jean-Honoré Fragonard, known for his delicacy and tiny details, in the shadows!

The frame is too big and ornate. The first time I saw it, the frame cried out for replacement. I mistakenly thought that a Parisian art merchant would have a better grasp of style and proportion. However, the painting *is* by Fragonard. I can make out the signature in the lower right corner. And his identifying skills — the blazing talent that set him atop all other French artists — are here. In the ray of sun piercing darkening clouds, I see his bold use of contrast between light and dark. The angel's slight smile over the shoulder, hinting at a secret, shows Fragonard's coyness. His teacher and mentor, Boucher, painted angels who were beaming with lightness and joy. Fragonard is much more subtle.

Yet something stirs in the pit of my stomach.

Ever since I was a child, watching my grandfather at his easel, I've worked hard to learn the technique of the artist. I venerate skill and learned craft. But I also go by instinct, whether choosing my next subject or selecting a shade or brushstroke. Today, standing here, my instinct keeps telling me something is wrong with this painting. What can it be?

If pressed to give my reasons, two things about the painting concern me. One is the level of detail of the white tunic worn by the angel. It is well done, but the folds lack the depth I'd expect from such a celebrated artist. I'd rather not think about what the dirty tunic looked like hanging off Zophiel's pasty-skinned limbs.

The second is the shade of blue Fragonard chose for the top of the painting, above and to the side of the cloud pierced by a sunray. It's darker than I would have selected. A lighter blue would create a more exciting contrast with the darkening cloud. However, I'm not an expert on the artist's preferred palette.

The door slams below, and I hear men talking, their voices indicating some urgency. I hurry down the main stairs.

"Tell me every single word Zophiel said to him," Sir Humphrey Willoughby demands of his operative, a sandy-haired, handsome young man named Henry.

"I wrote it all down, Sir Humphrey."

"Wrote it? That's fine, man. But *tell* me."

"The boatman is back?" I ask, excited. "The one who had Zophiel as a passenger?"

"He took him fairly far, then turned around." Sir Humphrey frowns. "Why are you here? Howard, I thought I told you …" He breaks off to snatch the paper containing Henry's notes from his operative's hands, unable to postpone reading it even to scold me. His eyes move down the page and then widen. "That miserable bastard," he says.

"Sir Humphrey, what is it?" asks Captain Howard.

He waves the paper and roars, "He told the boatman his name was Humphrey Willoughby, and he'd just enjoyed a glorious holiday at Strawberry Hill."

A giggle nearly escapes me, but I manage to suppress it just in time. The great Sir Humphrey Willoughby has been made a bit of a fool. I don't think I've encountered anyone in my life with the cheekiness, the bravado, of Zophiel.

"He talked about seeing the paintings … the garden … and a fine suit of armour," says Sir Humphrey, his lips white with fury. "Then he was quiet for a while before talking about getting right with the Saviour and a lot of other rubbish. The servants heard the same religious fears from him before Longfren unlocked the door."

Sir Humphrey tosses the paper onto the table. "The clothes don't say anything about where he's from, and now this! Damn it!"

Captain Howard picks it up and starts reading. However, I get that strange stirring in my stomach again, as I did when staring at the Fragonard painting.

"That part doesn't fit," I say, thinking aloud. "The pious part."

Captain Howard says, "Henry wrote 'Saint Saviour' here. That's what Zophiel talked about."

Sir Humphrey barks a mirthless laugh. "England's most hard-hearted criminals cry for a priest before the scaffold."

"He's not at the scaffold now," I say. "Did he say he wanted to get right with saints and saviours or with Saint Saviour?"

Henry says, "Saint Saviour, that's what the boatman said, Madame."

I bite my lip, my thoughts tumbling over one another.

"Have you got something, Genevieve?" demands Sir Humphrey.

I say slowly, "There's a church in Southwark called St Saviour's. I think Zophiel might want to go there."

Captain Howard says, "It's his parish church? But isn't that a common name for a church? How do you know that's the one?"

I tell him that St Saviour's has a special place in the lives of the poor of South London. "His accent strikes me as belonging to someone from south of the river," I say. "It fits. I just thought of something else. Remember you threatened him with prison? What did he say? 'Some of my friends are sent to the Clink.' That's the name for the terrible prison in Southwark. The Clink."

"Where he disembarked, it's not far from Southwark," says Sir Humphrey. "I suppose that supports your theory. But how many people live south of the Thames? Many thousands. We can give Zophiel's description to the priest of St Saviour's. I think now that you mention it, I've heard of it. But it's large. That will work against us."

"Yes, it's enormous," I say. "I've seen St Saviour's with my own eyes. It's amazing what they do. Especially because that entire area is …" The words die out as I remember why I went there that day and what else I learned about the area.

"Captain Howard, is there anything in the notes about Cross Bones?" I ask, my voice rising.

"No."

I turn to Henry, who is looking bewildered. "Did the boatman mention Zophiel saying anything about Cross Bones?"

He shook his head. Sir Humphrey says, "What's that? Some sort of pirate business?"

My heart pounding, I say, "It's the name of two things near St Saviour's. One is a graveyard for the most wretched poor, the unclaimed bodies, and the other is a tavern near the graveyard. It's known to be a place where criminals meet — and find work."

Sir Humphrey whips around and calls for Margaret and Emma. When they appear, he questions them closely about what they heard Zophiel ranting about in his makeshift cell. We learn not only that it was St Saviour's he shouted about but also, Emma confirms, Cross Bones.

"He sounded angry about the Cross Bones, sir," says Emma. "He said they were going to be sorry. I thought it was him being a lunatic and I didn't want to repeat rubbish."

Emma looks abashed, and I quickly tell her that she has done nothing wrong.

Now Captain Howard's blood is up. He wants to call for the carriage and make all speed to London. "Won't Zophiel be surprised to find us waiting for him outside his lair of miscreants?" he says, rubbing his palms.

But Sir Humphrey puts a stop to that idea. "By the time we arrive in Southwark, it will be very late, and we will be in an unfamiliar place without a clear plan and not many men."

"It's not unfamiliar to her," says Captain Howard, jerking his chin in my direction. "She says she knows where the tavern is. It's a shame we can't bring her."

"You can't?" I ask.

Howard shakes his head. "You'd slow us down. We'd have to look after you in a dangerous part of the city rather than search for Zophiel."

I am so angry I have trouble forming the words. "I would *slow you down*? I beg your pardon. I'm the only one here who's been to that part of Southwark! You may know your way around Westminster, Captain Howard, but you'd not know the first thing about talking to someone at Cross Bones!"

"Enough bickering, you two," barks Sir Humphrey Willoughby. "Genevieve comes with us. We go to London in the morning." He takes a breath and says in a more measured tone, "This means your trip home with Pierre will have to be delayed. I am sorry. I will see to the new arrangements myself once we are on the other side of all this."

That night, when I finally make my way back to the Willoughbys' house, I break the news of needing to stay longer in Twickenham to an ecstatic Pierre and a smiling Evelyn.

"I adore having you here, so selfishly, I am glad that all of this fuss over the Strawberry Hill ghost has led to one benefit — you must stay longer," my friend says. "It is so good of you to help, Genevieve. I'm sure Sir Horace will be grateful."

While bathing, I have a moment to myself for the first time, and some uncomfortable questions press in. As I scrub my weary arms with lavender soap, I wonder: Am I taking advantage of the "fuss over the Strawberry Hill ghost" as Evelyn put it, to postpone returning to my regular life? No matter the strain in my marriage to Thomas and boredom with Lichfield, that is where I belong. Coming to the aid of Sir Horace Walpole might not be my chief motivation. I wonder if I'm so caught up in the drama of the ghost of Strawberry Hill that I've lost my grip on what matters most to me.

When I wake up just after sunrise, though, I find that, whatever the reason, I badly want to be the one to find Zophiel. I am flooded with worry that Sir Humphrey will change his mind in the light of a new day and insist I remain. I dress quickly and have just finished my toast and bowl of strawberries when Sir Humphrey materializes in the morning parlour. He nods and settles into his chair.

"Genevieve, I wonder if you'd care to take a look at this," says Sir Humphrey, sliding an open book of illustrations towards me.

I recognize the work of the illustrator immediately. There's no one else like William Hogarth. My throat tightens. How I worshipped the man who refused to take me on as an apprentice when I found a path to him.

This illustration, one of his last, is crammed with satirical figures engaged in outrageous acts in what looks like a courtroom.

Sir Humphrey says, "Its title is *Credulity, Superstition and Fanaticism*."

Though I'd already recognized it, I nod and say, "I'm rather surprised you're an admirer of Mr Hogarth's."

"Why do you say that? Because in another of his prints he showed William Pitt as a warmonger happily fanning the flames of conflict with France? Ha! No, I'm not a particular admirer of the Hogarth's, but he is the one who captures the controversies of the greatest interest to the British public. This one mocks belief in the Cock Lane ghost, the obsession of all London for months. The point is that anyone who believes in ghosts that make knocking sounds is a fool."

"Yes, I remember that it caused a great fuss when Mr Hogarth published it. A lot of people found it amusing."

"Genevieve, you'll be interested to know that one person who was prominent in his amusement was none other than Sir Horace Walpole. He said publicly that *Credulity, Superstition and Fanaticism* was unsurpassed in Hogarth's canon and would help him 'achieve immortality'. And my friend Horace wrote letters to many people scoffing at the Cock Lane ghost. I have one myself. So, for anyone who was paying attention, Walpole was known to be a sceptic of ghost stories, even though he wrote *The Castle of Otranto*. He didn't start to question any of it — and seek out people like Lars Longfren — until his house was in an uproar over these sightings."

Tearing my eyes away from Hogarth's print and all its wonder, I say, "I suppose then that whoever hired Zophiel to haunt Strawberry Hill wasn't paying close attention."

"Really, Genevieve? You think that the man who planned this, who hired Zophiel and went to such great lengths, wouldn't have paid attention or done his research?"

For a minute I can't understand what Sir Humphrey is trying to say. But then I begin to see the circuitous path he's charting.

"You think that whoever is behind this *knows* that Sir Horace is not a personal believer in ghosts. But then why in God's name stage a haunting?"

"Genevieve, that's what I intend to find out."

Chapter Eleven

Two carriages set out from Twickenham that morning, bursting with men assembled by Sir Humphrey. We will arrive in Southwark in force.

Sitting in the Willoughbys' carriage, across from a grimly determined Captain Howard, I must wonder if this is the right approach. The sort of men who slink in and out of the Cross Bones Tavern will melt away into impenetrable hideaways at the first sign of such an invasion. I think I should share my opinion with Sir Humphrey, but is this the right moment?

Sir Humphrey has a request for me first. He asks me to describe everything I can remember about the day I went to Cross Bones. "I'm curious — why did you go there?"

After taking a moment to recollect what happened, I tell them. "One winter morning, a young woman was found dead, sitting against a building a block from my house on Fournier Street. No one claimed to know her. The fathers of our church arranged for her poor remains to be sent for burial in Southwark at the graveyard for the nameless and forsaken, the one known as Cross Bones. That upset me, how no one put much effort into learning who she was. They had decided she was a fallen woman and worth no account. I hired a hackney carriage, a driver familiar with Southwark, to take me there to find her grave."

"And did you find it?" Sir Humphrey asks.

"No." I grimace at the memory. "It was naive of me to think I could."

When he urges me to explain why, I try my best to recreate what I saw that day. The hackney carriage turned onto one of the most desolate streets in Southwark. We slowly moved past what I thought was an abandoned tavern, the wooden beams of its Tudor-era walls rotting into glistening slime. The driver told me that deep inside, men willing to commit crimes gathered. When I stepped out of the hackney, all I could see was another barren lot bordered by an iron gate and, next to it, a warehouse. Peering through the gate, I saw no gravestones or monuments. There were dozens of long wooden boxes strewn on the ground. To the right yawned an open pit containing many more wooden boxes. Coffins. No names.

As the men contemplate my dire tale, I look out the carriage window. I can feel the change in my blood as we get closer to London. The streets teem with other carriages, chaises, wagons and those riding horseback. Buildings of wildly different shapes crowd every single street, and signs shine brightly. People spill out everywhere.

London is the city I was born in, the city where I spent most of my life. I've tried to deny it. I've said I agree with Thomas every time he says how fortunate we are to find a home in the country, but the truth is, I've missed London with all my heart.

Coming from the west, we could approach Southwark taking one of several routes. However, Sir Humphrey is firm about using London Bridge because it was my route three years ago and he wants to recreate it so that I have the greatest familiarity.

Once we are in Southwark, I again see the shipyards, fields and windmills that dominate the land near the Thames. We pass St Saviour's gathering of spires and squat buildings, but immediately I see something has changed. Where I remember street pedlars there is a line of pitiful prostitutes — I hate the word "harlot" — turning this way and that, offering their wares. It could be a matter of my being here in the summer rather than on a dismal winter day. I hate to think that London and Southwark are aswarm with even more women selling their bodies now than when I lived in London. Such a lamentable life and often a short one, stricken with the pox or drowned in gin.

To my surprise, the carriage jerks to a halt several streets shy of Cross Bones, and Sir Humphrey and Captain Howard prepare to get out.

"But we've not arrived yet," I say.

Sir Humphrey Willoughby says as patiently as if he were explaining it to his daughter, "Genevieve, we decided it would be too obvious to drive the carriage up to the door of the tavern. It will attract attention. We need to continue on foot. Weren't you listening?"

"That makes good sense," I say, relieved that they are showing practicality.

After we've left the protective chamber of the carriage, the harsh air stings the back of my throat and turns my stomach. It's the combination of the ever-present smoke of London with the tanners' fumes *and* the rotting refuse piled in the streets. Sir Humphrey coughs for almost a minute, and Captain Howard wipes his eyes while muttering, "Zounds."

I'd insisted that I could cope, and I am determined to do so. I set out towards Cross Bones in a direction that I believe to be correct. Sir Humphrey Willoughby walks alongside as if we are a couple, and Captain Howard follows. The others in the second carriage string out behind.

The men are correct that the sight of the Willoughbys' grand carriage pulling up on one of the most wretched streets in Southwark would cause great suspicion. But our midday stroll won't go unnoticed either. Should genteel people care for a walk south of the Thames, there's the

Vauxhall in Lambeth. No well-attired outsiders walk without purpose here. The sharp-eyed must be wondering about our purpose at this very minute.

As I walk, I'm trying to study the buildings without appearing to do so, which would make things worse for us. Sir Humphrey peers down at me with a questioning tilt of the eyebrow as we approach a cross street. I shake my head. It all looks a bit familiar, but the switch from winter to summer has thrown me.

Beads of sweat gather under my bonnet.

Two men appear, coming from around the corner that's one block ahead and heading straight for us. Sir Humphrey pauses, his hand on my elbow. I see his other hand reaching for the pistol in his coat. Now I know why he wore this coat in the heat.

The two men come so close I can see the shine of the sweat on their faces. Sir Humphrey pulls me from their path, and Captain Howard pushes forward to stand with us. But the men dash into a shabby two-storey wooden house to our left, crashing through the front door, completely ignoring us. I hear raised voices in the house.

Exhaling slowly, Sir Humphrey says, "Let us go on."

In the next few minutes, we see more people running, women *and* men, all of them coming from around the same corner.

"What are they fleeing?" asks Captain Howard.

"I have no idea," says Sir Humphrey.

We edge closer, and I recognize the corner. Cross Bones, both the graveyard and the tavern, lie down this street. I rub my eyes. It could not be less like the forlorn street I ventured down three years ago. It is chaotic and loud, with people dashing everywhere. Not only that — the first two men who nearly collided with us reappear. They are running back to this street and bringing two *more* men with them, as if they secured reinforcements. Through the mayhem, I spot the Tudor-era tavern halfway down.

Amid my confusion, I breathe a sigh of relief that the tavern door is flung open. The building's wooden beams look close to buckling, and its shutterless windows are both broken, but Cross Bones Tavern is *not* abandoned. In fact, people are leaping out its door and onto the street.

"Are they aware of our coming?" asks Captain Howard.

"No one's paying us a bit of attention," I say.

Sir Humphrey Willoughby says, "Is that the graveyard across the street, Genevieve? Whatever it is, it seems to be the source of the drama."

"Drama?" I repeat, incredulous. "This place is brewing a riot."

"It will be hard to find Zophiel in such chaos," says Captain Howard, peering around.

"Genevieve, lead the way," orders Sir Humphrey.

I move far enough down the street that I can confirm the gap leads to Cross Bones graveyard. This is all so strange. Why would a cemetery for the forsaken attract such a crowd? The beads of sweat on the back of my neck are joining to form a damp patch. Dread is rising in my throat like a sickness.

A growing crowd is running past us, pushing to get to Cross Bones. Many seem distinctly disturbed.

"Not Jemmy!" cries one woman. "Not our Jemmy!"

We go forward in a tight trio. As we join the stream turning into the graveyard from the street, a cry goes out. "Give the call! Sound the alarm!"

Someone else shouts, "Someone send for the law."

"I am the law." His voice a clear bellow, Sir Humphrey Willoughby declares himself to the Cross Bones crowd. If they knew an under-secretary of His Majesty's government had planted himself among them, I'm sure they'd be shocked to bits. As for me, I must respect his courage.

Heads whip around. Some faces are grateful, but others scowl. The woman who shouted about "Jemmy" grabs Sir Humphrey's hand and pulls him forward. I'm seized by an intense need to know, and I follow Sir Humphrey despite Captain Howard hissing that I should get clear.

But as I get closer, my steps falter. The awful sense of living a topsy-turvy nightmare grows stronger. A tight group looks at someone sitting on the ground, just as they did on Fournier Street that winter morning.

But this time, it's not a young woman. It's a young man propped up against a cheap wooden coffin. And no one would mistake him for sleeping at first glance. His throat has been cut ear to ear, with dark blood drenching his shirt. His eyes are mercifully shut, but his mouth hangs open, showing those brown lower teeth.

I'm looking at Zophiel.

I stagger backwards. The angry roar of the crowd fades to a distant hum inside my head as my stomach roils. Dots dance before my eyes. I am losing consciousness.

Captain Howard brings me back, seizing me by both arms and shouting my name. My surroundings come back into focus.

I hear Sir Humphrey order Howard to get me back to the carriage. I half-stumble there, wordless and numb, but not so I can't remember Howard's caustic prediction of the day before about being forced to look after me. I brace myself for criticism, but I realize Captain Howard is upset himself by the time we make it to the carriage. "Poor sod," he mutters. "This is a rotten business."

Sitting in the carriage, I feel out of all danger of fainting. I am mercifully alone but for Sir Humphrey's retainer Henry, who looks in every ten minutes or so, quite concerned. I hold the cup of tea in my hands that the young man gave me. Sir Humphrey is questioning people about the murder. The constable and other people of authority have been sent for as well.

"Extra sugar for shock, just like Captain Howard ordered," Henry had said when pushing a chipped cup into my hands.

"I don't have shock," I say, annoyed over being treated like a weak child.

He says nothing out of politeness. My stomach, however, is in a sorry condition. I cannot drink the tea because of it. After a few sips, I feel like gagging.

Nobody of my party knows, except Sir Humphrey Willoughby, that this reaction is out of character. I've seen the corpses of the murdered before and not fallen to pieces. When Sir Gabriel Courtenay devised a plot to kidnap Thomas and take him to France, violence was part of it. And later, after the loathsome blackmailer Hervé Gaynard threatened me, I crept up the back stairs to his Covent Garden lair only to find Gaynard sitting at his desk, a dagger plunged into his chest.

Today is different. The death of Zophiel — I now know his real name is Jemmy, but I can't use it in my head yet — affects me. What he did at Strawberry Hill was wrong, of course. Still, in a way that I tried to keep strictly to myself, I admired him. He had guts and audacity. How did he come to such a gruesome end? People are murdered in Southwark just as they are in the dangerous parts of London, but the near-riot in the street suggests outrage. Perhaps it's due to the killer leaving Zophiel's body for anyone to find in Cross Bones graveyard, his throat gaping open.

And it's entirely my fault.

I hadn't been in the carriage for fifteen minutes when the realization hits me like a slap. Zophiel wouldn't have been in Southwark yesterday, but for me. I was the one who suggested we trap the person terrifying

Sir Horace Walpole the night of the dinner party. I should have said, "Very well" when Sir Humphrey argued that men of his choosing best do the investigation in a professional manner. But I'd been impatient, stubborn, sensitive to slights and anxious to assert myself — all my most difficult traits. And I was eager to postpone my return to Lichfield by delving into this matter. Had Sir Humphrey's men been assigned to it and snatched him in Strawberry Hill a few days from now, he'd have landed in jail. Zophiel would be spitting mad but … alive. He wouldn't have ended up in some violent dispute and dumped in Cross Bones.

"I haven't stolen a thing or hurt nobody. What's the crime in having a little fun?"

Zophiel's words keep going round and round in my head. An aching misery threatens to take hold, but I fight it. My throat is tight, and my eyes are brimming. I cannot, *will* not, weep in this carriage.

Henry taps on the carriage door. This time, he must not only inquire about my health but also ask for the cup back. "A woman across the street brewed tea when she heard you were ailing. I need to return it."

"Of course," I stammer. "I'm sorry. I hadn't given any thought to where the tea came from. I'm so selfish, so terribly selfish."

Henry winces. "Mrs Sturbridge. Please. It's just a cup."

Sir Humphrey reappears just after I hand Henry the cold tea. I've never seen him look this grim. His eyes are hard and angry, and new lines are etched from his mouth. He leaps in, and the carriage begins moving. I ask about Captain Howard. "He's staying to serve as a liaison with the Bow Street Runners."

"Ah, yes. The men that John Fielding sends to investigate murders." I think for a minute. "But whatever happened to Zophiel — what led to his murder — has to do with Southwark, some argument or grudge. What could Captain Howard contribute? Background?"

Sir Humphrey says nothing.

My stomach seizes up as if I'm about to gag all over again. "You think Zophiel's murder has something to do with Strawberry Hill?" I whisper. "That's impossible. He just got here last night."

"And walked right into the path of the man wielding a knife, I'm afraid."

Frustration shreds my rattled nerves. "You're not making a bit of sense! How could someone be waiting for him in Southwark who had *anything* to do with the business at Strawberry Hill? It's only the master of all this, his boss, who would know about Walpole and the haunting. Do you think Zophiel came scrambling back to confess he'd been caught, said he was lucky enough to escape without telling anyone a thing — and the consequence of this is he gets his throat slit? The penalty is death? Over a failed prank?"

Sir Humphrey looks pointedly at the carriage floor. He's under no obligation to answer my questions and I can see he doesn't care to.

Our carriage slows to a stop to take its place in the long line crossing London Bridge. Sir Humphrey taps his fingers impatiently at the delay. His face holds the same furious intensity as when he entered the carriage.

The back of my neck tingles.

Why is Sir Humphrey Willoughby so determined to return to Twickenham with all speed? His reaction is more venomous than it should be to the murder of a Southwark criminal who bedevilled Walpole. If he were incensed over the killing, he would be insisting on remaining in Southwark himself. Instead, he is hell-bent on returning to Twickenham, not even stopping for food before hurrying west.

"Tell me what is happening," I say quietly. "Sir Humphrey, what have you learned?"

Chapter Twelve

Sir Humphrey's hazel eyes study me more coolly and dispassionately than since that day eight years ago when he told me about Sir Gabriel Courtenay's true loyalty to Louis XV and turned me away from Courtenay.

"If I share with you certain facts, Genevieve, they must be kept in strictest confidence," he says. "Your husband cannot be told. Ever. Do you understand?"

I can't imagine how this could have anything to do with Thomas, but if I argue, I'll learn nothing. I nod.

He says quietly, "Jemmy Maylie was quite a favourite in this part of Southwark. You probably gleaned that from the reaction to his death. That's why I found three people willing to talk to me. They told me a stranger came around looking for Jemmy four days ago — two whole days before we went to dinner at Strawberry Hill. The man offered money to anyone who could tell him where Jemmy was and what he was up to. The problem was, Jemmy disappeared from Southwark seven weeks earlier. He told a few friends he had a high-paying job out of London — other than that, he was tight-lipped."

"So the man didn't learn what the job was at Strawberry Hill?"

"I don't know. Jemmy might not have been tight-lipped with

everyone. But then, on Sunday, Jemmy came back, and by Monday morning, he's dead."

"It couldn't be his boss who killed him, that just makes no sense. But then, why didn't Jemmy go to him — for protection?"

"Unclear," Sir Humphrey says curtly.

Our carriage has entered London Bridge, and we are plunged into dimness. Houses and shops cover the old bridge. I can no longer read Sir Humphrey's face so well. Everything I just learned has left me chilled, but I sense that the most crucial point, the fact that has hurled Sir Humphrey into his present state, is still being withheld. How can I pry it out of him?

I say, "I assume every effort is being made to locate this man who was searching for Jemmy, whether he killed him or not."

"Of course."

I can no longer control myself. "But what is it that concerns you so greatly? *Why* are you so keen to get back to Twickenham rather than direct the search for the man who murdered Jemmy? I want to be of service — how can I do so without all the facts? *Must I beg you?*"

He sighs. "Very well. But again, I must tell you, no one else can learn this."

"You can trust me, Sir Humphrey."

"We've learned that the man who was searching for the whereabouts of Jemmy Maylie had a distinctly French accent. Which leads to my belief that the French are involved."

I am no longer mystified by why Sir Humphrey is so angry. The war that William Pitt championed ended with a victory for England three years ago. From all I have heard, France took its defeat badly and desperately wants to regain its lost prestige and territories. And Sir Humphrey is the man charged by the ministry with protecting

England from the damage wrought by French spies and any other aggression from the kingdom across the Channel.

"And you think that it's not just the murder of Jemmy? That they have malign intentions towards Sir Horace Walpole?"

Clenching his fist, Sir Humphrey says, "I shall find out as soon as possible. We also know this Frenchman has a scar on his face, just above his chin. It's a description that could get us somewhere."

France. The mere word puts a chill in me like nothing else. I am a Huguenot. My great-grandparents were driven from their ancestral home because of their Protestant faith after Louis XIV revoked the Edict of Nantes. The torments that Catholic France inflicted on French Huguenots are difficult to believe. But they happened, from the petty persecutions for practicing our faith to the ruination of our livelihoods and to imprisonment, being made to row in the galley aboard ships — and death. However, I know one way I can help.

"Sir Humphrey, I need to examine the Fragonard painting. Walpole bought it in France. Our unknown enemy comes from France. There *must* be a connection. The angel is not right — something is not right. You must help me. I have been tormented by suspicions since I first glimpsed it."

"How can I help you look at a painting?"

"Persuade Sir Horace Walpole to let me take the painting off the wall and examine it in the light. Preferably full daylight. Not by candlelight — and not in the *gloomth*!"

Sir Humphrey agrees to make the arrangements I require. Despite our hours in the carriage and the shock of discovering Jemmy's murder, I'm eager to look at the painting today. But the sun is nearly set when our carriage arrives in Twickenham. There's no point in an inspection. Sir Humphrey lets me off at his house before pushing on to share the day's disturbing news with Walpole, though only some of it. He says Sir Horace must not know a Frenchman is involved.

When I join Evelyn and the children, an incredible weariness ripples through every inch of me; I can barely keep my eyes open long enough to eat supper. I tell Evelyn some of what I know out of earshot of Pierre and Diana. Sir Humphrey had been so firm about secrecy that I hesitate even to enlighten his wife!

The next day is cloudy, but I don't require full sun. I just need strong natural light to inspect a painting properly. Invigorated by a deep sleep, I ride with Sir Humphrey to Strawberry Hill.

I confess I was dreading my next meeting with Walpole. I thought the news of Jemmy's murder would send him into hysterics. But the owner of Strawberry Hill is calm and composed, ready to weather these new storms. I learn that his two house guests have left — Mrs Campion to her home in the country and Lars Longfren to travel on the Continent — and the servants have been instructed to be watchful and cautious about strangers.

To my relief, Sir Humphrey has persuaded Walpole of the value of my plan to examine his Fragonard painting. He even has a good suggestion of where I can scrutinize it. On the ground floor of Strawberry Hill is a "Cloisters" space, full of light and tables to work on. Some of the objects he acquired need cleaning and mending, so a cabinet of brushes, scissors, glues and other liquids stands in the corner.

Sir Horace and I use tremendous care to remove the painting from the wall together. It can be tricky to hang a painting and even more so to remove one. I lift the Fragonard off its wall hooks as he lends a hand, and Walpole closely accompanies me as I walk the painting down the stairs and to the Cloisters. I move slowly because the large, ornate wooden frame makes it challenging to wrap my arms around it and hold my grip. It's not a heavy frame, nor an old one. I fancy I can smell pine wood beneath the gold paint.

"It's not a forgery, Mrs Sturbridge, if that's what you fear." Walpole can't resist saying it as we make our slow progression. "I admit I may not be extremely familiar with Jean-Honoré Fragonard — he is, after all, a new artist. But no one acquainted with Madame du Deffand would dare to commit fraud against one of her friends!"

"I'm sure you are right, sir."

"Forgery is a sore subject with me because it's been attempted several times before by those who know I'm a collector," he explains with a rueful smile. "Unscrupulous people who hear the name 'Walpole' get ideas about extracting a fortune from me. But it usually has to do with concocted letters rather than art. Forging the work of someone like Fragonard must be extraordinarily difficult as well as risky. And I believe I told you I paid a good price for my angel, but nothing outrageous. I can't imagine who would go to the trouble."

And that's the part about art forgery I don't understand. I've heard only the vaguest rumours about people creating copies of great art to be sold as originals. It requires years of training and, ideally, apprenticeships and travelling through places like Italy to reach the level of an artist who could even begin to create something that would fool anybody.

"May I ask what excites further interest?" persists Sir Horace, his keen curiosity preventing him from leaving the Cloisters.

If I'm to proceed, I really need Walpole to go. But how can I say I'm driven by a nagging feeling that something about the painting isn't right? As he stands before me, waiting, a quizzical look on his face, a word pops into my head. A message. There's a message in this painting. But it's the last thing I can say. I have no choice but to lie.

"My motives are selfish. I do not know when I will have another opportunity to study a Fragonard, Sir Horace. While I know you want the angel to watch over Prince Arthur, there simply isn't good light in the armoury for me to examine it and learn."

Sir Horace nods and says, "Ah. Well, I'll leave you to it."

Finally, the master of Strawberry Hill leaves. I stare at the painting lying on the wooden table before me. The angel stares back at me, his beatific smile forever threatening to turn into a smirk. The tunic's folds aren't that impressive in better light, and the blue at the top is still too dark.

But these are not significant mistakes. If this painting is a forgery, it's a good one. I'd have to consult a Fragonard expert — and possibly Fragonard himself! — to confirm it.

"A message, why would I think there's a message?" I mutter to myself. There are no words anywhere on the painting but the artist's signature. No page from a book or letters glimpsed in a mirror.

But spies deal in hidden messages all the time. Sir Gabriel taught me that.

Just because I can't see a message when I look at the surface of this painting doesn't mean there isn't something here. Why should I consider only the surface?

My heart beating faster, I turn over the Fragonard. When I removed it from the wall, I saw no writing on the back or along the frame. But this large a frame covers the borders of the painting by an inch or maybe two. I might find something underneath. I'd not thought of this before, because why would anyone deliberately hide a message where no one could see it? But I am groping towards a linear perspective now.

Making my way over to Walpole's supplies cabinet, I select tools to remove the frame. It takes about fifteen minutes because

I keep my movements small and careful. I can't damage Walpole's possession.

Once the frame is off, I move the canvas down so I can see the top. To my surprise, it is not painted to the edge. There is an unpainted border of at least an inch.

My heart leaps in my throat as I read a phrase in French on that border: *Avoir une peur bleue?* In English, it means, "Do you have a blue fear?"

In smaller letters is another sentence I read, *Regarde sous le bleu.* That means: "Look beneath the blue."

I whip around to see if I'm alone in the Cloisters. No one is here; no one watches. I still feel vulnerable. Written in distinct script, the question seems meant for me — not for Sir Horace Walpole. He knows nothing about the blue formula my husband invented. That shade isn't found here. It couldn't be. They destroyed the pigment years ago and suppressed the formula.

Or was it?

My legs tremble as I return to the cabinet and search its drawers and compartments. After no more than a minute, I find what I was hoping for: a bottle of turpentine. I moisten a rag and return to the painting. I rub a two-inch-wide area along the top — a part that will be hidden by the frame after I put it back on.

It emerges slowly, inevitably, as I rub. It's the deep yet dazzling shade I thought I'd never see again. The colour that people were quite willing to kill for. Once the darker topcoat is removed, it shimmers undimmed.

This is the colour blue that my husband, Thomas Sturbridge, invented over eight years ago.

Chapter Thirteen

I make my way to the upstairs parlour at Strawberry Hill. Sir Humphrey must be told immediately.

The sight of Thomas's colour reminds me of the powerful allure attached to the search for a blue that can be used in art. There is not a genuine blue pigment found in nature. When people think they see a blue bird or flower, it's a trick of the light. For many centuries, the mineral lapis lazuli, found in Afghanistan caves, was one of the few sources of blue to be used for painting, but it was extraordinarily costly. Various chemists have discovered other solutions for blue, but nothing compared to Thomas's formula, a pigment created for porcelain and painting. It drove the French mad that a superior colour — one that would transform the art world and potentially make a fortune — might originate in England, and they took action.

I can hear the two men talking on the other side of the parlour door.

"If William Pitt returns to power, my friends in France are certain that we will have another war by next year," Sir Horace says. "Their letters are full of it."

"You know the obstacles to resuming war, my friend."

I badly want the sound to be gentle and unobtrusive, but my nerves are in such a state that my knock sounds urgent.

"Come in," calls Sir Horace Walpole.

I push open the door, and, to my relief, Sir Humphrey sits across a table from Walpole. "Mrs Sturbridge, how goes your Fragonard study?" Walpole asks.

I call upon the skills of a play actor and smile. It was drummed into my head, over and over, that Thomas's formula for the colour blue is a state secret. "Very well. But I remembered something that I need to relay to Sir Humphrey right away." I turn to Willoughby and say, "It's a private matter concerning my trip to be rescheduled to Lichfield. I apologize, but could I have a word with you, Sir Humphrey, out here?"

I have Sir Humphrey by the arm a moment later and am racing him to the Cloisters. He shows no surprise. He knew my excuse to remove him was nonsense.

"What have you found?" Sir Humphrey demands.

"You need to see it — you'll grasp the crisis at once." And he will. Sir Humphrey is one of the few people in all of England who could recognize Thomas's colour. He saw pieces of porcelain painted this dazzling shade in Derby, where Thomas had his private laboratory. And he personally negotiated the parts of the treaty agreement, sponsored by the Dutch government since France and England were then at war, laying out that production of the colour following Thomas Sturbridge's formula must desist in both countries.

I had covered the canvas with several parchments while I ran to summon Sir Humphrey. I look at Sir Humphrey's face when I lift the parchment atop the revealed blue. I am rewarded with the peculiar satisfaction of witnessing the under-secretary going into deep shock. His eyes widen, and his mouth falls open. When he finds his voice, he says, "How did you even know it was there?"

I point at the French question and tell him what it means. "Someone can take it more than one way. When I saw it, I felt immediately it was a question meant for me. That made me wonder again about the blue in the painting. But it's also a well-known phrase in French. I don't think that, in English, it has the same significance. 'Blue fear' means, well, it means to feel terror. The worst terror of a lifetime. Once I saw it …"

He slams the side of the worktable so hard the painting shakes, and I snatch the turpentine bottle before it tips over.

"They broke the treaty — damn," he explodes. "And now they're taunting us!"

Sir Humphrey is so furious that I would normally say nothing and give him time to regain control. But so many questions swirl in my head that I can't wait for his rage to pass.

"What does it mean if the French broke this treaty?" I ask.

"Obviously it's not anywhere near the importance of the Treaty of Paris. It's not as if the French are trying to take back Canada! The Sturbridge agreement is a separate document, executed under very different circumstances. The French have long been known to bribe British workers and inventors to come to France and use their knowledge in French industries. But a kidnapping connected to murder? That went too far. King Louis agreed to Thomas Sturbridge's request to leave France but only if he swore not to continue the production of blue in England. We didn't have to say yes to that, but we wanted to recover Sturbridge alive — and you, Genevieve — so it was part of the agreement. As was the French destroying the formula developed at Sèvres Porcelain. I believe King Louis's pride was offended at the thought that his chemists could not surpass the achievements of a British inventor."

I swallow and say, "You still haven't told me what the consequence could be."

"Very technically speaking, a treaty violation can lead to declaration of war," says Sir Humphrey.

At the shock he must see in my face, he hastens to add, "England would never go to war over a colour alone!"

"Who knows about the treaty?" I ask.

"Very few people. The cabinet box isn't opened to anyone in the cabinet except for the Secretary of State for the Southern Department and of course the Prime Minister."

While the treaty's obscurity should reassure me, I note that Sir Humphrey looks quite troubled. He says, "There are many tensions between our two countries, Genevieve. This is the last thing that anybody needs to be told about now."

I stare down at the painting lying on the table. It seems inconceivable that this angel in a cloud could push two countries closer to renewed conflict.

Questions pulse in my head. "How could the person who sold Sir Horace Walpole this painting know that I would be invited to Strawberry Hill and see it and doubt it?" I ask.

"No one could have predicted that," he says after a moment. "You should have been in Lichfield. Both you and Sturbridge. Well out of it. There was one chance in a thousand you'd ever see this painting in Strawberry Hill." He takes a shuddering breath. "The message was meant for me. I'm known to be Sir Horace Walpole's friend and his neighbour in Twickenham."

"I don't know," I say doubtfully. "This is too ... Byzantine. How could anyone count on you taking apart one of the paintings in a friend's collection, removing the frame and reading this? And why on earth would anyone in France ever want to let you know that this is happening at all?"

Sir Humphrey frowns as if working something through, then straightens and says briskly, "Here is what we shall do. Put the frame on. If you do so, no one will be able to tell from looking at it that you've removed some paint to reveal the blue sky underneath — am I correct?"

"Yes."

"Then get it back on the wall."

"But Sir Humphrey, I'm convinced this must be a forgery. Jean-Honoré Fragonard wouldn't be mixed up in all this."

"I agree."

I need help understanding this. "Sir Horace Walpole would be terribly distressed to know he bought a fake. We must tell him."

Sir Humphrey shakes his head. "No. We can't tip our hand quite yet. You've exposed their secret, but it's too soon to let the other side know, and I have a feeling they've got Strawberry Hill under observation. I need more time."

"But don't you want to take the painting with you and … ?"

"Not yet. I need to ride to London and consult with certain people in His Majesty's government. This is more than a murder case now. It's an incident between countries. Sèvres and the French were supposed to destroy any written record of your husband's formula."

I remember the complexity of the formula Thomas created and how difficult it was for him to keep it stable enough to produce pigment. Yet here the blue is, pulsing with its terrible beauty. I murmur, "This isn't like a recipe for cake. A great deal of it was in Thomas's head. I don't — I don't know how anyone else could have done it."

"Clearly, the French have found a way," says Sir Humphrey, who urges me to put the frame back on this minute while he watches. I comply, even though I disagree with putting it back up on the wall and pretending all is well. My movements are jerky and clumsy. Handling the canvas makes my skin burn. I don't want to touch the same wood, paper and paint as the person who scrawled the message of a "Blue fear".

He turns around to search the corners of the Cloisters with his eyes, much as I have. No sign of a servant, Walpole or anyone else. "We must give no hint that today you have discovered what someone meant us to discover," he says. "Horace … Evelyn … for now, they must be kept in the dark, do you understand?"

"You keep saying that, and I keep telling you the same thing," I snap. "I *am* discreet. Have you proof otherwise?"

I move to pick up the painting, but Sir Humphrey Willoughby seizes it first as if he's afraid I'll do some damage to it. Together we walk up to the armoury to replace it on the hooks hanging from the wall. I've never seen such an uncomfortable expression on his face. I wonder if Sir Humphrey dislikes touching it as much as I do. The smiling angel has become a warning of malevolence.

Sir Humphrey returns to Walpole's study to continue our pretence that all is well. In the carriage on the way back to his house, I ask Willoughby what all of this could have to do with Jemmy's death.

"I'm not sure," he responds. "But in Paris this past winter, whoever sold Horace the painting — and I have the name of the man who made the sale — wanted him to doubt the authenticity of his new art."

"It did have certain strange aspects to it," I say thoughtfully. "The foremost clue was the frame. It was the wrong size for the painting. They may have hoped he would have it reframed and see the message."

"Yes, that was done with cunning — quite deliberately," Sir Humphrey Willoughby says with a wry smile. "But Horace didn't care! He just desired a painting of an angel in the place where he honoured his precious Arthur Tudor. He didn't think to replace the frame and see the message and find it curious enough to notify me. So after a few months pass, and no alarm is raised, a certain skilful little criminal named Jemmy Maylie was hired. The objective was to get Walpole to pay serious attention to the painting. He pretended to be a spirit, knocking on the wall like the Cock Lane ghost and running through the house to the painting. Always the painting with its frame that is crying out to be removed. Maybe it could have worked. You connected this business to the painting right away. But then Jemmy was caught."

Hot tears sting my eyes. I've not by any means recovered from my grief over Jemmy's pitiless murder. It's unbearable to know that my actions shortened someone's life, especially someone who tried so hard to work his way up from the worst poverty of the London streets. I press my eyes with a handkerchief while Sir Humphrey Willoughby tells me what will happen now.

"I don't know how long I will be gone, Genevieve. We are in the middle of an upheaval in government. People will be distracted. Some are far from London. It is summer. But I need you to remain here in Twickenham. You're the only one who knows about the creation of the formula, how the French spied on us and then kidnapped and committed violence to obtain the blue. You know what it looks like, can recognize it. You'll tell the story when the time comes."

"But what about Thomas? He knows everything about it. He *invented* the formula!"

Sir Humphrey Willoughby takes my hands in his and squeezes them. "No. I realize this isn't easy, but for your own good — and for his — you cannot communicate with your husband. He must have no involvement whatsoever."

"You can't possibly think that Thomas knows of this, that the resurgence of his formula is his fault," I say hotly.

"I don't think he is responsible for the blue, the painting of the angel, or for Jemmy, no." He squeezes my hands harder. "But he must be kept out. Listen to me — and help me."

Sir Humphrey leaves in a whirl of activity, talking to Evelyn alone and telling her God knows what. Once his trunk is packed, he leaves with his valet and two other men to reopen the Willoughbys' London residence for at least a week.

He says only one thing more to me alone, drawing me away for a moment.

"I will also write to Thomas Sturbridge," he says. "You communicated that you would be home soon, correct? Within the week? You'll send him another one. I'll say my wife needs you to stay with us longer. Don't indicate otherwise in yours. Do I have your promise?"

I nod shortly. It's not until Sir Humphrey has left that I realize he didn't ask me for Thomas's address near Liverpool. Somehow, I think bitterly, he knows it already.

In some ways, the next five days are a reprieve. I return with relief to the company of Evelyn and the children, pushing out of my mind the terrible sights in Southwark and the feel of the painting I took down from the wall in Strawberry Hill. I admit it is also a relief not to be back in Lichfield quite yet. Sir Humphrey shall return with a decision on how to proceed, and at that time, I will need to revisit it all, informing the necessary parties of my husband's formula and, unfortunately, my role in a spying operation. Until that time, I would rather not torment myself.

That sound approach to the situation doesn't prevail in the middle of the night, when unanswered questions about the painting gnaw at me. Who in France found Thomas's formula? How could they overcome its complexities and produce the pigment without his leadership? Why alert the British that they have broken their word and are reproducing it? Are the French taunting us, as Sir Humphrey said? I'd think it's the last thing they would want to do.

What's worse, I feel weighed down by guilt over Thomas. I wrote him a lamentably brief letter explaining Evelyn still needed me in Twickenham and I must stay longer. To write any more than that would be a lie, and while we are not as close as we once were, I will not lie to Thomas.

It's on the fifth day that everything changes. It begins when Evelyn and I go with the children on a day trip that yields a new piece to the puzzle the false Fragonard presents.

On a cloudy and unusually cool morning, we set out for Hampton Court Palace to see the castle and grounds after Evelyn obtains permission for us to visit. It was built in the reign of Henry VIII. Following the Tudors, after adding something here or knocking something down there, the royal family gave up and ceased living there. It hasn't been abandoned exactly. We hear that retired servants and distant relatives of the royals are living in grace and favour apartments, though I see no sign of any of them during our tour.

I enjoy King William's Great Fountain Garden and Queen Caroline's Staircase. When I stand in Henry VIII's Great Hall, I tilt my head back to absorb the engineering feat and artistic triumph of the hammer-beam roof, made of carved wooden beams that look like the hulls of massive ships.

"King Henry was inspired by Venetian designs," says a voice to my right. "His castles, his tapestries and definitely his clothes." A white-haired, black-eyed gentleman bows and smiles and proceeds, in a strong Italian accent, to inform me that Henry VIII may have broken with the Church of Rome but nonetheless appreciated the Italian states' artistic genius.

I proceed to enjoy a thoroughly enjoyable conversation about architecture and art with Signor Antonio Pierro, a Florentine merchant visiting London.

"I am so glad that I travelled here to see Hampton Court and to converse with such a knowledgeable lady," he says. "Now I feel my own private Grand Tour is complete."

I laugh. "That's what the English do — they must go on the Grand Tour of the Continent. Did you set out to do the opposite?"

"Ah, you've caught me, Madame. That was one of my objectives, though business is what brings me to London first. I was curious to see the home of the young men who trample my country, holding their guidebooks and insisting that they see everything that Rome, Venice and Florence have to offer."

I wince. "Trample? Oh, but that doesn't sound very nice."

He bows again. "Too strong a word, forgive me. They do not mean ill. And I fear the English pay a price for their eagerness to see Italy in the last few years."

"What price is that?"

"The coins, sculpture and paintings they buy to send back to England? I would say only one piece in three is genuine."

I swallow hard, thinking of the fake Fragonard hanging in the vestibule of Strawberry Hill. I may, quite by chance, have stumbled on someone who is an expert on forgery. Trying not to seem *too* interested, I ask Signor Pierro about the skills of those who copy art and other valuables.

"Such mischief has been with us since the Renaissance!" he exclaims. "My dear Madame, Michaelangelo copied a Roman sculpture of a cupid and buried it in the ground to make it look older and then tried to sell it to a cardinal!"

After a few more light-hearted anecdotes about the adventures of copyists, my friend grows more serious. "It has become a business now," he says. "I am a businessman myself, so I appreciate the practicalities even if I cannot approve of the crime. I have heard rumours about a man, rarely seen, who began in Rome using art students. His ring of talented forgers has spread to his own city of Geneva and even to Paris."

I'm reluctant to tip my hand, as Sir Humphrey would say, but I am close to hearing the name of the master forger who could be behind our false Fragonard.

"How tantalizing a rumour!" I say, smiling at Signor Antonio Pierro. "He's rarely seen, but what do people call this man?"

He laughs. "You might find this strange, Madame, but he is known simply as 'the Abbé'. I don't think that this means he is a man of God! It is — what is the English word? — a nickname."

"And you have heard that the English travelling on the Continent, seeking to buy great art, are special targets?" I ask, thinking of Sir Horace Walpole.

"I fear so. And now I have taken you away from this young man for too long!"

Pierre tugs at my dress, eager to point out the wooden heads carved into the ceiling of the Great Hall. Signor Pierro explains that those distant faces are known as "the eavesdroppers".

"We never know who may be watching and listening," says our Italian friend.

Chapter Fourteen

The harm that can be caused by watchers is made plain by the news we learn shortly after returning to the Willoughbys' house. The major-domo, Joseph, tells Evelyn that a messenger came from Strawberry Hill an hour after we left for Hampton Court. When the messenger heard that Sir Humphrey had gone to London, he said that the news was so urgent that his instructions were to ride on. Sir Humphrey *must* be located, no matter how difficult a journey.

"What is this urgent news?" asks Evelyn. I feel a nervous pull, but she is perfectly calm. It occurs to me that she must face a good many emergencies as Sir Humphrey's wife.

"There's been a theft at Strawberry Hill, my lady," says Joseph.

Evelyn's eyebrow rises. "I hardly think that's worth pursuing Sir Humphrey and pulling him from his duties. It's a matter for the constable in Twickenham."

"What was stolen?" I ask, dread building.

"A French painting, Madame. It was stolen overnight from the vestibule just off the staircase. The armoury, I believe. I think it was of an angel. Somebody got into the house, took it right off the wall and walked off. And didn't take anything else!"

The rest of the evening passes as a blur. Evelyn takes this news in stride, adding to my conviction that she is accustomed to urgent messages arriving at her household. But she doesn't know the terrifying implications this theft carries.

Sir Humphrey didn't want to give any hint to the people who might be watching Strawberry Hill that we'd detected the blue, so he left the painting up. He thought it would be easier to identify and catch the spies if they were lulled into a false sense of security. But if we were going to do that, I should have matched the topcoat paint and hidden the discovery. Now, if the thief removes the canvas from the frame — and I have the feeling he will as soon as possible — he'll see that two-inch-long stretch of the blue I exposed and realize the truth is out. They will be alarmed by the unveiling of the blue, but if we no longer possess evidence, what can we do?

I find it interesting that Sir Humphrey made this costly mistake. He is always determined to control everything. "Our opposition," as he calls it, defies his control. Now, things have become quite complicated and difficult.

However, is that really my problem? I wonder wearily. Without the blue to point to, I've got nothing to tell anyone. My expertise is not needed. Sir Humphrey will no doubt decide to push on without me. How will I cope with being excluded from the investigation? I picture myself waiting with great impatience for the letters to arrive from Evelyn, forced to follow the latest developments from far away. It won't be pleasant.

When I'm preparing to change into my night clothes, I hear doors opening and shutting, male voices and other noises that indicate the master of the house has returned. I suppose when he heard there was no evidence to present, these planned meetings with high government officials seemed pointless.

The only thing to do is go to bed and find out what happened in the morning. But I can't seem to take the necessary steps: take off my day dress, clean my face, climb into bed. I ache with curiosity about Sir Humphrey's reaction to the theft. It doesn't seem possible to sleep tonight without knowing.

When I knock on the door to the parlour downstairs to announce myself, I find Sir Humphrey sitting in his favourite chair, holding a brandy, candles blazing, but he's not alone. Captain Howard stands at the window, curtains drawn back, though it's night.

Neither of them speak to me for a moment.

"I told you she'd be down," says Captain Howard, an odd gleam in his eyes.

"Yes, you have a sense of her." The last time Sir Humphrey used that expression it was to describe my affinity for Jemmy Maylie.

"Why on earth are you talking about me as if I'm not here?" I ask, trying to laugh but not able to. The way they look at me makes me wish I hadn't come down.

Sir Humphrey says, more briskly, "The theft of the painting changes everything, of course. I told Horace to keep the place locked tight and double up on servants, and he did, but that was not enough. I should have posted my own men. That was my first error. Actually, no. The painting shouldn't have been left hanging there. I didn't think they'd be so audacious as to break in and steal it out of the house of Sir Horace Walpole. You thought it should have come down, correct?"

I nod, uncomfortable. I do think Sir Humphrey made a critical error, but no one likes a gloater.

He says, "Howard has been kept busy in London investigating a matter that may — or may not — be connected. Another death."

Alarmed, I look at Captain Howard, but he has turned around to stare into the blackness, his hands linked behind his back.

"Genevieve, I told you in the carriage from London about the tensions rising between England and France. Their loss in the war rankles the French. You might even say it torments them. They make a great noise about supporting the colonists in America. As if the despotic French king would tolerate any hint of disobedience in his own colonies! We have caught spies for France making a study of our Navy's readiness for another war and even writing down the best route through the home counties for invasion. But that is what all kingdoms do. They spy on one another from outside and inside. We arrest — and we hang — when we capture enemy spies. But that does not violate any treaty. What was drawn up concerning the proprietary formula of Thomas Sturbridge *is* a treaty."

I nod. "Since the painting was purchased in France, the blue originated there. But you don't have the angel painting. So what do you plan to do?"

Sir Humphrey puts down his glass of brandy.

"If I make any form of official inquiry, the government of France will deny involvement. So I'll have to get my proof."

"Oh? How? Through your spies in France?"

Sir Humphrey's eyes darken. Without meaning to, I have touched a nerve. "The situation in France is … complicated," he says. "Our ambassador and his staff in France refuse to take counsel from me. Their attention is mainly on diplomatic alliances. I've been forbidden to place my own people in Paris or Versailles."

"So what do you intend to do?" I ask.

I spot Captain Howard turning to look at me out of the corner of my eye.

"I intend to send you to France, Genevieve," says Sir Humphrey Willoughby.

For the first second, I assume this is a terrible joke. But no one is laughing. And Sir Humphrey doesn't blink when I say that is the worst idea I've ever heard.

"Why?" he asks.

"You'd want me to go to Sèvres Porcelain, correct? Find out if they've started up again with Thomas's formula? I am the *last* person on this earth, except for my husband, who should set foot in that place. Someone could recognize me. And won't I be arrested? Isn't it part of the treaty that I not set foot in France again?"

"No," says Sir Humphrey. "Only Thomas Sturbridge is forbidden entry. Both countries wanted that. We put it in to prevent another kidnapping, and the French did because they didn't want him back looking for the records of his work. You're not mentioned, Genevieve. You weren't married at that stage."

If only they *had* included my name, I'd not be in this position now. France. The mere word puts a chill in me like nothing else. I am a Huguenot. My great-grandparents were driven from their ancestral home. If this weren't enough, I endured harrowing experiences in France when Sir Gabriel forced me to go there. I had no freedom, and at times I feared I'd never make it back to England alive.

Captain Howard says, "How many people even got a good look at you? Our information is the French brought you into the porcelain factory for one day only. And it was seven years ago. Who spent time talking to you? Jean Hellot, Sèvres's chief chemist, is well over seventy years old. He can't hold the position today. And Madame de Pompadour, the king's mistress, is dead."

I note that no one mentions Sir Gabriel himself. If I'm in danger of anyone recognizing me, it's him. But as far as I know, he disappeared in 1759 after losing the favour of King Louis. Before that, Sir Gabriel was one of the French king's most prized spies, one of *le Secret du Roi*. Without such employment, he was unwelcome in both France and England.

I explain, "The two people who knew me best were a brother and sister, Victoire and Sophie, who lived with me at that cottage in Versailles for weeks and weeks. They were guarding me. They were kind, though. They helped Thomas and I leave the country when the time came. It's been seven years, but Victoire in particular would recognize me."

Captain Howard says he'll ensure inquiries are made about Victoire and Sophie before we leave.

"And there might still be people at the porcelain factory who know my name and remember what happened. Hellot may be seventy, but if he sees me, he'll recognize me. If it's not enough that I am asking dangerous questions about the colour blue, there's the fact I'm a Huguenot. Someone might decide to throw me in prison just for that."

"That's ridiculous," Captain Howard murmurs.

"Is it?" I round on him furiously. "What do you know about being condemned and persecuted for your faith?"

"Quite a bit, actually," he shoots back. "An Act of Parliament had to be passed so that my brother and I could take commissions in the war and bear arms. Why? All English Catholics are assumed to be secret traitors, slaves to the Pope and Bonnie Prince Charlie."

"Stop it!" Sir Humphrey says. "How can this plan work if you two do nothing but argue?"

"What plan?" I ask, a new uneasiness forming. "I suspect you have concocted something more elaborate than simply sending me across the Channel."

Sir Humphrey and Captain Howard exchange a glance, the sort of wordless communication they've practised all along. My tolerance for it just ended.

"Stop," I shout. "I *despise* your meaningful glances. I will hear your proposal, leave nothing out. And if I have questions, you'll answer them honestly. Agreed?"

"Agreed," Sir Humphrey says, smiling. He may be heartened by the fact that instead of refusing immediately, I've said I will listen to the proposal. I'm not sure why I said that. This is a ridiculous idea, born of desperation.

He says, "You've never appeared to favour brandy, Genevieve, but will you join us tonight?"

"I believe a brandy would be just the thing." I sigh.

Captain Howard pours me a drink. "Here you are, Mrs Sturbridge," he says politely and returns to his place at the window. He is making an effort. It must be because Sir Humphrey urged us towards greater harmony, though I don't know why.

Sir Humphrey says, "You're correct that should Genevieve Sturbridge make inquiries in Paris and Versailles, it would sound the alarm. But you are the one to send. You are the only person in all of Great Britain who can recognize the shade of blue in question, knows its history, possesses knowledge of art and speaks excellent French. *And* you've already been taught the basics of spying."

My cheeks warm. I say, "I'm not completely sure, but I believe I should say thank you." I sip my brandy.

"But as you say, Genevieve Planché could be known at Sèvres Porcelain. The name Genevieve Sturbridge would also sound the alarm. The solution is: you would go as someone else."

"Pardon me?"

143

"We are making arrangements so that you can travel to Paris for several weeks to gather intelligence. But you will go under a different name. You will present yourself as a widow, formerly married to a British lord of a prominent English family, interested in buying paintings and porcelain. Sir Horace Walpole can send a letter to be used as an entree to the salon of Madame du Deffand. That's where he announced that he wanted a Fragonard angel. Someone set the wheels in motion at Madame du Deffand's salon. We need to find out who. The Vicomte Antoine-Jean de Breteuil contacted Horace a month later, saying he had just such a portrait. We need you to meet this viscount and the man who handled the purchase as well. If we follow their trails, eventually, it will lead to the blue."

All I can do is sit back in my chair and laugh. It's not a stupid plan — there's a slim chance of success — but they have the wrong idea of what I can do.

"This is absurd," I say. "I could never be convincing as the widow of a 'British lord of a prominent family'. That's not my world, as you well know. Do you think the French are ignorant of the English nobility? Between my bad manners and using a concocted name in Madame du Deffand's salon, it would be the work of an hour to unveil me as a fraud."

Sir Humphrey says to Captain Howard, "Go ahead."

He pulls away from the window and takes a position directly in front of me, feet close together, standing tall, as if he were about to make a special presentation of something: a shot pheasant? A piece of jewellery? This is unnerving. I grab my glass, downing more a gulp than a sip.

"Your identity will *not* be concocted," he says. "You will travel under the name of Lady Jane Howard, my sister-in-law. You are the same age and height and Jane rarely leaves Stanham Castle. She's never left England in her life. You'd dress as she would and wear a wig. That should go a long way towards creating an effective disguise. No one in Paris whom you meet would suspect you aren't her, especially with me there."

"You?"

"I will accompany you on the mission as myself. It would be strange if Lady Howard travelled without anyone in her family. Her children are too young. But her late husband's brother is the ideal escort. As Lady Howard, you can attend a salon, go to the opera, arrange to see paintings, or view porcelain, do whatever English ladies always do in Paris."

Captain Howard and I, pretending to be closely connected by family? An image leaps into my mind: Howard introducing me at a salon, showing the solicitude of a brother-in-law, his hand on mine. This is too much to take in. I stare at my lap.

Sir Humphrey jumps in to say, "Howard has been to Paris. You'll have him by your side and three of my trusted men posing as servants. And I have a maid for you who's more than a maid. They comprise my finest intelligencers. Genevieve, we need you to be the person in front: talk about art with the viscount and chat with those in charge at Sèvres Porcelain. You'll be able to produce leads. Howard and his men will follow up and do the real investigating. You'll be perfectly safe the entire time."

The word *safe* jolts me from my stunned state, and I remember they mentioned a second murder. How can they make promises that I'm in no danger in the wake of not one but two murders?

"I have to know what you know," I say.

Captain Howard tells me that the city wardens fished a body out of the Thames the day after the Cross Bones crowd found Jemmy.

He did not drown; the dead man had had his throat cut just like Jemmy. Although he'd been in the Thames for a few days at least, he was identified as a middle-aged man named David Fletcher. Fletcher was suspected, but never imprisoned, of various clever crimes, ranging from tricking elderly people out of their savings, to counterfeiting bank notes, to a bit of blackmail.

"We think he might have been one of the men who hired Jemmy," says Sir Humphrey. "Fletcher had associates in Southwark. And there is some indication he might have told this other party, the murderer, about Jemmy and where he could be found."

"What makes you so sure?" I ask sceptically.

Captain Howard says, "I'd rather not say."

I put down the brandy and rise to my feet. "I *insist* on honesty. Hold nothing back. I must be treated as an equal in this investigation."

Captain Howard waves at me to calm myself. "The corpse was in bad shape. Worse than Jemmy's. At first, they thought it was because he was in the water, maybe because a boat hit him. But there were ... things done to him *before* he died, the coroner said after examining him. It looked like pressure was applied to obtain facts."

I sit down, feeling wobbly. "Torture. You're talking about torture."

"You insisted on being told," pointed out Captain Howard.

"Yes. Yes, I did." I take a breath and continue. "It is not the danger of the mission that deters me the most. I cannot disappear from England for weeks at a time. I have a husband and son. To even consider this feels ... wrong."

"Your trepidation is natural, Genevieve, but this mission is the opposite of 'wrong'," says Sir Humphrey earnestly. "One reason I have protected you and championed you when others were furious over your entanglement with Sir Gabriel Courtenay is your loyalty.

That is the truth. When I told you that Courtenay was spying for King Louis, you ceased your activity immediately. And I know that in France, you persuaded Sturbridge to return to England. If it weren't for you, he may have submitted to French pressure to remain at Sèvres Porcelain. You are a patriot, and that's what I appeal to now."

It's true that I'm fiercely loyal to England, but I also share my husband's distaste for war. I say, "Sir Humphrey, I must be truthful with *you*. I don't feel comfortable gathering intelligence for the ministry to use as a reason for war."

Sir Humphrey grimaces. "Ah, you've misunderstood. Or perhaps I have not been forthcoming enough. I want to find out what the French are doing with Sturbridge's formula and put a stop to it to *avoid* any escalations. We may be able to deal with this quietly once we know who is responsible. The trail is cold in England. Both Jemmy Maylie and the man we believe hired him have been killed. The painting came from France. There's no choice — the investigation *must* continue in France."

Clutching my hands, I say, "I understand, but I am beginning to feel like an animal caught in a trap."

"Humphrey, Genevieve, are you aware of the hour?"

Evelyn, wearing a dressing gown and loose hair on her shoulders, stands in the doorway. We all apologize, while Evelyn listens.

"We should not disrupt the household. All I can say in my defence is that the matter is urgent," says her husband. "I'm bound for now by strict secrecy, or I would tell you about it, my dear, and you'd understand what provoked a heated discussion."

"Oh, I hate this secrecy," I lament. "Evelyn, keeping things from you is agony for me. Please know that."

She says, "As I am not deaf, I know that my husband and Captain Howard would like you to do something. You are not sure if you can agree. All I can say, Genevieve, dearest friend, is that I sometimes think of our days together in Derby, friends working at the porcelain factory. I've never known anyone else who had your spirit. You were determined, talented and so full of life and laughter. Mocking laughter, but laughter all the same. Mistakes were made in Derby, you were misled, no question. But if there were a chance for you to put that same spirit to a cause again, a righteous cause this time, how glorious that would be."

I stare at her, stunned.

"And now, I will say good night. Please lower your voices. The children shouldn't be disturbed, no matter the urgency." And with that, she goes back upstairs.

All I can do is tell the two men that I require the night to sleep on the matter and will inform them of my decision in the morning. They accept it with surprising grace.

Once in bed, though, my thoughts are so fevered that sleep seems impossible. I do feel a desire to respond to this call to serve my country. But how can I, a wife and mother, depart on a mission that will be difficult and, no matter what Sir Humphrey says, dangerous? The French worship beauty and honour talent, but it is a country steeped in violence and depravity. If there ever was a time in my life to attempt something like this mission, surely it is in the past.

But a dull ache closes around my heart when I think of that spirited, mocking, ambitious girl whom Evelyn knew in Derby. The truth is, that person is still me. I've tried my best to live as someone else, and it has not brought me happiness.

Chapter Fifteen

In the morning parlour, when I ask Joseph for his master's whereabouts, he tells me Sir Humphrey is in the garden. I find him kneeling before a bed of yellow roses, wearing trousers and a plain cotton shirt, a pair of shears in his hand.

"I've never seen you like this," I say.

"I enjoyed my father's gardens when I was a boy. He took such pride in them," Sir Humphrey says, wiping his forehead with the back of his hand. He stands up straight. "May I have your answer, Genevieve?"

Taking a deep breath, I say, "The answer is yes, Sir Humphrey, I will go to France. But I do have a condition."

Relief floods his face. "Thank you, Genevieve, thank you. We have many arrangements to make and things to plan and prepare for. We will leave as soon as possible, since Paris empties by late July." He remembers what I said and stops. "And what is your condition?"

I say quietly, "You have to stop hiding things from me."

"Such as?"

"You must tell me what troubles you about my husband and why you are keeping an eye on him and the rest of the Lunar Society. And why you opened my mail."

He looks down at the shears. "Let's make use of that bench under the beech tree. I think this conversation requires shade."

After we settle on the cool stone bench, Sir Humphrey tells me that while defending England from foreign enemies is his charge, in times of peace that takes different forms. Frenchmen can come to London any time they wish — and they do. Which ones are here to see the sights of London and enjoy its theatres, gardens and more risqué pleasures? Which ones are sharply observing who is rising and falling in the British Army, how many new ships are being taken to the water, and what is our munition readiness? These questions are crucial. But that sort of spying is not the only way that France can try to gain an advantage.

"For fifty years, we've been dealing with a significant problem," he says. "Our mills and factories and workshops are being weakened. Foreign agents lure away the most skilled English workers — especially the inventors — with large bribes. They are being spirited away to foreign factories — ironworks, shipbuilding and other businesses. We have problems with the Russians, but the most relentless spies are the French or certain Englishmen who serve the French, like Sir Gabriel Courtenay. You remember how good Courtenay was at learning about the inner workings of Derby Porcelain?"

I nod, humiliated to remember my part in the effort to steal Thomas's formula from Derby Porcelain. But I asked for the truth from Sir Humphrey, and I will hear it all.

He continues, "Our country's most urgent problem is finance. It's not widely known that Great Britain was left with a debt of over seven million pounds. We won the war with France, but British citizens pay the highest taxes in all of Europe — and the colonists in America refuse to pay their share. On top of this, the cost of everything keeps rising. If we have a bad harvest this year, there could be riots. We can *not* afford another war."

"But what does any of that have to do with Thomas?"

"Since the war's end, a new group of men are conducting research that is considered so brilliant, so revolutionary, that it could transform England's fortunes. This could be the answer! Unfortunately, none of them hold positions at our colleges, where they can be watched and protected from spying and corruption. No, they are independent men of science — doctors, chemists and teachers — living hither and yon. They have just begun to come together and ..."

"And meet in Birmingham," I finish for him. "You're talking about the Lunar Society." I was *right*. Sir Humphrey had his eye on Thomas and his friends.

"I am," says Sir Humphrey. "With so much at stake, we have to ensure that the Lunar Society is uncorrupted."

"You don't have to worry about French spies getting hold of any of *these* men," I break in to say. "They're too intelligent, and though money may always be a consideration in life, there isn't a possibility of any of them selling themselves to France. They have enormous integrity."

Sir Humphrey says, "Bribes and financial corruption are not the only matters to worry about. I rarely share my methods with anyone not working for me, but by taking on this assignment with Howard, you are doing just that, so I will proceed."

Am I working for Sir Humphrey — and, through him, the British government? I had not thought of it quite like that.

"The members of the Lunar Society like to meet in a certain coffee house in Birmingham. We pay coffee house workers and barmen in various cities to listen to the conversations of their patrons and send reports to us if the talk starts to venture into areas of alarm. Birmingham is one of those cities."

"You are spying on Englishmen?" I ask, appalled.

"Most of the time, it's rubbish and rants from men who like the sound of their own voices. I received a report from Birmingham that a man from the Lunar Society said that the war just finished was a farce that did nothing but trade territories among spoiled countries, that the British East India Company was evil incarnate and that the American colonists were right to oppose the Stamp Act and should continue to do so with all vigour."

"Those are Thomas's words, I know them well," I say impatiently. "But what is the danger to England's security in coffee house debate? He's not saying the Americans should defy the king."

"Genevieve, as you ask, Captain Howard and I were in the Midlands to receive further reports on men in the Lunar Society. Thomas Sturbridge was one of them, but not the only one." He waved me away with both hands. "Do not explode. We heard nothing to indicate that any group member was on the verge of pulling away from England to deal with France or any other foreign country."

"I could have told you that and saved you a great deal of time and expense!"

Sir Humphrey swats an insect and says, "I had to make the special effort with Sturbridge and Priestley because of the sensitivity of their research."

"Sensitivity?" My pulse jumps. "They are working on a book about electricity."

Sir Humphrey pats my hand and says gently, "Genevieve, you don't have to pretend any longer. I know the scope of their experiments. For as long as it takes, I will put all the resources available to me into protecting their efforts. Even Cavendish's work pales in comparison. Joseph Priestley and your husband are getting closer to discovering the deeper truths of the natural world and finding the connections that have eluded men of science until now."

In those first stunned seconds, my pride, always ferocious, will not allow me to reveal my ignorance. "Their work could be revolutionary," I say lamely.

"Imagine it," says Sir Humphrey. "We are about to understand the hidden properties of the air that we breathe."

A pair of wasps circle each other before landing on the hedge three feet away. Rose fragrance fills my head. It's a beautiful moment in the garden; all I can do is hide my pain, which runs deep. My husband has been lying to me about the work that is close to his heart. Why wouldn't he share his plans with me? He knows that while I have no training in science, I am keenly interested in its potential to unlock the many secrets of the universe. He is on the verge of unlocking one of those very secrets with Joseph Priestley, but I am shut out.

Now that I have officially agreed to gather intelligence in France and have "taken a briefing" as he puts it, Sir Humphrey launches into the practicalities. I am glad of it, for I can fix my mind on the steps to be taken rather than on this latest revelation about Thomas.

It will take five days for a team of seamstresses to sew new gowns for me to wear in Paris. Apparently, a borrowed dress of Evelyn's and my own clothes will not persuade French society of my rank. Also there is the matter of my being a supposed widow. It is explained to me that while few French noblewomen are faithful to their husbands, they do adhere to the conventions of mourning attire as carefully as if fearing a Bastille prison cell should they err. They don strict mourning dresses and even veils for two years, followed by half-mourning for another year at least. After that, muted colours and styles are permitted.

While these fashionable yet slightly muted dresses are stitched, I am to learn everything there is to know about Lady Jane Howard and her two children. My "brother-in-law" cannot start the lessons for two days — he is gathering the group of men who will accompany us.

Before he left, Captain Howard gave me several books to read. After a tiring few hours of being fitted, not to mention my scalp pulled this way and that during wig measurements, I retreat with the books and dinner to my room.

Each book is more appalling than the one before. The first volume is devoted to the triumphs of the Howard family. Dozens of family members claim to have saved England by leading armies and flotillas of ships into fierce battles won due to Howard courage. The Battle of Flodden ... the Spanish Armada. Am I expected to memorize the details of these encounters? I've always recoiled from descriptions of battles. I'm the least likely woman to marry into a military clan.

The second book is slim — a history of Stanham Castle, where I have supposedly been living since I married at the age of eighteen. I cannot stop staring at the illustration of the castle, displaying turrets and battlements. The words "grim" and "foreboding" spring to mind. I understand why Sir Horace Walpole was inspired by Stanham when he conceived Strawberry Hill.

And I again marvel at how poor a fit I am for this. I grew up in a narrow townhouse on Fournier Street in Spitalfields. I can't even imagine what anyone would do with the number of rooms in Stanham Castle.

The third book is separate from the others. The first two are bound together with a string and a neatly torn piece of parchment bearing the word "Howard". This one has another folded and torn parchment attached to it with the word "deportment" in that flourishing hand.

The Lady's Companion lists a numbingly long list of recipes to oversee and health cures to administer, along with advice aimed at character. With growing disbelief, I read, "The grand element … essential to woman … is modesty. It is the most important characteristic for this sex, as courage is to the other … Meekness is our salvation … To what end did God give us intellectual faculties? Surely not to amuse us but to enable us to thoroughly understand religion and the necessities of our families, and to assist us towards Moral Improvement."

What complete drivel.

The next day, when Captain Howard returns to the Willoughby house, I corner him, the book on female deportment in hand. "May I ask, Captain, how am I to accomplish anything in France if I am a meek and mute ninny as recommended in these pages?"

Scoffing, he says, "A mute is of course not what anyone wants. But you must learn the habits and practices of a lady so that you will not arouse suspicion while you are drawing out information."

Evidently Captain Howard does not consider me a lady at present. Why that should sting so, I am not sure. Yet it does, and I find my temper rising.

"Have you considered that France is home to women with brains, Captain Howard? Are you acquainted with the story of Voltaire and Émilie du Châtelet? She was a talented mathematician, and they lived as intellectual equals for over fifteen years."

Captain Howard shakes his head, exasperated. "That's well and good, Mrs Sturbridge, but my brother, an intelligent man without question, was no Voltaire. And Jane is no 'talented mathematician.' You are to play the part of his widow, a lady living in the north of England for years. If this mission is to succeed, you must enter into the spirit of it."

"By pretending to be a modest creature without a mind — or, as you describe it, a lady? Why must you make this more difficult than it has to be?"

"Ha ha — rich indeed!" he roars. "That is my exact question for *you*."

To prevent this quarrel from deteriorating further, I hurry out of the room. At this moment, the whole plan seems doomed to fail. How are we to persuade anyone of a family connection when Captain Howard and I can't abide each other?

It is Sir Humphrey who seeks me out. I expect him to hector me into submission. Instead, he says, "I know this is a great deal to ask of you, Genevieve. But when Howard suggested it, I thought it was an excellent idea."

Surprised, I say, "This was Captain Howard's idea?"

"Of course it was. I'm not likely to force him to travel to France and pretend to be your brother-in-law. Howard has every confidence in you. He feels that, with you involved, we will succeed."

As I mull this over, it hits me with force the strange situation I find myself in. I am entering into a mission with a man who sometimes behaves as if he does not respect me, yet he holds me in high esteem. And I am married to a man who has always said we are equals and that he adores and respects me, but he does not behave as if that were truly the case.

I know what this means. There is only one person I can rely on and that is myself.

Chapter Sixteen

After Sir Humphrey tells me that the plan to send me to France originated with Captain Howard, I decide to give the lessons my best effort. I am aware that the captain is a difficult person, and the lessons are not without challenge. We argue several more times. Voices rise. I confess that I throw a book across the room. Once Captain Howard kicks a tree.

But we push forward. He does not praise me, and I don't expect him to. I do sense grudging approval.

On curtseying, however, we persist in disagreeing. I see nothing wrong with how I dip and bow my head. "Surely it's passable by now," I say.

"Are you serious? Even when you execute a full curtsey properly and rise with grace, you can't help but roll your eyes. No more of that!"

I say, "Lady Jane Howard has never rolled her eyes?"

"No."

His arms folded, Captain Howard shows the stony face I see whenever I mention his sister-in-law's name. If I am to believe him, Jane Howard has led a blameless life: obedient daughter, motherhood before the age of twenty, dedication to the needs of her two children after becoming a widow. Rarely venturing into society, Jane finds pleasure in needlepoint by the fire and an occasional hunt for grouse.

In other words, a dull paragon.

How am I to convincingly become Lady Jane Howard if I don't understand her? We will leave England in two days' time. The haste is because Paris empties itself of all members of high society by late July, and they stay away for all of August. Anyone with a chateau or any form of country house escapes during the hottest weeks. There will be no one to question in the city of Paris: the nobility, the artists, the philosophers and poets, even the bourgeoisie, will disperse. Before that happens, Captain Howard and I, with our "servants", will take up residence in the Paris apartment owned by the Duke of Norfolk, the head of the Howard family. The duke rarely went there and agreed to our request without asking troublesome questions.

Throughout my "training" with Captain Howard, I've realized that while I am capable of spying — and have unfortunately proven that to the world — the impersonation of another woman is quite difficult for me. Before I fall asleep each night, I think, "I am not going to succeed." When the morning comes, optimism returns, more or less.

But we are running out of time and I am unsure that I can do this. I wish Captain Howard would open up to me, if only a little. If there's one thing I know about Jane Howard's brother-in-law, he is always restless. We need to get out of this room.

I suggest we take a walk in the grounds. He agrees, but only after insisting that we set aside time in the parlour later for becoming more proficient with fans. If my curtsey is clumsy, my fan technique is atrocious. I've never been one to flutter a fan before my face, but Captain Howard points out that not only are they commonplace among gently born ladies, but a fan could prove helpful if I'm trying to hide my expression.

I decide the moment has come to push for more personal details. Walking quickly to keep up with him, I say, "Tell me more about her family of birth, the Dormers."

"They are a respected and honourable family," he says.

"Oh, *please*, Captain, I need something more."

After a long silence, he says, "You might find it useful that Jane is the youngest child, and her family indulged her as the pet. They'd even agree to participate in the little plays she would put on."

"She organized plays?" I say, delighted. *This* is something I can work with.

"Jane would write the scripts, assign us our parts, make the costumes and arrange the sets. It was remarkable, actually."

"Find 'us' parts? You mean you were in her plays? But I thought she put on the plays when she was a child."

"She was. We were. I was ten years old when I played Ariel in *The Tempest*. Jane was Miranda, of course. My older sister Madeleine wouldn't join in unless she played Caliban."

I nearly crash into a maple tree, picturing Captain Howard as Shakespeare's sprite. It requires effort to stay with my original line of inquiry. "I didn't realize you knew Jane when you were children," I say.

"Our families were close," he says, and seems to want to say something more but stops.

Resisting the urge to shake him, I say, "Please go on."

His face darkening, Captain Howard says, "There was only a small group of families who *would* associate with us. Catholic families. The Dormers are devout Catholics."

"Ah. So the marriage between Jane and your brother was arranged?"

"No," he says. "It was not. If ever two people loved each other, it was Jane and my brother, Robert. It was the sort of love that most people can only imagine and never find for themselves."

At that moment, I grasp two things. The first is that Captain Peregrine Howard has not found love, at least not the devotion his brother experienced. The second is that he would be mortally offended if I made any allusion to his romantic life, wanting or otherwise. Though I find this direction in our talk intriguing, I know better than to press Captain Howard on affairs of the heart.

Unsure what to say, I ask if his sister has married or if she lives at Stanham Castle with Jane and the children. He peers at me warily.

"Madeleine never married," he says in a way that indicates the subject is closed.

Is even the life of a sister out of bounds for conversation? How maddening Howard is. But the captain says, in a very different voice, "Something must have happened."

Following his gaze, I spot Sir Humphrey hurrying to us. We start towards him, and the closer we get, I can feel that, as Howard says, there's been some discovery or turn of events — and it's not good.

"Genevieve, your husband is here," he says, a bit breathless.

Although I don't see how he could be mistaken, Sir Humphrey has it wrong.

"Thomas is finishing his work with Mr Priestley many miles away," I say.

"No, he's not. He broke off early and has hired a barouche to fetch you and Pierre."

"He stopped his work to come here?" I say numbly. I still find this hard to believe. Thomas's research means everything to him. And he hates smoke-shrouded London and the towns surrounding it. Yet he must have cut short his work with Joseph Priestley to be here now.

"He's in the parlour now, talking to Evelyn. I said I'd fetch you from your walk." Sir Humphrey studies my face. "Did you write anything, anything at all, in your letter that would make him suspicious?"

"No." My disbelief recedes, replaced by a wave of dizzying uncertainty. "What am I to say? How can I explain that I'm on the verge of leaving the country? He may not want me to go."

"You *cannot* tell him," Sir Humphrey says, his voice rising. "He must not learn that the French may have broken through on replicating his formula and are manufacturing it. And he can't know of your mission with Captain Howard."

With fervour, I say, "Listen to me, on the question of the blue, the colour he created, you can trust him absolutely to help us, to put England first."

"Perhaps I can. Perhaps I can't. It's risky. There is strength, an advantage, in restricting knowledge. Right now, we three are the only people in England who know that an illegally manufactured shade of blue — the colour of France — was painted on a forged work of art, concealed and sent here with a message meant for me. I haven't even told Horace Walpole the full story — he loves gossip too much. We can't inform Thomas Sturbridge at this stage, see him ride back to Lichfield and then hope he keeps quiet while his wife is in France."

"But you're putting me in an impossible position," I cry, turning to Captain Howard. "Don't you see?"

Howard looks from me to Sir Humphrey, frowning uncomfortably. "Yes, this is difficult. But I have to agree. Your husband knows so much about the formula — and he knows so many people. The Lunar Society. He's a powder keg that could explode."

My frustration boils over into anger. "Thomas is my husband, and I can't lie to him. I absolutely refuse to do so."

I stare at Sir Humphrey defiantly. I know he needs me. He confessed that only I possess the necessary background and knowledge to succeed at this. I'm not without leverage in this situation.

"If you tell Thomas Sturbridge about the mission, he will have to be confined until you return from France," says Sir Humphrey, hard as iron.

If the news that Thomas has arrived without notice shocks me, Sir Humphrey's threat leaves me reeling.

"You'd — you'd do that? Put an innocent man in jail?" I stammer.

"Not jail. The quarters would be comfortable, and the food would be well prepared. It's just a matter of someone not being permitted to leave."

It's time for me to call Sir Humphrey's bluff.

"Sir Humphrey, you cannot expect me to carry through with this mission under such circumstances."

He eyes me for a few seconds before saying, "Then Captain Howard will go alone, and you'll be the one to be confined until he returns to England. You have been told too many secrets of state. It's up to you if your husband joins you in confinement. And your son."

How could I hope to out-manoeuvre Sir Humphrey Willoughby, Under-Secretary in His Majesty's government? I should never have agreed to do this at all. When I picked up that bottle of turpentine in Strawberry Hill, I set myself on this path from which I cannot deviate.

Until I reach the end.

The three of us return to the house in unhappy silence. How much of my motivation to go to France is tied up in the responsibility I always feel for spying on Thomas years ago? My actions in Derby were part of a chain that resulted in Thomas never being able to share with the world his triumph over inventing the blue. Now I am into this affair so deeply that I must lie to the very man I wronged in the beginning.

Just before we walk in the door, Sir Humphrey says, "If you do this, I will make sure he understands. I'll speak to Sturbridge myself and explain when it's over. I'll take all the blame. Things will be made right, Genevieve. For now, tell him you need to stay longer. Evelyn needs you to stay longer."

My heart hammers in my chest as I walk with Sir Humphrey into the entrance hall. The parlour door is open. I hear my husband, that low, even voice, never a drawl to his sentences, never a fashionable affectation.

He's sitting across from Evelyn, in the middle of a sentence, but when he sees me in the doorway, he springs up. I move towards my husband without a second thought. I've been angry with him the last month, and hurt as well. But now the memories flood: our first kiss, Thomas's belief in me even when I admitted to spying, our passionate months in France and the Netherlands, our wedding, our joy at Pierre's birth.

His wavy dark red hair is tied back as always, but his face is a little leaner and his features are a trifle sharper than when we said goodbye in Lichfield. His eyes glow with affection but worry too.

Our embrace is tight. Nothing could be more natural than to go with Thomas today, to jump into this barouche with Pierre and head north. All the insanity — the haunting at Strawberry Hill, the discovery of blue hidden in the fake Fragonard, Sir Humphrey's mission — falls away like a fevered, made-up story. It takes every bit of control I possess to do what I must. I cannot bear the thought of Thomas confined for weeks. Nothing is worse than that.

Pressed against each other as we are, I can feel the sharpness of his ribs and his shoulder blades. He hasn't been eating as he should; that always happens when he throws himself into work. He kisses my cheek and, in doing so, shifts the embrace a few inches, and that's when I feel his heart beating quickly. Fearing he can feel mine doing the same, I pull away.

I see we are alone. Evelyn has tactfully withdrawn. Captain Howard and Sir Humphrey never came into the parlour. This is going to be supremely difficult. Thomas knows me better than anyone else on this earth.

"I am happy to see you, but I don't know why you came yourself, cutting short your work," I say. "The travel coach is fine, and Sir Humphrey was going to make the arrangements."

Thomas frowns. I've already erred.

"I don't need him to make arrangements for *my* family," Thomas says. "You've been here for weeks already. I feel we've intruded enough on the Willoughbys' hospitality. How long will it take you to pack? I want to start home today."

My throat dry, I say, "I can't leave yet. Evelyn needs me to stay."

"What?"

"You know her health has been poor. I need to stay here another few weeks." My husband is highly intelligent, and he knows me better than anyone. So I shouldn't be surprised that he sees inconsistencies immediately.

"I just conversed with her for fifteen minutes, and she seemed perfectly well," he says. "Genevieve, what's happening? Your letter was so short and odd. The very next day I received an officious letter from Willoughby also saying you would be delayed. I could tell something was wrong. I couldn't rest until I found out what."

I've rarely known Thomas to take such drastic action. I am both moved, and alarmed. He won't accept whatever excuse I offer. This is impossible. But somehow I must send my husband back to Lichfield without me.

"Nothing," I say, more loudly than I intend. "Nothing is wrong. I am spending time with Evelyn. Many women make trips to see friends in the summer. I have been lonely in Lichfield — you know that. You shouldn't have cut short your time with Mr Priestley, Thomas."

He reaches for my hand and says softly, "You're not acting like yourself, Gen. What are you keeping from me?"

I feel as if my heart is jumping out of my body. If I tell Thomas about his colour, he will not stand by and permit the mission to France without him. I know him that well. But to hurt him like this is a terrible, unjust thing to do. I cannot speak.

An incredulous expression spreads across his face. "Are you … leaving me?"

"No, *no*, of course not."

"Then why—?"

The door crashes open. A joyful Pierre tumbles into the room, thank God. Pierre is followed by Diana, Evelyn, Sir Humphrey and, last of all, an uncomfortable-looking Captain Howard.

"Papa! Papa! You're here! No one told me, why?" He jumps into his father's arms. Thomas's searching stare changes to delight. After his son's first hug, he gives a polite nod in Sir Humphrey's direction. His gaze lingers on Captain Howard, and he glances back at me.

"I've come to take you home, Pierre," says Thomas. "I have a barouche for the trip. I picked it out with you in mind."

Our son does not object — the Twickenham holiday has run its course for him — and he turns to me. "Mama, did you hear? We are leaving in a special barouche!"

My throat dry, I say, "You'll be going on ahead with Papa, Pierre. I'll follow you shortly."

Thomas does not dispute it; we do not argue in front of our son or anyone else. I go upstairs to help Pierre pack his things. I hear Thomas's voice downstairs mingling with that of the Willoughbys', which I find so disconcerting that I have trouble folding Pierre's clothes properly.

More than that, it provokes a memory. I remember one spring night, when, after putting Pierre to bed, I couldn't find Thomas in the cottage. I peered outside and there he stood, not even wearing a coat, his face turned up to the stars.

"It's too cold," I cried, as I joined him. "Are you recording the constellations tonight?"

"The stars?" he asks, surprised, as if he hadn't noticed them. "No, I am not here for them." He laughs and beckons for me to come closer. "Have you heard the expression 'Revolution is in the air'? There's an entirely different meaning to it, one that no one realizes. If only I could put it into words for you."

But instead of intriguing or amusing me, my husband irritated me at that moment. Pierre had been quarrelsome all evening and I was close to giving up on a sketch I'd been fiddling with.

"I will survive not knowing this," I remember snapping as I retreated into the cottage.

I have been nurturing hurt feelings that Thomas excludes me from the important part of his life, but is that fair? I may have withdrawn to the point that he thought I simply was no longer interested.

As I turn over this possibility, my husband appears in the room, saying, "Are we ready for me to bring down Pierre's box?" So typical of Thomas to want to carry this himself. He is never one to insist on servants.

The crust of anger and dissatisfaction in my marriage splits open and the tender affection I feel for Thomas bubbles up. While I can't tell him everything for his own wellbeing, I long to convey to him my feelings. Just at that moment, his eyes alight on the table of wigs set up in the room. The three powdered white wigs that I must wear in France to conceal my hair are in plain sight. My heart is in my throat. Thomas knows I never, ever wear wigs. I find them ridiculous. He will surely demand the truth.

My husband looks at me, perplexed, but says nothing.

I put Pierre in the barouche and kiss him hard. When I turn to Thomas, he puts his arm around me to pull me off to the side. Speaking just above a whisper, he says, "You haven't told me everything, Genevieve. I do not know what I've done to deserve this lack of trust. But I do know this: you have a history of impulsive, rash action. I see you don't want me with you. After all these years, I am pushed away. Remember, being apart now means it might be beyond my ability to help you."

Thomas kisses me lightly on the lips, steps into the barouche and rides away with our son. Pierre turns around and waves until they are out of sight. But Thomas does not turn around once. In his rigid shoulders gripping the reins, I can feel my husband's pain and confusion.

That night, alone for the first time in the bedchamber without Pierre, Thomas's hurt face swimming in front of me, I feel more wretched than I thought possible. But the next day, the last one before we begin our ride to the coast, brings a sharper fear.

Messengers from London thundering to the house on sweaty horses convey the latest news to Sir Humphrey. He takes me aside to explain what has happened.

"It's over — the ministry has fallen," he says in a low voice. "King George has said he will ask William Pitt to form a new government. Pitt knows all about Thomas's colour and the treaty — he signed it! I must tell you: he is the one who wanted both you and Thomas put in prison when you made it back to England. It took me many hours to dissuade him. The following year, he was no longer in power. But he's returned. On the thirtieth of July, William Pitt will officially become prime minister. And all of the ministerial boxes will be opened for him."

I stare at him, confused as to what this means. "But all he will see is that treaty of 1760, the one that said the formula could never be used again."

Sir Humphrey grimaces. "No, there is another paper in the cabinet box. It's the report I wrote after you discovered the colour blue in Walpole's painting and the murders connected to it. Your name is included — and your husband's."

"*Oh, no.*" The thought of the man highest in the British government reading my name, being reminded of my crimes as a spy, makes me feel sick to my stomach.

"What do you think the prime minister will do?"

"He isn't telling anybody his plans. But rumours are already flying that Pitt will want to persuade Prussia to ally with us again in hostilities against France and Austria. And that would bankrupt England. The human cost? I've seen estimates that one million people died around the world in the last war. No. This is the worst possible time for provocations."

Putting his hands on my shoulders, Sir Humphrey says, "Before the thirtieth of July, you and Captain Howard must discover who has begun making the blue again and why they hid it in the painting. Is this a taunt or a warning? Perhaps someone in France wants to stop this as much as I do."

I nod at this faint hope. I, too, have wondered why someone went to such incredible trouble to alert the British to the resumption of the blue formula.

"Genevieve, we have to learn the intentions of the French so that I can try to defuse this disaster before it becomes too hard for anyone to control. Not just for the sake of you and Thomas Sturbridge, but for the sake of us all."

PART TWO

Chapter Seventeen

France, July 1766

The first time I crossed the Channel, when Sir Gabriel Courtenay forced me to go to France, I was frightened every minute. When I board the small boat with Captain Howard, I feel nervous but also determined. I have spent many hours memorizing the details of Lady Jane Howard's life and practicing how she would curtsey, walk across a room and speak to others.

Within an hour, my anxiety over what awaits me in France is replaced by the misery of a churning stomach. I take note that Captain Howard feels it not at all. Worse, he suggests that after we arrive in Calais, I consume a hearty dinner at the inn to speed my recovery.

"I will never eat again," I inform him as I stagger onto the dock. "Not even the choicest Parisian chocolate could tempt me." But Captain Howard insists I sit down to a stew and a goblet of Burgundy. After the first bite, I will revive, he promises. To my irritation, he is correct.

Thus restored, I am curious to see something of the famous walled city of Calais, but our party sets out before dawn. Time is not on our side. Changing horses frequently, we reach Lille in two days. But then comes the even more gruelling journey from Lille to Paris. For me, it is a blur of dusty roads, bustling villages, dinners of cold meat and stale bread, and hard, insect-ridden beds. We travel much faster than we would if we were enjoying a visit of pleasure.

With Captain Howard often preferring to ride atop the carriage with our men, I enjoy the company of Louise, my maid during this mission. Sir Humphrey promised me a "maid who is more than a maid" — and Louise is undoubtedly that. Her skills range from tending to dresses and ladies' hair to deciphering codes and writing in invisible ink. She has completed several missions for Sir Humphrey, none of which she could speak a word about, quite rightly. Aged about forty, Louise is intelligent, sharply observant and resolute. She never utters a syllable of complaint. On the days of our carriage ride to Paris, we endeavour to make the time pass faster with French lessons, as Louise's grasp of the language is unfortunately modest. She confesses that she can't understand ordinary French conversation in the travel inns we pause at.

"If only they would speak the words slower, I would do better," Louise says.

"That's like asking raindrops to stay inside the clouds," I tell her. "The French speak quickly. The only solution is to throw yourself into it. I promise you, the language will become more decipherable."

As much as I had struggled with becoming Lady Jane Howard in Twickenham, I am glad of my false identity the deeper we push into France. Being in the country is worrying enough. I do not want to fight to protect the secret of my Huguenot heritage on top. Just as much as the first time I was in France, I am struck by how the Catholic Church dominates every mile. At the centre of each village and its numberless cottages rises a church, with priests, monks and friars — and occasionally nuns — milling about. Every time I glimpse a French soldier from our carriage window, I wince, thinking of all the family stories of the Dragonnades policy when soldiers were encouraged to mistreat Huguenot families, at the command of king and church. And of course, Paris was once the city of the greatest crime against Huguenots in history: the St Bartholomew's Day massacre. We have almost come to the two hundredth anniversary of that tragedy. The Catholics lured us to their capital city to celebrate a royal wedding and then murdered thousands of Protestant men, women and children.

Fortunately, Genevieve Sturbridge isn't making her way to Paris. Lady Jane is. Even though our two countries had most recently waged war for seven years, the French appear to welcome well-off visitors from England, just as the French are given free rein in England.

Finally, late on a cloudy Wednesday afternoon, we reach Paris. Our destination is a district unknown to me until now: the Faubourg Saint-Germain. When Thomas and I stayed in Paris, waiting for permission to leave France, it was on the right bank, in one of the city's oldest districts. We lived briefly in rooms facing a winding, narrow street. Little light filtered down, as the buildings on either side of the street sagged towards each other, nearly meeting. It was always noisy, from heavy carts rumbling past and hand carts bouncing along, the ringing of bells and the sound of clogs on cobblestones. Neighbours gossiped all day long. I can especially remember the pungent odour of our street: dust, filth-encrusted cobblestones, rotting fish and burned brown bread.

Faubourg Saint-Germain could not be more different. It seems that the French nobility, seeking better air and empty land, have begun flocking to the left bank of the Seine to construct their Paris mansions. These grand chateaux, called hôtels, rise behind stone walls and wrought-iron gates, a fringe of young trees sprouting on the outside of the walls and exquisite gardens on the inside.

Six years ago, the Duke of Norfolk, Howard family patriarch, took a lease on the third and fourth floor of a hôtel. On the fourth floor are the two main bedroom suites, with a sitting room between. I will occupy the larger suite, sharing with Louise, while Captain Howard occupies the other suite. It gives me a moment's pause to sleep so close to him, but it's all part of our pretence of being family.

I must admit that the rooms are furnished with more of an eye to luxury and grandeur than I expected. Cream-coloured paper covers the walls, set off by dark gold mouldings carved in the shape of roses. Side tables are made of marble and walnut. The chairs are like nothing I've seen: delicate yet comfortable, they have curved legs, arms and backrest, creating a silhouette of perfect harmony.

I am surprised not just because these rooms are rarely occupied but because of the Duke of Norfolk himself and who he is. I'm told that this eleventh duke, Charles Howard, is in some ways the premier duke in England. Due to hereditary privileges, a Duke of Norfolk oversees each English coronation. The fact that all these Howard dukes are Catholic confuses me. Captain Howard and his immediate family bear the full brunt of Catholic prejudice — they cannot buy property, attend a university or serve in Parliament. Incredibly, the head of the Howards *opens* Parliament. Doesn't Captain Howard resent that Norfolk lives so far above the rest of his clan, and from what I can see, does little to help the rest of them? The captain doesn't seem to.

How am I to successfully impersonate a Howard aristocrat if at a fundamental level I don't understand them? I put that question aside to pitch in and work.

The Howard quarters come with no standing servants. So we spend several hours cleaning and airing the rooms and sending out for food, firewood, bottles of wine, cut flowers and other necessities a noble

English family would require for a stay of several weeks. We had agreed to hire no French servants, not even a scullery maid. We could not take the chance of a French servant spying on us. Therefore, Vincent, the oldest man Sir Humphrey assigned to our mission and the one who has spent the most time in France, will cook our meals. I bathe in water scented with lavender oil that first night before having supper at the time Parisians favour for this meal: ten o'clock. Captain Howard joins me at the table, set with a fresh tablecloth and brass candlesticks, for roast capon, chestnuts and peas. Captain Howard always ate on the road with his men while I'd shared meals with Louise. But now, in the Faubourg Saint-Germain, just as with our sleeping arrangements, we must conduct ourselves like a gently born widow and her devoted brother-in-law, even if no outsiders witness our meals.

"The capon is tender — Vincent is a fine cook," I say, smiling. The truth is the meal is passable, no more. A capon cries out for more seasonings. But I am relieved to have made it to Paris, to put the hard, dusty roads, stale bread and flea-ridden beds behind me. I am resolved to do my part to make the mission run smoothly.

"Yes, Sir Humphrey selected each intelligencer for this mission because they have two sets of particular and complementary skills."

"What can Vincent do besides cook?"

Captain Howard swallows a mouthful of peas and says, "He is an excellent shot with a cool head. If I were facing long odds in a fight, I'd want Vincent and his long pistol beside me."

A shiver runs through me.

"Are you expecting such a fight in the coming days?" I ask.

"Simply because we are here to find out about pigments and porcelain, don't deceive yourself that such an education will prove peaceful," says Captain Howard. "To obtain your husband's blue colour the first time, the French countenanced kidnapping, murder and coercion. They may have set up an elaborate chain of forgery, deception, theft and murder again."

If his intention is to unnerve me, he succeeds. Dealing with the exhaustion and difficulty of rapid travel to Paris has gone a long way towards displacing the anxiety of the mystery of the blue. But now that we are in place, I must face the challenge head-on.

"Captain Howard, shall we discuss Vicomte Antoine-Jean de Breteuil? He is the viscount who wrote to Sir Horace Walpole saying that he had found exactly what was desired: a painting of an angel by Jean-Honoré Fragonard. I've always thought it odd that a viscount should intervene in this and address Sir Horace personally. Please remind me what we know about him."

Captain Howard drinks his wine and says, "Not as much as I would wish. We've learned he is from a distinguished family — his cousin, Baron de Breteuil, serves as the French ambassador to Russia. And the viscount's wife is the principal lady-in-waiting to Madame Adelaide, a coveted position."

"Who is Madame Adelaide?"

His eyebrows shoot up. "The oldest daughter of King Louis and by all accounts his favourite. It's said that Madame Adelaide hunts with her father and takes coffee with him every day, now that Madame de Pompadour is dead. But I thought you were acquainted with Louis XV and his circle."

I shudder to remember that tall, haughty monarch, his bored expression flickering to petulant annoyance, everyone around him poised to pounce on the person who had transgressed.

"*Acquainted*? I was in the king's presence on the last day at Sèvres Porcelain. But Madame de Pompadour, the king's mistress, engineered the entire event, so the king's wife and children were hardly present. I'm amazed you could think otherwise."

"Be at ease, Mrs Sturbridge," he says, grinning. "I was only teasing."

My mouth falls open. "You? You are teasing?"

"Yes. Why not?" He pours himself more wine. "I'm known for my sense of humour. And my Howard nose."

A giggle escapes me and then another. I can think of few men more serious than Captain Howard. Does he not realize that?

"What is it?" he demands, while still grinning.

"The latter, yes," I say. "The former, not so."

"Ah, you are cruel, Madame, but no doubt correct." He wipes his mouth. "So, to return to the topic at hand, we do know something of interest. The viscount seems to have little to do with his virtuous wife, who is always in the company of royalty. She has a room in Versailles to be close to Madame Adelaide. He has no court position — perhaps by choice, perhaps not — and spends his time in Paris. They have a child, being raised in the country."

"But in France, the husbands and wives of the *ancien régime* often live separate lives, don't they?"

Captain Howard nods. "In certain circles in England, it's the same."

I ask, "What of the *marchand mercier* who handled the sale for Sir Horace? The viscount put him forward."

"Sir Humphrey made many inquiries and all that he could determine was that Monsieur Lionel Rolandeu handles the sales of paintings, porcelain and furniture. His store is on rue Saint-Honoré, as are his competitors. If he is suspected of criminal connections, it's not noted in any records that any Englishman can read. Sir Humphrey found other purchases made in the last year through Monsieur Rolandeu, and everything appeared to be in order."

A memory stirs. "What's interesting is that for the elite of France *and* England, even during the war, there used to be one man who everyone wanted to do business with: Monsieur Lazare Duvaux. He was by far the most esteemed *marchand mercier*. What no doubt helped his standing is that he was a friend of Madame de Pompadour."

Captain Howard reaches under the table for something. "I have an ignorant question to ask, but if I share this box with you, it may receive less scorn and ridicule."

He presents me with a cream box wrapped in blue ribbons.

"Blue, Captain Howard? Really?"

"The colour holds no significance beyond its being what the confectionery had on the counter to sell. As you like to remind me, blue is the colour of France."

I untie the ribbon and lift the box's top. Inside nestles a dozen chocolate bonbons. "Ah, these are perfect!" I cry. "You can ask me anything — what is the source of motion on the physical plane? — and I will do my utmost to answer. But you needn't bribe me with chocolate to dodge ridicule."

"Putting that aside, my question is: What is a *marchand mercier?* Doesn't it mean 'a merchant of merchandise'? Why are they a thing in France?"

I nibble my first bonbon. Captain Howard is full of surprises. First, attempting levity and now arranging sweets for the table. I am rather touched that he remembered my bonbon remark in Calais.

I plunge into explanation: "Diderot himself said they were 'Sellers of everything, makers of nothing'. I know they started as shopkeepers, people who sold objects to those who wanted to fill their homes with porcelain, paintings or a beautiful cabinet. Some of them specialized in repairing fine objects too. But in the last fifty years it became a more prestigious calling. They would work with an owner of a chateau, even a palace, to commission pieces to fit the decor. They had to be careful since they operated outside of the Parisian guilds, which exert great power. But if a *marchand mercier* had the most discerning taste, he could command high prices. As Sèvres porcelain prices went up, the *marchand mercier* could command more. I know that Monsieur Lazare Duvaux had his business on the rue de la Monnaie, the same street where Sèvres opened its porcelain shop. But he's been dead for several years, just like Madame de Pompadour."

Captain Howard says, "Wouldn't someone of discerning taste have questioned the too-large frame and noticed that the blue of the painting's sky was darker than what Fragonard himself might have chosen?"

"Yes, if Rolandeu had a background in art, he should have noticed." I think for a moment. "So these men could be part of a plot to make Thomas's blue, up to their elbows in corruption and crime, or they may have nothing to do whatsoever with an illegal colour or art forgery or anything that happened in Strawberry Hill and are being used by the true criminals. They are tools, even victims."

"Yes, you've got it," says Captain Howard, tipping back in his chair, still unaccountably good-tempered as he bites into a bonbon. "We will focus our efforts on the viscount and Madame du Deffand in the early days. Once we have gathered as many facts as possible, we will visit Sèvres Porcelain and finally, Monsieur Rolandeu to clinch it. I hope that if no one else cracks, Rolandeu will."

I raise my glass. "Here's to 'it' then," I say, and we drink together.

Still fairly sober, we go over the details of the plan. First, we will send Henry, brought on the mission for his youthful good looks and his quick mind, to deliver my card and the letter of introduction to

Madame du Deffand tomorrow morning. This is the most important of our objectives: to find out who overheard Sir Horace Walpole at that salon and decided to act. Now, it's only possible to appear at one of Madame du Deffand's weekly salons with an invitation. And invitations are rare. Even if I were to see Madame du Deffand in society, I could only address her if someone introduced us first. French etiquette has rules that can't be broken.

However, our great advantage is Sir Horace Walpole has struck up a close friendship with Madame du Deffand. His letter on our behalf cannot fail.

Henry's second stop will be the Louvre. Sir Humphrey's operatives had learned that King Louis granted Jean-Honoré Fragonard a studio to work in at the Louvre Palace, once a home of the monarchy but abandoned for Versailles by Louis XIV. Only the most celebrated and talented artists are invited to be in residence in the Louvre. Fragonard will be given my card too. When we meet him, we shall pose as admirers of his talent with a hunger to buy and then learn what we can of his commissions for rich Englishmen.

Henry's third destination, bearing my card, will be Sèvres Manufactory Works. He'll inquire on our behalf when the next available time is to visit the factory in Versailles and see the latest creations for sale and, hopefully, be granted a tour. Once on the premises, using my memory, I'll try to determine if anything seems markedly different, or any employees act suspiciously. This is the only place I run a slight risk of being recognized if the master chemist Jean Hellot materializes. But it was seven years ago, and I'd be putting forth a different identity.

Suddenly, Captain Howard coughs, his face turning red. "Bonbon," he gasps. "Stuck in my throat."

I fetch him water, which he gulps. "These chocolates are too sweet," he says, his voice raspy. "Make my teeth hurt and hard to swallow. Who could eat this frippery every day?"

Ah, just when my "brother-in-law" was becoming more congenial, he reverts to the Captain Howard I know all too well. I tell my dinner partner I must retire.

Seeing this wide bed, set on a walnut frame with brocade curtains, fills me with awe. I've never occupied such a bed in my life. I assume I will lapse into sleep within a minute of climbing into this luxurious expanse. However, even with the curtains pulled back, I can't draw a comfortable breath. The warm bedchamber serves as an unpleasant reminder that summer is already upon us, and 30 July is only three weeks away.

Something else makes me feel uncomfortable. Sleeping in luxury in Paris, enjoying a fine meal with bonbons, teasing Captain Howard — this doesn't have the tenor of a mission with the fate of two countries riding on it. I am enjoying it much more than I should. My husband certainly had no notion that this is how I would occupy myself while away from him. It makes me recoil to think of the look on Thomas's face when he said, "I don't know what I've done to deserve this lack of trust."

After at least an hour of tossing and turning, I make my way across the smooth floor to the tall windows. The air is cooler outside. I tie back the curtains as far as I can and open the windows wide. I discover it's possible to step outside the bedroom and onto a narrow balcony. Although a lady should never show herself to the world dressed in night clothes, it is dark outside. A large tree stands in front of the window. And the oil lanterns fixed to the street posts have been extinguished.

No one will be able to see me, I tell myself.

A delightfully cooling shiver runs up my bare arms as I step onto the balcony. The scent of the roses planted in front of the house drifts up to meet me. Glancing to the right, I observe that Captain Howard's suite has a matching balcony. As I watch, there's a shift in the darkness. I can just make out his profile. The captain is enjoying the night air as well, dressed in a white linen shirt. I don't want him to see me — I couldn't bear that.

I hop back into my room, and hurry to bed.

Chapter Eighteen

When I finally find sleep, my rest is deep. I awake refreshed and dress quickly, with Louise's help. There must be goals I can accomplish today.

Our fourth-floor rooms are quiet. No sign of Captain Howard or any of our group.

When I make my way to the third floor, the location of the other men's sleeping quarters and the kitchen and pantry, I see no one waited for me to appear before plunging into their tasks. Henry is a few minutes from setting off. He wears his specially made black-and-red Howard livery. Like Louise, Henry has never been to France before this. Fortunately, Simon, our driver, is familiar with Paris. Sir Humphrey assigned Simon to our group for his knowledge of France, his experience with horses and his skill with a sword, I've been told.

Captain Howard gives the men their final instructions. Henry and Simon listen with rapt attention, quivering to obey his orders. He has this effect on others — well, except for me. I must wonder what the men's response would be if I gave orders one of these days.

I know that their last stop, Sèvres Manufactory Works, is several hours from Paris, which means they won't be back until late. After Henry and Simon disappear down the stairs to the street, I ask Captain Howard our plan for the day.

"There is little we can accomplish of importance without our carriage." He shrugs.

Thinking of his relentless pushing through France to arrive in Paris, I say, "I can't believe you would wish to sit idle all day, Captain."

"Mrs Sturbridge, we don't have much time for this mission, but to flail about without purpose accomplishes nothing. Once Henry returns with the responses to our cards, we will set up our approach and move as quickly as possible. I know it's not easy, but there are times when we must be patient."

I don't care for his condescending tone and say, "If we *did* have a carriage this morning, what purpose could be accomplished?"

He thinks for a moment. "When I told him I was coming here, Sir Horace Walpole gave me an idea of how people spend their time. He said that English visitors to Paris — and leading members of French society — promenade in the Tuileries Garden many mornings. That might be worth the effort. The viscount could be among the promenaders. But the Tuileries is on the right bank. Obviously, we cannot walk all the way there."

I am loath to give up and, when I remember something, I present an idea. "There's a splendid garden on the left bank not far from here — the Jardin du Luxembourg. I would expect that French society would show themselves there as well. We could walk to it without it looking strange. I believe Parisians walk about more than Londoners. Not long distances, of course, but they aren't as dependent on carriages here."

Captain Howard shows no enthusiasm.

"Why do you oppose my idea?" I demand. "Do you have knowledge I don't about the Jardin du Luxembourg?"

Scowling, he says, "For God's sake, you imagine me a connoisseur of gardens? I've never been to the Tuileries *or* the Luxembourg. I concentrate on more important matters than trees and flowers!"

I've become well enough acquainted with Captain Howard to know that there's sometimes a matter of pride simmering behind his scowl. After a moment, I say, "When were you last in Paris, Captain Howard?"

This is when I discover that Howard came to Paris with his family when he was seventeen, stayed a fortnight and has not been back since. I am amazed at how he's worked to conceal this from me, always determined to possess every advantage.

"A war broke out ten years ago between our countries, may I remind you?" he says. "I could hardly visit then."

"Quite true."

Instead of continuing to bluster, he says, more quietly, "Travel on the Continent requires wealth. I have been on an officer's half-pay since the war ended."

I think of the chairs in the Duke of Norfolk's room. Probably four of them cost more than the captain's yearly wages. This is not the time to bring up such comparisons, however. I take it as a good sign that he's opening up to me. "Captain Howard, why on earth should you try to hide your lack of familiarity with Paris — in front of me of all people? You know that I have never had much money. Am I not your partner in this endeavour?" He nods, but unsmilingly. To prevent a spell of brooding, I fetch the guide to Paris I'd spotted in the Duke of Norfolk's sitting room. It shows the Jardin du Luxembourg is within walking distance.

"Very well." Captain Howard groans. "As I'll have no peace otherwise."

And so, with my powdered wig atop my head, wearing a cream-and-grey dress and carrying a parasol, I set off with Captain Howard.

I want to see the elegant gardens created for Marie de Medici, queen of Henry IV, and, most importantly, try to get a sense of the aristocracy of Paris. If I am to make the acquaintance of Vicomte de Breteuil and move among the finest porcelain factories, artist studios and merchant shops to hunt down signs of the blue, I must fit into this world.

It's a bright morning, not too warm yet. The well-swept streets of the Faubourg Saint-Germain seem even more removed from the Paris neighbourhood I stayed in with Thomas. There is none of the wheels clacking on cobblestone and the shouts of the carters that I recall. Here noises are muffled. The Faubourg smells of carriage leather, lightly burned sugar and an absolute explosion of flowers: not just roses but narcissus, lilac, violet, lily and iris.

"Don't you think this walk could prove an ideal method of letting Paris know that Captain Howard and Lady Jane Howard have arrived?" I ask, relishing the exercise.

"Oh, it's known already."

I peer at him uncertainly. "How?"

"I sent a formal letter from London to the British embassy in Paris. We are all supposed to inform the embassy when we are in France, those of us who are gentry. When it comes to everyone else, if they take rooms in Paris, the innkeeper must report their names to the department of Antoine de Sartine and the secret police or be fined."

"That sounds ominous."

"We do not want to attract Sartine's attention — that would be a catastrophe. It's said that when three people talk on the street, one of them is likely to be his man."

I pause to look behind us. Captain Howard chuckles. "I believe I'd know if anyone is following us or trying to listen. No signs. I want to keep it that way as long as possible. We should use our 'Howard' names now, just to be sure. You must call me Peregrine, and I will call you Jane."

The signs of great wealth gradually disappear during our walk. Regular houses replace the hôtels rising behind wrought-iron gates. The front steps of these whitewashed houses are dotted by children enjoying the morning, and their front walls by window boxes crammed with pink and white geraniums. The self-conscious, remote grandeur of the Faubourg gives way to the homes and shops of living, breathing French people. I even spot a few poles hanging from back windows, laundry fluttering.

And then, past a row of chestnut trees, stretches the Jardin du Luxembourg. I read in the guide that the Luxembourg covers over fifty acres. It is one thing to see such a number in a book and quite another to take in all the pathways, hedges, flowering trees and, most of all, the famous fountains.

Captain Howard's sharp eyes detect a line of beautifully dressed people strolling up and down a walkway mostly shaded by a row of towering trees. No lady wants the sun to brown her complexion. These could be some of Paris's finest, taking the morning air.

We find our place in the line of people slowly moving up and down the pathway. They are mostly couples, with some pairs who look like friends or could be mother and daughter. They greet one another, toss a joke and pause for chatter. Occasionally, I feel the eyes of the promenaders on me and Captain Howard as they pass. But we do not elicit as much as a nod or smile, much less a "Bonjour". I was warned about the strictness of French etiquette. We simply cannot speak to anyone without an introduction. The viscount could very well be one of these fashionable men dressed in brocade and silk stockings sauntering past me, and I have no way to discover it.

"Cease those sighs of frustration," says Captain Howard in a low voice. "You have no reason to look disappointed or to sigh. You are Jane Howard, seeing Paris for the first time in your life. Look happy."

I force myself to smile as I whisper, "You recognize no British lord or lady who could make introductions for us to their French friends?"

"No."

"Well, let us make one more turn and then we shall return to the Faubourg? And no harm done. We've seen a beautiful place," I say.

Halfway down the walkway on our last promenade, a new group emerges. A tall couple, followed by people that look like functionaries, stride towards us.

"What a surprise," says Captain Howard quietly. "That's the Earl of Rochford and his wife. He's a British diplomat. I wonder why he's come to Paris in July. Ready yourself."

My pulse quickens as the Rochfords draw near. He's tall and aloof, this earl. He looks about fifty, his wife is perhaps ten years younger, with an expression of distinct displeasure. I mentally prepare my curtsey and smile. This is what the lessons were for. But how low should I dip for an earl? An inch higher than a duke? I don't have time to ask the captain.

The Earl of Rochford's gaze alights on us but instead of moving on without recognition or interest, as the French promenaders have, he stops short and says, "Howard, isn't it? I saw your letter in the embassy papers yesterday."

"Yes, my lord. Captain Peregrine Howard." He bows. "It's a pleasure to see you and Lady Rochford in Paris." He turns and with a flourish of the hand says, "May I present my sister-in-law, Jane, Lady Howard, of Stanham?"

I murmur, "A pleasure, my lord … my lady." Then I bend my knees, dip, and bow my head, keeping my arms straight at my side. Captain Howard needn't have worried about my rolling my eyes. I've never felt less amused in my life as I rise and gaze at the Rochfords. The countess scans me from wig to shoes. Did my curtsey fail? Should I have said something else?

The earl nods in my direction, turns to Captain Howard and says, "We arrived four days ago from Spain — Pitt has asked me to serve as ambassador and we had to move with all possible speed."

"We had to find a house in Paris with *no notice*," complains the countess.

"Though as soon as I get the royal summons, I expect we'll have to live at Versailles," says her husband. "Pitt needs me to get the French in hand."

"The Queen of France sees almost no one, and the king allows few entertainments," says the countess, still vexed. "He's *still* mourning Madame de Pompadour. Can you imagine?"

Her husband says, "Yes, I'm told that since Pompadour's death, Louis has shown himself in Paris just twice — once it was to lay the foundation stone for the new Abbey of Saint-Geneviève, up over there." He points vaguely past the fountain.

The countess gives an elaborate yawn. "Saint Genevieve, patron saint of Paris? Oh, all of these saints and feast days, so *medieval*. How anyone makes sense of it is beyond me."

To hear my name feels strange. But of greater concern is her mockery of belief in saints in the middle of Paris — and in front of Captain Howard.

The Earl of Rochford snaps, "My dear, the Howards are Roman Catholic. They I suppose do make sense of it." The countess shrugs and pouts, and he turns back to us. "So why *are* you here? There are few English visitors in Paris at present. It's too hot. No one with a title would care to be trapped here besides us ... and now you."

Captain Howard says, "We are here to buy porcelain and paintings. Lady Howard is keenly interested in both."

"Yes, I am," I chime in. "If you have recommendations, I'd be most grateful."

The Earl of Rochford snorts. "I'm the last man to ask about French art! I believe that English painters deserve our patronage, Lady Howard. Joshua Reynolds is hard at work forming a Royal Academy of Arts for Great Britain. Might I point you in that direction?"

I nod, trying my best to not show how unhelpful I find his words.

"Lady Howard, I may have something for you," announces the Countess of Rochford. She confers with a woman behind her and then hands me a card that says "Madame Alice, Dressmaker."

"She is the best dressmaker in Paris, I saw her yesterday. Madame Alice is the one best able to help you."

But I said I wanted art, not a new dress! I want to retort but manage to stay silent. It takes me a few seconds to grasp that the countess is lobbing an insult at my appearance, but it would not serve our mission to show offence. "Thank you," I manage to say.

The Earl of Rochford delivers his own piece of advice. "While you are in Paris, don't have anything to do with French troublemakers. I know they whisper about wanting to prop up the Stuart pretender to the British throne."

For the first time, Captain Howard looks offended. "Charles Edward Stuart is an incoherent drunk, dribbling in his cups in Rome. I would not tolerate such whispering, my lord."

"I'm glad to hear it, Captain, though I didn't realize the fact was so widely known that this past January Stuart moved into the Palazzo Muti in Rome after leaving Paris for good. I wish you a good morning."

With a long penetrating stare, the Earl of Richmond, his wife and their party continue past us on their walk.

Captain Howard curses himself for his stupidity for much of our return walk to the Faubourg. While the whereabouts of the Catholic Pretender, Bonnie Prince Charlie, are not a state secret, it was Sir Humphrey who told Captain Howard about his Rome residence. Ordinary Englishmen might not have heard. For weeks we've been focused on what I should say while in France. I never imagined that Captain Howard would slip up instead and reveal knowledge he should not have.

"Any question of my loyalty provokes me," he admits. "When Bonnie Prince Charlie invaded England, my family thought that we could be arrested for our faith to prevent us rising with him. I was thirteen and I still remember that fear."

"When the Stuart prince invaded, I was fourteen," I say, surprised. "And I was afraid, because Bonnie Prince Charlie was backed by France, and my grandfather said if France had its way and put him on the throne, the Huguenot refugees would suffer. Even though we were Protestants, just having French names was dangerous for a while."

He nods, and I feel a new bond with Captain Howard. For very different reasons, we've been shadowed by fear of the French and not always felt that we were safe and secure in our country.

"I've been subjected to sneers about my Catholic faith all my life," Captain Howard says. "That is no excuse. And now Rochford will have his eye on us."

What makes this situation worse is I feel responsible for it happening, because I insisted on the stroll through the Luxembourg gardens. If I hadn't, we would have been spared the encounter with the Rochfords. While posing as a Catholic, I could feel their distrust and contempt turned on me. What will it mean for the British ambassador to monitor us? This is something we do *not* want.

In the Duke of Norfolk's rooms, I do my best to practice the patience that Captain Howard counselled. When our men return, we will know the next steps to take.

Finally, when the sun is low in the sky, Henry appears. One look at his face reveals that things did not go well.

"At Sèvres Porcelain, they said there would be no private viewings for the next month or any special tours — he said we must go to the store in Paris if we want to see the porcelain," says Henry.

"But I must get inside the Sèvres main building!" I cry, dismayed. "When I was there before, they showed their porcelain lines to people who asked to see them in a special viewing room. They wouldn't make arrangements for someone presenting a card as Lady Howard?"

"We shall deal with this," Captain Howard promises me before moving on to ask whether we have an appointment with Jean-Honoré Fragonard. That's when we learn the artist is unavailable. He is working on a commission at a client's home, which is far from Paris. When would Fragonard be back? No one could say.

"So much for that as well," I say, deeply disappointed. "Please don't tell me that Madame du Deffand refused to have us at her salon."

Henry says, "A man accepted the card. He said he would give it to Mademoiselle Véronique, who is the assistant to Madame du Deffand, and if we are welcome, we will receive an invitation."

"And what day is the next salon?" I ask.

Henry, miserable, says, "I asked. He didn't answer. After the man explained how he would dispose of the card, I was bid a good afternoon."

I sink into a chair, reeling from this string of bad news. "How are we to proceed?" I ask. "It almost seems as if there is a concerted response to our requests. We are frustrated or put off everywhere."

Captain Howard refuses to join in my dejection, rather to my surprise. He points out that we haven't been spurned at Madame du Deffand's. She has our address in Paris. A messenger should knock on the door very soon and extend an invitation.

No sooner are the words out of his mouth than we hear a rapping at the door. My entire body sags with relief. Louise hurries to answer and returns with a sealed message in her hand.

But it bears the insignia of the Earl and Countess of Rochford.

"I'll open it," snaps Captain Howard. He breaks the seal and reads aloud, "Lady Howard, I have made arrangements with Madame Alice to see you tomorrow morning at her shop in the Faubourg Saint-Germain. Lucy, Countess of Rochford."

A burst of laughter escapes me, then another. It isn't from joy but from the realization that our mission in Paris is off to a terrible start. I had flattered myself that I, Genevieve Planché, could play an important role in righting a wrong, investigating the crimes of the devious, even in preventing hostilities from breaking out between these two countries. What a painful joke.

Chapter Nineteen

The next day, I hadn't had a bite of breakfast when Captain Howard and I fall into an argument. No matter how much I strive for harmony with the man, disagreements arise. The only way to prevent them is to submit completely to his will, which of course I cannot do.

"I don't need a new dress, Captain," I say. "There's nothing wrong with the ones we brought from Twickenham. The Countess of Rochford is only trying to humiliate me."

Last night, when he suggested that I take up this offer from the countess, I assumed Captain Howard was not serious. But it seems he is.

"It may offend the Rochfords if you don't keep the appointment with Madame Alice," he says. "While that is not a huge concern all things being equal, we are trying to not attract notice from the ambassador, remember? If you disdain the arrangement made, it will provoke such notice."

I tear off a piece of bread from the platter on the table, furious that it looks as if I may have to endure an appointment with Madame Alice.

Louise says, "I understand that when they come to Paris, English women are keen to order dresses and English men to order suits and shoes. This is very much expected. I'll go with you, Mrs Sturbridge, acting as your maid."

Captain Howard throws her a grateful glance and tears into the bread from his side of the table.

Growing desperate, I say, "What shall we do if the invitation comes to attend Madame du Deffand's salon and it is to be held today but I am at the dressmaker's?"

"Her salons always begin at five, Walpole told me," Captain Howard says. "You will be back here long before that. Madame Alice's shop is in the Faubourg."

With that, I give in. Donning another stylish dress made for me in Twickenham, I set out with Louise. It isn't as sunny this morning, but the air is thick. I slow my steps for I don't want to look like a sweating disaster when I reach the shop.

As expected, I find not a moment of pleasure at the hands of Madame Alice, an imperious woman wearing heavy rouge and a galaxy of beauty spots. She says, "The countess is a valued customer of many years. Due to her patronage, I agreed to see you without notice."

While taking my measurements and displaying fabrics and ribbons, she conveys that I lack what a desirable Frenchwoman possesses: natural grace and appealing curves. That both things are true does not make it easier for me to hear.

"Our Madame de Pompadour was ethereal and sophisticated, and she set a style of slenderness for the court," says Madame Alice. "You are very slender, Lady Howard, in that you are impressive. But, alas, Pompadour is gone. The fashion is for buxom ladies in Paris this year. I will see if I can compensate with the shaping of your bodice and extra panels."

"Thank you, Madame," I say, gritting my teeth. "I'm most grateful for your expertise."

"Padding is out of style, so I regret that I must do this. In Paris, you understand, women's gowns are simpler. Fewer bows. The sleeves are gathered around the elbow, not hanging. I expect it takes a good while for the English to catch on."

On our way back to the Norfolk rooms, Louise confesses, "I didn't understand more than a dozen words anyone said."

"You're the fortunate one," I tell her. "That's the last dress I order in Paris. If it's finished after we leave, I could not care less."

"I'm sorry she was unpleasant," says Louise. "But I may have a consolation. When we were buying foodstuffs, I heard about a café catering to well-born women that's on Boulevard Saint-Germain. It serves chocolate, Turkish coffee and pastries. With your skill with the language, Mrs Sturbridge, you might be able to pick up something interesting from the ladies there."

"Lead on," I say, intrigued.

We find ourselves in a chic establishment serving food and drink at small tables. And we are surrounded by beautifully dressed women of all ages, chatting as if they've known one another all their lives. No one speaks to me or Louise, not because of a particular rudeness but for the fact that, yet again, we have no one to make introductions. I can pick out snatches of conversation. They talk about clothes, wigs, skin treatments, jewels and parties. I know there are intellectual women in Paris, among them Madame du Deffand, who devour Voltaire and Rousseau and debate exciting new ideas. But they're not in this café.

After finishing my cup of Turkish coffee — a bracingly strong concoction I would like to see in London — Louise and I return to the Norfolk rooms. There I receive two pieces of unwelcome news. The first is that we have not received a message from Madame du

Deffand or anyone else. We don't know when her next salon will be held or if we are invited.

The second development is that Captain Howard left hours ago in the carriage, driven by Simon, without telling anyone his intention. I scrutinize every single thing I remember him saying this morning, and yesterday evening as well. No plan for the day was mentioned.

The afternoon crawls by without a message from Madame du Deffand. She's had my card and Walpole's letter for over a day. Sir Horace said we should hear back shortly, since her salons are held every week and she would have to adjust her guest list. What could be the problem?

When the church bell rings four o'clock outside, my anger flares. He's been gone since ten o'clock, I have gathered. I can't believe that Captain Howard is pursuing his own plan without telling me, much less including me. But what other conclusion can be reached? A dark suspicion takes form. Did Captain Howard push me to go to Madame Alice's shop to get me out of the way?

The sound of his firm, quick step on the stairs sends me to the sitting room to confront him.

"Where have you been all day, Captain?"

An eyebrow raised, he says, "Out looking for contacts to lead us to the viscount or to Sèvres. My assignment."

"Your assignment? It is *our* assignment. I do not appreciate being left here all day without purpose. I demonstrated in the Luxembourg that I am convincing as Lady Jane Howard. I am the one who needs to see the blue with my eyes. I'm unlikely to find it in a cupboard in the Duke of Norfolk's rooms."

"Enough!" He holds up his hand. "There are places I can go where people are more disposed to conversation but women are not permitted. I was at Lapérouse, a new restaurant on Quai des Grands

Augustins. It's a place where men gather to buy wine, drink wine and have a bit to eat. Vincent heard about it."

"And did you learn anything?"

"Yes, Mrs Sturbridge, as you ask, I did. That Italian you talked to at Hampton Court was right — there is a master forger whose centre of operation is Rome. In the last year or so he has begun doing business here too. The man is known only as the Abbé. I tried to find out more, but that's all I could glean from this young comte. He was so drunk as to be nearly incoherent. He said the Abbé takes delight in selling forged old masters to gullible English tourists and I should be careful with my money."

"Fragonard is not an old master, and I can't believe anyone would describe Sir Horace Walpole as gullible," I say. "But I suppose you think the Abbé is the man responsible for Walpole's forgery?"

"It's possible. But of even more interest is something I heard about a certain Mademoiselle Veronique, the assistant to Madame du Deffand. She does not enjoy a good reputation, especially when compared to her predecessor. That young woman grew restless with being an assistant and formed her own rival salon. Veronique is not as intellectual a woman, which is understandable. Madame du Deffand must want to prevent creating another competitor. The key thing is Veronique is said to be susceptible to a large bribe so that she'll put in a word with someone aching to be invited to Madame du Deffand's exclusive salon. It's just a matter of finding a way to meet her."

I would think that would be only slightly less difficult than finding our way into the salon itself. Aloud, I say, "These are the things you learned in six hours spent at this restaurant?"

"I did not spend six hours there."

When I ask where else he spent time today, Captain Howard treats me to an icy stare, the like of which I have not seen since the earliest days of our acquaintance. He says, "I do not need to seek your permission for my actions, Mrs Sturbridge."

Stung, I say, "I'm aware of that. But it was my understanding that we would function as a team."

"When possible, we will. Do you have ideas apart from parading up and down the Luxembourg?"

I am certain he is attempting to intimidate me — to relegate me to the side. But I push forward. "We could go to the theatre together, no? Lady Jane enjoyed theatricals when young, you told me. Wouldn't she be eager to go to the theatre or opera in Paris?"

"I thought of that this morning and sent Henry to purchase tickets at Comédie Française. No box seat is available for any performance in the next two weeks. Most people secure their admission months ahead. And we can't stand in the pit. That would be inappropriate for someone of your rank and station. I'll send Henry to the opera tomorrow to see if we will have better luck. But tonight I am going out alone to the sorts of establishments to which no man brings his sister-in-law."

"I see." I decide to match his cold, aloof manner. If Captain Howard expects me to burst into angry reproach, he's mistaken. After a couple of hours spent talking to his men, the captain leaves again for his date with the debauched of Paris.

I take a simple dinner alone, trying to come up with my own ideas for the mission, but I am rewarded with nothing. Afterwards, I station myself at the bedchamber window, hoping for a breeze. The air is even thicker than before, an unwelcome reminder that we are occupying the peak of the summer. We are meant to succeed in our mission within the next two weeks, yet I can't say we've made any progress besides scraps of gossip that Captain Howard picked up in a restaurant. There's no question that this seems much more daunting than I expected in Twickenham. What will happen if we fail? This is the first time I have asked myself such a question — and faced the fact that we may fail. We can't even find a way into Madame du Deffand's salon.

I step out onto the balcony, resting my arm against the railing. The heat is beginning to fade as the sun sinks low in the sky, though darkness and the lighting of the Faubourg's oil lamps are still hours away. Before me stretch the elegant hôtels of the aristocracy, with more being constructed. From here, I can see boats unloading materials from the Seine. Churches dot the district too, and a few monasteries.

Just below, I watch a gaunt friar in plain brown robes walking slowly, his arms folded, past two well-dressed fops in wigs and silks. The aristocracy and the Catholic Church move hand in hand, while the poor of the city toil far beneath their notice.

Suddenly, my hand itches to seize a brush and paints and capture what I see. The contrasts of Paris inspire me to paint, a longing I haven't felt in well over a year. I wonder if I might sketch in pencil some of what I see here and complete the work after I return to England. Ideas for colour and composition jostle in my mind. I have missed this rush of excitement.

That night, I am in the middle of a dream when I hear my name. Is it Pierre — is he sick? But he always says "Mama" and the word I hear is "Genevieve".

Struggling out of my night fog, I mumble, "I'm coming, Thomas." My eyes ease open, and it comes to me: I'm in Paris on a mission for Sir Humphrey Willoughby, far from my family. Someone else calls for me.

I find a dressing gown and stand by the door, waiting to hear my name again.

"Genevieve?"

I recognize that speaker. It's Captain Peregrine Howard.

When I open the door, I'm confronted by the captain, swaying on his feet, reeking of strong wine, tobacco and the scent of rose oil, a woman's fragrance.

"I'm sorry, please say … say you accept it, Genevieve," he says, his words slurred. Has he ever used my Christian name before tonight? I don't think so. The high and mighty captain is as foxed as any elbow crooker on Brick Lane. I try to stifle a laugh.

Peering past him, I can make out the outlines of the furniture in the drawing room. It's not the middle of the night. Dawn is about to break. Simon, presumably Howard's servant during the night's excesses, slumps unconscious in a chair near the door.

"I was rude to you. Awful."

"It's forgotten already, Captain," I say. "I possibly was rude to you as well."

"Aw, I'm a rotten bastard. So, so rotten."

Oh, dear. He's that sort of drunk.

"You must find your bed, Captain Howard. It's the only thing to do."

Not till you say you're not angry … with me," he says, his lower lip quivering in a pout. "I have secrets, but so do you … so do you."

I can hear stirring on the stairs. It cannot be five o'clock yet, and he's waking the household. I need to calm him down, though I expect that the captain will soon be terribly sick. I'd like to head that off if possible.

"I am not in the least angry," I say briskly. "I could make you tea, Captain. Would you like that? Just give me a minute to light the fire."

Holding a candle, our cook and pistol wielder, Vincent, appears and says, with the discreet wisdom of an older man, "Madame, I think I should be the one to get the captain to bed. I've managed worse cases. It would help if you retired to your room. This is for men to manage."

"Thank you, Vincent."

He puts his arm around Captain Howard's waist to lead him to his room, but not before the captain mumbles, "I like … her hair when it's down."

Men say all sorts of things when they are drunk, I tell myself. The important thing is that we carry on with the mission. I'll make no reference to this behaviour later today, and if I know him at all, he won't either.

Still, what did he mean when he said we both have secrets?

Chapter Twenty

I am unable to fall back asleep, no matter how hard I try. I hear various voices on the other side of the door throughout the morning, but not Captain Howard's. And thank heavens, no retching noises.

Midway through the morning, I send for Louise, and she helps me dress.

"Is Captain Howard himself?" I ask.

"More or less," she says, a grin appearing.

When I come face to face with Captain Howard, he is haggard with bloodshot eyes. However, he smells as if he's scrubbed himself vigorously with mint soap, his hair is flat and damp and his clothes are fresh. He couldn't have found more than a few hours of unconsciousness but somehow seems to have shed the worst signs of drunkenness. I can smell coffee. I imagine he prevailed on Vincent to make a lot of it.

"Good morning, Madame." There is a flash of pleading in his eyes. How important it must be to him that I make no reference to the night's behaviour.

"Good morning," I say. "Did you manage to obtain any titbits last night?"

"I did. More than titbits. Very helpful information. I think it's safe for us to assume that the viscount is friendly with, and could be doing business with, corrupt persons."

"Tell me!" I'm exhilarated that finally we may be getting somewhere.

"At the second club I visited, I met an Englishman also visiting Paris. Bruce Chilton. Not the sort of young man who would have sent a letter to the British embassy. And not a young man anyone would want their sister or daughter to marry. Stupid. Lecherous. Lazy. Drunk most nights of the year, I expect. He took a liking to me and insisted on serving as my guide to the best places in Paris. And by best I assume you comprehend he had in mind the worst. But I played along."

I ask carefully, "I don't mean to offend you, but is this man Catholic?"

"I don't blame you for asking. Bruce Chilton was not raised Catholic, but he's definitely High Tory, so he's well disposed. But really, I could have been an evangelical Protestant, and he'd still have wanted to impress me with all the people he knows in Paris. I let him go on and on, telling pathetic stories, until he mentioned that he's met Vicomte Antoine-Jean de Breteuil."

"Now you have my attention," I say.

"Mrs Sturbridge, here it is. The viscount is part of a certain circle. A notorious circle. One of its leaders is a Comte du Barry. Bruce tells me that du Barry owns a casino that has a brothel upstairs. And he's not a secret owner or investor. He can often be found on the premises, talking to the customers and the women."

"A count behaves so?"

"He comes from an old family that's run out of money." Captain Howard glowers, and I wonder if he's thinking of Stanham Castle. "Chilton also tells me that du Barry is the worst libertine in Paris. He has a nickname: Le Roué. His young mistress is a beautiful blonde girl, Jeanne, who used to work in a milliner's shop. Now she lives openly with du Barry in Paris, even though he's got a wife somewhere."

"If Vicomte de Breteuil associates with du Barry, he can't be a respectable person," I declare. "That is a piece of gossip that could prove useful. Good Lord, imagine stepping inside that casino."

Captain Howard takes a deep breath. "I don't need to imagine."

"You went there last night?"

He nods. "I told Bruce I *had* to go at once. I made him think I wanted to see du Barry's mistress for myself. I hoped to find the viscount, but he didn't make an appearance. I spent about three hours there waiting."

"But you did meet the Comte du Barry?"

"We spoke twice," Captain Howard says uncomfortably. "He was rather busy."

I learn that while Captain Howard had decided to use the young rake Bruce Chilton to pursue the trail of Vicomte de Breteuil, he came to regret joining forces with someone so unreliable. After they were both in place at the Comte du Barry's casino, he noticed, while playing faro at the gaming table, that Chilton and du Barry were in deep conversation in the corner of the room.

Perhaps a half hour later, du Barry beckoned to Captain Howard to go upstairs.

"I did so only in hope of learning more of the viscount. I assure you, Mrs Sturbridge, my brother and I never patronized such establishments."

I know that whenever Captain Howard mentions his beloved older brother, Robert, he is in the grip of his most intense emotions. I pat his shoulder lightly and with encouragement.

He continues: "After I was there a while, Comte du Barry said to me, 'I understand you are interested in a friend of mine, Vicomte de Breteuil.'"

"Ah. He said that?"

"I don't know what that fool Chilton said to him. So I made light of it. I said I'd heard the viscount was a man to meet in Paris. What happened next is what worries me. Du Barry said, 'I cannot produce my friend for you here. But I can offer you the prettiest girl in Paris. You may borrow Jeanne for the night.'"

I had assured Captain Howard that I was aware of the goings-on in such establishments, but this sort of depravity is new to me. A nobleman who is a pimp?

Seeing my expression, Captain Howard says, "I would shield you from this, Madame, if it were not for the implications to his offer. On our way out, Chilton expressed his jealousy and surprise. He said that du Barry lends his beautiful mistress, Jeanne, to others but only to make men indebted to him in some way."

I feel startled.

"Why would he want you indebted to him? You are an Englishman on holiday."

"I don't know." Captain Howard's large brown eyes mirror my bewilderment. "Du Barry said something else. It's even more appalling to a lady's ears, but I have reason to repeat it."

"Captain, how bad can it be?"

Captain Howard covers his eyes as if he can't look at me while repeating it. "'My Jeanne likes a good long ride and you are a handsome cavalry officer, so you should suit her.'"

My cheeks flaming red, I say, "Your reason to repeat this is … ?"

Taking his hands from his eyes, he says, "I never told the Comte du Barry I was a captain of the cavalry in Québec. Nor did I tell Bruce Chilton. The day before, at the restaurant, I had a tense moment with a Frenchman who had served under the Marquis de Montcalm in Québec, and I resolved to be as vague as possible with everyone going forward unless forced to specify my commission in the war. Chilton didn't care about it. The man has no interest in the military."

"So how did the Comte du Barry know?"

Captain Howard shakes his head, more at a loss than I'd ever seen.

"Did you ask the woman herself?" I blurt.

"I did not converse with her, Mrs Sturbridge. Good God, did you think I took up du Barry on his sordid offer?"

"I'm sure I don't know, Captain," I say with a shrug. Even through Howard's offended glare I feel a twinge of relief, though I don't know why. What he does in these places is none of my business.

Clearing my throat, I say, "Is it possible that you have been … discussed in these clubs, and the details of your conversations from the restaurant reached du Barry? But that would mean from the beginning we are being watched and followed. I'd hate to think so!"

He says, "It is possible that we *are* being followed in Paris, Mrs Sturbridge."

"Why would you think that?" I ask, tensing.

Captain Howard explains that when he and Chilton stumbled onto the street outside du Barry's casino, where the patient Simon and his carriage waited, Chilton laughed and pointed at a man wearing a tricorne hat peering from a doorway. He announced, "Sartine has him following me. He likes to have all significant English visitors shadowed. The more significant the man, the more skilled his shadow. So you can see I'm not worthy of his best men," Chilton howled.

"Yes, you said that Sartine was to be feared in Paris."

"He is indeed. We have nothing like his force of secret police in London — and nothing like the Grand Châtelet. It's a police head-quarters, prison, morgue and torture chamber, all in one."

I swallow and ask, "Have you noticed anyone shadowing you?"

"No. But I might not … if the person was very skilled."

I point out that we haven't gone anywhere since arriving in Paris that would arouse suspicion. And his night-time prowling is what someone would expect for an unmarried army captain. He nods, but I can tell he's barely listened to what I said. Some concern nags him. I wonder where else he went yesterday besides the restaurant, the stops he refused to disclose to me. Why is he so worried that the secret police followed him?

"A knock at the door," announces Simon.

"Ah, finally, our invitation to the salon," I say relieved. I am eager to plunge into the mission and not be left, bored and restless, in these rooms.

When Simon brings me the messenger's sealed paper addressed to me, I pause at the sight of the seal. It is a large "C". That doesn't seem right. But Captain Howard says, "Her name is Marie Anne de Vichy-Chamrond. It might be her preference."

Lady Howard,

I seek the honour of your company and that of Captain Howard in my private box at tonight's performance of Tartuffe, at the Comédie-Française. If you could favour me with a reply as to your intention, I'd be most obliged.

Your servant, the Honourable Bruce Chilton.

I recoil from the thick paper as if it might bite me. "Why is this invitation directed at me?"

Captain Howard says, "Lady Howard is of higher rank than me. It's only proper. But the man never, ever said he had a box at the

Comédie-Française. How? Boxes are expensive, and the French nobility hold on to them like death. Chilton is next to a nobody."

"So we shouldn't go? You painted such a disagreeable picture of him."

He looks at me, surprised. "No, we must go. I very much doubt that this is his idea. He is a fool and could never possess the connections for such a box. But he is English, like us, and I believe they are using him as a pawn to lure us in."

"They? Even more reason to refuse to go. We can't trust Chilton."

"Of course we can't trust him! But this is how the game works, Mrs Sturbridge. Spying is sometimes like fishing. We put a line into the water, a bit of bait on the hook. We see who nibbles. I've already stirred things up in the clubs and casinos. This invitation is the result, and we may get a face-to-face encounter with our quarry. Yes, tonight, we shall make our first appearance, the two of us, before French society."

Captain Howard jumps to his feet — and stumbles, his face gone white. Those hours at the casino of Comte du Barry took a heavy toll.

I tell him he must rest for at least a few hours. "You are not in fit health for the challenge we face tonight." After the expected amount of arguing, he agrees. Fifteen minutes after Captain Howard disappears, I hear heavy snoring from the other side of the door.

Now is my chance. Captain Howard needs sleep, but I do not. There is something important I can do during these spare hours.

I tell Simon to fetch the carriage, bracing for him to question me or insist that Captain Howard sanction it. I'm quietly pleased when he does not.

Wearing my wig and fashionably dressed, Louise safely at my side, I tell Simon to take us to the Louvre. Henry said that while he learned Fragonard was not in residence, the Louvre housed the Royal Academy of Painting and Sculpture. For over a century, artists have emerged from this academy. When I asked him whether he had seen any paintings exhibited for the public, Henry said, "I *believe* so." Perhaps I will be able to see a Fragonard work.

If nothing else, I enjoy the opportunity to cross the Seine and escape the oppressive luxury of Faubourg Saint-Germain. I want to see for myself the famous statue of Henry IV on his bronze horse. Edging slowly over the crowded Pont Royal, I peer out the carriage window. The Seine is so crammed with every conceivable size of boat I can barely describe the water's colour. Is it brown perhaps? Once again, my fingers itch to hold a brush and paint what I see.

At the river's edge, a bevy of laundresses shout at the man trying to stop them from washing their clothes in the river. It makes me smile.

On the other side, I notice a crowd of men reading notices nailed to a tall board. Behind the board, a man waves to another, and, when they meet, a booklet is exchanged, but surreptitiously, a blur of paper from one pocket to another.

We don't have far to go on the right bank. The enormous white brick Louvre Palace is impossible to mistake for anything else. What takes time is finding someone to direct us to the Royal Academy of Painting and Sculpture inside it. At two of the entrances to the palace, people are selling clothes and trinkets in makeshift booths. I spot two men trading papers bound together like crude books besides one of the booths.

In a wing of the Louvre, we find classrooms and studios and an office ruled by a trio of serious older men. They scrutinize me with suspicion. What's a well-dressed lady and her maid doing here? Bitterly aware that the academy has never allowed females to take classes or exhibit, I force a smile and move on.

As I'd hoped, the academy hangs sketches and paintings on the walls outside the artists' studios and classrooms. It isn't an exhibition with artwork to sell. These are examples of work by former students of the Academy. And the best painters in France studied here. I could spend all day — and all night — studying these creations. But with limited time, I search for anything by the Academy's most brilliant recent student, Jean-Honoré Fragonard.

After leaving Louise to rest on a bench, I find success. Two Fragonard ink sketches are mounted side by side. They are not portraits or classical figures. These are landscapes showing fantastic detail in the trees, hills and brooks.

I feel someone's curious gaze alight on me.

"You savour Fragonards without colour?" asks a young man, short of stature, with lively wide-set eyes and a wispy brown beard. "That's like eating a cake baked without sugar."

"There's a huge amount of talent evident even without colour," I dispute. "Look at the shape of the forest in this sketch and how it seems wild, yet Fragonard controls its thrust."

I plunge into the most enjoyable conversation I've had with anyone since I came to France. I have finally found someone who does not require an introduction before we may converse. The student and I analyse and debate Fragonard's art in great depth. It does not surprise me when my bearded friend confesses, with the passion of his years, his contempt of the "deep frivolity of Boucher and Fragonard".

"You should moderate your words," I say, laughing. "Does not the man himself have a studio in the Louvre?"

"I hear he's nestled in the country, Madame. Gorging on poached truffles while painting the mistress of a rich man." He sneers enjoyably before admitting, "If Monsieur Fragonard were less dismissive of the youth coming up behind him at the Academy, we might judge him differently."

Thinking of Joshua Reynolds, I say, "We expect generosity from the most successful, but alas, it's the last place you shall find it."

Nodding, the student says, "You are wise, Madame. But do you think it possible to change the order of things and melt the ice in the heart of the prosperous painter? When will that happen?"

I think for a moment before a wicked smile explodes, and I say, "When women are allowed into the art academies!"

I'm still smiling a half hour later as our carriage prepares to cross the Seine. I loved seeing art and debating it rather than sitting in the Norfolk rooms waiting for Captain Howard to return.

Louise remarks, "Debating that student put pink in your cheeks."

"Yes, it did." I take in the bustling chaos of the Seine, not so different than the Thames. It comes to me that this is what it was once like with Thomas. We loved nothing more than debating ideas by the hour. I say softly, "My husband says that those who study science find common ground regardless of country. I think it is the same for artists."

Louise says nothing, and when I glance at her, I'm taken aback to see her mouth pinch with disapproval. Too late, I remember how Sir Humphrey always hated it when Thomas preached an international brotherhood of science. And while we might enjoy a cordial connection, she is Sir Humphrey's loyal operative.

"The French are our enemies, no matter their special talents," Louise says.

"Of course," I say, chewing the inside of my lip. I wonder if part of Louise's job is to watch the wayward and impulsive Genevieve and report back to Captain Howard when I'm safely out of earshot. He and Sir Humphrey spied on the Lunar Society after all. It's what they do: observe and report. When we return to the Duke of Norfolk's rooms, I signal to Simon. "Did you see anyone at all who you might think followed us to the Louvre or back?" I ask.

"No, Madame. Captain Howard told me to be sharp at all times. I noticed no one."

Upstairs, I find a revived Captain Howard — quite revived indeed.

"You left no word for me on your plan — I have been going mad here," he says angrily. "Every time you leave these quarters without me, you face elevated risk, Mrs Sturbridge. *You* are the one whose true identity we must conceal, not mine. Your destinations must be chosen with extreme care."

"Captain Howard, I know you see my role as nibbling chocolate and gossiping with dressmakers, but I had a better idea: confirm that the painting Sir Horace Walpole bought was no Fragonard by looking at some undoubted originals. I can make that judgement with complete confidence now. It's a good painting — and an excellent forgery — but it doesn't match Fragonard's mastery of fine details."

"Hmm," says Captain Howard. "Yes, that is good. But still, I wish that you had—"

"Asked your permission?" I cock my head and wait for his response.

"Point taken," he says. "Shall we agree on this: the next time you take it into your head to leave these quarters, you will consult me? May I ask that of you?"

"Yes. If you do the same with me."

His eyes blazing, he opens his mouth to refuse. Something stops him. After a moment of tense silence, he mutters, "Very well."

I do my utmost to hide my triumph.

Chapter Twenty-One

Two hours later, dressed in the finest apparel we brought to Paris, Captain Howard and I set out for the Comédie-Française in our carriage.

"You look uncomfortable, Mrs Sturbridge, why is that?" Captain Howard asks when we face each other in the carriage. "You wore a gown much like this one to Strawberry Hill."

Our string of quarrels does not put me in a frame of mind to confide in him, but he presses me. This is an important evening, and I must be confident and ready.

"I'm growing used to it all — a corset keeping me from drawing deep breaths, my scalp aching from pins and my face stinging from heavy paint. But I've never in my life worn a weighty necklace like this one. Sir Humphrey went to some lengths to obtain it for this purpose — a night at the theatre or a ball." I lay my fingers tentatively on the gold links weighing on my bosom. "But it presses so. I feel like the edges will leave a mark. At least the central amethyst jewel is nice — smooth and cool. Don't worry, when we are at the theatre, I'll try to look as if I've worn such jewellery all my life — in character."

Captain Howard says, peering out the window, "Jane never wears anything like that. She inherited family jewellery, a few pieces from my mother. All very old-fashioned."

I wonder how it feels to pretend in Paris that his family enjoys prosperity in England. We are only able to succeed at this charade because he and his real sister-in-law conceal their reduced circumstances with such vigour.

"We know that someone wants to find out more about us and they are using this invitation to the theatre as a means to do so," says Captain Howard. "Whenever possible, we must turn the tables and try to find out more about *them*, without confrontation of course. We need to tread a careful path to the viscount. He may have nothing to do with this invitation, but my instinct says that either the man or those who associate with him are making a move."

"I'm ready for them," I assure Captain Howard.

When we alight, we are swept into the crush of an excited crowd surging towards the tall, grey-stone theatre at 14 rue des Fossés-Saint-Germain-des-Prés. The doors stand flung open, welcoming all to the House of Molière — the oldest theatre troupe in France, perhaps in all of Europe. Within moments, the entranceway and lobby are packed so tightly that no one can move more than a handspan.

The air is suffused with the thick, intoxicating swirl of perfumes — a hothouse of human flowers blooming all at once. Tuberose mingles with jasmine, sandalwood with lavender, each fragrance distinct yet lost in the alchemical medley. The women's silks and satins catch the light, their dresses' smaller hoops and *ruche*-cuff sleeves whispering of Madame Alice's latest dictates. Around delicate throats glint chokers of lace ribbons or pearls. Jewels flash at every turn, but the question rises: are they genuine treasures or imitations, like the Fragonard angel Sir Horace bought last spring? The truth glimmers just out of reach, hidden in the gleam of paste and crystal.

Most striking of all are the women's *poufs*. Unlike the quarter of us who wear wigs, the majority flaunt their natural hair, piled high in extravagant arrangements of curls and waves, threaded with feathers, ribbons and improbable artistry. Some towers are adorned as if to challenge the chandeliers themselves.

As the press of bodies tightens, a flicker of unease brushes my thoughts — perhaps flaunting borrowed jewels in such a public venue was unwise. But I remind myself where we are: the Comédie-Française, a symbol of French prestige since Louis XIV merged two rivalrous actor troupes. The murmured excitement around us confirms it: tonight's offering is *Tartuffe,* once banned for its affront to the Church. The anticipation crackles, a frisson of forbidden delight coursing through the crowd.

I lift my chin and move with the poise expected of a bewigged and bejewelled lady. My hand rests lightly on Captain Howard's outstretched arm. He stands out even among this gilded throng. French fashions have evolved for men as well — waistcoats shorter, breeches tighter — and he can carry that off, but it is his military bearing, his broad shoulders and his narrow waist that command attention. Not to mention his haughty gaze, which is by no means put on for the requirements of our Parisian mission. He once stared at me like this in my broken-down Lichfield barn. Behind us, Henry's solid presence in red-and-black livery is a quiet reassurance.

My blood sings as we press forward. I do not shrink from what lies ahead. Our invitation tonight, strange and unexpected, came from the hand of a man whose weakness may very well make him a pawn of our enemies. And yet, that is precisely why we are here: to confront the unknown, to uncover the truth.

Captain Howard steps forward, his voice crisp as he addresses an older theatre employee. "We are bound for Box Number Three."

The man's eyes widen, his expression flickering between surprise and unease. "Monsieur, are you certain of the number?"

Captain Howard shows him the numbered card that came with Bruce Chilton's invitation. Still, the employee hesitates, as if running through a series of unpleasant scenarios in his head. "Is there someone else I need to speak with?" asks Captain Howard. His French is good, but I assume his English accent is discernible.

The employee apologizes and, holding a lit candle in a brass dish, leads us up a surprisingly shabby set of stairs. Rudimentary maintenance is not being performed. Are we heading to an undesirable private box? I suppose I shouldn't be surprised.

Once off the stairs, Captain Howard, Henry and I follow the employee down a narrow corridor with numbered doors on the left. It, too, verges on dilapidation. The employee opens the door to our box, near the end of the corridor.

Captain Howard says to Henry, "Wait out here." I can tell from how Henry nods that the two men discussed a plan earlier.

Not three steps into the box, and I hesitate. It isn't a second-rate patron's box. It is large and positioned perfectly at height and near the curtained stage. It might be the best box in the house. How could this Bruce Chilton possibly have secured such seats? Captain Howard described him as a young wastrel of little social importance. And still no sign of our "host".

Glancing into the main theatre, I take in the private boxes arrayed opposite. They are all decorated with blue and gold *fleur-de-lis* carved and painted onto wood just below the bottom ledge, as ours must be as well. The national symbol of France.

Four empty chairs stand before us in two rows. Captain Howard and I exchange a wary look and move towards the chairs in front. What else can we do? It might look strange to take the others. Below us, people are finding their places, whether it's a seat in a row or jostling for the best advantage in the standing pit.

Less than a minute after I ease onto this red velvet chair — rather lumpy, to be honest — I feel the first wave of attention. I would like to prepare to enjoy this controversial play. But I see faces tilt up and towards us from the main floor. People nudge one another. I even see some people pointing at Captain Howard and me.

At first, it strikes me as absurdly funny. I had thought of tonight as my debut in Paris, but I'd not expected to draw *this* much attention. The humour of the situation dies when I notice that the boxes opposite ours are filled with people wearing silk, brocade and jewels, and they are lifting their monocular glasses to get a better look at me. Dozens of French people stare with unconcealed curiosity. What if they knew the woman wearing a wig and jewels was Genevieve Planché, a Huguenot from Spitalfields? For someone who has struggled with the fear that I don't belong in the English nobility and would have a difficult time persuading anyone that I do, this is a nightmare coming to life.

"Steady, Lady Howard," says Captain Howard softly. "Talk to me, but show no concern. They've got their glasses on us."

I turn slowly to see a smile pasted on his face. He, too, realizes that we are attracting an enormous amount of attention for two strangers sitting in a box at the Comédie-Française.

"Have we played into someone's hands?" I ask and smile back.

His reply, coming through clenched teeth, is "I'm going to wring Bruce Chilton's fat neck."

With that, the lights dim. The curtain rises.

Although I've always wanted to see *Tartuffe*, I couldn't have described the production I sat through at Comédie-Française if asked about it afterwards.

I laugh at the odd joke, recognize a line said with verve and originality and appreciate the workmanship of the stage sets. But concentration on a play is next to impossible with what else happens in Box Number Three.

Next to me, Captain Howard swivels sharply in his chair at the sound of two men talking in the corridor, their voices raised. The door opens a few inches and Henry says, "Captain, I—"

"Howard, be so good as to instruct your personal guard that I am your host and not here to rob you," says an irritated drawl.

"Let Mr Chilton through, Henry."

In steps a portly young man dressed as a dandy, though his waistcoat is unbuttoned on top and the bunch of lace at his throat is flattened, as if someone had already made a faint attempt to throttle him.

He slides into the chair behind Captain Howard with a loud thump. "I am so, so sorry," he says, tapping the back of Howard's chair before bowing to me. "My lady, please forgive my lateness." An unctuous smile spreads across his face. "The Honourable Bruce Chilton at your service. If I'd known that I'd be sharing a box with such a vision of loveliness, I would have pushed my way through the lobby with brute force. Your brother-in-law did not do you justice, Lady Howard."

I nod to him, trying not to roll my eyes at his oily flattery. I turn to look at the stage, but I can feel Chilton's eyes on me. A speculative mood pulses.

After a few minutes, Captain Howard asks, his voice calmer, "Chilton, I must ask you, who pays for this box? It can't be you."

"Oh, no, no. It was a gift for the night. Splendid view of the stage, agreed?"

"A gift from whom?"

"I'll tell you later, Captain. I'm trying to give the play my full attention."

Although I would also like to wring Bruce Chilton's neck, Captain Howard and I manage to control ourselves. No more is said. We are both burning with curiosity about whose box we are sitting in, but we can't bear down on Chilton while half of Paris watches. Every so often, I hear a lid open and shut and a snorting noise as Chilton busies himself with his snuff. Who would choose this weakling as their instrument?

My attention becomes divided between the actors on the stage and a man sitting in a box directly across from us. The many candles flickering onstage provides enough light to see him. A tightly coiled white wig atop his head, he wears a dark green jacket — and he persistently watches us through monocular glasses. Everyone else in his box appears to be watching the play. Not him. I don't know which of the three of us he is observing so openly.

I wish we had thought to bring these glasses, or there had been some in the box. Hating that the man in green can see me with much more clarity than I can see him, I force myself to confine my attention to the stage. After what seems like an eternity, the interval arrives. Bruce Chilton is out of the box like a shot to secure wine for the box. Down on the main floor, candelabras are brought out to light people's way as they mill about, chatting happily.

A moment later, Henry opens the door a few inches and says, "Captain Howard, a gentleman asks to pay his respects to you and Lady Howard."

Howard rises, and I do, too. We glance at each other, and I nod. I am ready to play my part of a lady receiving a guest.

It's no shock to see the man in dark green step into our box. Up close, he looks to be in his late thirties and strikingly handsome, though his mouth has a cruel set. His brocade jacket and waistcoat are expensive — I know that one can only achieve that colour green through a series of difficult dyes. His shoe buckles sparkle with diamonds, and he holds a thin ebony cane under his arm as he steps towards us.

Whoever the stranger is, with this incredible dedication to fashion and the money to fuel it, he's a man of importance with undoubted connections. We should take him seriously.

"Forgive my intrusion," he says. "But I understand that you wish to make my acquaintance, Captain Howard. I am Vicomte Antoine-Jean de Breteuil."

Chapter Twenty-Two

Here is the man who wrote to Sir Horace Walpole and arranged for the purchase of the Fragonard painting. He must know some of the secrets we are here to learn.

The man bows to Captain Howard, although it is more a tilt of the shoulders and an inclination of his head.

Why is the viscount coming to us? Meeting him was the best outcome I could have hoped for tonight. But this feels strange. I can only wonder if he knows we are investigating him for wrongdoing and is trying to take his measure of us.

I have rarely felt more admiration than I do for Captain Howard at this moment. He smiles, makes a quick bow and says, quite casually, "How very good of you, my lord. As you know, I am Captain Peregrine Howard. May I present my sister-in-law, Lady Jane Howard?"

The viscount shifts towards me, lowers his cane and executes an actual bow this time. I sink into a curtsey, not the lowest one possible — that is reserved for royalty — but the one Captain Howard taught me to do when meeting someone from the nobility.

"I'm enchanted, Madame," he says. That cruel mouth forms a smile, one without warmth.

We exchange bland views about *Tartuffe*, followed by observations about travel in July and the differences in accommodations between London and Paris.

"I am certain you've been to France before, am I right, Lady Howard?" he asks.

"No, sadly," I say. I am careful not to show dismay. This is the kind of question I've been hoping I would not hear. Is it possible he knows who I am and is going to try to trap me into confirming his suspicion?

"But your French is excellent." His eyebrow rises.

I have my explanation ready, the one we prepared in Twickenham. "I had an excellent French governess growing up, one I retained for my children. I have enjoyed years of conversation with her. I'm delighted that all those talks have produced the desired result."

"They have indeed." He holds my gaze a few seconds longer than is comfortable. With that chilly smile, he says, "And so, Lady Howard, do you like our theatre?"

"Very much."

"That's gracious of you, but it has seen better days, I'm afraid." He makes a dismissive gesture to the pit with his ivory cane. "They built this on an abandoned tennis court years ago. Appalling to see the decline. We put on the finest productions in all Europe, and we have some treasures to protect. Do you know that backstage, in the green room, is the armchair Molière sank into when he uttered his last word onstage nearly a century ago? I hope when you return to Paris the next time, Lady Howard, our beloved Comédie-Française will be in a new theatre building. A truly splendid new building. Well, I must return to my seat. The interval is ending. I just had one more question." He turns to Captain Howard and says with the same offhand charm, "Why did you wish to make my acquaintance?"

I prepare myself. Captain Howard will have some facile answer ready, for he shows an ability to think on his feet. Whatever he says, I'll echo it.

"My lord, I understand from a friend of mine, Sir Horace Walpole, that you are the man to talk to about paintings."

I stiffen in disbelief. Why is Captain Howard tipping our hand now? This sounds confrontational to my ears!

While I struggle to compose myself, the viscount thankfully looks only at Captain Howard. He shows no surprise, no revelation of dismay. I detect only one possible sign of stress: a swift swallow.

"Ah, yes," he says. "I recollect that I did assist the prime minister's son in obtaining a painting quite some time ago."

Captain Howard thrusts the dagger deeper. "If I may refresh your memory, it was an angel painted by Jean-Honoré Fragonard."

The two men regard each other in silence. I can hear someone making an announcement from the stage. Interval is over.

Vicomte de Breteuil walks to the door. Standing just outside and listening, no doubt, Henry opens it for him immediately.

The viscount's eyes travel between Captain Howard and me. He's no longer within the sphere of the candles and I can't make out his expression. "I know many people. I enjoy making introductions and it pleases me to be of service to friends from England." His hand twirls the cane. "If I hear about something that is … special, I will send word. You are staying in the rooms of the Duke of Norfolk, are you not? Good. This way I know where to find you."

A chill ripples through me. We didn't say where we were staying in Paris, but he's gone out of his way to show us he knows. How would he learn this? I silently curse the absent Bruce Chilton. He must be the source.

After the viscount leaves, Captain Howard steps out and confers with Henry before returning to his seat. The play has resumed.

Having no choice, I've retaken my seat. I whisper to Captain Howard, "He knows where we are staying!"

"Yes. Yes, he does."

"Why did you tell him so much?"

"Quiet. I'll explain when we are in the carriage. Breteuil is no doubt watching. And others may be too. We are on display at this moment, and it's important to be calm. We must look indifferent to his visit, especially you."

I know I should not do it, but after a few minutes, I can't resist. I steal a glance across the theatre. Although he's shifted position in his box, I can make out the viscount by his unusual green coat. He watches the stage, not me.

For the remainder of the play, I do the same. I watch the actors, laugh when others do and clap with the rest of the audience. I don't want anyone who's watching — "*and others may be too!*" — to detect that I am unnerved by the smiling, cane-wielding viscount. But also I am able to pay closer attention to *Tartuffe*. I have survived a challenge. Or rather, Lady Jane Howard has.

At long last, the play ends. Rising, my back to the audience, I comment, "Chilton never came back."

"He's a tremendous coward. But also, they may fear he couldn't stand up to my questions."

"They?"

Captain Howard calls for Henry without answering me and asks him, "What did you learn?"

"The box is paid for by Louis Jean Marie de Bourbon, Duc de Penthièvre," Henry replies. "He is the grandson of King Louis XIV and …" Henry bites his lip.

"What is it?" demands Captain Howard.

"The duke is said to be the richest man in all of France."

No wonder everyone gaped. How could strangers sit in the duke's box? Everyone's curiosity was set aflame as they wondered why we deserved this honour. Captain Howard curses softly. Rallying, he directs me to put on my best face all the way to the carriage. "It could not be more important that you look as if you've enjoyed a night at the theatre, nothing more."

I attempt to do just that as we descend the shabby stairs and join the melee in the lobby. We draw some appraising looks. Some of the people wielding monocular glasses must recognize us. I don't see the Vicomte de Breteuil. One tall woman wearing a pale pink wig and who stares at me quite openly is with a group near the doors in a protective half-circle. Someone in that half-circle shifts, and I spot a small, frail-looking woman in the centre. She wears a cap with a long white-lace veil in front of her face. She couldn't possibly see through it. A younger woman has a book open and is reading from it aloud to the veiled theatre patron.

It hadn't occurred to me that she might attend the play. But this woman appears to be blind.

I nudge Captain Howard and whisper, "Is that Madame du Deffand?"

After a moment, he says, "It may be."

"This is our moment, then. I shall speak to her and try to coax an invitation."

He seizes my elbow. "If you're wrong about who she is, you'll be cut dead. Even if you're right, she may not want to speak to you."

"I've been scorned by my 'betters' all my life, Captain Howard," I whisper. "I don't fear it, be assured. Don't you want me to try? It could be chalked up to bad English manners."

With that, I make a path to the half-circle, hurrying to reach them before they leave the theatre lobby, Captain Howard and Henry in my wake.

"Madame du Deffand?" I say loudly. "May I speak to you?"

The little lace-covered head turns towards me. I must be correct in her identity. But Captain Howard is also correct, as the others in her party stare at me, horrified.

"I am Jane, Lady Howard," I say, just as loudly. "My brother-in-law and I are visitors from England and friends of Sir Horace Walpole's. He sends you his warmest greetings."

"You are friends of Sir Horace?" asks the veiled woman, her voice surprisingly strong. There's an edge of disbelief. I don't blame her. Walpole is the most sophisticated man in England — how could friends of his behave boorishly in France?

How can I prove it? I rack my brain in a near panic until an idea strikes.

I say, "Yes, I was recently enjoying dinner at Strawberry Hill, and he said he was going to write to you about acquiring the clock that Henry VIII gave Anne Boleyn."

Madame du Deffand makes hand motions that are incomprehensible to me but not to the women standing between me and her, who swiftly create an empty path so I can move closer. "I received that letter about the clock three days ago, it was a marvel of wit, just like all of my friend's correspondence," Madame du Deffand says. "If you are recent visitors to Paris, why didn't you drop off your card, Lady Howard? In France, that is our custom.

We don't shout at people we haven't been introduced to in the theatre, my dear."

I can feel my cheeks redden. Captain Howard moves forward protectively and says, "We did that straight away, Madame du Deffand. I am Captain Peregrine Howard. My man delivered Lady Howard's card and a letter of introduction from Sir Horace to your home three days ago."

The woman is transformed into fury. "How can this be?" she snaps. "Veronique, why was I not informed of a letter, hand-delivered and written by my close friend Sir Horace Walpole?"

A pretty and petite young woman with bright brown eyes says, "I'm not aware of such a delivery, Madame."

"Well, we shall find out what happened. I am mortified, Lady Howard. Mortified. I assure you that courtesy is paramount to me. Veronique, I want to leave immediately so we can commence finding out what happened."

"Yes, Madame," says Veronique, bending down to pick something up. As she rises, she shoots me a glance of resentment before attending to Madame du Deffand.

I suspect that Veronique is at the bottom of why my card never made it to Madame du Deffand. Either she mislaid it or purposely kept it from her employer. But why would she have done the latter?

I say nothing until we are in our carriage. Then I half-collapse into the seat and say, "Captain Howard, why do I feel that half of Paris is conspiring against us?"

To my amazement, he laughs. "Not quite half. But definitely a significant few. We've learned quite a lot tonight. You were magnificent!"

"Why, thank you," I say, sitting up.

"You *are* fearless," he says, pounding the seat with his hand and his eyes flashing with triumph. I feel the pleasure he takes in the evening and share it wholeheartedly. I also feel stunned — I don't believe I've ever got this kind of reaction from the captain.

Growing serious, Captain Howard says, "The viscount may not be fully involved in the crimes we are investigating, but he has some involvement, I can communicate that to Sir Humphrey. I know you were shocked that I confronted him in the theatre box by bringing up the painting. I had to see his reaction. Now I can say with assurance that I believe Breteuil knows that the painting is a forgery. And he's aware of a threat — that we pose a possible threat to their schemes to produce the blue formula. He arranged with Chilton for us to be taken to the box of the duke."

"But why would he do that?"

"To better observe us, to intimidate us. He was probably hoping we'd make fools of ourselves. He can't be happy we didn't."

"And the Duke of Penthièvre? Is *he* involved in this affair?"

"I sincerely hope not. He's a cousin of King Louis. He has the power to crush us, and there's nothing Sir Humphrey Willoughby could do about it."

I shake my head. "All this occurred simply because you asked Bruce Chilton, in some seedy little club, if he knew the Vicomte de Breteuil? You could have been an ordinary social climber making the rounds of Paris trying to ingratiate yourself with people who have titles. The viscount acts as if he knows everyone important in Paris society."

Captain Howard grimaces. "I wonder if their suspicions were aroused the minute anyone heard of the Howards arriving. The fact that I am English and came so soon after the painting was stolen could put the scoundrels on alert, I'm afraid. Sir Humphrey didn't want to wait another couple of months when people start to come back to Paris from their August holidays. Especially not with Pitt returning to office and reading that file before summer's end. I was worried about the timing of coming so soon. But there was nothing else we could do."

He grins. "Your presence is of particular interest, I've noticed. They are curious about how much you know, if you are an English lady buying gowns and going to the theatre or …"

" … or if I am a spy," I finish. "Why would they assume I am not?"

"Because it's so rare. In France, King Louis's Secret du Roi, that exclusive circle of spies reporting only to him that your Sir Gabriel Courtenay was part of, there were no women, correct?"

"No. At least not that I know of."

"Sir Humphrey employs only one woman in any spying capacity, and it's your maid, Louise."

Something Captain Howard said has me bristling with annoyance and I can't let it pass. "Don't call him *my* Sir Gabriel Courtenay. I broke with him and disowned him years ago and haven't had a moment of contact since." For a second I remember Sir Gabriel's sad gaze the last time I saw him, at Sèvres Manufactory Works, but quickly banish the vision.

I can't read Captain Howard's expression in the darkness of the carriage. I didn't want to reopen our earlier quarrels, but I had to set this matter to rest.

"I apologize, Mrs Sturbridge."

"Thank you."

First praise and then an apology? This is a new Captain Howard. I'm anxious to move on. "I must admit to being baffled as to why Veronique would stop my card from finding its way to Madame du Deffand. Unless she hates the British, which is very possible."

He sighs. "No. I find it hard to believe that a girl like her would suppress a letter from one of Madame du Deffand's friends for personal prejudice. We can't even be certain that she's the one behind this. It might be anyone in that household. Perhaps the card and letter never reached Veronique. Remember, that's the place where Walpole announced he wanted a Fragonard angel. The Vicomte de Breteuil himself might have been at her salon that evening — or someone else in the entourage of Madame du Deffand could be Breteuil's contact. But I don't think we can avoid the fact that they know why we're here and they don't want us to learn more. That's why they went to the lengths of preventing our card reaching Madame du Deffand. Walpole announcing he wanted to buy a Fragonard angel was the beginning of everything."

Our carriage slows as we near the Duke of Norfolk's apartments. Yet I find I don't want to go upstairs.

"I suppose we couldn't find new rooms?" I say. "I hate the thought that Breteuil knows where we sleep at night."

"To leave here would be an admission of fear. We absolutely can't show fear. You understand that?"

"I do. But there's a difference between showing no fear and feeling no fear. Do you think the viscount is behind all of it — the colour blue, the theft of the fake Fragonard and the murder of Jemmy Maylie?" I think of that twirling cane and smiling chat about Molière's armchair. Did I meet a murderer? It's hard to believe.

The coach stops. Instead of getting ready to hop out, he moves to the other seat next to me and takes my hand. His grip is strong and warm, and his fingers have lines and ridges I wasn't expecting.

"I honestly don't know," he says softly. "That's why this is such a sensitive stage in our mission. We must watch every single word we say, every single move we make. It's more important than ever that no one in France discovers that you are Genevieve Sturbridge."

Chapter Twenty-Three

The following day, we've just finished our breakfast toast when a knock sounds on the door. A messenger extends an envelope, one bearing the undoubted seal of Madame du Deffand. Captain Howard does the honours and says, "We are invited to her next salon. And we don't have long to wait. She's holding one tomorrow at five."

While it is a relief to finally be invited to the Paris salon where this mystery was born, we have enough information gleaned from the theatre to be sure of the viscount's involvement. Still, there's no question that we will attend. Perhaps the Vicomte de Breteuil will be among the other guests, giving Captain Howard and I another crack at him. He is the key to finding out who inserted the blue in the false Fragonard. We must learn the identities of his associates.

As if reading my mind, Captain Howard says, "Now the places we need to go to are those that house the viscount's possible confederates: Sèvres Manufactory Works and the shop of Lionel Rolandeu. I wish we could find a way to insert you into the porcelain factory. As we have not yet accomplished that objective, we can concentrate on Monsieur Rolandeu.

"How about we plan to go to Rolandeu's shop on Tuesday, the day after we attend Madame du Deffand's salon?" I'm pleased that we are in motion now. "But I have to say, I'm burning with curiosity about

Sèvres. I cannot understand how the porcelain workshop could begin production on Thomas's formula under the nose of the master chemist Jean Hellot. I tell you, even if Hellot were retired, they wouldn't dare. He took the plan to King Louis of sending Thomas and I back to England and cease use of his formula. No one else had the respect of the king and Madame de Pompadour to that degree. Someone may have stolen the formula from Sèvres, and the secret blue has to be produced somewhere else."

There is much to do and preparation to make. However, that afternoon, Captain Howard insists that he and I take a long, leisurely walk to the Church of Saint-Germain-des-Prés. It is one of the oldest churches in Paris, founded in the sixth century by Childebert, the son of Clovis, King of the Franks. We finish our walk in the park adjoining the church, among the well-trimmed hedges and banks of flowers. While Captain Howard pays attention to everything I say, his eyes constantly scan the street and every inch of the park for signs that we're being followed. "Did you suggest this long walk to the church to watch for someone following?" I ask.

"That was one of the reasons," he admits. "But no sign of a watcher."

"Well, this is the day for God," I say, pointing past the hedge at the worshippers who stream in and out of the church. "Maybe the watchers don't report to duty on Sunday."

He smiles at my little joke. "If *only* such men were good Catholics."

A thought occurs to me. "If you wish to go to Mass, you should, Captain Howard. It must hold appeal for you to attend Mass in a church that's over a thousand years old."

He shakes his head. "It would look odd for me to go alone, and I couldn't ask you to attend Mass. I know that Protestants are distraught at the very idea of a Catholic Mass. Let them think we are content to pray the Rosary in private."

I silently study the profile of Captain Howard. Will I ever understand this hard-headed man who behaves with such arrogance while occasionally showing me moments of quiet consideration?

On our walk back to the Faubourg Saint-Germain, I ask Captain Howard to tell me everything he knows about Madame du Deffand.

"She's from a noble family in Burgundy and had, I believe, a convent education before marrying, by her parents' arrangement, the Marquis du Deffand. The marriage was not a success. She was the mistress of the French Regent, Duke of Orléans, when in her early twenties. He's said to have been the most degenerate man in all of France. Quite an achievement! There were other romantic liaisons, but books became more beloved to her than men."

"That seems a wise decision," I comment.

"Her letters are said to be brilliant. Of course they are dictated — and she has to be read to and to go to the theatre and opera to listen, now that her sight is gone — she lost that more than ten years ago. She is a favourite correspondent of Voltaire's. Madame du Deffand began holding these salons to elevate the level of conversation above frivolity and invites people from different parts of society to participate. They are quite exclusive, as we know all too well. What else do I know? Her husband is dead, and she has no children."

Absorbing all this information, I say, "Her salon is admirable, especially considering her disadvantages. I'm curious what Madame du Deffand lives on and how she pays for these entertainments."

"According to Sir Horace Walpole, after losing her sight, she was granted a pension by the Queen of France at the suggestion of a relative of Madame du Deffand's who is favoured by Her Majesty. She receives six thousand livres until her death."

I reflect on the unfair advantage held by the aristocracy. If an ordinary woman of seventy were widowed, childless and blind, her situation would be dire indeed. For those of noble birth, a relation or a friend can always be found to cushion life's blows. But I decide not to share that observation with Captain Howard just now, in the spirit of harmony. We need to be on the best of terms to continue our mission at the salon tomorrow.

Captain Howard points out, "Sir Horace Walpole says that she is grateful for her pension and lives carefully. Her salon is not held at Versailles or in the library of a chateau, as one would think. She lives in rooms provided by the Convent of Saint Joseph on the rue Saint-Dominique — where she also holds her salon."

I shrug. "I've never been inside a convent before. But it's just another thing to pretend to have knowledge of, for Jane Howard would know her way around a convent, wouldn't she?"

"I believe so," he says, a shadow passing over his face. I am burning to know what preoccupies him at such moments, but I have learned the futility of asking probing questions about his family. I am supposed to pretend to be a Howard while he withholds certain facts from me.

The next day, I wear the same gown to the salon of Madame du Deffand as the day I went to Strawberry Hill. It seems fitting. I only wish I didn't have to wear a wig for every outing. It's a hot afternoon, and I'd love to scoop up my own hair with pins, no heavy wig pressing down.

"I hope the viscount will be at Madame du Deffand's salon," says Captain Howard as we ready ourselves to leave. "We still don't know if he overheard Sir Horace say he wanted a Fragonard or if someone else conveyed that desire to him. At the theatre, he confirmed that he arranged for the painting to be sold to Walpole. There is no longer a trace of doubt. But did he know it was a forgery from the beginning? And did he know about the blue being painted on the edge and covered up? He didn't strike me as someone who would want to warn the British that something is afoot. We need to unmask his confederates all the way to the person who is creating your husband's formula. When we get these answers, I can communicate that to Sir Humphrey."

"I just wonder ..." My words trail away. My heart quickens as I consider a new possibility.

"You have something?" asks Captain Howard. "Tell me."

I say slowly, "We've assumed that the person responsible for the forgery is the same person who made sure that the forbidden blue was there, though hidden, and who wrote a message warning of a Blue Fear so it wouldn't be hidden for long. What if it's two different people who are *not* working together? The person revealing the blue is operating independently, trying to fulfil his own purpose. Somehow this person, this second person, was able to subvert the forgery and use it to ... to deliver a message."

"Why would you think that now?"

"To forge a painting and get paid for it by a member of one of Great Britain's leading political families is one thing. The way that the viscount said 'the prime minister's son' with a bit of contempt makes me think that he would draw pleasure from playing such a trick. But he certainly wouldn't want the forgery to be revealed — or for his part in it to be made public."

Captain Howard's eyes widen. "And so when Sir Horace didn't seem to realize what he had, it was the *second* person who set up the haunting of Strawberry Hill to force him to pay attention to the message?"

"Yes … I think that could have happened. These two persons — or groups of persons — could be at cross purposes."

Captain Howard takes a deep breath. "This is a mission with more shadows, more mysteries and complexities, than any other. But we are progressing, Mrs Sturbridge. We are progressing. And I think you may be right about the parties being at cross purposes. It may explain the violence we saw in Southwark. The two persons came into direct conflict."

I try not to let him see my shuddering at that reminder of Jemmy, propped on the ground with his throat cut in Cross Bones.

"Let us hope we witness no such similar violence in France," I murmur.

"Amen."

I don't know what to expect of a salon in a convent. Tall, dark walls covered with ivy rise off the street. With visions of Sir Horace Walpole's Strawberry Hill fresh in my mind, I prepare for stained-glass windows and plenty of "gloomth". But we do not at any point intrude on the confines of Saint Joseph. The rooms of Madame du Deffand seem to be separate from the quarters of the sheltered brides of Christ.

We enter the small antechamber to her living quarters through a private cobblestone court. When I hand my card to the ferret-faced young serving man at the door, and he reads, "Jane, Lady Howard," it elicits a reaction I've yet to see in France: fear. The effort to block us from coming to the salon has led to very unpleasant consequences, I suspect.

Cowering before us, the serving man says, "You are welcome, so welcome, my lady — my lord."

"It's captain, not my lord," says Howard.

"A thousand apologies!" The serving man pushes open the door. The long room occupied by perhaps a dozen people is the opposite of austere; there is furniture of brightly polished wood, tapestries on the walls and freshly cut flowers in vases everywhere.

A glance around the room reveals that Vicomte de Breteuil is not here.

"Ah, Lady Howard, Captain Howard, you've arrived, Madame du Deffand will be so pleased." Curtseying before us is Veronique, smiling sweetly. "Did you have difficulty finding our little salon? No? How nice. Madame wishes to be apart from the convent, yet close to it too. Do you know what she likes to say? By occupying her time, the practice of religion banishes her ennui, but she wishes that she could deeply believe in its principles for that could provide a lasting distraction from knowledge of the advancing evils of existence."

I have no time to untangle that idea, for Veronique is relaying the names of the other guests as she leads us across the long room. As her words are soft and quickly spoken, I can hardly retain the names, all of them unfamiliar. They are not all titled aristocrats; some people are "Madame" or "Monsieur". Veronique lets us know that among the company is "one fine poet and two natural philosophers".

Madame du Deffand sits in a large chair against a tapestry halfway down the room. She is listening intently, her veil gone but her eyes closed, to a woman sitting to her left. A small black spaniel sits at Madame du Deffand's feet. Veronique pauses before her, as if waiting for an opportune moment to announce us. The dog looks up at us, blinking with interest, but Madame du Deffand speaks to the other person, and Veronique continues down the room. She takes us to the only two empty chairs left. They are in a group of three at the far end, near a window. Captain Howard and I will be seated on either side of a man who looks about thirty years old, slim, with unpowdered dark blond hair. He looks at us more welcomingly than anyone else so far. With his smile, short nose and bright brown eyes, I am reminded of a friendly terrier.

"This is Giles Descoteaux, one of our natural philosophers," she says. "May I introduce Lady Howard and Captain Howard?"

"Ah, this is propitious. I am to enjoy conversation with the source of the excitement," our new companion says.

"Excitement?" repeats Captain Howard as he takes his seat.

Giles Descoteaux leans towards the captain and whispers, "Madame du Deffand dismissed her old serving man Francois for not passing on your card and letter of recommendation. He'd been with her for ten years."

"Madame had no choice, for I never received such papers," chimes Veronique.

"Of course you didn't," Giles Descoteaux says.

I understand why Veronique is pushing this so hard — worried for her position, she's emphasizing that she had nothing to do with hiding my card and Walpole's letter — but I wonder why this Giles Descoteaux is trying to help her. What is it to him?

The ferret-faced servant hands Captain Howard and me glasses of sherry.

This time, Descoteaux swivels to me to say softly, "The first glass of sherry is the best. After that, I think they open a worse vintage. May I offer you another piece of advice? Don't try to pet the dog should she wander this way. Tonton looks gentle, but she bites. Hard." I should laugh, but there's something about his whispered knowledge that is not to my taste.

Veronique says, "That dog … oh, that dog."

Madame du Deffand calls out, "Veronique! Who are you talking to? I insist you tell me."

"I'm talking to Monsieur Giles Descoteaux. I've brought Lady Howard and Captain Howard to sit with him."

"I'm so glad you are here, Lady Howard. Sir Horace Walpole's letter of introduction was found. I dismissed the incompetent servant who misplaced it. Sir Horace wrote to me that this is your first visit to France. I hope it's off to a pleasant start."

After I assure her that ours is a most enjoyable visit, Madame du Deffand says, her tone rapturous, "The letters I receive from Sir Horace have no model and cannot be imitated. They are the sublime of naturalness." As Strawberry Hill is the least natural house I've ever been to, I am surprised but also glad that Walpole can form such a friendship.

She continues, "I am perturbed by something, and I wanted to bring it up. Do you know that Sir Horace, not in the missing letter but another one, urged me to be discreet and cautious in all my letters to him? He says a very good friend of his, a man positioned to know, told him that the mail of important people is being opened in both countries and read by the authorities. In France, my letters could even be sent to Versailles for additional scrutiny. Have you acquaintanceship with a man Sir Horace may know who is an authority on the practices of spying? Should this advice be followed?"

How horrified Sir Humphrey Willoughby would be to know that his discreet counsel to Walpole is being repeated in a Parisian salon! I say, resisting the urge to look at Captain Howard, "I do not know who that could be. How … interesting. Caution does seem prudent in correspondence."

"I find the very thought of spying so sordid," says Madame du Deffand firmly. "What kind of person would do something like that?" Without waiting for an answer, she thankfully dives into another topic. The news from Versailles is that the dauphin, the grandson of Louis XV, will be betrothed to the youngest daughter of Maria Theresa of Austria.

Madame du Deffand says, "This daughter, Maria Antonia, is a controversial choice."

This is the only conversation in the room for a while. Everyone has an opinion on the Austrian archduchess whom the French chief minister promotes as wife to the dauphin. Everyone joins in except for Captain Howard and me. I can summon up no opinion and have little interest in Maria Antonia, a ten-year-old girl in Vienna, and whether she would make a good Queen of France. I am more concerned with how, in the absence of the viscount, we should learn anything of value in the salon.

"Lady Howard, I am sorry if this is uncomfortable for you," whispers Giles Descoteaux. I have noticed that all side conversations, if not part of the main topic, are whispered.

Dismayed that I am allowing my emotions to show on my face, I deny the topic displeases me.

"But didn't your husband die in Québec in the war? That's what Madame du Deffand said before you arrived. And now everyone is talking about the worth of Austria as an ally of France because of what happened in the last war, when our nations allied to fight England."

Descoteaux smiles, but I don't feel the warmth of sympathy. There is something else behind his wide brown eyes. I think he is trying to provoke a reaction from me, testing me for some purpose I've yet to identify. Any comparison to a friendly terrier has vanished.

"Political conversations do not trouble me," I say coolly, to put an end to the topic. I pointedly look to Madame du Deffand, who is still talking about the Austrian royal family.

"But do you miss him?" Descoteaux persists. "I'm speaking of your husband. I'm told that some women, when they become widows, welcome their freedom. Do you?"

Gazing past Giles Descoteaux, I see Captain Howard's legs tense. If there's one topic I fear he could not handle calmly, it's speculation over the death of his older brother. I say quickly, "Of course I miss my husband."

Descoteaux nods and thankfully returns to silence. Why did he ask such an appalling question? I know that "natural philosopher" can mean "chemist", and I've met certain of Thomas's friends who lack tact and knowledge of etiquette. Is this the reason for his behaviour?

Madame du Deffand calls out, "Lady Howard, is that your voice? I meant to ask you something. I am told you occupied the box of the Duc de Penthièvre at the performance of *Tartuffe*. What an honour! But how did it come about? Since his wife died, the duke does not see many people."

"It was a gift," I say and, seeing an opportunity, I add, "I believe it was the Vicomte de Breteuil who arranged it."

"The Vicomte de Breteuil?" Madame du Deffand begins to fan herself vigorously. "I would approach that association with caution, Lady Howard. But how could you know his reputation? You've just arrived. I have not invited him to my salon for at least a year. If the Vicomte de Breteuil's wife were not a dear friend, I would cut him completely."

So the viscount was not at the salon the same day as Sir Horace Walpole. Then who told him that Walpole announced he wanted an angel painted by Fragonard for his Gothic castle? He didn't deny he'd arranged the sale. I take out my own fan and use it, trying to hide at least part of my face. I don't want anyone to be able to read my reactions.

Madame du Deffand says, "Giles, didn't you say that the duke's son, the Prince of Lamballe, shall be coming to view your line of new pieces in a special show the day after tomorrow?"

"Yes, Madame," says the rather rude young man next to me. "He is coming with the Duc de Chartres."

Madame du Deffand says, "Ah, another man of no virtue. And he's such a strong influence on young Lamballe. The poor Duc de Penthièvre. What's to be done?"

The conversation jumps to the sorry morals of the young aristocrats of France. I don't follow a word, a suspicion having formed in my head.

I whisper, "New pieces, Monsieur Descoteaux? What did Madame du Deffand mean by that?"

He turns to regard me with those limpid eyes. "Pieces created at Sèvres Manufactory Works, Lady Howard. You've heard of it?"

Fanning harder, I nod.

"I have the honour of holding the position of chief chemist at Sèvres," he explains.

"But how can that be?" I say. "What about Jean Hellot?"

A second later, I realize my error. But it's too late to correct.

A slow smile spreads across his face. "You *have* deep knowledge of Sèvres if you know the name of the chief chemist. How remarkable that the status of the employees at our factory has reached a castle in the north of England."

I peer past Giles Descoteaux to Captain Howard. I can tell by how he's tilted his head that he's listening. But I don't know if the captain understood every word.

My heart hammering, I say, "I like porcelain very much, and it's a famous place. The colours Jean Hellot created are well known. Some say Sèvres is the finest maker of porcelain in all Europe."

"Oh, it is, Lady Howard. It is. Be assured. Jean Hellot was the chief chemist for twenty years. But he died five months ago after a long illness."

"I see." Ah, this explains so much!

Descoteaux leans even closer to me. "His was not a quiet death. The cause was apoplexy. First there were headaches, then loss of sight. He bled from his extremities. His body became paralyzed. At the end he could use only his sightless eyes to try to let the physicians know he was in agony. And they could do nothing for his pain, nothing at all."

I twist in my chair, recoiling from this description of Hellot's suffering, and drop my fan on the floor. Giles Descoteaux picks it up and places it gently in my lap.

"How I've distressed you," he says, his eyes no longer innocent. "Hearing of his demise most definitely upset you. Even more than discussion of losing a husband. One would think you had met Jean Hellot, that you knew each other. But of course, that's impossible. You were clear that you've never been to France before in your entire life."

I can feel perspiration trickling down my back in this warm, stuffy salon. Determined to throw this chemist off the track, I say, "I lost a loved one to apoplexy, Monsieur, so your description of Jean Hellot's suffering made me relive those sad days."

The gloating dims in his eyes. He must know that he went too far in what is supposed to be polite conversation and murmurs, "My apologies, Madame."

"I do accept, and, as you are aware of my avid interest in porcelain, I wonder if you would have time for a visit to Sèvres? I would love to see the factory."

He shakes his head. "I wish I could, but we no longer offer the tours of Sèvres for the public. That's impossible."

"Oh?" I am desperate to push my way inside the porcelain factory and a way to do so occurs to me, though I could alienate this chemist. Fortunately, his wishes and feelings don't matter to me a whit.

I turn in my chair to Madame du Deffand. "Did you say that two esteemed noblemen would be paying a visit to Sèvres the day after tomorrow, Madame?"

"Yes, Lady Howard. Why do you ask?"

"It would be a highlight of my visit to step inside Sèvres and see its talented craftsmen and chemists at work. Madame, will you help me persuade my esteemed seating neighbour, Monsieur Descoteaux, to allow Captain Howard and myself to visit? If the porcelain factory is open to these other esteemed visitors, could we come too — perhaps afterwards?"

Madame du Deffand says, "Why would he need persuading? Doesn't Sèvres have public hours, Giles?"

Descoteaux says, without looking at me, "Only rarely, but if you wish it, Madame, I can make an exception for our English visitors. The day after tomorrow it is."

Chapter Twenty-Four

"I'm a fool, a fool," I cry in anguish when Captain Howard and I are safe in our carriage. "I shouldn't have shown any reaction at all. I practically wept on his shoulder over Hellot's death."

"Descoteaux delighted in telling you the details of his illness, I heard that part," says Captain Howard, shaking his head.

"Have I ruined the mission?" I demand. "You said the most important thing was that I convince everyone I am Jane Howard. I told you and Sir Humphrey I couldn't convince anyone that I'm an English noblewoman! I bungled it with that horrible man."

Captain Howard doesn't answer for a moment to my mounting dismay. "No, it's not ruined," he finally says. "He may chalk it up to you being a female. Most men believe women to be inferior, weak and incapable of governing their emotions. He struck me as that sort. No one could attribute your irrational outburst today to you being Genevieve Planché, Sir Gabriel Courtenay's spy and Thomas Sturbridge's wife. It's too great a leap."

"How delightful — prejudice against my sex protects me."

"Just so," says Captain Howard. He points out that attending the salon served a useful purpose. No, we don't know who informed the viscount that Walpole was eager to buy a Fragonard. But we were able to force a promise of a tour from Giles Descoteaux. And we know

now that Jean Hellot died five months ago after a long incapacitating illness. With Hellot out of the picture, it would be easier for someone at Sèvres Porcelain to ferret out Thomas's formula and begin work on it. First Madame de Pompadour, then Hellot. The people who used to oversee Sèvres Manufactory Works are gone. This could present an opening to the unscrupulous.

I put the question to him that has been bubbling up in my thoughts ever since I met the chief chemist. "Do you think it is Giles Descoteaux who is responsible?"

Captain Howard doesn't answer. Instead, he turns it back on me. "You know some of the most brilliant chemists and physicists in England. Not only your husband but the others in the Lunar Society. Did he seem on par with them?"

"The way you phrase that question, I can tell that you think he doesn't. All I can say is chemists exhibit character that doesn't always seem as if it would be one drawn to science. Some are recluses and others are leaders of society. He didn't seem like a leading inventor but ..." I shrug.

"Well, we will be inside Sèvres the day after tomorrow to get a better sense," Captain Howard points out. We will attend a private showing of the Sèvres collection at three o'clock, following the appointment made for the Prince of Lamballe and Duke of Chartres.

"I look forward to it." But then I sigh. "If only the thought of seeing that man again didn't make my skin crawl."

"You'll feel differently after a night's sleep," says Captain Howard. "And we shall be kept busy the day before. You won't have time to fret."

"What are we doing tomorrow?"

"We go to the shop of Lionel Rolandeu on the rue Saint-Honoré."

This decision surprises me. "Ah, yes, you said you wanted to go. But something about this troubles me. You and Sir Humphrey are always saying not to tip your hand. But what reason do we have to visit Rolandeu's shop? It is supposed to be the last stop. Will we be asking him to buy something on our behalf?"

Captain Howard assures me he has an excuse all worked out that won't strike anyone as strange. While plunged into such discussion, we can find out more about who he does business with, finding the trail leading from the painting Walpole bought to those who tampered with it.

"Can't it wait until the day after we travel to Sèvres?"

Captain Howard bites his lip. "No. We should move quickly. Lionel Rolandeu must know something. The viscount and perhaps Giles Descoteaux may realize we are on their trail. I need to talk to him and get what I can before they reach him and tell him to keep his mouth shut."

Although Captain Howard encouraged me to get a good night's sleep, it's the opposite. Nightmares trouble me over and over. The description of Jean Hellot's agony was too searing. The kindly chief chemist was one of the few people who helped us while we were kept in France. My husband had looked up to Hellot while at Sèvres. Thomas was being groomed as Hellot's successor, before the decision was made to send me and Thomas back to England. Instead of Thomas Sturbridge, the position was eventually given to the disagreeable Giles Descoteaux.

The first thing I think after waking up is that I wish I could say something to the mistress of Louis XV. *"Madame de Pompadour, you wouldn't like the man creating colours at Sèvres Porcelain now."*

As unpleasant as I found him, would Giles Descoteaux be brash enough to defy the order of the absolute monarch of France? That I can't accept.

It's a cloudy, thick morning and hotter than any other since we arrived in Paris. It promises to be the kind of day when my dress sticks to my skin. Captain Howard perceives I am not well rested and offers to go alone to the shop on the rue Saint-Honoré.

"Absolutely not," I say.

I'm silent while Louise dresses me for going out and helps me with my wig. Was it less than a week ago that we arrived at these apartments and enjoyed a dinner of capons and wine? I had thought, in my ignorance, that as we obtained answers and advanced closer to the mystery's solution, that I would become elated. Instead, a feeling of nervous dread threatens to dominate.

"I wish we had time for another stop today — the Academy in the Louvre," says Captain Howard in the carriage. "I would like to see you show the same spark today as after you spent time with those paintings."

"There were drawings. Hmm. Does that mean you are in a mood to argue?"

He says, "If you would stamp your foot and tell me how wrong I am, then yes."

"Captain Howard, put your mind at rest. I won't fail you at the shop today."

He grimaces as his eyebrows shoot up, an expression I've never seen before on Captain Howard's face. "Mrs Sturbridge," he says, "you believe the only reason I could take an interest in your wellbeing is that I demand that you succeed as a spy?"

When he puts it like that, I realize I am being unfair. "No, goodness, no."

We ride in silence for a while. "Actually, Captain Howard, you could do something for me that would ease my mind."

"Name it."

"When you came back to the apartment after making the acquaintance of the Comte du Barry, you said we both have secrets. Since I'm at risk in this country, I'd like to know your secrets."

His mouth falls open. "Zounds, hasn't anyone told you that on a sober morning, you can't toss back at a man what he has said when he's drunk?"

"No, no one has ever told me that." I smile to lighten his embarrassment.

"Well, I am relieved to see your spirits revive, even if it's at my expense. The answer to your question is I am not keeping any secrets from you that pertain to our mission in France."

I know he has a real secret, but I won't press. *Not this morning anyway.*

Rue Saint-Honoré is very long. It is one of the main arteries of the city and used by wagons and carts bringing their wares to the markets and shops most mornings. For a while, when I look out the window, we are rumbling neck and neck with a heavy wagon stuffed with barrels of salted fish. Later I notice many signs advertising the establishments that make their living out of the French love of fashion: dressmakers, haberdashers, jewellers, tailors, watchmakers and milliners. Three streets show nothing but drapers' shops. They even have display windows boasting bolts of cloth of many colours.

As we alight from the carriage near our destination, just the two of us this time, a bit of rain spatters our faces. There are other people milling about, going in and out of shops, and some dart into doorways to keep from getting wet.

We move as quickly as we can to Lionel Rolandeu's shop. This street has other signs that look as if they belong to fellow *marchands merciers.* His is one of the smallest. And while the others boast large, attractive signs for their establishments, Lionel Rolandeu's sign is muted. Next to the door of Rolandeu's shop, a large card is posted: *Sells all sorts of trinkets, mirrors, pagodas, lacquer and specimens of natural history and tasteful paintings, vases and statues.*

I say quietly to Captain Howard, "The trinkets come first, and the paintings come near last? Why would the artwork of Jean-Honoré Fragonard ever be associated with this shop?"

We ring the bell hanging next to the door and wait for someone to let us into the shop. The rain still spatters, and we stand under the few inches of cloth awning that stretches above. After a minute passes, no one opens the door, so Captain Howard rings the bell again, harder.

Following a period of waiting that would allow anyone to wrap up an immediate task to open the door, I suggest, "Perhaps they have already reached him, and he is avoiding us by not opening his shop."

At that, Captain Howard tries the doorknob. To my surprise, it eases open. We step over the threshold to find an unoccupied shop with a clean, gleaming counter. Behind it rises shelves populated by green, red or grey pagoda statues — miniature temples of the East that seem to be in fashion now. Adorning a special cabinet are four vases with figures that look to be of ancient Greece. These are even more the rage: vases reflecting the new passion for excavation of sites in Italy and Greece. I've seen them in London too. Interest in classical vases began in France, and naturally the English leaped in to compete. Our kingdoms' fierce rivalry rages everywhere.

"Monsieur Rolandeu?" calls Captain Howard. Silence. We've come here for no purpose. The owner is not here. But then, why leave open the door to the street?

"Is this some sort of trap?" I whisper.

"I highly doubt it. We've made no inquiries about Rolandeu. None of our men have come by to ask questions. How would our enemies know we planned to come this morning?"

"But you were worried someone was going to try to shut up Rolandeu before he could talk to us," I point out. "That's why we are here."

Captain Howard tries the handle of a door in the corner leading to a private office. When that, too, opens, I shake my head, baffled.

Two steps in, I can tell from how his back quivers that now Captain Howard is the one who is surprised. I hurry to follow him in.

The first thing that strikes me is how different this chaotic space is from the neat shop in front. Papers are strewn everywhere: across the large desk, on the floor, hanging from a bookshelf. Ledgers are pulled out from their places. It could be the office of a man who does not value neatness.

I detect a heel mark ground into a paper lying on the floor. Has someone ripped through here?

Captain Howard kneels on the floor on the other side of the desk. For a second I wonder why he's picking up the mess. No, that is not a book or a mess of papers next to the captain. It's a man's shoe on a foot … attached to a man's stocking.

I jump back. A man is lying on the floor.

"What's wrong with him?" I whisper, though there's only us in the room. "Asleep? Ill?"

"He's dead. There's no pulse and his skin is cold. We are too late."

"Murdered?" My voice rises.

"No evidence of that."

I take a few steps closer, frightened but consumed with curiosity. This man is a stranger. It couldn't be worse than seeing Jemmy Maylie, who *was* murdered.

There is no blood. He hasn't been stabbed or shot. But it's still horrible. The man's eyes bulge. His face is suffused with a purple colour and a dark red tongue protrudes. I find one aspect particularly tragic: his balding head, the skin smudged and scabbed, is exposed to view, with his white wig lying at his feet. It must have been knocked off his head when he collapsed.

I kneel to pick up the wig, an expensive one originally, with three tight curls on each side but a bit dirty now. For some reason, I find that achingly sad. Turning it over, I see something loosely stitched into the back, a few words and a number scrawled on a narrow slip of paper. There's something about the writing … my pulse quickens.

I tear the paper from the back of the wig.

Hearing the noise, Captain Howard, who had been examining the man's face, says, "No! Don't touch anything."

I drop the wig where I found it but hang on to the slip of paper.

"We have to get back to the carriage as soon as possible," says Captain Howard.

"But should we not summon the authorities? We have an innocent reason for being here."

"There could be a coroner inquest, and we don't want to be mixed up in that," he says, seizing my arm and leading me out of the office.

We hurry through the front of the shop, still empty. But when Captain Howard puts his hand on the doorknob, he hesitates. Frown lines deepen across his forehead. He just said he wanted to flee this store as quickly as possible. Then why aren't we on the rue Saint-Honoré?

"If this *is* a trap, they could be waiting for us outside," he says softly. "Walk normally when we get onto the street, show no distress."

He takes a breath and pushes open the door.

Chapter Twenty-Five

My first thought is that the number of people on the rue Saint-Honoré has doubled in the few minutes we were inside the shop. Yet no one hovers right in front. People are everywhere — men, women and even children — and they all seem to have somewhere to go. It must be because the rain has ceased. They are caught up in the pleasure of buying goods at their favourite shops: a vase, a bolt of silk, a loaf of bread. No one knows that behind one of the doors is a dead man, his wig knocked off his head.

I hold out my arm, and Captain Howard takes it. We walk together, our steps steady, to the carriage down the street.

But after we are safely inside, Captain Howard tells Simon to wait. He positions himself at the window where he can best see Rolandeu's shop.

"What do you expect to see?" I ask. He points. "This." I sidle close to him. We both watch a group of men rush into Rolandeu's shop while the curious gather outside.

The captain signals to Simon for the carriage to leave.

"Where did they come from?" I ask, horrified. "If they'd come fifteen minutes earlier …"

Captain Howard says grimly, "Exactly."

"But you said you didn't think he was murdered. This could be in response to a worker finding him, perhaps just before we arrived, and it took a while to find the police. That's why the doors were left open."

"If this were England, I'd ask a physician to open the body and investigate," he says after a few minutes.

"Did you see signs of violence?"

"No. And Rolandeu was not young. It could have been a failure of his heart. It's just I've never seen a face that colour …"

I spend a moment trying to take all this in. "What about the state of his office? It was in such disorder. How could a *marchand mercier* do business like that?"

"Do you truly believe that was Rolandeu's doing?" Captain Howard asks.

"Ah, so you think it *was* foul play. Or perhaps someone else was there before us who, seeing him dead, searched his office. You were intent on speaking to Lionel Rolandeu before someone shut him up. Did we closely follow a visit from one of his compatriots in this plot?"

Captain Howard says thoughtfully, "And that compatriot was then good enough to leave the doors unlocked. The whole affair felt very strange."

"Strange indeed. I have something to show you."

I reach into the bodice of my dress and remove the piece of paper I discovered in the dead man's wig. I hold it out, and Captain Howard reads aloud:

"Blue Colour 17. The Versailles Formula."

He says sharply, "This is written in English. Perhaps *that* is why someone tore apart the office! But they missed it. What significance do these words hold? Is the Versailles Formula your husband's shade of blue?"

After a minute, I say, "Colours are always numbered, so that's not significant. Neither is Versailles being attached to a colour formula. Sèvres Manufactory Works is but five miles ride from Versailles Palace. Sèvres works with many shades of blue."

"Then why did you take this?"

"It's not the individual words — it's the script. It's familiar in how the 'B' forms in *blue* and the 'F' in *formula*. The tiny flourishes in ink at the top of those letters? They are distinctive. I've seen them before."

"Where?" demands Captain Howard, his dark eyes blazing in a white face.

"On the back of the false Fragonard when I took off its frame. The message was 'Do You Have a Blue Fear?' It was the same script for the 'B' and I recognize the 'F' because it is identical to the one in 'Fear'."

Captain Howard exults, "We've got them! If only we still had the painting itself. With the painting and this piece of paper, Sir Humphrey could intervene and try to stop them and no denial would be believed."

We are finding the connections between the people responsible, although not the origin of Thomas's formula. I ask, "Do you think Lionel Rolandeu wrote on the back of the painting? We know he shipped it to Sir Horace Walpole."

"Or it was another party, but Lionel knew all about it. And he knew it was forbidden. Why else hide the slip of paper? Genevieve, without you, this wouldn't be happening. You were able to get us into the salon of Madame du Deffand. You found the piece of paper and recognized the handwriting and put it all together. You see now why Sir Humphrey was adamant that you go on the mission?"

Captain Howard must be excited indeed to use my first name, something he has not done since the night he was inebriated. I wonder if I will ever say his first name. It seems most unlikely.

Peregrine.

But the new spirit of unity — our respect for each other's talents — comes close to dissolving that very night. Vincent draws Captain Howard aside on the third floor to show him the results of his own efforts, undertaken when he wasn't driving, guarding or cooking for us. He is an excellent investigator. Vincent is the one who learned that the brother and sister who guarded me while I was confined in France last time are employed in a chateau far from Paris. The last two nights, Vincent plunged into the heart of the city for another reason, sticking his head in taverns and coffee shops. He found material to bring back and share with Captain Howard. One thing I've found remarkable is that there are no newspapers printed in Paris. London is awash in them. But in Paris there is only the circular of official news from Versailles. *Everything* else is underground. No wonder Parisians are addicted to gossip.

"What are those booklets?" I ask, trying to see what's spread across the table. "Are they pamphlets? I saw these being passed around outside the Louvre and on the bridge as well with subterfuge."

"You don't want to see these, Madame," says Vincent.

"I don't?" I laugh. "Why not? Aren't they political? I'm accustomed to political satire."

Vincent still hesitates, but when I persist, Captain Howard says, "Suit yourself."

I pick up the first one. It's devoted to Louis XV and his daughter, Madame Adelaide. The first illustration shows them in a tight embrace and progresses quickly into lovemaking. I put it down after seeing the third page. It hardly seems necessary to continue.

The second pamphlet is devoted to Louis XV and his mistress, Madame de Pompadour, who is now dead. Their saga begins with the two of them, but after the French king fails in the bedroom, Madame de Pompadour procures him young girls while she watches through a keyhole or joins in.

"Well," I say, trying not to show my repulsion. "These artists are no Hogarth, in either artistic skill or satirical content. I suppose you collect them to try to assess the mood of the capital city towards the monarch?"

"It's interesting to see how far they travel and how fast," says Captain Howard.

"But how would you know that?"

"I saw the Pompadour one in April. They were printed in England. Not by Englishmen, let me assure you. Frenchmen opposed to their king are coming to London to set up small presses. Our laws on expressing political views are not as harsh as in France. If they're caught printing here, it's the Bastille."

I laugh with scorn. "Political views? These are nothing but obscenities."

Captain Howard shrugs, and in that scornful gesture, I see the side of him I despise.

"How would you like it if someone printed terrible things like this in France about George III?"

Vincent says, "But Madame, our king is an honourable man, a devout man, a good husband and father." As Vincent is the only man in our party who speaks of a wife, I know how much King George's values mean to him. That's why it's even more important to me to make him understand.

"King Louis isn't a good man — I'm not arguing that, Vincent. But this … ? These pamphlets are demented — grotesque. It's unfair for us to look the other way when filth is printed."

Captain Howard says, exasperated, "We don't enjoy looking at these pamphlets, and we despise the men who drew them and printed them. You can't demand fairness when two countries are locked in a struggle like ours with France. It shows naivete, Mrs Sturbridge."

"To try to have integrity is naive?" I shoot back.

"In dangerous circumstances such as these, *yes*." He loses his temper at last and slams his open hand on the wooden table. "The discussion is over!"

I retreat from the table. Louise and the others have gone dead silent, and none of them meet my eyes except for Henry, who, to my surprise, sends a tentative smile my way.

I find myself in the kitchen later while Vincent is chopping vegetables for meat pies. He beckons me to listen. "Captain Howard sometimes has a strict manner, Madame, but a great deal of that stems from his concern for you and his wish to protect you."

"I understand that. But Vincent, I'm not a fragile piece of porcelain." I pick up one of his knives and brandish it as he laughs. "You might be surprised to learn of my abilities."

"No doubt," he says. But his grin fades. "Sir Humphrey Willoughby made each of us take an oath to be personally responsible for your safety."

The sound of this makes me feel uncomfortable. "Anything in particular I should know about the oath?" I ask.

"'She is a mother. You must see her reunited with her son.'"

My emotions prevent me from speaking for a moment. Leave it to Sir Humphrey to force me to go to France on this mission but then make my safety everyone's most important responsibility. Hitting me harder is the guilty realization that I have been relishing the challenges of the mission and feeling my adventurous spirit and hunger to paint return and not thinking of Pierre for long stretches of time.

"I love my son very much," I say, struggling to keep my voice from breaking.

"I love my children too," says Vincent. When I look at him, surprised, he says, "I like to keep my family private."

"Then we must keep each other safe."

Whether this was Vincent's intent or not, I resolve to argue with Captain Howard as little as possible from now on. I might not always agree with him, but upsetting everyone and undermining him accomplishes nothing. And we seem to finally be gaining momentum. I have the slip of paper on the *Versailles Formula*. I do think it is possible that I will spot Thomas's formula at Sèvres and learn who is responsible.

We are polite to each other when we set out for Sèvres. The journey from Paris to the porcelain factory, near Versailles, takes several hours, so it is best there is no tension.

"Have you given more thought to Rolandeu's death?" I ask.

"Little else," he says. "It would be most helpful if I could coordinate with the Paris police, but that's impossible. His death could have absolutely nothing to do with the Versailles Formula. If he was part of that forgery ring, he was probably involved with other legally dubious activities."

Henry raps on the side of the carriage door. For some reason, he and Simon would like Captain Howard to ride atop with them.

For most of the rest of the journey I am alone, watching the crowded streets and closely built houses of Paris fall away. The road to Versailles takes one through the countryside; I remember that from eight years ago.

However, my thoughts do not stray to the past as much as to the future. If I see anything at Sèvres Porcelain suggesting that Thomas's blue is being produced, I believe we have succeeded in gaining the necessary information. We can prepare for the journey out of France and back to England. Sir Humphrey can meet with the French ambassador in England or some other officials, share these proofs and exert pressure to get the French to stop making the formula. By the time William Pitt becomes prime minister on 30 July, the crisis will be averted.

For the first time, I wonder if I should wait for Sir Humphrey to send a letter explaining the mission to Thomas before I return to Lichfield. With a pang, I remember how, when I fell in love with Thomas and I feared he was about to be told that I was a spy at Derby Porcelain, I ran to him, desperate to be the one to tell him myself. How things have changed. Now I feel nervous about how my husband will receive my return and hope that Sir Humphrey can prepare the way. It still stings that Thomas accused me of impulsive actions that plunge me into trouble. Nothing about my presence in France is the result of an impulse. But even if I were someone who acts quickly, isn't that what Captain Howard praises? Ah, such comparisons are unfair. A wife is different to a spying partner.

My brooding comes to a halt when Captain Howard rejoins me during one of the carriage's stops. I can tell something is wrong at once.

"Much as I hate to relay this intelligence to you, our carriage is being followed," he says, staring out the window. "Henry's sharp eyes saw another carriage trailing us on the outskirts of Paris. It's almost impossible to tell if you're being followed in the city. For all I know, they've had an eye on us for days. But on a road such as this …"

"The road between Paris and Versailles is frequently travelled! How do you know we have a pursuer?"

"We deviated from the main road a bit and did a few things that should have put him ahead of us. Instead, he keeps reappearing and stays a certain distance behind — just close enough to follow. He's well experienced at this sort of thing."

The menace I've felt in Paris has emerged from the shadows and come out into the light.

"Are these the people who forged the painting and sent it to France and followed that with murders in London?"

He grimaces. "I'd prefer that choice to the alternatives."

"*What*?"

"The French police. If Sartine's men enter the picture, we are in the kind of trouble it's hard to get out of. We have no sanction for any investigation. Our enemies who seek to exploit the formula have their suspicions of us to be sure. But they don't dare take action. If they have pursued inquiries in England, they will have learned by now that there *is* a Lady Jane Howard of Castle Stanham, and she has a brother-in-law, Captain Peregrine Howard, a veteran of the war fought in North America. We are not people to be interfered with. That's why Sir Humphrey was so set on you impersonating a real person and for me to come to France as myself. My service to Sir Humphrey is not public."

Is Captain Howard fooling himself? Didn't he go to Strawberry Hill openly as a friend and associate of Sir Humphrey Willoughby, the spymaster of England? Walpole at least knows of some sort of connection. In some ways, of the two of us, I am the one who is safer — as long as no one finds out I'm Genevieve Sturbridge.

"Why are the French police so hateful to you?" I ask. "At least we know they won't try to murder us!"

"I very much doubt that *anyone* would dare to harm us. Banish that thought. The truth is, relations between England and France are strained to say the least. We cannot embarrass the British government."

A thought occurs to me. "You said 'alternatives'. Could the British ambassador whom we met in the park — the Earl of Rochford — have ordered us followed because he thinks we are conspiring with 'Catholic troublemakers'?"

He meets my gaze unhappily. "Yes, that has occurred to me. Whigs like him think English Catholics are sympathetic to 'Bonnie Prince Charlie', even though we've always been loyal to the Hanoverian kings. It was a risk with this plan. If it comes to it, evading the suspicion of the French police or the British ambassador is our priority. It would be preferable to return to England empty-handed. I'm sorry."

I pat his arm. "Do not worry about me."

He laughs bitterly. "I *do* worry about you." He looks out the window again. "You must remember that Lady Howard adores porcelain and has followed its achievements from afar. You know a lot about porcelain because you've enjoyed looking at it and reading about it. That's how you knew about Jean Hellot. The fact you worked as a porcelain painter in Derby — it's paramount to hide that expertise."

"I will, I promise."

"I suppose it would be fitting that I, your doting brother-in-law, should know a little something about the magic of Sèvres," he says, with the sarcasm I've not heard lately. I welcome it, as a sign that Captain Howard is mastering his nerves over our being followed. "Tell me the basics."

"It's named after the small town of Sèvres, but the location was chosen for its proximity to Versailles," I explain. "Madame de Pompadour was behind it. She made all the decisions regarding the porcelain-making and wanted to be able to visit at any time. It was to please her that Louis bought Sèvres and made it a royal manufactory. The king's mistress was beautiful, but she also wanted everything around her to be beautiful, and she took that ambition as far as a person could. She sought to create exquisite perfection to entertain the king, and what better way to do that than with porcelain?"

Captain Howard's eyebrows go up. I sense scepticism. I think it possible that he has never spent time examining a piece of first-rate porcelain. He may have no idea of Thomas's difficulty in developing a pigment that would dazzle the eye when painted on porcelain. That I would like to remedy. I am proud of my husband, no matter what has taken place in our marriage. His brilliance, combined with his kindness and his passion for righting the wrongs committed against the common man, are the qualities that made me fall in love.

I explain, "At Sèvres, each piece is a marriage of creativity in the shape of the object and spectacular beauty in the colours. The colours must all be good."

"Isn't that obvious? If you expect someone to pay a fortune for a piece of fired clay, the colours would have to be good."

I shake my head. "You don't understand that the word has a special meaning in this circumstance. When you create a colour for pigment — to be used on canvas or clay — what you must try for is a 'good' colour."

"Ah, excellent," he says, smiling. "I'm grateful you are overcoming your aversion to discussing the topic."

"I have no such aversion, Captain."

"I'm not imagining it. You always pull back into yourself whenever your husband's colour is mentioned. The thoughts you reflect on during those moments do not appear to be pleasant. But please, I don't want to discourage you from educating me. Proceed."

I don't like his scrutiny. But I push my annoyance aside in the interest of the mission. I tell him, "There are three requirements a colour must meet before it can be deemed good. It must be attractive, it must be easy to produce and it must be permanent. In the first category, his blue succeeded beyond expectations. No one who has seen it denies that it is the most brilliant shade of blue ever seen. The problem is that it is not easy to produce — that is an understatement. Thomas was the one to discover a mineral below a mountain in Saxony that, when processed, can yield this shade. But only if someone combines it with other elements at certain temperature and in exactly measured amounts. The process is enormously complicated and delicate."

Captain Howard says, "This is why it's so unstable."

"Yes. And an unstable colour cannot be permanent. Although when he was kept at the Sèvres Manufactory and forced to work on his colour, Thomas did achieve stability, and when it was applied, it was permanent. At Sèvres, and I'm afraid at Sèvres only, his colour was consistently good."

Captain Howard, who seems to grasp the principles of science, asks, "The chief chemist, Giles Descoteaux, do you think he is capable of getting hold of the written formula for the blue and starting it up again to the needed requirements?"

"I can't tell."

Peering out the window, Captain Howard says, "What a shame it's raining again. I believe we are arriving. Isn't that Sèvres Manufactory behind the gate?"

I lean so far over to see it that my shoulder presses against Captain Howard's chest. At the sight of the elegant building, I gasp. I'd planned for this moment of return for days, for weeks, ordering myself to be calm, but a flood of difficult memories throws me into turmoil.

It resembles a manor house surrounded by stately trees, not a manufactory organized into work spaces for design, moulding, firing and, most relevant to us, painting. Years ago, after spies filtering through China managed to break the centuries-old codes of secrecy safeguarding how porcelain is made, the European nations leaped into rivalry to see who could produce the choicest luxury products themselves. France triumphed over the Germans and the English with Sèvres, the most exquisite porcelain of all.

Right now I am thinking of Sir Gabriel. After not seeing him for months, I was thrown together again with Sir Gabriel Courtenay on the one and only day I was brought to Sèvres. I was so afraid of him because he was the one behind ordering me confined in a nearby house, separated from Thomas but used as a point of pressure to ensure Thomas worked on his formula. Yet I learned just before we were brought inside Sèvres that it was Sir Gabriel who had also arranged for paints and canvas to be delivered to the house so I could continue to produce my own art during my captivity.

"Courage," Captain Howard says softly. "I'll be with you."

I move away from the captain in the carriage and sit straight. The last thing I would ever want is for Captain Howard to know that I am thinking of Sir Gabriel at this moment.

By the time the carriage draws up, I'm calm and controlled. As Captain Howard and I mount the steps leading to the front entrance, I ask, "Is our unknown friend still following?"

"Oh, yes. But don't turn around to look. We must go forward."

Inside the reception area of Sèvres, we give our names and are immediately directed to a room to the side. No one looks at all familiar, but that day I was brought here, I didn't speak to anyone at Sèvres except for Sir Gabriel Courtenay, Madame de Pompadour,

Jean Hellot, my husband Thomas and, finally, King Louis. Of that group, two are dead, one's whereabouts is unknown, my husband is in England and, even if the King of France were to materialize suddenly, I'm confident he would have no idea that Lady Jane Howard is really Genevieve Sturbridge.

The room to the side is the same viewing chamber I stood in before, where Louis XV beheld the collection of Thomas's work. It seems smaller today. Four pieces are mounted on a long table for display.

"Lady Howard, Captain Howard, welcome to Sèvres!"

My stomach turns over at the sight of Giles Descoteaux, walking up to the porcelain display and smiling widely. Even though he's at his place of business, the chief chemist is dressed much the same as at Madame du Deffand's salon. His blond hair is unpowdered; his clothes are simple. If he's gone into business with the viscount and others to produce Thomas's blue, he's not spending his money on clothes.

As he approaches, he holds up one hand and says, "I have a surprise. The Prince de Lamballe and the Duc de Chartres are still here. They wanted to meet you. They are being summoned now. They're taking refreshment."

We are to meet the two spoiled young noblemen Madame du Deffand spoke of in her salon? I assumed there would be no overlap. My nerves stretch tighter. But I make sure there's a smile on my face while Captain Howard murmurs that it is an honour to make their acquaintance and goes on to thank Descoteaux for making this porcelain viewing possible.

While Captain Howard is speaking, I take the opportunity to study the four pieces of porcelain, ranging in size from six inches to perhaps two feet high. They are painted with precision and delicacy in many shades — and none of them are Thomas's blue. I didn't seriously think that Descoteaux would be so brazen as to display porcelain painted with the forbidden shade, but still, I feel a thump of disappointment. I wonder if evidence exists in the laboratories or workshops upstairs.

There's a stirring at the door. The two men who saunter into the room, holding wine goblets, are so unlike other males that I feel as if I am meeting unicorns. Giles Descoteaux introduces them formally as Louis Alexandre de Bourbon, Prince de Lamballe, son of the Duc de Penthièvre, and his cousin, Louis Philippe Joseph d'Orléans, the Duc de Chartres. They are both tall, very young, wearing the most expensive coats and waistcoats. The Prince of Lamballe's ensemble is pearl grey with silver thread, and Chartres's is palest lavender. They both wear white silk stockings and jewelled shoes boasting two-inch-high heels. To finish, their heads are covered with outrageous wigs — they resemble sparkling white beehives — and they have beauty marks painted on their faces.

I make my most profound curtsey, and I must admit at that moment to gratitude that Captain Howard insisted I learn the different levels of curtseying in Twickenham.

"You sat in my family's box at the Comédie-Française," says the prince, who has a boy's voice. He cannot be more than sixteen. "I heard that everyone in the theatre was talking about you and couldn't understand who you were. What a supremely funny idea from the Vicomte de Breteuil!"

He laughs loudly and spills some of his wine onto the floor, dangerously close to the nearest piece of porcelain.

Giles Descoteaux, I note, does not flinch.

The Duke of Chartres is a cooler young man, or perhaps he just carries his wine better. He studies me and Captain Howard for a moment and then pronounces, "They must come to the ball."

"Yes, you're right — they must!" the prince says.

The duke says, "It will be in two days' time at Château de Sceaux, belonging to Lamballe's father. Everyone will be in costume. The theme is … the *clergy*. You must come as a nun, a priest, a monk, a friar, a bishop or …"

They both exchange a knowing smirk. "An abbé!" the Prince of Lamballe howls. "You could come as an abbé! Perhaps if enough people dress the part, the real one will make an appearance after all."

Chartres nudges him and says, "Shut up. We promised, remember?"

"Oh, yes. You're right."

To whom did they promise to keep the Abbé's presence a secret? I wonder.

Captain Howard says, "Your Grace, we appreciate the invitation, but I don't think it will be possible to attend. We don't have costumes with us and—"

The Duke of Chartres says, "Oh, costumes and masks will be supplied. Two will be sent to the Duke of Norfolk's apartments tomorrow. Isn't that where you're staying? We must have you. Whenever possible, we want to include our Catholic friends from England."

And with that, the two young men of royal blood drift out of Sèvres. I am filled with suspicion. A shared Catholic faith shouldn't be enough of a reason to invite strangers to their ball at such short notice.

Giles Descoteaux clears his throat and says, "I assume you'd like to see our latest pieces now, Lady Howard?"

Captain Howard and I move towards the table for closer inspection, and I force myself to pay close attention.

No matter whether they contain Thomas's blue or not, each of the four pieces is ravishing and yet fantastical, just as I remember. All of this elaborate artistry devoted to simple objects! It's like a laudanum-fuelled fantasy made reality. As Captain Howard mentioned, I am fully aware of what went into these creations: the passionate perfectionism, using skill acquired from years of training. But I shove all of that out of my mind. Lady Howard wouldn't know exactly what it takes to produce porcelain at this level.

The first piece is a large white soup tureen with a milkmaid and her flock painted on its side. "That's the colour Pompadour Pink found in the milkmaid's dress," Giles Descoteaux says. "It was invented here expressly for Madame de Pompadour. Pink was her favourite colour. Is it yours, Lady Howard?"

"No," I say. "But it's very beautiful. When I see this pink with my own eyes, it is richer than I'd expected. A little deeper."

"My favourite reaction! Depth of colour is what we're known for at Sèvres. Do you like the next pieces, Lady Howard? They are a matched set of covered vases."

Why does he keep addressing me alone? Descoteaux seems to take some delight in toying with me and has since we met at Madame du Deffand's.

I make a show of scrutinizing the two large vases with handles. No figures of ancient Greece here. They are decorated with vines and leaves and flowers and, in the centre, another human depiction, this time of modern young lovers intertwined. The dominant colour is deep blue, and it's nothing like Thomas's shade.

"Truly gorgeous," I say.

Giles Descoteaux says, "Yes, this pair is exceptional. And painted a shade of blue that Monsieur Hellot also created. He named it *Bleu Céleste*. One of his most celebrated — it's very hard to make. Let me guess what your favourite colour is, Lady Howard. It's blue, isn't it? I know I'm not wrong!"

I take my eyes off the vases and turn to look at Descoteaux. A bit of spite dances in his eyes. A smile hovers. I am nearly convinced he knows that we are here in search of Thomas's formula and he's letting me know that to draw me out. But I won't go silent out of fear. I'm here for a reason.

"Blue is a beautiful colour," I say. "I appreciate you showing me these and pointing out Monsieur Hellot's contributions. But what about you, Monsieur Descoteaux? May we see any of the colours you've invented?"

The insolence fades. "I'm working on a number of new shades, Lady Howard," he says, turning towards the last piece on the table, a jug. "I expect you will hear of them some day."

"I hope we do," I say politely.

Giles Descoteaux peers at me sideways. "You know that the sales we make at Sèvres benefit France? This manufactory belongs to King Louis."

"That's interesting," I say. I know this fact all too well — Louis made the manufactory a royal enterprise to please Madame de Pompadour — but would Lady Howard be aware? Doubtful.

"Our nation has many debts," says Descoteaux. "And France cannot tax its people as heavily as England does. We have no Parliament and many groups are exempt." His tone is bitter. But then he gazes past us at the porcelain pieces and says, fervently, "It is through advances in science and art that we may hope to fill our Treasury."

This is so close to what Sir Humphrey shared with me as his vision for England overcoming its debt! My heart pounds faster. I can't help glancing at Captain Howard to see if he understands the significance. This, here, is a motivation for the French to start production of a dazzling blue. Money for their kingdom. The captain looks at the porcelain with politeness, tinged with boredom. My heavens, he is *good* at this. What a skilful intelligencer.

When Giles Descoteaux finishes his comments, Captain Howard says, "We very much appreciate seeing these pieces, Monsieur. And now we may see a little more of the manufactory? A short tour?"

"No," Descoteaux says sharply. "We cannot give any tours today. I'm sorry. I thought you understood that this would be a private showing only. The artists and other workers have complained about people watching them at work. That's why I made this change. I can't have them slow down with so many orders."

Captain Howard looks dismayed, an emotion I know is anything but feigned.

"Oh, that's a shame — we came so far today, Monsieur," I say, jumping in. "Can't we see anything else of Sèvres?"

"No, Lady Howard, it is not convenient. Not today."

We have no choice but to leave. Descoteaux smiles again, as if he knows he has thwarted our plans. I realize that even if he escorted us through every room, the chances of my seeing Thomas's blue are very, very small. Still, after this afternoon, I do know one thing: Descoteaux is involved. I just don't know how to obtain physical proof that we can show Sir Humphrey.

"Well, we wouldn't want to affect your business, Monsieur," I say. "We shall say goodbye."

"You will see me again, Lady Howard. Count on it. I'm also invited to the Prince de Lamballe's ball. I'm so looking forward to it. I understand they have certain surprises planned. It should be unforgettable."

273

Chapter Twenty-Six

"I don't see the need for a ball," I announce as our carriage rumbles back to Paris. "When the servants of the Prince of Lamballe bring these costumes and masks, I think we should refuse them and send regrets. The way he promised to see us again at the ball was nothing short of menacing."

Captain Howard smiles. "After you baited Giles Descoteaux, you're not going to the ball to enjoy another go at him?"

"I didn't bait him. I was simply trying to come up with something to say. Is it wrong of me to ask to see what the chief chemist has created?"

Captain Howard scoffs at my protestation of innocence.

"You were needling him, and he didn't like it. It was very well done! I had to fight to conceal my pride in you."

The captain grins at me with a wink — a *wink*! — before turning to his analysis of these developments.

"I do think he knows about the Versailles Formula. You heard him on the importance of science and art for the royal treasury. Whether he's turning a blind eye to the formula being produced or he's behind it himself, he's doing it to help his king and country."

"That is precisely what I think," I say. "I'm not sure what Giles Descoteaux is guilty of, but he's not innocent in this affair."

"I know you find the man disagreeable, but I think we should bear down harder. He's a weak link. Louis may relish the money that Sèvres porcelain brings in — and it would bring in even more if the most beautiful colour blue the world has ever known were used — but I don't believe the King of France is ready to break a treaty with England over this."

"If Giles Descoteaux seeks honour in what he's doing, I think it would make him *more* formidable, not less," I say.

"But he can't fall back on aristocratic connections. As the chief chemist at Sèvres Manufactory, he has a lot to lose if this goes wrong. I don't think our mission is at an end. We may be able to get him to admit what he's doing at the ball. Let's see what happens when you next cross swords."

Captain Howard has great faith in my ability to extricate admissions out of Giles Descoteaux. Once my severest critic, now he is a staunch believer. There's a part of me that takes pride in having gained his confidence. But I wonder if Captain Howard underestimates Descoteaux because he is a chemist without "connections". If Giles were a viscount or an officer in the French army, would Howard relish future encounters?

"I'm not fond of the sound of Descoteaux's 'surprises'," I say. "Are you?"

"Knowing this is a ball put on by the Prince of Lamballe and Duke of Chartres, the surprise is likely a room set aside for … certain entanglements."

"What sort?"

"Oh, please, Madame, you know what I am referring to," he mutters, looking away.

"Captain, I do not."

"Very well. There is likely to be a room set aside for orgies. Dressed as monastics, the guests will experience a more intense thrill. At all the British officers' gambling tables, they talk about the notorious orgies of Paris, preferably with nuns and monks involved, costumed or otherwise. We've got nothing in England that compares, not even the Hellfire Club."

"Surely those effete young men we met are not capable of that kind of depravity," I say, shocked.

Captain Howard laughs a little. "I heard about the Duke of Chartres at Comte du Barry's casino. He has a string of mistresses already and a taste for just such activities. Don't worry — only willing participants are involved. You and I won't have anything to do with *that*."

I find I can't even look at Captain Howard now. I stare at the passing villages out the carriage window trying to think of a subject to bring up — anything. After a moment, he says, "I apologize. I must say I find it hard to predict when something will embarrass you and when you will chastise me for trying to shield you."

That assessment provokes a smile. "Huguenots are raised a certain way, so acting jaded in this realm can be a challenge. But you're right, I can't ask for shielding when we're here on an important mission. I do want to be honest — I have a bad feeling about this ball that I never had about the Comédie-Française or Madame du Deffand's salon. Many people will be there, none of them our friends, some who may wish us ill. And they will be masked so we won't know who we are dealing with."

Captain Howard says, "But you must see that we need to exploit all opportunities. We have not obtained proof of anything, and that's what we need to take back to England. Proof. We don't know who told the viscount that Walpole wanted a Fragonard. And we don't know for sure who is recreating the blue. If I could have turned that office upside down on the rue Saint-Honoré, I might have found evidence. But who knows what the French police would do if they found me tearing apart an office with a corpse in it? We are not going to be invited inside Sèvres Manufactory again either. Giles Descoteaux made that clear. I think our only course of action is to attend this ball to see if we can establish any more information."

"What do we need in hand to complete the mission, Captain? I know you wanted me to see the blue porcelain and hopefully bring a sample back to England along with a report. We don't have it, but we do have the 'Versailles Formula' piece of paper from the office of the man who arranged the sale to Sir Horace Walpole. The viscount admitted that he arranged the painting's sale. And we know that Jean Hellot is no longer at Sèvres. We can relay the information on the new chief chemist as well as his suspicious behaviour."

But Captain Howard is dubious that we have met the needed expectations of proof.

"If we can get the identity of the forger and establish his involvement, then we have enough proof," Howard says. "The prince suggested the Abbé would be there."

"We've both heard that the Abbé is rarely seen by anyone. And yet he plans to appear at a ball?"

"We'll all be masked. When you think about it, this is the ideal social setting for the master forger."

I've met my match in stubbornness in Captain Howard. Not even our being followed all the way to the Faubourg — that small carriage stays with us, always far back on the road but never disappearing — can dampen his enthusiasm.

I find no allies among the rest of our group. They agree with Captain Howard that the ball represents a golden opportunity.

No one agrees with me that it is too dangerous, not any of the men or Louise. They perceive my reluctance, and each tries to reassure me in their own fashion. Henry promises to stay inches from me the entire night. Simon says that he and Vincent will remain with the carriage but will be well armed with swords, daggers and pistols.

"The sooner we can obtain the proof required, the sooner we can return to our families," Vincent points out.

Louise will not come to the ball, even though the presence of a lady in attendance would raise no eyebrows. She has a task to perform. We intend to report in person, but we can only move so fast when trying to race from Paris to London. Sir Humphrey had said that as soon as we have something to report to send a letter ahead. While the rest of us are at the Château de Sceaux, she will ready the secret messages for Sir Humphrey, using her skills. Both Captain Howard and I will first write letters home — as mine is from Jane Howard, it will be to my oldest child — in our own hands. Then Louise will write in invisible ink in the spaces between sentences. When we return from the ball, there may be more for her to write — clearly, Captain Howard hopes so. As soon as she's finished, Simon will take a single horse and ride to a place north of Paris where we've arranged for mail to be sent.

"Madame, thanks to your perseverance, we have news to convey to Sir Humphrey," she tells me quietly. "This French ball does sound distasteful to a proper Protestant wife and mother, but there's no help for it. We must swim in filthy water when we undertake this work."

Distasteful is not the word I would choose. It isn't prudishness that prompts my aversion or a disdain for Catholic costumes. I know all about the degeneracy of French aristocrats. Captain Howard tells me of gossip picked up by Vincent that the Duke of Chartres is actually trying to ruin the Prince of Lamballe's health because the younger man is heir to France's largest fortune. Were Lamballe to die young, the money would go to his sister, a young woman Chartres is angling to marry. But are the English much better? We've also heard that there's an addition to the Earl of Rochford's French household: his illegitimate daughter newly arrived from England. As the childless Countess of Rochford is famous for her many lovers, she's agreed to help raise the girl, as long as she could continue to amuse herself elsewhere.

I am proud to say this is not my world, but I am here to perform a task and must mingle with the debauched nobility. In fact, when the costumes and masks are delivered, I must acknowledge the workmanship. My costume is a long white habit with a black cape; it comes with a tight white cap and a black veil attached. Captain Howard will also wear a long white habit and black cape.

"We are meant to look like a nun and friar of the Dominican Order," Captain Howard says. "I must say I have less of a problem with our costumes than with these masks."

"Oh, really? I think they're quite impressive." The masks stretch from the middle of the forehead to just below the nose. They are black with gold letters and gold ribbons attached to tie them on. "They're Venetian in design. Mine is a Colombina — you see the embedded gems? — and yours is a Columbine."

Now it is Captain Howard who for the first time shows apprehension. "It doesn't matter to me where they were made — I don't like how much of the face they reveal. And you won't be able to wear your wig."

"I'll keep the cap and veil on every minute," I say dreamily, running my fingers along the mask's edge. "No one will know me."

I hear an exasperated groan and look up to see Captain Howard waving his arms as if he wants to give up. "You suddenly lost your terror of this ball because you'll don a Venetian mask?"

After a moment, I say, "I will be honest with you. Venice is the one place in Europe where a woman could receive some formal artistic training and exhibit paintings without having to pretend they come from a man's brush. In France, no woman can be admitted to their Academy. It's impossible to receive serious training in England. When Sir Gabriel Courtenay recruited me to take the position of porcelain painter in Derby to spy, the payment was money to go to Venice so that I could set myself up there. I can't believe that we would be in danger wearing something from the city that champions artistic freedom."

I wait for the questions and the condemnation, but if I've surprised Captain Howard of late, he surprises me by saying nothing. He seems to accept what I've told him.

Putting on a nun's habit is strange, so loose and floating. I wish I could wear something beneath it and on top of my chemise, but Louise says it would look ridiculous. "Besides, you'd expire from the heat," she points out. We plait and bind my hair as tight as possible so that it's invisible under the cap and veil.

However, just before we leave, we receive a jolt that revives my apprehension about the ball and much more besides. Vincent brings in the underground news pamphlets, and they mention a coroner's inquiry into the suspicious death of Lionel Rolandeu.

Wearing my white habit, I'm careful with handling the pamphlets to avoid being smudged with print. But handle them I do, since I read French the quickest of us all. One pamphlet, which indulges in more speculation than the others, makes me drop the sheet on the table as if it bit me.

"*Nous soupçonnons un* poison," I whisper. "Suspicion of poison."

If this is true, we are bound for a masked ball in the company of at least one person who knows how to administer sophisticated poison and evade the French police. A thick silence stretches for at least a minute in the drawing room of the Duke of Norfolk. Henry breaks it by saying, "The ball might be unsafe for you."

"We are still going," Captain Howard explodes. "Of course it's unsafe, every place we go to in France is unsafe for English people to some degree. But by God, any Frenchman who dares to lay a finger on Genevieve Sturbridge will wish he'd never been born. I will *not* allow it!"

His vehemence takes me aback. He speaks only of my safety — why not his own? Out of the corner of my eye, I spot Louise and Vincent exchange a look heavy with meaning. What conversations have they been having? But no one says a word. We make final preparations for the carriage ride to Château de Sceaux in tense silence. It feels wrong to leave Louise all alone for the evening, but she points out that her work will benefit from solitary concentration, and she'll keep the doors locked and bolted.

Vincent urges us to eat before we leave because, at most balls, supper is served an hour or more past midnight. All I can manage is an apple and a slice of bread, but at least it's something.

I am alone inside the carriage for the first half hour or so, various frightening scenarios jostling in my thoughts. Château de Sceaux isn't as far from Paris as Versailles, but it will take at least an hour to reach. Captain Howard, Vincent, Simon and Henry crowd up top or ride on the sides to better assess whether anyone is following.

When the carriage stops, and Captain Howard joins me inside, his eyes are burning with frustration. Asking if our shadow is still present isn't necessary. Everywhere we go now, someone trails us.

My nerves are so taut I feel as if I will snap inside this carriage, on the move again. But fretting or falling into hysteria won't solve anything. Perhaps a joke will help.

"I think if we only drink wine from a new bottle, we should be fine," I say. "And no bonbons, needless to say."

He stares at me for a long unblinking moment, some emotion churning within him.

"I have something I must tell you," he says. "I am determined to protect you no matter what, but if you must take charge of this mission because of what befalls me—"

At last he shares my dread of the chateau, but we are moments away. I jump from my side of the carriage to his and grab him by the shoulders. "Stop this — stop it at once. Nothing can happen to you. *Nothing*. You won't allow it for me, I won't allow it for you. And I'm not one to be crossed."

He flashes a smile. "I know you're not." He pulls my hands from his shoulders, but instead of letting go, he squeezes them. Once again, my pulse quickens. I should pull away. I do not. Curiosity burns as I feel these strong calloused fingers ...

"Genevieve," Captain Howard says, his voice thick.

The carriage jerks to a halt. Henry raps on the door, and Captain Howard and I leap apart. Whatever he was about to say, he's changed his mind.

I've seen Kensington Place and Hampton Court. I've seen the Palace of Versailles. But if pressed to select the most dazzling residence I've ever beheld in my life, I'd have to pick Château de Sceaux. Built of brick and stone, with many, many windows, it is surrounded by vast gardens: hedges, statues and reflecting pools.

Our carriage joins a line of others rumbling up the dusty road to the chateau. An orange sun trembles on the horizon, casting a shimmer of light that reflects in at least a dozen windows. When our carriage reaches the curved drive that's in front, violin music pours out of the ground-floor windows thrown open to the warm night.

"Sixty rooms inside, I'm told," says Captain Howard. "We should keep to the main ones."

Anger flares as I take in the full magnificence of the chateau. Why should royal blood entitle anyone to live like this — and the spawn of royal playtime at that, for the Prince of Lamballe is descended from Louis XIV and not his queen but his mistress, Madame de Montespan.

Everywhere I see servants scrambling to make this ball a success, in the garden, on the drive, bursting out the front doors. "The comfort of the rich depends upon an endless supply of the poor," I say, quoting Voltaire. Captain Howard frowns, not following my point. At that moment, I think of my husband, how we read Voltaire and Rousseau to each other and burn with the same passion for justice for all people, as elusive as that is. There's so much I want to tell Thomas that only he understands. I miss him with an ache.

Simon leads the carriage to a bank of elms, and Captain Howard, Henry and I step out.

"Goodbye, Lady Howard," says Vincent, sitting beside Simon. When I nod to him, he sticks his hand meaningfully in his front coat.

"I'm grateful he brought his pistol, and I'm glad that Vincent is a champion shot, but I pray that there's no cause for it tonight," I say.

"As do I," says Captain Howard quietly. He extends his arm, and I take it. The laughter and music grow louder as we approach the front entrance. It seems like a night shaped for frivolity.

Yet I cannot help but wonder: *Is there a murderer inside?*

Chapter Twenty-Seven

My fears prove justified in the first minutes. Two masked men dressed as priests refuse to permit Henry to enter because he has no costume. The black-and-red livery of the Howards is not a religious order.

"You're telling me no guests have brought menservants to this ball?" demands Captain Howard.

"None without costumes," says the taller priest. "It is a strict rule for the Prince de Lamballe's affair."

Since we can't insist Henry comes without creating an uproar, Captain Howard reluctantly sends him back to the carriage. Henry looks at me before turning and walking into the purplish dusk and towards the line of waiting carriages.

"Henry had a long dagger in his jacket," I say a moment later, when we are out of earshot of other guests. "Are you bearing arms in your monk's habit?"

"I was able to squirrel away a hunting knife," says Captain Howard. "But I hope my physical activity tonight is dancing rather than fighting. Are you game?"

"Only if I absolutely must," I say. "I'm not the best dancer. I didn't have many lessons when I was young."

"Really?" He laughs. "My lessons, as I recall, were unending. Not yours?"

My voice just above a whisper, I say, "You keep forgetting I'm a Huguenot. I heard so many sermons raging about this. John Calvin himself preached that dancing is vile. He said it could only be a prelude to fornication."

"You don't say."

Blushing beneath my mask, I say, rapidly, "I do know an English country dance or two."

"I'm unlikely to have a chance to see you do that. We should at least have practised a minuet. Everyone can dance one."

"A minuet? Oh, yes, I can manage. In Lichfield, the dances we attended had minuets, and I picked up the steps."

Saying "Lichfield" drives home even harder that I am a married woman, one who realized outside that I miss my husband. This banter is wrong, and holding hands in the carriage was wrong. I am not going to reject Captain Howard, or chastise him in any way, but this must be dealt with later. Much later. For now, we need to preserve our lives in this chateau and try to get information if at all possible.

Braced for what is to come, Captain Howard and I step into the ballroom — or what was likely an expansive drawing room now cleared of furniture. It must be one of the largest rooms I've ever seen, spanning more than sixty feet and illuminated by dozens of candelabras. The walls are adorned with intricate moulding in the shapes of shells, while the polished marble floor gleams under the flickering light. On the wall opposite the tall windows, which have been thrown open to the warm night air, a mural catches my eye. From my knowledge of Greek mythology, I recognize it as the tale of *Leda and the Swan.* The sight of all these costumed priests, monks, bishops, friars and nuns cavorting across the floor is quite bizarre. There must be close to a hundred people dancing while the orchestra plays. Most of the costumes are brown, black or grey, with a splash of red or purple worn by a handful of the men.

After a pause, the orchestra starts a new song. Couples form new groups, and a complicated dance begins. As they join the others, I hear a couple delight in the "quadrille", but when I look at Captain Howard, he shrugs. This French dance is new to him too.

After observing the entire dance discreetly, we pass through side rooms where others talk and sip wine. Gradually, it becomes clear that even though they are masked and costumed, most of the guests seem acquainted with one another. How are they able to identify each other? Did they all say what they'd be wearing before the ball? Or do they whisper their real names in each other's ears, and I never see it?

No one whispers in our ears or is so forthright as to ask who we are. We are very much outsiders. Yet I feel eyes examine me through holes in these Venetian masks. I do not know if we walk past Giles Descoteaux or Vicomte de Breteuil. After about an hour, we recognize the Prince of Lamballe by his laugh. Dressed as a Benedictine monk — or so Captain Howard identifies his order — the prince runs past us laughing, chased by a nun. It's by his drunken laugh I know him. He is so very young, it's unfathomable that such vast riches will be his someday. Something tells me that, should he survive his wasted youth, the Prince of Lamballe won't spend his fortune wisely. To concentrate such wealth on shallow and silly aristocrats feels more than wrong. It's cruel to those who labour hard for next to nothing.

I notice that one of the costumes worn by several male guests is different from the rest. It's less religious in its outline: a long black jacket and waistcoat and black stockings, with the only lightness a bunch of white lace at the throat. The hat distinguishes this costume: short and wide with an enormous brim.

"That's the dress of an Abbé," Captain Howard confirms, for I'd already suspected as much.

"What does an abbé *do*?" I ask.

"I'm not exactly sure," Captain Howard admits. "I think some abbés are scholars at the monasteries. A high-level clerk or a low-level diplomat. It's ambiguous."

"And do you think one of these abbés is our master forger, his business stretching from Geneva to Paris?" I whisper, remembering what I heard from my Italian friend at Hampton Court.

"It would be the finest achievement of our mission if we could identify him."

Whenever one of the abbés passes close by, I study him. One abbé is stout, another is tall and elegant. A third is an enthusiastic dancer. None of them strike me as an obvious candidate for master forger.

As the night advances, I begin to feel more and more foolish. We were invited at the whim of a boyish prince. The ball is no trap. My fears seem unwarranted. But while it's a relief to be safe from harm, it will be unfortunate if this ball proves to be a waste of time. I can't even work out who Giles Descoteaux is, the one person I'm sure is coming besides our host. Perhaps he can't tell who I am either.

Captain Howard is the one to point out something I find ominous. While he has seen two other Dominican friars at the ball, I'm the only Dominican nun.

"Do you think there's a purpose to that?" I ask.

"Probably not," he says, but he moves even closer to me. "Perhaps we should dance. The orchestra played a minuet before. We may get another. We must do something while we wait for supper. I hope we'll work out who some of these people are when we sit down to eat."

I smile in agreement. But no matter how he tries to reassure me, the truth is that, to those who organized my costume, I am easily identified as Lady Howard because I am the only Dominican nun here. And since I am unable to wear a wig, this is the closest I have come to my real appearance while in public since we touched French soil.

The orchestra plays a minuet, and Captain Howard and I join the others on the ballroom floor. We blend in, but it's not my doing. Captain Howard moves in perfect time with the orchestra, and every step is fluid and well measured.

"You are an excellent dancer, brother-in-law," I say when the orchestra finishes the piece. "I only had to follow you."

"Am I?" he responds. "Well, I am doubly grateful to hear it. You *are* sparing in your praise, you know."

"Is that so?" asks a man. "How sad. Praise can be so pleasant, I always say."

Captain Howard and I turn as one towards the person addressing us. My heart leaps. It's an abbé, the tall one.

"Would it be possible for me to claim the next dance?" he asks me, extending a courteous bow of the head to Captain Howard. There is a slight accent to his French. Is that Swiss?

"Yes," I say and hold out my hand. "I would enjoy that."

Shooting me an approving glance, Captain Howard steps out of the way.

My partner's touch is light and cool. When the candelabra light reflects on his clothing, I realize that the abbé is not dressed in black but in the deepest violet. We exchange bland pleasantries as we find a place on the floor.

For the first minute, I could not speak to him again, as the dance would not allow it. His movements are more languid than Captain Howard's, but he, too, is a fine dancer.

"You are a visitor to Paris, Madame?" he asks when the opportunity presents.

I decide to toy with my dance partner, as various men have toyed with me since I came to France.

"Do I seem so provincial?" I say. "Perhaps I have lived here all my life, Monsieur l'abbé."

We part with the music, and when next drawn together, he says, "Not provincial. But I think you come from another country due to your French, though it's very good."

It's time to release his cool hand, but when we can next converse, I say, "I think you, too, come from another country, Monsieur l'abbé. Shall we exchange guesses?"

Although his mask covers his face, unlike mine, I detect a smile as he says, "If it amuses you, Madame. I am at your service."

I admit to enjoying this repartee. But at the same time, suspicion stirs. There's something about his voice. Not the accent. Something else. Is this man a touch familiar? Could it be the Vicomte de Breteuil behind the mask, putting on an accent to throw me off? The height seems about right. This man's eyes are brown. Were the viscount's? I'm disappointed I won't be able to converse with the mysterious forger. Still, to talk to the viscount could bring some result.

When next we come together, the abbé says, "I would wager that you are English, Madame."

That settles it. This *must* be Breteuil. The music parts us, giving me enough time for my response, which is: "That's an unfair wager, don't you think? One unworthy of an abbé."

Instead of looking offended, his brown eyes spark with amusement. I feel another tremble of familiarity.

"Why?" he asks.

I answer, "You know who I am. But it is a night for games, is it not? I believe I know who you are. I confess I find this subterfuge a bore."

The music ends, and he says, "I think you are mistaken, Madame, on knowing my true identity. I wish to converse with you and explain myself. Shall we find another room?"

My pulse quickens with alarm. I have no intention of being alone with the abbé. I glance around, but Captain Howard is not visible now.

"Yes, let us converse, but we shall do it in the ballroom — the far corner by the window will serve," I say firmly.

"You wish to stay within sight of your escort? That's no doubt prudent. He has been watching us every single minute. He seems highly protective."

"As would befit a brother-in-law," I say coldly.

A dry chuckle emanates from behind the mask. "If you say so."

What is he suggesting about my connection with Captain Howard? There is no possibility that we have revealed anything at this ball. I do have feelings for the captain, feelings I am desperately trying to extinguish. I fear that something about the way I speak to him or dance with him is giving me away. But a stranger wouldn't know how to read my innermost feelings in public, especially not while I am masked.

I refuse to be rattled, particularly by a man who could be trying to trick me into a weak moment and do me harm.

By this time, we've reached the corner. Our steady progress is drawing attention from the people still dancing. Masks keep turning in our direction. Why? Is it interest in me or in the abbé?

With a shudder, I wonder if every single person in the room is conspiring against me and Captain Howard, but I shake it off. These fancies do harm by frightening me when I need to be strong.

The abbé touches my elbow to position me so that my back is to the dancers. The touch, the way he steers me, feels even more familiar. But Vicomte de Breteuil has never put a hand on me.

"Do I know you, sir?" I ask, becoming frightened.

The abbé stares at me for what must be a full minute before saying, "He should not have sent you. You're a brilliant choice for the mission, but haven't you realized yet how dangerous your situation is? I am not in control of all parties. I cannot protect you, as much as I would want to."

A cold wave of horror crashes through me as realization forms. I know the voice. I know who speaks to me.

The man in the abbé costume is Sir Gabriel Courtenay.

"My God," I whisper. "My God, it's you. It can't be. It can't."

"Compose yourself. Keep your voice low. They can't know what you know, do you understand me? And they absolutely can't learn your real name. Summon your captain and leave the chateau. Immediately. Your lives are at risk."

Chapter Twenty-Eight

I must find Captain Howard. I make my way past the dancers swaying and whirling, trying to prevent panic from taking over.

Sir Gabriel Courtenay is here. Sir Gabriel Courtenay may be the Abbé that is the mastermind of an art forgery ring. And Sir Gabriel Courtenay could be the one who's responsible for the colour blue being painted in the false Fragonard.

"Your lives are at risk."

I find Captain Howard and, even with his mask on, I can see he is alarmed. "What's wrong?" he asks.

"It was him," I whisper.

"Which one was it? My God, what did he say? Are you hurt in any way?"

"Don't ask me who it is now, but we need to leave the ball," I stammer. "I'll explain outside."

"Why?"

"Peregrine, it's our lives," I say. "*Please.*"

He takes my arm, and we are out of the ballroom, walking quickly down the main marble floor corridor in the direction of the front entrance.

A man says, "Oh, but you can't leave. It's much too early."

The Franciscan friar who looms in front of us is the real Vicomte de Breteuil. He lifts his mask to reveal himself.

"Lady Howard is unwell," says Captain Howard. "She needs to take the air."

"Oh, yes? Don't you think she would benefit from a rest upstairs? I know the perfect room."

"I appreciate the offer, but we're leaving."

The viscount does not move.

This is it — the moment they reveal themselves. Every moment of suspicion, every shiver of dread, was justified. Moving as one, Captain Howard and I try to rush past him, but three other masked friars appear, forming a barricade between us and the door.

"If you keep quiet, no harm will befall you," says Vicomte de Breteuil. "Don't think that creating an uproar will help you here. There are many in this chateau who harbour hatred of British officers."

"If you harm her, I swear to God, I will kill you," says Captain Howard.

"Who would dream of harming Lady Howard? I may not be one of your famous English gentlemen, but I have no intention of hurting a pretty widow."

Hands clamp my arms, and I am whisked off my feet as the men force us off the corridor, up two flights of stairs and down another, narrower passageway.

My panicked thoughts turn to Strawberry Hill, where an old castle and dark passageways were a fond tribute to shadowy scares concocted by Sir Horace Walpole. Here it's something else indeed.

"This will create an incident that will reach the ears of your king, I promise you," Captain Howard says in fury. "We are Howards. Do you know what that means?"

"I am confident that neither King Louis nor anyone else will hear a word of what happens to any Howards tonight," says the viscount, and he nods at his men. A door opens, and they push me inside. In the room, bright with candlelight, I make out a group of people sitting on couches and chairs. The door behind me slams.

A man curses on the other side of the door. Whipping around, I see Captain Howard is no longer with me. By the crashing sounds that follow, I can tell they're dragging him away. Henry and Simon are outside the chateau, without any idea of what's going on.

I am alone.

"Yes, we thought it would be interesting to separate you," says the Vicomte de Breteuil. "Our original plan was to concentrate on Captain Howard, but after your impassioned conversation with our abbé, this seems a more fruitful course."

"Can't we see what she looks like?" asks a priest sitting on a divan, his arm around a nun. She still wears a half mask but no cap or veil. Her golden blonde hair cascades over her shoulder. I have no idea who they are, but they all know me as Lady Jane Howard.

Someone unties my mask and removes my cap and veil. One of the viscount's men roughly pulls loose the pins in my hair.

"Each and every one of you will regret this, I promise you," I say.

Mocking laughter rings throughout the room.

"I hoped she'd be younger," says a man sitting in a corner. He wears a cardinal's costume.

"She has a trim figure, you must admit," says the voice of someone I know. It's a nasty jolt to see him in close alliance with the Vicomte de Breteuil.

"Monsieur Descoteaux, you disgrace yourself in taking part in this," I hiss.

Giles Descoteaux removes his mask. "How nice that you recognise me," he says, smiling. "But take part in what? We have no intention of harming you, Lady Howard. We simply want to talk to you."

The nun says, resentfully, "You promised me a séance. Not this — whatever this is."

Her priest companion says, "Couldn't we fit that into the night's entertainment? I did promise Jeanne a communication with the spirit world."

The viscount speaks. "Oh, I am sorry. I forgot to mention it. The séance I promised won't work. The travelling scholar we met says that he can't contact the dead, that all of our ideas about the Swedenborg philosophy are wrong. He's in the other room now, asking for something to eat."

"No!" It's a single word that escapes, but it draws the attention of the viscount.

"Tell them to bring in the Swede," he says, smiling at me. "I have a feeling …"

I twist my head, desperate to avoid the encounter. I'm still wearing a nun's costume. It's been several weeks since Walpole's dinner party. It might be enough for him not to recognize me.

A door opens at the other end of the room, and I hear Lars Longfren's voice. I shut my eyes.

Rough hands shake out my hair and lift my chin. "Herr Longfren, do you know this lady?"

After a few seconds, Lars Longfren says, wonderingly, "Mrs Sturbridge, what are you doing in Paris?" Only then do I meet the puzzled gaze of Herr Lars Longfren, who shared a table with me at Strawberry Hill.

I can hear the sharp intakes of breath. And then comes a thunder of activity. The viscount's men hustle Longfren out of the room. Giles Descoteaux steps towards me, so incredulous his mouth is agape, while the viscount takes two steps backward, shaking his head in wonder.

"The wife of Thomas Sturbridge," says Descoteaux. "*The wife of Thomas Sturbridge*. Mother of God. What devils the British are! They no longer had the painting, so they sent his wife to find the blue. *Of course.* In the treaty, he can never enter France, but Sturbridge's wife can. She knows it by sight. She's been posing as a Howard while trying to find evidence."

"She's not only the wife of the genius," says Breteuil, laughing. "Don't you know the whole story?"

"Don't call him a genius — you know how I hate that," Giles Descoteaux half snarls.

"Before she was the wife of the English chemist — does that make you feel better? — she was the operative of Sir Gabriel Courtenay. He sent her to find the formula in England. I suppose there's no one better qualified for this job."

"That explains their conversation in the ballroom."

As they exult over my capture, it keeps repeating in my head: "You are safe as long as they don't know you are Genevieve Sturbridge." Whatever protection the veneer of Lady Jane Howard gave me is stripped away. What did Sir Gabriel say? "It's your lives."

I take a deep breath. I may not be a noblewoman, but I am a human being, and I will fight to survive.

"I demand — I demand — that you release me and Captain Howard this minute," I say, stamping my foot. "We haven't done anything wrong. We are visitors to France. *You* are all criminals."

"Nothing wrong?" says Giles Descoteaux, laughing in disbelief. "You're in France now, Madame Sturbridge, and here under false pretences."

"And you think there will be no repercussions if you make us disappear?"

The viscount says, "Who said you would disappear? No one. We simply wanted to talk to you, and now that we have discovered who you really are, it reveals nearly everything we desired to know. You came here to find out if your husband's formula has been restarted. Who sent you? I would like to know that. Was it Sir Humphrey Willoughby?"

Giles Descoteaux says, "I want to know what Courtenay told her."

"I'll tell you *nothing*," I spit.

The viscount cocks his head to the side. He asks the time and, when someone tells him, he nods.

The cardinal says, "She's been quite rude. Don't you think we should teach this woman manners before we release her? I don't like being called a criminal."

"No, I don't think so, Donatien," says the viscount. "Best to confine yourself to harlots and maids. This woman is something special."

"She doesn't look special to me," sniffs the cardinal. "And now we know she's not even of noble birth, she's fair game."

Breteuil grins. "She's a highly trained spy who knows a great deal about science and art. Worth her weight in gold. I'll wager she's the reason they've got as far as they have. I wish I had two of her."

Descoteaux says, with that taunting smile I despise, "What a shame all those efforts will come to nothing. You will not succeed at stopping anything to do with the formula, if that is your intention."

Furious, I say, "It isn't *your* formula. You are stealing the work of another man. Is that because you don't have the talent to come up with your own colour?"

"No one speaks to me like that," he says, his teeth bared.

I brace myself. If I am to be attacked, I will go down fighting.

The viscount says, as if we were two children, "Now, now, you two. None of that. I think it's time for us to have a private conversation, Mrs Sturbridge. I do have a few questions about your mission and how much your government knows. Most of all, yes, I want to know exactly what Courtenay said to you."

"No," snaps Descoteaux. "The captain can leave the chateau. But not her. Bring her back when you're done."

"Giles, do you forget we have some special guests among us tonight, courtesy of Sartine? There can be no bloodshed. But that doesn't mean we can't use some — hmm, shall we say zealous persuasion?"

Hands clamp around my arms again, and a man marches me out of the room and down the passageway, the viscount behind us. Fear courses through me. How am I to withstand what he has planned?

Suddenly I hear voices at the end of the passageway and a man laughing.

The viscount won't want to hurt me in front of witnesses, I know that. I try not to react to the laughter. Not quite yet. I can feel the man's fingers loosen around my arm, however. They know this won't look proper to be forcing a woman anywhere.

Two more steps and I wrench free and spring towards the door at the end of the passageway. With a curse, the man and the viscount come after me. But the door opens, and a new trio of guests appear. I smile brightly, say, *"Pardonnez-moi,"* and hurry past them.

To my relief there are even more guests coming. I continue to hurry along, my eyes down, until I find some stairs and hurtle down them. No one follows. I see a plain-looking door at the bottom and shove it open with all my strength.

I'm outside the Château de Sceaux, near the vast gardens.

I should feel relief to be alive and unharmed, but I'm deeply upset and flooded with shame. How could I let them learn my real name? Is Sir Gabriel Courtenay the Abbé everyone whispers about? At first I couldn't believe that he could be the notorious forger mastermind, but is that worse than being a traitorous spy? Why didn't I realize earlier that Sir Gabriel was the one? He was an art connoisseur and always praised my ambitions to paint. When we were outside Sèvres, I remembered how he sent me art supplies . Why didn't I put this together earlier? He was never an artist himself, but he had tremendous knowledge about painting. Of course he could oversee a vast network of forgers.

"I cannot protect you as much as I want to."

What does that mean?

Tears spill from my eyes, and I dash them away. I have to determine where I am. This is the worst time to disintegrate. I need to find the carriage and then, with our men, try to find Captain Howard. They said no bloodshed, but I don't trust these terrible men. And I've not only ruined my cover but the captain's as well. They'd only release me if they thought he was no longer a force to be dealt with and that makes me go cold and shaky.

What has become of Captain Howard?

I stumble past a tall hedge. Far ahead, I see some torches blazing and a line of trees. That must be where the carriages wait. I can't find him alone. I'll get the others, and we will search.

"Lady Howard! Lady Howard!" I hear my name in English. I see a man about fifty feet away.

My heart leaps.

"I'm here!" I shout at the figure of the man rounding the side of the chateau. He's tossed off his friar's robes and carries a sword.

Captain Howard pivots and then runs towards me full out. When he reaches me, he throws down his sword, seizes me by both arms and says, "What did they do to you?" He pushes my hair off my face and frantically scans me in the darkness. "Your mask, your veil. Gone. Are you hurt?"

"No. No. I was so afraid for you," I cry, collapsing into him.

"For *me*? Afraid for me? My God, if you knew what I've been going through."

I make another sound, half sob and half laugh, and then I take his face in my hands and press my lips to his.

He throws his arms around me, running his hands up and down my back and kisses me back, harder than I think any man has ever kissed me in my entire life. We cling to each other as if to part us would kill us.

I hear it faintly at first, then louder. "Captain Howard! Are you there? Lady Howard?"

With a groan, he pulls himself away. After a moment, he shouts, "We're over here."

Vincent and Henry run to us. As soon as they confirm I'm unhurt, we all make our way to the carriage. Simon appears, and within seconds, the horses are pulling our carriage down the drive, and we're rushing from this hateful place.

Simon manages the horses alone, for Henry and Vincent are desperate to hear what happened inside the chateau and ride in the carriage with us. It turns out that no Frenchman asked Captain Howard a thing. They just dragged him outside and threw him onto the lawn, cursing him as an English dog, and said he would be beaten if he tried to re-enter the chateau. "Lady Howard will soon join you," a man sneered. Howard ran to the carriage, armed himself and circled the place, searching.

"Captain, we must leave Paris tonight," Vincent says.

"First we rest the horses or they'll soon be no good to us," says Captain Howard. "We leave after dawn." He turns to me and says, "Tell us everything. Are you ready to do it?"

I take a breath. "The first thing is that I know who the Abbé is. It's Sir Gabriel Courtenay. I believe he is the master forger. He knows why we are in France. And the others in the room knew his real name."

I repeat everything Sir Gabriel said.

"'He shouldn't have sent you.' Do you think he meant Sir Humphrey? Ah, some of the pieces come together."

And then I relay, word for word, what happened in the room with the Vicomte de Breteuil and Giles Descoteaux.

"Who were these other men, and the woman?" asks Henry.

Captain Howard says, "From their words and actions, I'd say it was the Comte du Barry and his mistress, Jeanne, and the cardinal just might be the Comte Donatien de Sade. I heard about him from Bruce Chilton. Sade is a friend of the Duc de Chartres. He likes to imprison and torture women. He's already done a spell in Vincennes Prison."

"I wish I could say this surprises me," I say.

Vincent points out that neither the Duke of Chartres nor the Prince of Lamballe seem to be directly involved. It's true that neither of them were in the room, and no one mentioned their names. A masked ball gave the viscount and Giles Descoteaux cover for trapping us. But they went to such great lengths to seize us and then separate us — why are we unharmed and escaping with all speed now?

Captain Howard looks deeply troubled.

"What is it?" I ask. I want so badly to take him by the hand, and it demands all my self-control not to act.

"I don't understand why they let us go," he admits. "Two men are dead in England. They poisoned Lionel Rolandeu. All of that was done to prevent us from learning about their activities. But we know just about everything now. And yet we are free to go? Free to return to England and inform our government?"

I think over everything said in the room upstairs. "They were concerned about the time," I say. "It seems like they were no longer concerned about something once midnight had passed. But I don't know why that should matter — and I agree with you. Letting us go makes no sense." I remember something. "The viscount mentioned that Sartine's men were there somewhere. That must have been a deterrent."

Captain Howard says slowly, "Perhaps. But I have to think there is some reason that they are sure we pose no threat. And I don't think we will care for the reason when we find out."

Henry says, "I wager they are following us now."

Captain Howard bangs on the carriage door to stop. He and Henry spend the rest of the ride to Paris atop the carriage while Vincent remains with me.

"I'm fine," I keep reassuring him.

"You've been through something worse than you realize," he says and insists I drink brandy from a flask.

When we finally reach the Duke of Norfolk's rooms, I stumble from the carriage. The brandy has lessened my distress and fear, or perhaps it's exhaustion. "The horses need rest, and we need a few hours' sleep," Captain Howard announces.

"Were we followed from the chateau, Captain?" asks Vincent.

Captain Howard shakes his head, but that news does not please him. Instead, it seems to trouble him further.

"Why don't they care where we are and what we do now?" I ask, fear surging once more. "Shouldn't our next move concern them more than ever?"

"Exactly," he says.

Henry shouts, "What? The door is open! But I heard Louise bolt it behind us."

The rest of us rush to the door, hanging open. Vincent, holding up a lantern, charges up the stairs to the third floor, with Simon, Henry, Captain Howard and I following.

"Louise!" shouts Captain Howard. "Answer!"

With a sickening rush, I understand why they lured us to the ball, kept us a certain number of hours, released us and didn't bother to follow. Because our home base was the target all along.

Chapter Twenty-Nine

We run upstairs and pour through the rooms. I'm torn to pieces with anguish and self-loathing. All I can think is what fools we were to leave Louise alone unguarded. Everyone was worried about protecting me.

Louise is in the corner of the fourth-floor sitting room, her hands and feet tied and her mouth covered by a knotted cloth. She wriggles in her ropes. Thank God she is alive.

More hurriedly lit candles reveal a bruised face and cut lower lip. Louise says, "They have the letters, my messages. They took everything. When I tried to fight them, they struck me and tied me up. I'm so sorry, Captain. They came up through the back stairs that lead to the privy. They must have come through the fence from the street and broken that door."

I make a compress for Louise's bruises, and Vincent checks her for other injuries, although she insists she needs no fuss.

"They began to question me, but when they found the letters and saw the invisible ink, they stopped because their leader said this was the gold."

"Leader?" asks Captain Howard.

"They were all at the chateau," I say, confused.

"I can describe him, Captain," says Louise. "Their leader was dark-haired, a man of about forty. He had a scar on his chin."

The chill of the realization moves through me in waves. The murderer of Jemmy is in Paris.

With all candles lit, we assess the damage. Our rooms are torn apart. Papers are strewn everywhere.

"Why do this?" Captain Howard says. "My God, why? Those messages with invisible ink didn't need to be taken. They must know we will leave with all possible speed for England. We will convey what we've learned in person."

"They are not going to let us leave France," I say.

"The best place to stop us was on the road between the chateau and Paris," says Captain Howard. "Drive us off the road, eliminate us all, hide traces. No one in England would ever be able to discover what happened. That would have been the best strategy."

Simon suggests, "They want to intimidate us."

Howard shakes his head. "It's almost like they're making a show of intimidation."

Henry says, "Then it's to slow us down, Captain. You're sure we shouldn't leave now?"

Captain Howard is silent for a few more minutes. "We are a far distance from fresh horses, and we don't have time to make new arrangements. If we are to leave in strength, these horses must rest, and so must we. We face a formidable opponent tomorrow. Don't deceive yourself that the danger is over. I know it sounds impossible, but everyone must get sleep. We leave this house at nine and begin our journey to the coast."

No one is more surprised than me to fall into a deep sleep after a night such as this. I know nothing until voices and banging sounds outside my door wake me. I hear Captain Howard's voice, and the memory of our kiss fills me with turmoil. What must he think of me, a married woman, throwing myself at him? I'm afraid he wished it had never happened. Do I wish it hadn't happened? I do. My marriage vows are sacred to me. Through the hurt, the loneliness, the guilt and the confusion I've felt, I know that Thomas has disappointed me — and I am certain I have disappointed him as well — but he has done nothing to deserve my behaving like this.

I have been struggling with these feelings of attraction to Peregrine Howard for days, perhaps for weeks. Our kiss was fuelled by a desire I've not felt for a long time. It could be prompted by my relief at surviving the ordeal at the chateau. If only I hadn't felt in his lips and his hands that he desires me just as much.

I splash cold water on my face furiously. These thoughts must be banished.

I'm here to perform a mission for the British government, not to make a fool of myself. But focusing on the mission makes me think of Sir Gabriel Courtenay, returning to my life after all these years. It shouldn't surprise me that he is the mastermind of a forgery ring. He was a traitor spy, too clever for Sir Humphrey Willoughby to catch until he ruined himself by going to extremes to get the colour blue for King Louis and Madame de Pompadour. Is he the one who is behind the blue's return? In a way the colour was his doom, and he may be seeking vengeance against both countries.

I check Louise's bruises, which have turned into a nasty bluish purple. She insists her hands are fine and won't take no for an answer on dressing my hair and putting on my wig. The last thing I want to do is wear it again, but she says Captain Howard wants us to depart looking the way we did on arrival.

Amid the fuss of packing and provisioning, Henry says a boy on the street handed him a sealed message for Captain Howard.

Frowning, he opens it. As his eyes scan the writing, the colour drains from Howard's face.

"No, no, no," he says hoarsely.

"What?" I ask.

To all of our astonishment, he strides into his room and slams the door. We hear him throw something against the wall and curse.

Vincent knocks on the door, but Captain Howard shouts at him to go away. Simon and Henry get the same response. We look at one another, disturbed and even frightened. Ever since our team was assembled in England, Captain Howard has led us with decisiveness and courage.

Louise says, "It's up to you, Mrs Sturbridge. He listens to you."

Nodding, I rap on the door and say, "I'm coming in."

"*No, you're not.*"

I push the door open. He is standing near the window, one palm flat on the wall as if to prop himself up. The unfolded paper lies on the table.

"Get out, Genevieve."

"What does the message say?" I ask.

"No one else can see it. I can't permit it."

I pick up the paper, but before I can read it, Captain Howard says, "She's been kidnapped."

I stare at him, utterly bewildered. There's no woman in Paris who matters to him. A truly horrible thought occurs. The kidnapping didn't take place in France but in England.

"Do they have the real Jane Howard?" I whisper. A second later, I reject that theory. At the chateau they thought I was Jane until Lars Longfren revealed my identity.

He takes a deep breath and says, "They have my sister Madeleine. She's in Paris. She's a *real* nun."

I rub my forehead, absorbing this shock.

"When she was eighteen, Madeleine took vows at the Augustinian order of sisters on rue des Fossés-Saint-Victor. It was her choice. My mother was still alive and wanted Madeleine to stay with her. A lot of Catholic families send a daughter to one of the French convents created for English women. But in her case, Madeleine had a calling and wouldn't accept any obstacles to her wishes. She's taken the name Sister Candida."

Now I understand something.

I say, "When you came to Paris with your family, it was to bring her to the convent."

He nods.

"And that day when you were gone for so many hours, you went to see her — that was the secret you kept?"

He nods again.

I read the letter aloud. "*Captain Peregrine Howard, we have your sister. If you report what you have learned in France to the government of England, her life is forfeit. Any involvement of the French police and any complaint made to the French ministries about this affair will result in her death. After one year, if nothing is heard from England, she shall be released. You have lost. You have no choice but to accept it.*"

Turning to look out the window, he says hoarsely, "It's my fault. They were following us from the day we reached Paris. Probably before. They saw me visit her convent. The reason they wanted us at the Château de Sceaux was to make sure of no interference. Breaking into this apartment was another distraction. Their target was my sister's convent. I should be horsewhipped for my stupidity."

"Stop this! You don't know how they found out about Madeleine. Your family is real, that was the strength of the mission but also its weakness. They could have found out about her some other way. There must be people in England and in Paris who know about Madeleine Howard. Or maybe someone intercepted your letter to the embassy in Paris and knew we were coming. That's not your fault."

He finally looks at me with a bleakness I've never witnessed.

"No matter how they discovered her existence, she will be killed because of me."

"Not if we do nothing about the Versailles Formula," I protest. "Her life is more important than any colour, surely!"

"This has never been about a colour, Genevieve. You know that. It's about two countries clashing on the battlefield over and over. When we are not in a state of war, we work to do the other side an injury. We are locked in mutual hostility. It's bankrupting both our countries. That's how a creature like Giles Descoteaux can find allies. This ring of scoundrels and murderers see a fortune being made from blue, the colour of France. Money *and* prestige. But if France breaks the treaty, even over something like production of an English formula, England feels it must act. And our new prime minister is the one who took England to war against France. Everything is in our hands right now. Everything."

My stomach churning, I say, "What will you do?"

"I must be alone to think. Give me that. And I beg you not to tell the others about my sister's kidnapping." He pauses. "You know I have strong feelings for you?"

This is the time for me to say we must forget about last night's moment. I can't. I can only nod.

"Then, Genevieve, I ask you to help me now and keep this secret."

I leave the room without a word. *Secrets, always secrets*, I think bitterly.

In the drawing room, where the others wait in fear, I say that

Captain Howard has a decision to make on something, and we will know soon what to do.

No more than half an hour later, Captain Howard emerges. His eyes are afire with anger — and determination.

"I must go alone to confront Vicomte de Breteuil," he says, seizing his sword and tucking his pistol in his coat.

"You will not go alone," cries Simon.

The other men chime in. "If it's a fight, you'll need every one of us," says Vincent. "We're with you. Always."

Captain Howard says, "I cannot tell you the cause, only that what he has done is an infamy and this is a matter of my honour, my family's honour. There is a good chance the fight will end in injury, even death, and, should I survive, imprisonment."

To my astonishment, this does not discourage the other three men. If anything, they are *more* motivated.

"No," I say. "You haven't thought this through, Captain. You can't throw your life away — or theirs." I indicate Simon, Vincent and Henry. "The odds against you, against you all, are too great."

Captain Howard says, "Stay out of this, Genevieve. Henry, you must remain here and protect the women and get them out of France by yourself if necessary."

Henry furiously protests, but Captain Howard will not listen to him — or to me.

"Wait — stop — this action will bring about the consequence you most fear," I cry.

"No. Direct attack is the only thing that has a hope of preventing it," he says. "They assume I am weak. They're counting on it."

While I watch, feeling helpless, the three who will confront Vicomte de Breteuil arm themselves and thunder down the stairs.

I fly down after them.

"Damn it, Genevieve, get back up there!" Captain Howard roars at the bottom of the stairs, more enraged with me than he's ever been before.

"I am your partner in this until the end, Captain," I say. "If necessary, I will follow you now."

Cursing me, he throws open the door. The three men charge up the street towards the stable where our carriage and horses are kept. Simon had no time to ready them.

"Halt! Halt at once! All of you!"

To hear a shout like that here, on the well-manicured streets of the Faubourg Saint-Germain, is so shocking that all of us freeze.

A stern-looking young man with fiery red hair approaches us, his sword drawn. At least ten men stand behind him.

"Monsieur de Sartine, the lieutenant general of the police of Paris, wants to see all of you. Get in your carriage and follow me. I will lead you to the Grand Châtelet now."

Chapter Thirty

It beckons to me after I step out of the carriage. The Grand Châtelet. Its jagged towers and sagging walls are a testament to centuries of fear. Fortress, prison, morgue and who knows what else — it squats on the banks of the Seine like a malignant city unto itself. Behind it, on Île de la Cité, the towers of Notre Dame shimmer in the sunlight, their beauty a painful mockery of our destination.

The cloudless sky traps the ferocious heat, intensifying the stench that rolls over us — rot, human waste and death. My stomach churns. Can the sewers of Paris really empty so close to the cathedral? It seems impossible, yet the reek is undeniable. I pause, pressing a handkerchief to my face, and glance at Captain Howard. His expression remains unreadable, his resolve unshaken. But that frightens me more than it heartens me. I suspect the man deludes himself that somehow he will still be able to reach the viscount with a drawn sword.

"Do you admire our Grand Châtelet?" jeers Hébert, the red-haired man who works for Sartine. Hébert had placed an English-speaking man in our carriage to keep us from forming a strategy. Now, he herds us towards the looming entrance. "Built to fend off the Vikings. Ever since, it defends France and our king against *all* enemies."

He jerks his head towards a large stone archway carved into the cluster of crumbling buildings. Beyond it, we enter a cobblestone courtyard, half-shadowed but still stifling. The shade provides no relief from the stench. To our left, a wide opening, barred with thick iron yawns. This, I think, must be the prison Captain Howard warned me about.

We head towards another doorway, but as we pass the barred entrance, a scream slices through the air. It is raw, inhuman, the sound of someone enduring unimaginable torment. My knees weaken. The courtyard spins, and I am gripped by the same disorientation I felt staring into Zophiel's gaping throat at Cross Bones.

A hand steadies me. "Jane, are you well?" Captain Howard's voice is calm, but there's a sharpness, a warning in his tone. Our enemies may know my real identity, but we will try to keep the façade alive with Sartine.

Summoning every ounce of strength, I gather myself and follow Hébert up a wide staircase. In England, I was assured I'd be in no physical danger on this mission, yet hours ago I was roughly handled, came close to torture and am now being marched through this temple of state-sanctioned suffering. Anger flares, but there is no use in directing it at Sir Humphrey Willoughby now.

At the top of the stairs, Hébert leads us down a dim hallway and knocks on a heavy oak door. Without a word, he slips inside, leaving us to wait.

"What a vile place," I whisper to Captain Howard in English. "Can you imagine subjecting foreign visitors to such a vision of hell in London?"

To my surprise, he smiles faintly. "A very effective way to shred one's nerves," he replies. "If only we had an entranceway like this."

No matter what far-fetched plans he nurtures, the man's resilience astounds me. I must match Captain Howard's courage, no matter what comes next.

When the door opens, I step into an unexpected oasis of calm. Antoine de Sartine's office radiates quiet luxury: wood-panelled walls glowing in the afternoon light, fresh flowers arranged in porcelain vases, and a row of powdered wigs on polished stands behind his desk.

Sartine himself sits at the desk, his features sharp and composed, a man in the prime of middle age. He studies us briefly before speaking. "Captain Howard, Lady Howard, I am investigating reports of a disturbance at Château de Sceaux last night. I am told you were expelled from a social occasion and that afterwards you armed yourself, Captain Howard, and patrolled the chateau's perimeter with your men."

Beside me, Captain Howard's haughty profile softens slightly, a minute shift that only I would notice. I suspect he feared he would hear about the blue formula or a kidnapper's threat, not this.

"Have you indeed?" Captain Howard replies, his tone measured, offering nothing more.

Sartine's lips tighten in irritation. "The chateau belongs to a nobleman of the highest rank, closely tied to our king. That ball hosted many prominent families. Any scandal involving British visitors to Paris could spark diplomatic tensions. I must know what transpired."

Captain Howard hesitates, and before I can stop myself, I plunge into the gap. "If I may, Monsieur de Sartine," I say, my voice steady, "I can explain. It is a delicate matter, and my brother-in-law is protective of my honour. That is why he hesitates to speak."

Sartine nods approvingly. "I can understand this. Please do enlighten me, Lady Howard."

"After dancing, Captain Howard and I attempted to leave. I was feeling rather tired. The Vicomte de Breteuil detained us and led us to a private room. But he refused to allow my brother-in-law to accompany me into the room. This led to strong objections, and he was expelled forcibly."

Sartine's lips tighten. "This is unacceptable behaviour on the part of the vicomte."

"Inside the room, I was insulted, Monsieur de Sartine. I would very much prefer to not share the details. But I was not … interfered with, and in light of my strong distaste for what was on offer, I was led out of the chateau. There, I found my brother-in-law, and we left."

"Who else was in the room?" demanded Sartine. When I name the Comtes du Barry and de Sade, he looks heavenward as if seeking divine help.

"This is appalling, and although he is a vicomte, I will speak personally to Breteuil," says Sartine.

"Monsieur, I would prefer you not do that," says Captain Howard.

"Would you?" says Sartine sharply. "Because you have some private action in mind? Wasn't that where you were headed this morning? Sir, I find it hard to believe you wouldn't seek satisfaction for the insult to the lady's honour, a member of your family."

"I am a captain in the British Army and am under orders concerning duels and other personal attacks," he says firmly.

"Of course you are," Sartine says, a slight smile curving his lips. But Captain Howard folds his arms and says nothing more.

After a moment of bemused silence, Sartine says, "There is another reason I assigned three of my men to the chateau. We have heard of the activities of an art forger, a man who operates in several countries. We want very much to capture him, as he damages French prestige with his crimes. Our intelligence was that he would appear at the chateau because it was a ball for those in religious costumes and he is known only as the Abbé. But why this ball? My informant heard that he operates in secret, trusting very few, and no one knows his true identity. He disdains polite society ordinarily. But there was a reason — some reason — he was willing to emerge from the shadows. There was another guest there he intended to meet, that was our theory. Captain Howard, Lady Howard, do you know about this Abbé and have any idea as to who the guest he wished to meet could be?"

I have never in my life worked harder to conceal my thoughts and emotions than this moment. I look at Captain Howard and he appears genuinely puzzled.

"I wish I could help you, Monsieur," says Captain Howard. "I don't know anything about forgers. But I do hope you capture him soon."

Sartine shoots him a glare, nods and says, "I think it best that you leave Paris, Captain. Can you and Lady Howard wrap up your visit in the next twenty-four hours? It is July, and the city is emptying. There cannot be much more planned for your stay."

"Very well," Captain Howard says tightly.

Hébert leads us to our carriage. Our two men, Simon and Vincent, looking subdued, wait nearby.

"I will escort you back to your apartments," says Hébert. "And Captain, you should know there will be police stationed outside your apartment until you depart Paris. Sartine does not trust your promise to be peaceable, and neither do I."

Captain Howard and I file into our carriage.

"You think quicker on your feet than any woman ever born," says Captain Howard quietly. "It is a shame that we cannot enlist Sartine. He's an intelligent man. I was expressly forbidden by Sir Humphrey from briefing him on our mission."

I nod wearily and settle into my seat. My left hand touches something, and I look down. It is a small piece of paper, folded and sealed, with something truly startling written on it: *Fournier Street.* That was the street I lived on in Spitalfields. I've never mentioned that fact to Captain Howard or anyone else during my stay in Paris. But one person in the city knows it very well. In fact, he has dined there. I am stunned that somehow someone was able to slip this into the back of the carriage, steps from the Grand Châtelet. I should have learned by now never to underestimate Sir Gabriel Courtenay.

My hand closes around the paper, and I slip it into my bodice to hide it. This has to be of great importance, and I will find a way to read it in private.

When we are back in the Duke of Norfolk's apartments, Captain Howard tells us his real plan. The rest of us will leave Paris tomorrow. Henry, he says, will wear Howard's clothes and impersonate him, which should be possible because Sartine does not appear to know that another man stayed in the apartments. It won't look like anyone is missing.

"It will seem that we've complied, and the scrutiny will leave with you to make sure the carriage is bound for the coast," says Captain Howard. "I will be able to investigate freely."

Simon says, "One man alone? And that man having disobeyed orders from the head of police to leave?"

Captain Howard says calmly, "I refuse to leave this country without achieving my objective. I wish I could tell you men the details, but it is impossible."

I know why he is staying. Captain Howard won't leave Paris before freeing his sister.

Vincent says, "Sir, I don't see how this can succeed. You'll be killed."

"If so, I plan to take with me as many of these bastards as possible," says Captain Howard. "No more discussion." His eyes turn to me. "And that includes you."

I insist on speaking to Captain Howard alone.

"I won't leave you, Peregrine," I say once we are in his room.

He says, much more calmly than I have heard so far today, "My mother, when she was dying, asked me to take care of Madeleine and Robert's wife and children. I consider this a sacred vow. You are not Catholic, but you can understand such a moral responsibility. I know you can. It's a promise I would die for, Genevieve. I won't add you to the list of people who've been hurt because of me. Give me this if you have any feelings for me at all."

I make as good a show as I can of arguing with him. Just as Captain Howard agreeing to not cause difficulties aroused Sartine's suspicion, it won't seem right to Howard if I don't object.

The truth is I am desperate to find a moment to read Sir Gabriel's message alone. Finally, I manage it in my bedchamber when Louise is in the drawing room.

"*I understand your party has lost something. If you want to find it, I can tell you how. Meet me at the Abbey of Saint-Geneviève, at the cornerstone laid by the king, no later than six o'clock today. You must come alone. If anyone else is with you or waiting nearby, I cannot speak to you.*"

There is no question about it. I will be there by the appointed time. The challenge is how do I slip out of these apartments without anyone noticing? And if we are being watched, how will I walk past a police guard?

It takes me a little time, but I put together my plan.

When Louise is elsewhere, I search through her satchel for her plainest dress. I fold it up and slip it into a sack along with Sir Gabriel's letter. There's one more thing I need to obtain and it takes more time to squirrel away a kitchen knife than I would wish. It's already mid-afternoon, and I don't know how long it will take me to walk to the Abbey of Saint-Geneviève.

Trying to look casual, I put the sack under my arm and head for the back stairs. Captain Howard is going over maps in his room. Louise is resting. Only Vincent and Henry can see me leave.

"Madame?" asks Henry. "Where are you going?"

"I need to use the privy," I answer and hold up my sack. "Ladies sometimes require rags, Henry."

He blushes and turns away, but I am free to walk downstairs. First, I search for the gap in the wall that the viscount's men used to break in. Boards are laid out next to it with nails. The ever-efficient Captain Howard must have already ordered the gap to be sealed. In another hour, this exit would have been impossible.

I tear off my dress, one of the pretty brocades stitched for me in Twickenham, and put on Louise's plain brown one. It's too big for me, but I can do nothing about that. I remove my wig and put it in the sack.

Next I shake out my hair and pin a small lace cap atop. A married woman shouldn't wear her hair down, but I want the police guard to see someone who looks as different from a wigged lady as possible. I put the knife in Louise's pocket along with Sir Gabriel's message. I will destroy this evidence somewhere between the Duke of Norfolk's apartments and the Abbey of Saint-Geneviève.

I grip the back wall and prepare to ease myself out of the opening in the board.

"Madame, I can't let you do this."

It's Henry, standing next to the privy, shaking his head.

"Why did you come down?" I ask, eyeing the opening. If I can distract him and jump out, I may be able to make it onto the street.

If he follows me, shouting, everything will be ruined. I pray he goes back upstairs to get Captain Howard first.

"I have three sisters," he says. "It shouldn't ever take this long."

"I am doing this to help Captain Howard," I say. "I received a message. The instruction is I must come alone. You have to believe me, Henry."

"Absolutely not. Captain Howard would shoot me if I let you go."

He takes three steps closer. I can only hurtle through this opening if I make an arrangement with Henry.

"What if I tell you where I am going? And you can tell the others once I am safely away? You can meet me there if you can safely make it past the police guard. But do not leave here until seven o'clock."

"How do I know you are giving me the correct location? Show me this message."

"Oh, when did you become so clever?" I moan. I fish the message out of my bag and hand it to Henry. "This is the only course of action that has any hope of success," I tell him. "I know who sent me the message. He can never be underestimated." I think of the plot Sir Gabriel created to find the colour blue, how he used me to that end, his brilliance and his ruthlessness. To this day, Sir Humphrey is haunted by his adversary and by how much damage Sir Gabriel did before he finally went too far in kidnapping Thomas and me. Yet he rose like a phoenix from his disgrace in England and France and became a mastermind forger, whispered about in the capitals of Europe.

Henry stares at me unhappily, Sir Gabriel's message in his hand. He's not sure what to do.

Before he can grab me, I dart out the opening in the boards. Edging my way down a narrow opening between buildings, I find the street that runs behind the Duke of Norfolk's apartments. This should be easier than I planned.

No. Sure enough, a man on the corner of this street looks very much like a police guard. Oh, Sartine *is* intelligent.

I walk the way women in Spitalfields walk, the way all women walk who don't own satins, slippers and fine wigs. I don't look away from him, but I don't stare at the man in the eye, either. I simply go about my business — and he appears to lose interest before I even reach the corner.

I set out towards the Luxembourg gardens, my path guided by a recollection of the Earl of Rochford pointing to a distant hill, saying it was where King Louis dedicated a church. Surely, once I find the gardens, the abbey will not be far. But as I press on, the streets grow unfamiliar. I had no chance to refresh my memory with the guide to Paris — it would have aroused suspicion — and now, I must admit I am lost. Instead of the grand expanse of gardens built for Marie de Medici, I find myself trapped in a maze of winding streets and narrow alleys.

When I stop to ask for directions, a young woman gestures to an elderly man sitting on a crate in the shade of a grocer's shop. "Thibault knows everything about the Abbey of Saint-Geneviève," she says.

I approach him with cautious respect. "Monsieur Thibault, can you tell me how to find the Abbey of Saint-Geneviève?"

I fear he's sleeping. His eyes flutter open, startled, and he studies me for a long moment. "Is there a crisis in the city?" he asks, his voice hoarse with age.

His question catches me off guard. "No," I reply, though my stomach tightens. "Why do you ask?"

"You must know why."

"I'm afraid I don't."

He sits up, his tone sombre. "Whenever Paris is in peril, the fathers of our church carry the reliquary of Saint-Geneviève through the streets, from the abbey to Notre Dame. It has always been so. My grandfather saw them walk when famine struck. I saw them when our king, Louis the Well-Beloved, lay dying of smallpox. Saint-Geneviève cured him."

The image of Sir Gabriel flashes to mind — his twisted obsession with King Louis and, no doubt, the resonance of this female saint's name. Of course he would choose this place.

"I wish to pray there for the safety of my sick sister," I say, forcing a humble tone. "Can you help me find the abbey?"

"It's on the highest hill on this side of the river. The king had the abbey torn down, Madame. They're going to build something even bigger there to honour her because Saint-Geneviève saved his life. I will give you directions."

"Thank you, Monsieur Thibault."

I follow the path he dictates. The streets widen and I pass what looks like a college. And then, just as the man said, I see a tall hill rising above all the surrounding streets. But I also note that the sun is lower in the sky. It might be nearing six. I speed up my walk. I don't want to draw attention to myself, but if I miss Sir Gabriel, then I have no idea what I will do, how to save Madeleine Howard.

Scrambling up the hill, I see the place where the abbey used to be and where they are now building a new one. The walls are about five feet high. Within the walls is a vast pit of construction next to a church and grounds. Why did Sir Gabriel pick this place? It's not deserted. A dozen workmen are busy within the walls.

I draw closer. I see that the workmen are putting away tools. Their work is nearly finished for the day.

"Monsieur, I have a question," I say to the man who could be the foreman. "Where is the cornerstone that King Louis laid for the new abbey for Saint-Geneviève?"

"It's in the centre, but towards the back," he answers. "It's not safe to walk in there now, Madame. We are digging the vault where Genevieve's relics will be kept. Come back when the abbey is finished."

I nod, retreat and wait until the workmen leave. As soon as the way is clear, I pick my way across this pit of stone and boards to the square stone in the centre. Once I reach it, I look around carefully. There's no one else in sight. Is it past six? Did he not wait for me?

While scanning the pit yet again, I see a gap where an archway may be planned. Beyond is a small cemetery and a cluster of trees. Standing next to the line of trees, I see a tall man, watching me with the careful alertness I remember all too well.

Chapter Thirty-One

It doesn't take me long to reach Sir Gabriel. Unmasked, he is as I remember: dark eyes, a firm mouth. He wears no wig, and I note with a pang the white hairs sprouting from his temple and new lines between his nose and mouth. He has aged since I saw him. Yet even here, standing in a cemetery to exchange information, the man possesses dignity. I can't believe even now that I am reunited with Sir Gabriel in these circumstances.

His gaze takes me in, top to bottom. "I've seen you wear some lamentable clothes, Genevieve, but never anything quite this atrocious."

"You are criticizing my choices in clothes? Even now? I had to wear a disguise to get away."

"Why?"

I tell him of Sartine picking us up and interrogating us — not omitting Sartine's interest in the Abbé forger — and their subsequent orders and ongoing observation.

"Kidnapping a nun is a despicable decision, even for Giles Descoteaux," Sir Gabriel says.

"Don't you mean for the Vicomte de Breteuil?"

"It wasn't his idea. The viscount is a willing follower of the master chemist. He thinks Giles Descoteaux will make him very rich. I am more than familiar with the viscount's character. Up to now he was content to be an occasional partner of mine in forgeries. He heard from Veronique, the assistant to Madame du Deffand, that Sir Horace Walpole, that spoiled rich boy grown old, required an angel painted by Jean-Honoré Fragonard. As if that was something Fragonard even specialized in! Breteuil suggested it would be a good idea to paint one for Walpole. It would serve him right. I took it from there."

Sir Gabriel watches me and waits, a slight smile curving his lips.

"It was you who had the blue painted at the top and covered over?" I ask. "And you asked Lionel Rolandeu to draw the warning about a blue fear and the rest?"

He simply nods.

"I must ask … why? Why did you do that?"

"Louis discharged me from the Secret du Roi, but I still retain respect for the king. I give loyalty to other human beings rarely, but when I do, I suppose it's for life."

Now I know for certain why he picked this place for our meeting.

"Louis wanted Thomas Sturbridge's blue destroyed," Sir Gabriel continues. "That was his wish in 1759. He didn't want France to have to steal formulas from Englishmen and kidnap their chemists. It offended his Bourbon pride, don't you remember? He wants French artists and chemists to be the best in the world without having to steal, as I learned to my great cost. So when I heard that Giles Descoteaux was trying to pressure Jean Hellot to retire, and then Hellot died and he took the spot, I knew the situation would require watching. Unfortunately, he was able to recreate the laboratory conditions of Sturbridge's formula well before Hellot died! When they're ready, they plan to convince the king it's their own formula, independently researched and developed, that simply happens to resemble Sturbridge's mix."

"Could that work?"

Sir Gabriel shrugs. "The king does cherish beauty — in women and in art. It may work. I felt compelled to do something. It wasn't easy, but I managed to bribe someone to secrete a batch of the blue for me. Then I gave it to my own artist to use. I insisted that an ugly and oversized frame be used, assuming Walpole would have it removed immediately. And I know that he and Sir Humphrey Willoughby are good friends, and whenever he's in a bad spot or faced with a mystery, Walpole turns to Willoughby. I couldn't believe it when nothing happened for months."

"So you came up with the idea of someone playing ghost and that way leading Walpole's attention to the painting?"

He nods, lips tightening. "Yes, but Zophiel performed week after week, and Walpole *still* didn't take down the painting to investigate why."

"I should have known you were the one who came up with the name 'Zophiel'. You always liked Milton, Sir Gabriel."

"I am sorry I couldn't meet the boy. It was all done through intermediaries. They found an ambitious, unscrupulous, brilliant street urchin from Southwark. He was perfect."

"I know. I was there the night Jemmy got caught. I have to tell you … I liked him."

For the first time, Sir Gabriel shows true anger. "When Giles Descoteaux found out that a batch was missing and it went to someone from my camp, he went wild. He should *never* have sent a murderer to England. Take the painting off the wall if you must to cover your activity, but why must throats be slit? The boy was no threat to anyone."

I tell Sir Gabriel about how we found Jemmy in a graveyard, one far less picturesque than the one we stand in now.

"Did he poison Lionel Rolandeu as well?" I ask.

"Oh, yes. I think Descoteaux has gone mad. The blue can have that effect. You should know that, Genevieve. Breteuil is a greedy fool to deal with him. I've tried to make the viscount see reason and failed."

I feel a stab of fear. "What about you, Sir Gabriel? How can you be safe?"

"I've made Breteuil so much money that he is motivated to believe my story that it was one of my operatives, in the pay of the English, who did all this, and not myself."

"And Giles Descoteaux? What will he do when we rescue Madeleine Howard? Will he know you betrayed him?"

He doesn't answer that question directly.

"I have three things to tell you, Genevieve. One is the address of the place where Madeleine Howard is being kept. It's 247 Boulevard Raspail. Can you memorize that? Repeat it twice. She will be moved tomorrow out of Paris. So you will have to act tonight."

Sir Gabriel always wanted me to repeat everything. He hasn't changed! I do so, and he nods, satisfied.

"The second thing to memorize is the name of the Parisian solicitor I visited today. I made out my will. You are my primary beneficiary. You'll inherit certain investments, property, stocks and cash, in France, Switzerland and Italy. I wish I had something to leave you in England, but as you know, prosperity never came to me on English soil except through spying."

He tells me the name, and I memorize it, but I am stunned. "Why would you leave me a cent, Sir Gabriel? This is a sudden decision, made rashly. You must reconsider."

"I've been considering it for almost a week — since I knew you were in France."

"But how could you know that?"

"When I heard that a Lady Jane Howard and her brother-in-law were in Paris a short time after the murder of Zophiel, I suspected. When I found out this Lady Howard was at the French academy in the Louvre saying women should be able to create art next to the men, it was obvious, I'm afraid."

For a moment I can't fathom how he knew my words. There was only one person I spoke to; I didn't see how we were closely overheard. "You are acquainted with that student?" I ask.

"Acquainted? He's one of my most talented artists!"

Incredibly, with all of the horror and fear I've gone through, I have to laugh. But Sir Gabriel Courtenay has never looked more serious. In fact, if I didn't believe it to be impossible, I would swear he looked nervous.

"Genevieve, the third matter to discuss is the reason I've made out my will. I have a daughter. I want you to act as her guardian should I die. You are, quite simply, the only one I can ask this of."

My head spins. "A daughter? You have a daughter?"

"Adele is four years old. My solicitor has her address. I have her safely hidden just outside Paris."

I swallow and say, "What about Adele's mother?"

"Dead," he says flatly.

For a moment I don't know what to say. My heart fills with pity for the master spy, the adversary of Sir Humphrey Willoughby, the wealthy art forger whispered about through Europe, with no one he cares for in his life except for a small child and no one to turn to now to safeguard her except for me.

"I am sorry," I say. "I hope you found some happiness with her mother before she died."

"It depends on how you define happiness," he says dryly. "Josette never gave me a moment's peace. I dearly love Adele, so in the end, our liaison was worth the pain."

Those grave, speculative eyes take me in. "No, Genevieve, I told you once that you were the only woman who could have saved me. It was the truth."

He reaches out and caresses my face. The memories flood me, of the fear, the attraction, the admiration and the hate I felt for him.

His hand still cupping my face, he says, "I don't believe in regrets, except for when it comes to Genevieve Planché. I'm sorry for what I did to your life. Look at it this way. If you inherit soon, you will have the means to do whatever you want, go anywhere. Even Venice, at long last." He smiles painfully. "It is my fault you married Thomas Sturbridge. He's not the man you were meant to marry."

I pull away from him. "Oh, no. Don't say that. I *am* happy. I have a son, you know."

"I know you do. But a schoolmaster's wife, buried in the country? It's the very last thing I wanted for you."

How does he know where I live? Ah, Sir Gabriel always knew everything.

However, he never appreciated Thomas's gifts. Sir Gabriel had a blind spot. Yes, he wanted me to find Thomas Sturbridge in Derby in order to steal the formula. But the revolutionary potential of science to explain the world always left Sir Gabriel unmoved. Which he proves with his next words.

"Your feelings for Thomas Sturbridge were born from the intensity of your mission, the one I sent you on. The life of a spy — there's nothing else like it. I wager that you have realized that by now."

I can't bring myself to speak.

329

"And I have another wager to make, that the feelings for a man you're thrown together with could be stirring here in Paris."

"No," I say quickly. "It's not like that."

Did the excitement and fear of the mission fuel my attraction to Captain Howard, as such a heightened reality once did for Thomas? No. I know that my feelings for my husband run deeper. And it isn't just respect for his brilliance in science. I love him as my soul mate, and I will find a way past the trials of everyday life to nurture that. I hadn't completely decided for certain until this moment.

Sir Gabriel says, "Well, it would be better for you if it's not. Unless you plan to get a new husband with every spy mission you undertake."

A man's voice says, "This is the last mission for Genevieve Sturbridge."

Giles Descoteaux steps out from his hiding place, a smirk on his face. "That was quite a conversation, Courtenay. You're right. I always knew it was you." The smirk changes to a snarl of hatred. "You arrogant, lying swine. You stole my blue and you tried to warn the English — our sworn *enemies*. No matter how often you've denied it, you're still at heart an English dog." He spits on the ground. "No Englishman — no Englishwoman — can ever be trusted!"

Sir Gabriel says, stepping in front of me, "There's no need to harm the woman. This is between us." He's reaching into his coat, I hope for a weapon to fend off Descoteaux.

"It is indeed. And I will finish it today." He turns his head and shouts to someone, "Take him — take him now."

Sir Gabriel shoves me back with all his strength, saying in English, "Run — I will hold them off as long as I can." I stumble farther into the graveyard before I remember my knife. I don't want to hide. I want to fight. Looking over my shoulder, I see a second man, taller, with a horrible smile on his face — and a scar in his chin — charging towards Sir Gabriel. He raises his sword and lunges.

At the same instant that I see Sir Gabriel crumple to the ground, I hear a shout. Three … five … ten men pour into the cemetery, brandishing swords and pistols. Leading them are Captain Howard and Hébert, the man who works for Sartine. Henry is with them, and Simon and Vincent and more police guards. Relief pours through me, but confusion as well. Captain Howard was adamant on not going to Sartine.

The mass of men overpowers Giles and his assassin in a few minutes. The last I see of Giles Descoteaux is him struggling with the ferocity of a madman, his talented-chemist veneer stripped away. But he's no match for Sartine's police.

I push my way through the melee to where I last saw Sir Gabriel Courtenay. I can take no joy in this rescue if Sir Gabriel is seriously wounded. Someone grabs my arm as I pick my way through the headstones, shrouded in gunpowder smoke.

"My God — Genevieve, my God," says Captain Howard, breathing heavily. "If we'd been here ten minutes later …"

"I had to do it," I tell him. "It was the only way. If I hadn't come, I'm certain Madeleine would have been killed — and I feared you would soon be killed too."

"I saw the message," he says. "Henry gave it to me."

"But why did you … ?" I look around us. It seems as if more police guards than ever are pouring into the area.

"I couldn't lose both you and my sister, treaties and ministries be damned. I went to Sartine."

I tell Captain Howard the address I memorized of Madeleine's location. "You must go tonight. That's what Sir Gabriel said."

Captain Howard says, "You're not coming with me?"

"Go — go — I will be with you later," I say. "I can't leave."

Captain Howard stares at me, inscrutable, before whipping around, calling for his men. They run down the hill, away from the abbey, back to the thick of the city. I hope that within the next few hours, Madeleine Howard is freed to become Sister Candida again. Does her brother understand why I can't leave yet? I doubt it — I don't know if I understand it myself.

To my relief, Sir Gabriel is no longer prone on the ground. He sits slumped against a tombstone; whether he pulled himself up or someone helped him, I don't know. But as I draw closer, I see dark red blood soaking his side.

"Sir Gabriel?" I say.

His eyes flutter. With a wince, he sits up taller. He is weak and in pain.

Hébert materializes and examines Sir Gabriel. "We could take you to the surgeon, Monsieur," he says doubtfully.

"Tell them to go, Genevieve," Sir Gabriel gasps.

"But you need medical treatment."

"No. It's over. I want them all to go. Just you. Just you."

Hébert catches my gaze and nods. Sir Gabriel is dying.

Sartine's men withdraw. After all the shouting and the violence, the graveyard grows quiet again. I feel numb and completely at a loss. What should I do? I sit on the ground next to him and try to staunch the wound, full of fresh blood.

"Stop," he says. "Pointless. I have to tell you what to do. Not much time. England, Genevieve. Take her to England. I couldn't return. Traitor. But Adele can go. You can take her. Protect her, please."

I take his hand in mine and press it to my cheek. The acrid smell of gunpowder mixes with the sweet fragrance of yellow roses rising above the headstone.

"You don't have to worry, Sir Gabriel," I say, tears pouring down my face. "I will take care of everything. I won't fail. How could I? You taught me so much. Trained me well."

A faint smile hovers, even as his eyes drift. He is losing consciousness.

"Ah," says Sir Gabriel. "It happened. How funny."

"What happened?"

His voice falters to a rasp. "I thought you were lost. I got you back. You saved me ... after all."

Chapter Thirty-Two

When there is no doubt that Sir Gabriel's life has slipped away, I rise slowly, trembling, to feel a hand on my shoulder. It is Vincent's.

"Captain Howard thought I should be the one to help you," he says softly. "Go wait over there while I make arrangements for this man. Then we will return to the Faubourg."

In the Duke of Norfolk's apartments that night, all of the intelligencers are present, full of concern for me. Louise, still bandaged and bruised herself, insists on putting me to bed. "Where is Captain Howard?" I ask.

"With his sister. Yes, he told us about her, Mrs Sturbridge." She pauses. "You saved her life, and the captain's too. The entire mission succeeded because of your courage."

Strangely, I don't feel pride in any of this or even relief that it is over. The criminals are captured, and I am alive. It is all too raw and confusing. Overwhelmed, I turn my face to the wall and find oblivion.

The next day, Captain Howard returns but only to fetch me. "Madeleine must see you this morning," he says briskly, as if it is just another day of the mission.

"Surely she needs rest and medical care after what happened," I say, surprised.

"They have very good apothecaries at the convent," he says. "Physically, she is unharmed. She will be fine. But she will give no one any peace until she speaks to you. She's a stubborn woman." A ghost of a smile. "The only woman I've ever met who is more stubborn — is you."

On my way to meet her, I reflect on the consequences of Captain Howard's bold decision to defy Sir Humphrey and share the mission's scope with Sartine. It's paid off handsomely. Sartine has not only agreed to oversee the destruction of the blue laboratory established by Giles Descoteaux but also ensured that a new letter can be written for the Sturbridge formula file in Whitehall. Certain parties broke the treaty in Paris but have been apprehended and imprisoned. France seems intent on honouring the agreement that Louis XV made in 1759. For now, tensions between France and England are easing, at least on this front.

Of course, these are two countries teetering on the edge of bankruptcy, driven by centuries of rivalry and their shared passion for waging war and building empires. Any peace is fragile. But I won't have contributed to the cause.

My only disappointment with regards to France's reaction is that Vicomte de Breteuil will escape punishment while Giles Descoteaux and his assassin face justice. The reason is infuriating. As the chief lady-in-waiting to the king's favourite daughter, Princess Adelaide, Vicomtesse de Breteuil is untouchable. No scandal can be allowed to taint the royal family, even through the misdeeds of a courtier's wayward, greedy husband.

At the convent, I find her not in bed but in the cloisters garden. Madeleine Howard, or Sister Candida as she is called, sits on a bench, wearing a black tunic and veil and white coif with a degree of dignity that makes me ashamed of how we imitated her calling at a chateau's ball. She has the same long nose and serious brown eyes as her brother. I find myself intimidated as I accept the invitation to sit beside her, until she smiles radiantly.

"Mrs Sturbridge, I want to express my gratitude in person," she says in English tinged with a French lilt. She has lived within these walls nearly half her life, Captain Howard told me in the carriage. It is inevitable she should seem French. "You risked your life to meet with this man, Sir Gabriel Courtenay, because you received a note saying he knew where I was held. Peregrine told me."

I glance at Captain Howard, who looks away, biting his lip.

"I am blessed and humbled by your courage," she says. "But I have questions."

I nod. "What can I do to help?"

"You accepted this assignment, to come with Peregrine to France and uncover a mystery about a formula for a shade of blue. I find this mystery very difficult to understand, though my brother has tried his best. Why would so many risks be taken for pigment? It is beyond me. But it is not for me to understand your intelligence mission, much less to sanction it."

She frowns and shifts closer to me. "There is another mystery that I really must understand. It is important for me to do so, but I can't without your help. After years of living by codes of treason and crime, why did Sir Gabriel Courtenay do this for me? Why did he want to save me and send this message to you?"

It's a question that plunges me into silence as I work to gather my thoughts. "Sister Candida, I am not sure. Sir Gabriel was a complicated human being, but I think he came to have regrets. While he had done many dishonourable things in his life, he reached a point where honour meant a great deal to him. He couldn't stand by. He had to try to intervene."

She mulls this over in silence. "This is more than a good deed, don't you agree? He knew it was highly dangerous to save me and to meet you. This was an … atonement. He sought to repent for his many sins by this action which he knew could be fatal to him. He knew the risks. He accepted them, and perhaps he welcomed them. It was penance. I know you are a Protestant and so was Sir Gabriel, but I see these principles at work."

I take a deep, shaky breath. "Yes, I agree with you."

She turns to her brother. "I want to talk to Mrs Sturbridge more about Sir Gabriel Courtenay and the kind of man my saviour was. She may be more comfortable if you are not present, as you can be very judgemental, Peregrine."

I try not to smile as he looks at his sister, eyebrows raised, but then retreats obediently.

She says softly, "I have no regrets over taking vows. I only wish I could have my brother in my life far more often. He is very dear to me." She looks me in the eye. "And dear to you as well, I think. I may not know anything about earthly love, but I recognize devotion in the way he spoke of you and in the way you look at each other here."

My oh my, she is as good at subterfuge as her younger brother. Sister Candida wanted to get me alone to talk about Peregrine, not Sir Gabriel. But I can't speak. She knows I am married. This can only be appalling and shameful for her.

Rallying, I say, "I have a great deal of respect for your brother. I will not lie to you. Other feelings may exist. But I will go home to England, to my husband and son. It's possible I will never see Peregrine again after we return. I think that is best."

My spirits drop to imagine a future without the furious, brave, arrogant yet thoughtful — and damnably attractive Captain Howard.

"You will never see him again, yet you risked your life to save his?" she asks wonderingly. "I am grateful for what you did, but I think it was your fear that he would die trying to free me that sent you to the Abbey of Saint-Geneviève, not the thought of my perishing."

"You make me sound so noble, like a tragic heroine," I say with a shaky laugh. "My husband, who knows me very well, would describe it as a rash and impulsive action."

"Perhaps the truth is somewhere between."

"No doubt." I think for a moment. "I was in terror of Captain Howard getting himself killed. He says I am stubborn, that you are stubborn. *He* is the most stubborn human ever born! I was determined to prevent his death, yes. But also I broke away and came to find Sir Gabriel Courtenay and where you were because it is something that I could do. Perhaps only I could do it."

"Ah. Now we come to it." She smiles again, calm and knowing, and in that moment, I understand why she carries a serenity her brother lacks. It's more than the peace that comes with choosing the life of a nun. She lives in a country that cherishes her faith and heritage, while Captain Howard wrestles with the need to prove himself in a country that disdains a fundamental part of who he is.

I take a breath and try to explain. "I am a wilful, striving woman, full of ambition, Sister Candida. It's my nature. While Sir Gabriel's mission was a criminal one and this assignment in France was a noble one, they both appealed to me. That's the truth. I want to be tested and challenged, and to meet the challenge. To use my wits and my abilities. My talent, if I have such a thing. This time in France I have felt truly … alive."

Horrified, Sister Candida says, "Mother Mary, you don't intend to put yourself through this sort of experience again, do you?"

I laugh. "I have no plans at present to do so. I must assume this opportunity was a rare one. But more immediately, I have a son to care for and there has also been a young orphan girl put in my custody."

I tell Sister Candida about Sir Gabriel's daughter and that Sir Gabriel has provided resources for me in a last will, resources that must go to her welfare and education.

"Now I understand fully," she says. "He knew his end might be coming soon and he chose you to raise his child. That's why he went to such trouble to reach out to you. He chose well, I must say."

"Thank you," I say. But I feel a shiver of nerves. Am I equal to the task of Adele Courtenay? I must do my best. What will Thomas say when he learns I am bringing her into our home — and that I possess a fortune bequeathed to me by Sir Gabriel? He is essentially a kind and caring person. I know that after the first shock, he will try to accept this little orphan and to even be a father to her as I try to be a mother. Perhaps I fell in love with Thomas because of the intensity of being caught up in the assignment to discover the blue. But I love him still for all his fine and good qualities. He is also an understanding person. I must try to bring something of the spirit of the mission to France into my life in England. I don't know how exactly. But I will find a way.

Sister Candida interrupts my contemplation to say, "I think we should summon Peregrine to take you now to where you need to go. These arrangements must be made for the child as soon as possible. But I think I have two regrets now. The second is not being able to see more of you."

She rises to her feet and looks down at me, shaking her head with a smile.

"I have to say, Mrs Sturbridge, there is certainly no one else like you in God's world."

THE END

Author's Note

The 1760s were a fascinating period in history, brimming with pivotal changes and escalating tensions. France's resentment over its loss of territory and prestige in the Seven Years' War, coupled with England's struggle to bear the immense cost of victory, set the stage for a decade of rivalry. Both nations seized every opportunity to undermine the other, actions that arguably sowed the seeds of the American Revolution and the French Revolution. It was a time of profound upheaval, with dynamics rising in ways that contemporary observers could scarcely comprehend. Remarkably, neither the words *espionage* nor *scientist* existed in 1766, yet international spying and the scientific revolution were already reshaping the world.

These characters are from my imagination: Genevieve Planché, Captain Peregrine Howard, Sir Gabriel Courtenay, Thomas and Pierre Sturbridge, Sir Humphrey Willoughby, Evelyn Willoughby, Giles Descoteaux, the Vicomte de Breteuil, Lars Longfren and Jemmy Maylie. In this novel, real people flit among them: Sir Horace Walpole, Madame du Deffand, Dr Erasmus Darwin and his wife, Polly, Antoine de Sartine, the Earl of Rochford and his wife, Lucy, the Prince de Lamballe, the Duc de Chartres, the Comte du Barry and his mistress Jeanne (soon to become the adored mistress of Louis XV) and, in a cameo appearance, the man known to infamy as the Marquis de Sade.

Two key historical figures remain "offstage": the Swedish philosopher Emanuel Swedenborg and the British inventor Joseph Priestley — credited with the independent discovery of oxygen. In this novel, I've imagined Priestley working alongside Thomas Sturbridge on experiments. While Priestley did publish a significant book on electricity in 1767, his groundbreaking work on oxygen lay in the future.

Sèvres porcelain and the art of Jean-Honoré Fragonard are integral to the era and entirely real. However, Thomas Sturbridge's "Versailles Formula" for blue pigment is fictional, inspired by the later invention of synthetic Cobalt Blue. This vibrant colour, eventually embraced by artists like J.M.W. Turner, Claude Monet and Vincent van Gogh, achieves breathtaking effect in Van Gogh's masterpiece *Starry Night*.

France and England spied on each other and did what they could to damage each other throughout the mid to late 1760s, but the countries did not resume war until 1778. In that year, France formally entered the conflict between England and its defiant American colonies. When William Pitt, who had championed the Seven Years War, returned to power in the summer of 1766, there were fears he would push for armed conflict then, but it turned out he was not at his best physically or mentally and could not master Great Britain's fiscal and political tensions.

I am forever grateful to editor Alice Rees for buying my novel *The Blue* in 2018 and allowing me to bring the character of Genevieve Planché to life. As a descendant of Huguenot refugee Pierre Billiou, who came to New Amsterdam (now New York City) in 1661, I longed to write a Huguenot heroine. I thank Aubrie Artiano and James Faktor for commissioning a third book in the saga of Genevieve Planché.

It is Becky Slorach who helped me develop this novel towards its full potential with her insightful edit. Without Becky and Katie

Seaman, *The Versailles Formula* would not push through to what I hope is an exciting novel for readers. I appreciate the fine work of Kate Ballard and Sarah Tranter and the rest of the staff of Joffe Books.

My deepest gratitude goes to Emilya Naymark for her notes on *The Versailles Formula*, and to Harriet Sharrard for her comments. Sophie Lechner came to the rescue with answers to my French questions. I am also thankful to these friends for their encouragement while I was writing the novel: Mariah Fredericks, Kris Waldherr, Hope Tarr, Dru Ann Love, Carol Goodman, Timothy Miller, Kate Braithwaite, Paulette Kennedy, Libbie Hawker, Barbara Claypole White, Erica Obey, Laura Joh Rowland, Elizabeth Kerri Mahon, Evelyn Nunlee, Elaine Devlin Beigelman, Donna Bulseco, Caroline Hwang, Thea Burgess, Sophie Perinot, Andrea Catalano, Judith Starkston, Mary Tod, Aimie Runyan-Vetter, Shawntelle Madison, Piper Huguley, Shizuka Otake and Triss Stein.

Once again, I must express my loving appreciation for my husband and children, who tolerated my obsession with bringing to life in a novel a couple of months in 1766 England and France.

The Lume & Joffe Books Story

Lume Books was founded by Matthew Lynn, one of the true pioneers of independent publishing. In 2023 Lume Books was acquired by Joffe Books and now its story continues as part of the Joffe Books family of companies.

Joffe Books began in 2014 when Jasper agreed to publish his mum's much-rejected romance novel and it became a bestseller.

Since then we've grown into the largest independent publisher in the UK. We're extremely proud to publish some of the very best writers in the world, including Joy Ellis, Faith Martin, Caro Ramsay, Helen Forrester, Simon Brett and Robert Goddard. Everyone at Joffe Books loves reading and we never forget that it all begins with the magic of an author telling a story.

We are proud to publish talented first-time authors, as well as established writers whose books we love introducing to a new generation of readers.

We won Trade Publisher of the Year at the Independent Publishing Awards in 2023 and Best Publisher Award in 2024 at the People's Book Prize. We have been shortlisted for Independent Publisher of the Year at the British Book Awards for the last five years, and were shortlisted for the Diversity and Inclusivity Award at the 2022 Independent Publishing Awards. In 2023 we were shortlisted for

Publisher of the Year at the RNA Industry Awards, and in 2024 we were shortlisted at the CWA Daggers for the Best Crime and Mystery Publisher.

We built this company with your help, and we love to hear from you, so please email us about absolutely anything bookish at feedback@joffebooks.com.

If you want to receive free books every Friday and hear about all our new releases, join our mailing list here: www.joffebooks.com/freebooks.

And when you tell your friends about us, just remember: it's pronounced Joffe as in coffee or toffee!